PRAISE

"Beautifully written and achingly romantic, fans of *Outlander* will devour this immersive Welsh timeslip. A stunning debut."
~Hester Fox, author of *The Last Heir to Blackwood Library*

"Fans of Diana Gabaldon and Susanna Kearsley will adore this intriguing tale of star-crossed lovers unbound from the limits of time. Sweeping, romantic, and evocative of the wild, Welsh countryside. Cozy up with a cup of tea and enjoy!"
~Paulette Kennedy, bestselling author of *The Witch of Tin Mountain*

"*The Wisp and the Wolf* is a beautiful debut, lush with historical detail, a truly magical landscape, and a slow burn romance that will leave readers swooning."
~Sarah T. Dubb, author of *Birding with Benefits*

"With beautifully lush world-building and poetic prose, *The Wisp and the Wolf* is a debut to be reckoned with. I was thoroughly enchanted and already want to reread it!"
~Erin A. Craig, #1 New York Times bestselling author of *House of Roots and Ruin*

The
Wisp
And
The Wolf

The Ellylldan Chronicles: Book One

JEANNE RENEE

The Wisp and the Wolf

The Ellylldan Chronicles: Book One

Copy editing: Jeni Chappelle Editorial

Cover design: Seventhstar Art Services, Stefanie Saw

Formatting: Starla DeKruyf

Amazon ebook: 979-8-9899321-0-8

Amazon paperback: 979-8-9899321-1-5

B&N paperback: 979-8-9899321-2-2

IngramSpark paperback: 979-8-9899321-3-9

For my parents, Merry and Bill Nebeker,
who gave me both roots and wings.

CONTENT WARNINGS

This book contains scenes depicting attempted sexual assault, death of a parent, spanking a child, homophobia, mild gore, and open-door consensual sex.

Take care, my dears.

"No coward soul is mine."

~ Emily Brontë

CHAPTER I

ELLYLLDAN

MARCH 19, 2002

Climbing onto the hood of my rental car in the drizzling rain hadn't been the plan. A normal person wouldn't even consider it. But when the tiny blue hatchback lurches to a halt on the sinuous, nearly empty road, it seems like the thing to do.

I wasn't exactly normal anyway.

Now, sprawled across the windshield like a beached starfish, I blink up at the ashen sky and wonder if people still die from catching a chill. It sounds like something this dank, archaic place of castles and dragons would conjure up. Maybe this is how I die.

At least I won't have to face Meredith.

Frigid wind smacks my face, scolding me for the cowardly thought. Knowing better than to ruminate, I squint into the murky afternoon and imagine myself back home, running along a desert trail, lavender cacti crowding the path, my breath steady and hot as a beating heart under a massive blue sky. I'm almost grounded enough to feel the warm, dry air on my skin when two fat rivulets of rain drip into my ears.

"God damn it," I hiss and sit up, spitting out the daydream like a cherry pit. I glower up at the sky. Only a handful of hours in Wales and I already ache for sunshine. It's going to be a long spring.

"Of all the places to run off to and get knocked up in, Mer," I grumble, thankful for once the bizarre connection I share with my identical twin has its limits.

I look around. No houses are visible among the dense green landscape, but it's not too far back to the village I just passed, although the trek promises to be unpleasant. And there's no telling how long a tow truck and repairs could take. Necessary tasks start to pile up, and my gut churns with dread. I'm tired, hungry, cold, and fucked.

No sooner do I resolve to start walking than headlights appear from behind like giant eyes in the falling dark. A rusted pickup truck rolls casually to a stop right behind me.

Heart thrumming at the prospect of rescue, I slide off the hood of the car just as a tall figure in a trench coat and wide-brimmed hat steps onto the wet blacktop. Hope shrivels into panic as the stranger starts forward, eclipsing the low beams. Pulse thrumming, I fling myself around the hood of the car, putting as much distance between us as I can.

The imposing figure steps closer.

"*Ti'n iawn?*" calls the shadow in a lilting tongue as it stops, lifts the brim of its hat.

I look up and encounter the open, rosy face of a woman well past middle age. Obscured by rain, her features are indistinct, but everything about her presence feels robust. Good-natured. She smiles.

"Hi," I say, hoping to indicate I don't speak Welsh and immediately feel like an idiot.

The woman clicks her tongue. "Are you well, love?"

There's no truthful way to respond, so I simply lie with a nod.

"Havin' a bit o' trouble?" Eyeing my general dishevelment, she gestures toward the car. She chuckles as if this is a rare accomplishment.

Rain drips into my eyes as I look between the woman, the dead rental car, and the long misty road. There's only one thing to do.

"Would you mind giving me a ride back to town?" I ask.

The stranger tilts her head at me like an owl before she gives a curt nod. "Aye, and a bit more to be sure. Come along." She waves at the sky and turns. "It's picking to rain old ladies and sticks, isn't it?"

"Thank you," I say, my voice feeble against the elements. Quickly, I grab my backpack from the front seat, shove every scattered item inside, and scuttle around the car as she hefts my bag with impressive strength.

"Oh, I can—"

"Lock up, love!"

I sigh, gratitude and embarrassment warring in my chest, and jam down the old locks before following.

"*Cwtch* in," she says from the driver's side.

With my suitcase occupying most of the cab, I squeeze in and slam the heavy door behind me. Pleasant, warm scents of leather, coffee, and dog envelop me. I'm damn near giddy to be out of the wet.

"Now then." She thrusts out her hand, abrupt and energetic. "I'm Mrs. Brenda Jones."

"Meg Quinn." I wonder what kind of woman still introduced herself as Mrs. as I shake her hand. It's calloused and warm, despite the chill evening.

"How do you do," she says, though it wasn't a question, and pulls onto the road without looking. She doesn't turn around.

I crane my neck back as the little blue rental disappears around a bend. "Sorry, but isn't the town that way?"

"Aye, but we aren't going to the village. I own Llangynog Inn just up the road. It's that much nicer than a wet car park, isn't it?"

A vague sound of protest gathers in my throat, but I can't find any words. Shit.

"Where are you traveling to?" Mrs. Jones asks.

"Bala." I swallow, clear my throat. "I'm supposed to be there this evening."

"Lovely. On holiday? Don't get many American visitors except for that."

I sigh, lean back against the worn seat. "Just visiting my sister."

I don't elaborate. Traveling against my will to fulfill my late mother's dying wish could be called many things, but a holiday isn't one of them. Hunger and fatigue twist my stomach, and I start to wonder how far 'just up the road' really is.

"Brilliant. Cymry blood, are you then? That's our word for ourselves, isn't it." Already exceptionally polite, she perks up at the prospect of my Welshness.

"Half."

Mom was born in Cardiff but moved to Hershey, Pennsylvania with her parents and two older brothers when she was eight. Ever after, she accused the rain of smelling like chocolate. My sister's unexpected wedding last summer had provided Mom with her first trip back to Wales. She'd been so excited about the wedding, traveling—all of it—that she ignored the pain in her abdomen until it was too late.

Not helpful.

Mrs. Jones purrs with satisfaction. "Well, it's no wonder you have the face o' a *Cymraes* then, is it?"

I force a wan smile, and Mrs. Jones falls silent. I'm being an ass but am too uncomfortable to know what else to say. Turning to the window, I stare beyond my mottled reflection in the glass until my gaze snags on a faint, blue light alongside the road. I expect it to disappear as we drive, but the orb seems to drift along in the rain at the same rate as the truck. It bobs and sways like a lantern or flashlight but otherwise keeps pace with us, its cerulean glow gently flickering.

"What's that?" I point. "That light?"

Mrs. Jones glances over and does a double take that would be comical except for the expression on her round face. Her eager smile flatlines.

"What?" I ask. The hairs on my neck bristle.

She jerks her gaze back to the road before answering. "Well, dear, that's an *ellylldan*."

"Oh?" I raise my eyebrows and wait, clearly not understanding the tangled Welsh sounds.

Mrs. Jones clears her throat. Her knuckles have gone white on the steering wheel. "I do believe you'd call it a will-o'-the-wisp."

"A will of the—oh," I breathe as my jet-lagged mind catches up. I can't remember what the term means exactly but think it refers to some kind of faerie or spirit in folklore. Right. I turn back to the mercurial light, brighter now. Beckoning.

"Best keep your eyes straight on, love," says Mrs. Jones. "It wouldn't do to be lead astray on the eve o' Ostara."

"Ostara?" I parrot.

"Aye. The dawning season. When the earth wakes up from her dark sleep and the Christ is risen, isn't it? Spring."

She's perfectly serious. With some difficulty, I give the phantom light one last look before turning my attention to the rain-splattered windshield and the dreary road stretching before me.

S tumbling through the back door of Llangynog Inn, I feel as anxious and disheveled as Piglet being blown across the Hundred Acre Wood. No sooner have I crossed the threshold of the imposing slate-roofed farmhouse than I'm waylaid by two enormous licking, barking balls of gray-and-white fur. Cold rain pelts my back as I submit to the ubiquitous crotch-sniffing and foot-stepping-on of large dogs while trying not to fall and eat shit in the doorway.

"Move! Get gone with ye!" Mrs. Jones commands, sending the dogs scampering to the far end of the room, their pink tongues lolling in oblivious joy.

I blow out an exaggerated breath and force my jaw to unclench. What in the actual hell is next?

Divining my thoughts, Mrs. Jones chuckles.

"Come by here, Miss Meg. The beasties won't gobble you down." She closes the mists out with a bang.

Too cold and wet and tired to argue, I take in my surroundings. It's a large kitchen boasting wood-beam ceilings, stone floors, and an ancient bricked-in stove. A stout table sits against one wall, where a collection of intricately carved wooden spoons hangs, each more detailed than the last. Every inch of the space is immaculate.

"Shall we have a cuppa tea and something to eat?" she asks, removing her hat and coat.

It's then I get my first good look at Brenda Jones. A Viking of a woman, her platinum hair is swept away from her face and pinned in a delicate bun at the nape of her neck. Her eyes are pale and clear, her round cheeks ruddy from the chill. She's wearing work boots under a long, wool skirt, floral blouse, and heavy cardigan. I couldn't have conjured a Welsher fairy godmother if I tried.

Without waiting for my answer, she puts a kettle on to boil and rummages through the refrigerator.

"Uh, yeah. Thank you. That sounds great, but could I use your phone real quick? I need to call my sister."

"Yes, yes." She gestures with a large, cured sausage from behind the open fridge door. "After."

Clearly phone-calls-first isn't the way to do things here. Waffling between relieved and annoyed, I slide onto a chair. Soon, two cups of tea and a plate of sliced meats, cheeses, and brown rolls, their tops bright with oil, appears in front of me. My mouth waters at the yeasty, buttery smell. I haven't eaten since inhaling a croissant in the airport in Cardiff, and my stomach churns with hunger, despite the awkward situation.

Doing the honors, Mrs. Jones fills a roll and hands it to me. "Are you at university then? You look o' an age to be."

"Thank you." I accept the treat. "No. Well, yes, I—I took some time off this year but start graduate school in the fall."

"Brilliant." She takes her seat at the table. "My son Dai is at uni now in Bangor. The lad wants to be an engineer o' all things." She shakes her head as if this is a shame.

I fill my mouth with sandwich and let out a little moan of delight at the salty, creamy goodness.

"And you?"

I'm so engrossed in eating it takes a moment to realize what she means. "Oh," I mumble through a mouthful of food. *Get your shit together.* I swallow. "Studio art."

Mrs. Jones rewards this statement with a chime-bell bright

smile. "An artist? Brilliant! Did you notice the love spoons then?" she says, pointing to the wall display.

I nod and swallow another mouthful of sweet bread and salty meat. It's ridiculously delicious. "I did, actually," I say, looking back up at the spoons. "They're lovely. Local artist?"

Ranging in size from a baby's spoon to a soup ladle, each russet wood carving boasts a unique handle. One is a Celtic cross, one a dragon. Another holds the leonine face of a daffodil. The smallest is also the simplest. Glossy, amber wood with two interlocking hearts.

"Aye," Mrs. Jones says, her voice reverent. "My late husband. Mr. Jones thought the dragon his best, but I'm a bit soft for the wee one." She gestures to the hearts. "Gave it to me when he proposed, he did."

The last bite of sandwich sticks in my throat.

"I'm sorry for your loss." I say this, polite and automatic, though little meaning remains. Like over-squeezed fruit, the words are hollow, nothing left but bitter rind. Still, what else does a person say when you've accidentally brought up a stranger's dead husband?

"Oh, don't worry yourself, *bach*. Been some time now." She offers me the generous, reassuring smile of the long bereaved. I'm not good at this yet.

I nod, and the conversation falls away as we sip our steaming tea. The cup is warm in my hands, and the spicy smell of bergamot and cinnamon soothes my frazzled nerves. I stand to clear away the plates, but Mrs. Jones shoos me off.

"Away with you, Miss Meg. Welcome you are to ring your sister from the lounge. Just through there it is. Let her know I'll have my neighbor, Evans the Tire, see to your car in the morning."

My expectation of getting back on the road tonight flops to

the floor, deflated. "Oh, you don't have to bother, really. I can call a tow truck myself or—"

Mrs. Jones swats away my protests. "Evans owes me a favor for introducing my nephew to his youngest girl, Iris. They'll be getting married in June. Her poor folks just about put the fiddle on the roof at the prospect of that one ever getting married, so it's no bother."

Unable to muster a response, I pass into the adjoining room and pinch the bridge of my nose, where a headache threatens to bloom.

The room is a butter-yellow Mecca of amateur watercolors and family photos. An ample floral couch reminiscent of its owner reclines under a large picture window trimmed with lace curtains, and along the opposite wall, a small fireplace yawns in the mellow light of a table lamp. My belly full of food and dread, I collapse onto the couch and dial Meredith's number on a landline. It only takes one ring.

"Hello?"

"Hey."

"Oh my God, I've been waiting to hear from you all day," my sister laments into the receiver.

"Yeah, sorry. I forgot to call from the airport, and then my rental car broke down—"

"Oh my God."

"—but I'm fine."

"Do you need John to pick you up? Where are you? Wait. How are you even calling?"

"No, do not send John. Seriously. I'm fine. Someone's grandma gave me a ride, and now I'm at some bed-and-break-fast off the main road."

"You hitchhiked? What the hell, Meggie? That's not safe. Not even here," she says, her voice pitching higher with each word.

"Will you relax? I will never hear the end of it if you pop those babies out on the couch because of my shitty luck."

"Facts." My twin's deep breaths come in a steady rhythm over the line. My own slow in unison. Even over the phone, our bodies sync with each other.

"Okay," she says after a moment. "So where are you exactly?"

"Llangynog Inn. I guess I'm staying here tonight and getting the car fixed tomorrow."

"You guess?"

"Yep." I look around the bric-a-brac-filled room. "I think I finally get why you like it here. The whole damn country is somehow super friendly and bossy at once." I lower my voice at the last bit so as not to offend my hostess.

Meredith snorts through the receiver. "I'll remind you of that when you're choking down a crow pie."

"If I don't drown myself in a muddy puddle first. Damn, it rains a lot here."

"Desert rat."

"Barefoot pod."

Silence radiates out of the receiver. Fuuuuuck. Too far.

I roll my eyes to the ceiling and wrap the phone cord around my finger, pinching off the circulation. "Sorry. That was harsh. It's been a stupid long day."

Meredith clears her throat. "Yeah, well, the car thing sucks."

I let the cord unwind. Watch the blood drain. "It doesn't matter," I say, anxious to sweep away my gaffe. "I better go, but I'll call tomorrow before I take off."

"Okay."

More silence. "You aren't going into early labor or anything, right?"

"Not on purpose," Meredith says, her voice returning to

normal. "The doctor says I gotta cook these little beans at least four more weeks to avoid major complications."

"See you tomorrow." I close my eyes and envision her stroking the vast expanse of her stomach, willing her babies to stay put.

"Bye."

I cradle the receiver without responding and hang my head between my knees. Why am I always such an ass? Despite minor physical differences—Meredith is slightly shorter and curvier with a deeper cleft chin and no gap between her front teeth—my twin and I couldn't be less alike.

When we were kids, our mom loved to dress us in matching outfits. Each morning, she'd straighten our socks and frost our tawny hair into identical, pig-tailed perfection only to have me fall apart like icing in the sun. Even then, I was sharp and unwieldy, a knife in hand. It's no surprise Meredith grew into the kind of woman whose lipstick stays on all day. Who's never needlessly unkind. This should make her easy to hate, but it doesn't. Everyone likes the shiny side of a coin. Even me.

Outside, the storm picks up, tossing rain against the dark window. At the thought of Mom, a familiar weight presses against my chest. I have to move, right now, or be rooted in place, held down by a wave of grief. Gritting my teeth, I stand and push open the kitchen door back to Mrs. Jones just as the wind begins to scream.

CHAPTER 2

MARCH HARE

I sense it hovering nearby, just out of reach like a tune half remembered. I grasp at it, but the edges morph and slip away, ephemeral as mist.

Suddenly I'm awake, and the dream is gone. Blinking, I run a clammy hand over my face and find the red-eyed alarm clock on the nightstand. 5:37 A.M. *Too early* is my only coherent thought as I nestle deeper into my pillow.

Then I hear it. Silence.

"Oh, thank God." Constant as a heartbeat, Welsh rain is apparently the kind of thing you only notice when it stops. Sitting up, I flick on the bedside lamp and flood the quaint room with a lemon-chiffon glow. The pervasive chill plucks at my bare parts as I reluctantly slide out from under the mountainous layers of chintz bedding and directly into a bathrobe and grimy bunny slippers. I'd bet my best drawing pencils Mrs. Jones wakes up ungodly early, but I try to be quiet as I gather my toiletry case and creep around the bed—where I promptly trip and go sprawling.

I aim a foul, ripe curse at the floor. More familiar with falling than a grown woman should be, I pick myself up and collect my scattered belongings. Palms stinging, I ease the door to my room open and find myself nose to chin with the much taller and more imposing Mrs. Jones. *Shit* is all my muddled brain can think as I look up. She's wrapped her ample build in a lavender floral Laura Ashley robe, and her eyes—blue as glaciers—are wide with surprise.

"Good morning," I say. "Sorry. For the noise. I was just ... and then I tripped."

She touches my rumpled hair freely as if I were a child. The casual tenderness of it presses on my heart like a bruise.

"Are you hurt, love? You look a bit bruised here, you do." She points to the soft skin under my eyes as her brogue tumbles the Rs around in her mouth like bits of hard candy. "Did you not sleep well then?"

"No, I'm fine. Sorry if I woke you."

Mrs. Jones waves this off as if the idea is ridiculous. It probably is. For all I know, she's woken up at 5 A.M. every day of her life.

"Well," she says with a brisk nod, "if you must be up at the cut o' dawn, I'll set out a proper breakfast for you. Just a bit o' a bird, you are." With a disapproving click of her tongue, she turns toward the stairs.

Desperate for several cups of strong, black coffee and a bowl of Frosted Flakes, I fake a smile and head for the bathroom at the end of the hallway. Locking the door behind me, I turn on the shower as hot as it will go and reluctantly shed my robe and night shirt. Steam fills the small room as I tuck my long, burnt-sugar hair behind my ears and, ignoring the pale smudge of my reflection in the grainy mirror, step into the water.

Stinging hot pinpricks slide down my small frame as I stretch into a luxurious yawn.

I groan at a sharp pain under my right ribcage. Absently pressing the spot, my mind jerks to my twin. I drop my hand, understanding. Damn, the little beans must be kicking hard today.

Dad was especially fond of our Twin Sense, as he called it. He loved telling the story of the first time I went to a sleepover without my sister. In the middle of the night, my friend and I crept into her kitchen for extra cake but only succeeded in slicing open my finger with a steak knife and waking up the family's basset hound. As the story goes, while I was across town watching my palm fill with blood, Meredith came barreling into our parents' bedroom, screaming. We were ten. It was only after the car accident that our connection took visual form as well. I drag a hand through my wet hair and wonder— what would Dad have thought about that trick?

Back in my room, I shimmy into jeans and a cable-knit sweater the color of oatmeal. After braiding my damp hair without ceremony, I don the only piece of jewelry I wear on a regular basis: a long, silver chain with our mother's ring hanging from it. Twin pearls perched between a delicate swirl of white gold, it had been a gift from our father when she'd given birth to Meredith and me.

I still can't bring myself to put the ring on but have worn it around my neck every day since she died. Meredith got Mom's engagement ring, but if she wears it, I wouldn't know. Tucking the chain into my sweater, I breathe more easily as the cool metal rests between my small breasts. A mooring post for my heart.

Outside, birds trill among the still-dripping trees, drawing my attention to the window. Lingering clouds smear the gray horizon and, just visible between earth and sky, hangs the faintest sliver of a young moon. Forgoing makeup altogether, I strap on my watch, lace up my walking boots, and head downstairs to face Mrs. Jones and her hearty meal.

Wrapped in all her cabbage rose glory, Mrs. Jones stands

sentinel over her stove, the snap and pop of grease in perfect concert with the steaming teakettle.

"Take a seat in the lounge, Miss Meg. Won't be but a minute."

Resigning myself to a sans-sugar-and-coffee breakfast, I move obediently into the adjoining room. A single place setting lies across the pedestal table in the corner, and a tidy fire smolders in the hearth. It's all incredibly charming, and for the first time in a while, I resent my numbness. But I'm grateful for the warmth and sit down, letting my attention stray to the conversation that had led to this moment.

"Of course you won't be in the way. Don't be *twp*," Meredith had chided over the phone.

"*Twp*? God, Mer, do you hear yourself?"

"Of course I do. But seriously, John is adding a nursery to the back of the house, so you'll have your own room and everything."

"It's fucking cold in Wales," I said, hoping to shock her into silence.

"Well, it's hotter than balls in Arizona."

I couldn't bite back the smile. The image of my immaculate sister standing in her kitchen talking about hot balls over weather reminded me of those vintage 1950s' postcards showing eerily perfect housewives saying things like 'Guess where I'm tattooed.'

"Look," Meredith said, the sugary fringe dropping from her voice. "I know things have been … hard, but it'll be warming up a little by March and you can go home any time."

I nodded at the phone as if Meredith could see me. Maybe she could.

"I'm telling you, Meg. Wales is in our blood. You'll feel it when you get back. And it's what Mom wanted in the end, yeah?"

I'd exhaled a bitter chuckle. "Right. Because you know so much about that."

The kitchen door swings open with a clang, jarring me from my thoughts.

"There is a proper meal for you, Miss Meg," Mrs. Jones says, placing a tray piled with tea, toast, sliced tomatoes, bacon, beans, a poached egg, and a pile of stewed seaweed in front of me.

"Thank you," I manage, genuinely grateful for the tea and toast at least. "It looks wonderful."

Hovering at my elbow, Mrs. Jones stares with an expectant smile. I get the message and lift the steaming teacup from its saucer. The rich tang of cloves reaches my nostrils just before I take a sip and scald my tongue. I take a huge bite of toast to cover the sting.

Placated, Mrs. Jones moves on. "Evans the Tire rang last night after you retired and said he's having the car towed to his shop and will ring this afternoon."

I grimace, unable to hide my annoyance and swallow hard. The toast is buttery and rich and scrapes as it goes down.

Mrs. Jones clicks her tongue for the second time this morning. "Now don't be spoilt for choice. Busy, busy Evans is on a Monday morning with appointments, you see, but he'll come by soon enough."

"I understand," I say, abashed. "I really do. And I appreciate the help. I'm just ... anxious to be on my way."

"It's no trouble, *bach*." Mrs. Jones presses a square finger to her chin and arches a pale brow at me. "Now, what to do with you. Can't have you moping about."

Tea sloshes into the saucer as I clatter the cup into place. "Please, don't bother yourself about me. I can just—"

"Melangell's," she interrupts.

"Pardon?"

"St. Melangell's. A lovely medieval church with a shrine, it is. Quite famous, actually, and just a short walk from the village. You should have a looks."

A medieval saint's shrine? Huh. I'm intrigued in spite of myself, but glance toward the window, hesitant.

Being an astute woman, Mrs. Jones solves the problem for me. "Oh, it's not picking to rain again. There's a little, little road see that leads to the church—oh, two or three kilometers up the valley," she rattles off. "I'll drop you at the car park on my way to market and retrieve you at half twelve, eh?"

Staying inside would be easier, but the chance to stretch my legs and get out from under Mrs. Jones's attention, without getting drenched, is too tempting to ignore.

"All right. Thanks," I say not wanting to be remembered as a complete asshole.

"Right. Well, I've chores to see to, so tuck in, love. I'll bring the lorry around for you shortly," she says and heads for the kitchen, victory billowing behind her like a cape.

Shaking my head, I stare at the plate. I can almost feel my mother's ghost prodding my back. I haven't had an appetite in months, and the rich smell of the food turns my stomach a bit. But I pick up my fork, determined to make a dent. Best not disappoint Mrs. Jones.

"Remember, stay on the path and mind the time." Mrs. Jones's moon face shines down at me from the window of her dilapidated truck.

"Promise," I say and give a small wave. She means well. Beyond that, Brenda Jones quite literally rescued me, so I'm only a little surprised when my stomach twists anxiously as she drives out of sight.

In a hurry to shake off the unease, I inhale the crisp air and look around. In the corner of the parking lot sits a red phone booth, bright as a tropical bird, with a weathered trail marker squatting at its feet. New-day light sloshes over the gray hills as I hitch up my backpack.

"Get a grip, Quinn," I say aloud and head down the rocky trail.

I don't expect a long hike, but since I've done little more than pace hospital corridors in months, I take it slow. Still, it isn't long before I have to stop and catch my breath as the unfamiliar valley comes to life around me.

In the distance, serrated, gray peaks rise to meet the pale sky, while little stone walls and low hedges crisscross the rolling hills around me, creating the patchwork pattern of a giant's quilt. Most trees are still leafless, their spindly fingers scratching at the sky, but a few bushy pines stand out in triumph against the cold. While far from warm, the weak sunlight ripens a scent I can't identify—something resinous and sharp—and I breathe it in. Closing my eyes, I focus on the scene around me and let thoughts about Meredith pass. About making amends. About the babies. About mum. About any of it.

When that doesn't work, I start walking again.

I'm still a good way off when I spy a steeple poking up from among the trees like a witch's hat, though the body of the church remains hidden by the enormous evergreens encircling it. Getting closer, I can see how truly massive the trees are and notice a large stone lychgate marking the entrance to the churchyard. I stop again, listening. Surely such a charming place has more visitors than me, but the valley is quiet except for the wind. With curiosity bubbling in my chest, I pass under the moss-covered arch.

"*Caw!*"

"Oh my God!" Startling violently at the sound, I leap backward and land in a puddle up to my ankles as a cluster of slick, black feathers swoops over my head.

"Fuck," I mutter, shaking the muddy water from my shoes before looking up.

A massive raven stares down at me from a low branch, its black eyes indignant.

"Stupid bird," I hiss and, without thinking, reach down for a stone, only to stop short. What the hell am I doing? Disquieted by the beast and my aggressive response to it, I edge away from the bird and turn toward the church.

Seated on a gentle knoll, the stocky, stone church boasts a bell tower on one end and a small apse at the other. Askew headstones flare out from the structure in a circle edged with evergreens like the frothy hem of a petticoat. The largest tree towers over the lychgate. Weathered and reddish-gray, its trunk twists in on itself, fissuring apart to leave a gaping maw in the center. Silver-green needles sweep the ground, and from one fractured limb, red sap oozes. The bloody wound of an ancient warrior.

For a moment—a single heartbeat—I long for the neglected pencils, pastels, and sketch pad buried in my suitcase.

Maybe here. Maybe it will come back to me here.

Then the moment, like everything else, dies and takes my desire to create along with it.

Filmy clouds trail over the sun, throwing the yard into deep shade. A shiver I'm not sure has to do with the chill skitters down my back before I head up the path, gravel crunching underfoot. Unsure how exactly to proceed, I stand outside the large, wooden door, feeling ridiculous. Why did I bother coming all this way again? What if Mrs. Jones was wrong and random visitors aren't allowed? Suddenly tired and irritated, I turn to leave just as that damned raven lets out a series of chortling caws. Even the bird finds me pathetic.

Well, that settles it. I push open the door. It swings with surprising ease, and I step inside.

I'm smack in the middle of a long aisle of pews with a baptismal font on my left and a gift shop farther down the aisle. To my right is the altar and what could only be the shrine behind it. A strange hybrid between a sarcophagus and the Arc of the Covenant, the shrine dominates the space and plays an eerie counterweight to the mundane scents of wood polish and moth balls. The sanctuary looks empty, so I step farther in and glance up.

My jaw drops. Mounted along the wall of the nave is a huge, scythe-shaped bone.

"It can be off-putting to some," says a raspy voice from behind me.

Startling—again—I spin to find a striking, middle-aged woman standing near the shrine. "Can't imagine why," I say. "Sorry, the door was open so—"

"My apologies," she says. "I didn't mean to startle you. Visitors are always welcome at St. Melangell's, they are." She approaches with an enviable grace, and I have the overall impression of sharp eyes behind dark-framed glasses and natural black curls above a scarlet scarf, which blazes against the deep tan of her skin.

I look back up at the bone. "What is it?"

"*Asen y gawres,*" she says, coming to a stop beside me. "It means 'the Giant's Rib.' It's from a great fish that was discovered in the Berwyn Mountains to the west, you see."

"Any sign of Noah's ark?" I tease.

"Not just yet." She's clearly having none of my sass, and I immediately like her for it.

I clear my throat. "It's beautiful here."

The woman nods. "Aye. Many a soul has worked hard over the years to keep it so." She extends her hand. "Reverend Clara Fitzwilliam. I'm the priest guardian for the church and cancer center."

The word "cancer" falls like a hammer between us, jarring me, but I push it aside and take her hand. "Meg Quinn. Stranded American traveler."

She smiles. "I gathered as much. Well, Miss Quinn American Traveler, do you have any questions?"

"No, but thanks. I'm just passing some time while my rental car gets fixed."

Arching an impeccable eyebrow, Reverend Fitzwilliam gives me a cursory glance, no doubt taking in the backpack and soggy shoes. "Walk in from the village, did you?"

"Guilty."

"Well, seeing as you're already here, I'll give you a tour whilst you wait."

Of course you will. Without another word, she launches into various aspects of the church's history. I trail behind, only half listening. Normally, I'd be fascinated, but nothing about me, or now, is normal. I find myself longing to sit in silence and soak up the church's peculiar ambiance.

"Now, the rood screen is fifteenth century," Reverend Fitzwilliam says, pointing to the large, intricately carved wooden partition that separates the body of the church from the altar. "It depicts the story o' Saint Melangell. Do you know the tale?" Her tawny eyes flick across my face, expectant.

When I shake my head, she slides onto the nearest pew and gestures for me to join her. Tired from the early morning and my walk, I slump next to her.

"It's a simple story at its bones. In the seventh century, a young noble girl named Melangell fled Ireland to escape a forced marriage and became a hermitess in this valley. One day, the prince o' the land, Brochwel Ysgithrog, was out hunting and pursued a hare that took refuge under Melangell's cloak. She protected the creature from the huntsmen, and even the hounds would not defy her. Prince Brochwel was so impressed with Melangell's piety that he bequeathed this valley to her. From that day to this, people have come here in search o' sanctuary."

Something about how she says the last word draws my attention away from the elaborate screen. "You tell that story well. Almost like you believe it."

"I have no reason not to believe it." The reverend purses her lips. "This valley is a thin place, you see." As she speaks, a shadow passes behind her eyes, and they glaze over. I stare, but it's as if the reverend is peering at the back of her pupils.

"A thin place?" I venture.

She blinks, and like a fleeing fish, the shadow darts away, leaving her eyes clear and focused. Every hair on the back of my neck stands on end.

"Aye. A thin place is a seam between worlds, isn't it? A fault line where God's presence is felt more strongly." She leans forward, whispering. "Some even say it's where *y Tylwyth Teg*—the Fair Family—pass through."

It's my turn to purse my lips. Apparently, farmwives like Mrs. Jones aren't the only people around here who believe in fairies.

My glass face betrays me because a chuckle leaps out from the reverend.

"Ah, you aren't the first to doubt and certainly won't be the last. Just think o' it as a place where all that happens cannot be explained." Still smiling, she looks fondly around the church. "A place where one can find peace amidst the beauty o' our Lord's creation."

"How do you know?" I ask, defiant against her ministering.

"The yews," she answers without hesitation and moves toward one of the windows scattered down the length of the church. "There are six trees planted in a circle around this site, you see. Five o' them are more than two thousand years old. The sixth, older yet. Ancient people recognized something here and—"

"Marked it." I remember reading in an art history textbook once about supposed Druid sacrifices and Celtic rituals enacted in the shadow of sacred groves. It all proved more than my Methodist imagination could digest, but the idea of something living and yet ancient in ways I would never truly comprehend moved me then. It still does.

"Correct." She smiles. "It is my belief that the energy that spoke to the early Britons, centuries before Christianity came to our island, is the same natural power that drew young Melangell. And is, in fact, what draws visitors still." Reverend Fitzwilliam's tiger eyes flash, her polite smile falling away. "Is there anything I can do for you, Meg? We have staff available at our cancer center if you'd like to talk."

That's all it takes. Heat floods my body as grief hooks its gnarled fingers between my ribs and scratches open my festering heart. Tears fill my eyes, and my throat burns as I viciously hold them back. I will not fucking fall apart here.

"I have to go." I stand abruptly, desperate to get away from the strange woman and the eerie pull of this place. Only when my fingers curl around the smooth iron of the latch do I look back.

Reverend Fitzwilliam stares right through me.

"Goodbye, Meg Quinn. Mind the yews." Her voice reverberates off the tile floors as the Giant's Rib smiles down on us.

Long repressed tears cloud my vision as I fling open the door, the odd warning clinging to my back like a broken spiderweb. All I can think is *away, away, away* as I stumble into the grass until my knees give out and I crumple in front of a large headstone. Struggling to breathe, I dump my backpack and press my hands to the cold, unreadable slab. I drag in one long breath and then another as thoughts of the bones beneath me flood my mind. The bones of someone's son, daughter, sister, brother, father, mother. Father. Mother. Images race across my vision until I'm no longer looking at an obscure tombstone but my own parents' graves, the memory of their deaths fresh as the turned earth of a burial mound.

Fisting my hands in the grass, I let the rage overtake me with a scream as I double over and sob.

I open my eyes to the sun resting at its noon high and find a glass of water sitting next to me. Blinking away from the vicious light, I sit up and stare in confusion at the glass until my befuddled mind clears.

The reverend. Of course. Embarrassment threatens to flood me again, but I shake it off. There's a dull ache behind my eyes, and my throat stings from crying. But I'm back inside myself at least. It's a relief.

"Enou—*hic*—gh," I say aloud and reach for the water.

Movement off to my left catches my attention, and I glance over.

"Holy shit." I gasp, flinching away from the large rabbit crouched not two feet from me. Scooting back, I wonder why the creature would come so close, especially in the middle of the day. Dabbing my eyes, I stare at the animal, water forgotten.

Clearly having more in common with Aesop's Hare than Peter Cottontail, the fur along its back and face is a deep, specked brown, while its underbelly fades to buff, marred only by little clumps of leaves. Its nose twitches, but with glassy, black eyes and rod-straight ears, the harmless beast looks surprisingly formidable. Still confused as to why it's come so close, I glance around and catch my breath. Laying in the grass at the rabbit's feet is my mother's ring. My hand darts to my neck only to find the broken chain snagged in the throat of my sweater.

"Shoo," I say, expecting the animal to dart away.

It doesn't.

Shifting onto the balls of my feet, I lean forward and swat at it. "Go—*hic*—away!"

Nothing. Locking its doll-like eyes with mine, the damn thing snatches up the ring in its mouth and bolts.

"Damn it," I hiss and take off after it, straight across the graves. It's heading for the trees. "No, no, no, no," I call impotently as the hare wriggles under the gnarled roots of the largest yew.

Skidding to a halt, I stoop down to look after it. Expecting the entrance to a warren, I'm pleased to see the roots simply vault over a small tunnel that leads into the hollow core of the tree. Scraps of light filtering through the canopy make the salt-white pearls gleam against the black earth. There's no sign of the little thief, but I heave a thankful sigh at not having to stick my arm down a dark rabbit hole. Standing up, I lean into the mouth of the primordial trunk, but the ring's still too far down for me to grab.

I'll have to climb in. If I lose that ring or get arrested for damaging antiquities, I will hunt that rabbit down and have Mrs. Jones put it in a stew.

Carefully, I hoist myself up the side of the trunk. The warm, knobby bark rewards my intrusion with a keen scratch. I suck in a breath and look down as a ridge of scarlet wells up across my wrist. *Now we're even.*

I step down into the belly of the yew, anxious to grab my ring and get the hell out of here. The hollow interior is just wide enough for me to retrieve the precious heirloom and slip it deep into my pocket.

The air around me hisses, as if someone lit the burner on a stove. Fear squeezes my gut, every nerve in my body screaming *run*. I grab the trunk to pull myself out, only to jerk my hands back. The wood is scalding. There's no smoke or flame, but the mercurial orange glow of an ember surges up from the knobby base just as the space inside the trunk bends, swaddling me with invisible arms, squeezing tighter and tighter, the pressure and heat mounting until my vision tunnels into a single white dot. I gasp and have the vague sensation of slipping down a long shaft until, finally, finally the thunderous snap of a suction cup being unsealed breaks the air. I crumple to the ground in a heap, the pounding of my heart amplified and echoing through the silence.

CHAPTER 3

THE WOLF AND THE LION

Cold. It's the first thought that slips past the fog in my mind. I ache with cold. Then the rhythmic *swish* and *splat* of blades cutting through soil catches my attention, exorcising the feverish dreams of Meredith that flicker around the edges of my awareness.

I crack open my eyes, blinking. What the hell happened? Am I sick? Drugged? I can't think straight and try to stand, only to have a wave of dizziness break over me. Oh God, I think I might be sick, but the nausea passes. I look around. I'm still crouched in the belly of the yew tree. The dank, musky smell turns my tender stomach as I look up into the canopy. Frosty clouds have erased any hint of sunshine, throwing the graveyard into deep shadow.

Swish, splat, swish, splat. The sounds anchor my focus, and with a tentative hand, I touch the tree. My fingers slide over the bark, now brittle with cold.

"It's just a tree," I say, gingerly standing up. "Just a normal, not-on-fire tree because that would be crazy."

My limbs are heavy and my head aches, but I seem fine and scramble out of the yew's hollow as fast as possible.

Swish, splat.

Stepping clear of the roots, I turn toward the sound and freeze. Not twenty feet away, two men stand with their backs to me. Both are wearing long, dingy shirts, trousers, and odd, fitted caps. I only see flashes of their hands and faces, but what I can see are filthy from shoveling a large pile of dirt back into a trench near the center of the churchyard.

As I watch the men work, unease twitches in my belly like the tail of a restless cat. How could they have accomplished so much in such a short time? Still unseen, I scan the ground for my bag, which should be visible from here, but see nothing. Another stone lands on the growing pile of fear in my gut. Did someone take it? Maybe Reverend Fitzwilliam picked it up?

My already cottony mouth goes dry as the June desert. What if people are looking for me? Shit. The thought of Mrs. Jones calling the police when I don't turn up—who would then notify my sister, who would then panic and go into early labor —has my pulse spiking. I cannot ruin anything else.

Breathing faster, I spin to face the church and gasp.

What the fuck?

Questions logjam my brain as I stare at what can only be a hallucination. The bell tower is gone. Thick shutters cover each window, while the door and porch have disappeared completely.

"But that's impossible."

A phlegmy cough is the only reply. I jerk around to find the two men staring at me. I can only stare back in shock. Neither look much taller than my own 5'2," which strikes me as odd for men, but their sinewy forearms and corded necks speak of deep strength. They continue to stare without reservation. Every intuition is screaming at me to leave, run, anything, but I can't make my body move.

I need answers. Sucking in as much air as I can hold, I

swallow hard and step toward them. "Excuse me. Hi. Sorry to interrupt your work, but do you know where I can find Reverend Fitzwilliam?"

The older of the two has a pockmarked chin, which he juts forward, while the second looks no more than a teenager, his face full of freckles and scant whiskers. They exchange silent, wide-eyed looks, the teen's mouth agape.

"I can see you're busy, but I could really use some direction," I ramble.

They continue to stare as if I've said something indecent. Clearly, I've crossed some local, unknown-to-me line, but with no one else to ask, I persist, stepping closer. "You see, I ... fell asleep ... and now I can't find my bag, and I think someone might be ..."

It's then I glance down, and my words evaporate.

A shrouded body lies in the trench, clumps of soil splattered across it like ink blots on paper. I look at the men. The scarred laborer coughs again, says something in rapid Welsh, and pokes his shovel in my direction, his meaning clear.

Go.

I reel backward. Heart slapping against my sternum, I hurry around the corner of the church and lean against it. I don't know whether to be reassured or terrified by the scrape of gritty stone against my knuckles—falling through a phantom wall would have proved I was dreaming. Apparently, I'm not.

Before I have time to think and properly freak out, shouts erupt from inside the church, and the heavy wooden door, now located at the end of the church, crashes open. I press myself against the wall as two new men tumble out in a tangle of punching, kicking limbs. Attempting to get away from the violence and find the reverend, I slip inside the church and ease the door closed with a soft *thud*.

I plunge into dense shadow. Stepping below deck on a

pirate ship would have been less disorienting, and I nearly lose my balance. Ahead, sconces scattered along the walls cut the darkness into long swaths but offer little substantial light. I shuffle forward, waiting for my eyes to adjust. When they finally do, I start to tremble. At the far end of the church, the familiar rood screen glints in the firelight.

Fear grips my throat so hard I can't even scream. Even still, utter, unabashed astonishment drives me forward, down the nave and through the smoke-tinged air toward the elaborate carving.

All I can do is stare up at the wooden structure. This can't be real.

Now painted in vivid shades of green and red, the stylized depictions of a harassed hare bounding through the green woods toward the virginal Melangell are identical. Either someone has restored the screen to its original splendor in a matter of hours, or I've gone mad.

I go through every possible argument as to why this is not the same piece of craftsmanship I saw earlier today with Reverend Fitzwilliam. But my trembling limbs and racing heart confirm what my mind wants to deny. It is. It can't be, but it is. The stone floor tilts beneath me, and I sit down hard.

Then I see him. Kneeling in front of the shrine, he first appears little more than a broad shadow in the flickering light. But as I watch, the man crosses himself, stands, and picks up a tall staff from the ground.

When he turns and stops short, I know I've been seen.

"I'm looking for Reverend Fitzwilliam." I force the words out as I struggle to my feet. I can't see him clearly, but as he steps forward, the edges of his cloak flap open to reveal dark woolen clothing and a pair of high leather boots. A dagger the size of my forearm hangs from his belt, and while he's not massive, he has the long-limbed amble of a tall man.

"Ha-have you seen her?" My voice is weak with panic. I edge backward.

The stranger advances, this time pausing under the amber glow of a sconce. Deep-set eyes stare back at me from their place between heavy eyebrows and a prominent nose.

"Be ye on pilgrimage?" His voice holds the gentle rumble of distant thunder and catches me off guard.

Despite his size and the stern set of his mouth, relief trickles down my spine; the man's English, though heavily accented, is a welcome sound. I force myself to go still and wait for any sense of danger to rise from his presence. Unexpectedly, the thrash of fear in my belly eases.

"Pilgrimage? No. I just walked from town. Please, I need to—"

"Town?"

"Yes," I say, frustration rising to replace the fear. "Llangynog. And I'm looking for Reverend Fitzwilliam. Do you know her?"

The man scratches at the dark whiskers along his jaw with an elegant, long-fingered hand and looks me over. I cross my arms and do my best to stare back until I realize he isn't ogling. More curious than predatory, the stranger gazes at me as if I were an exotic animal.

I stare back. "Right. I'll take that as a no. Do you know anyone else who might help me?"

Once more, my dark and brooding companion catches my eyes. Holds them. "I know not who ye seek, mistress. Make haste from whence ye came."

With that, he looks away and strides past me.

"Well, that's just fucking perfect." I fling my arms in frustration as the church doors open.

Literally crowing with excitement, a second figure saunters in with a burst of light. The energy of the newcomer announces his youth well before he pauses in the torchlight. As short and fair as the first man is tall and dark, the burly teenager sports a scratched cheek and a satisfied smirk. Tufts of grass and mud cling to his shoulders and hair, but he either doesn't know or doesn't care.

Mr. Dark and Brooding shakes his head. "I see fortune has favored ye."

"Methinks ye can thank my brawn for the favor, not fortune's bloody wheel, brother," scoffs the younger man.

"I shall remember that the next time yon *blaidd* tries to knife yer foolish arse o'er dice."

The fair youth shrugs as if this is a silly concern. It's then he finally catches sight of me and smiles.

"*Su'mae*," he greets.

The tall man slings the staff—which is actually an enormous wooden longbow—across his back before speaking into the fair one's ear. The teen's eyebrows shoot up and then pinch into a scowl.

"Hey," I say, letting my irritation and fear roil up. "Are you able to help me or not?"

Neither man answers.

Tears pinch my throat, but I swallow them down viciously. Enough of that.

"Fine," I say and push past them, ready to walk back to town and the comfort of Mrs. Jones's inn. Approaching the door, I look down so I don't trip and smack into someone in the archway.

"Oh! Sorry," I say, stumbling back.

In response to my courtesy, a thick hand clamps onto my wrist and wrenches it behind me as another wraps around my throat.

"Ow! Stop it!" I scream, my shoulder muscles burning in protest.

A coarse voice laughs behind me, and I gag at the stench of my attacker's sulfurous breath. Only then does terror truly take hold, and I lose myself, kicking at his ankles and wrenching myself forward. It's useless. He twists my arm harder, squeezes my neck, and brings my struggles to an immediate stop. Pain and desperation sweep over me as I hear my own breath leak out in a sob.

"*Gad iddi fynd.*" The dark man's deep voice sweeps over me.

I lift my eyes and see the brothers crouched in a battle stance. Dark and Brooding's unsheathed dagger glints in the wavering light.

"Forsooth, if another beating be yer wish," the younger, fair man says in English, his fists raised, "ye could have asked. Naught would please me more."

"Give back me purse, *bachgen,*" my assailant spits over my shoulder, "or I shall make good use o' yer bitch Saxon."

"I'm not—" I start, only to suck in a ragged breath as the man yanks my wrist between my shoulder blades. I pitch forward, no longer able to look up as every muscle in my back and right shoulder screams.

The dark man speaks a single, expectant word in Welsh. A snort of disgust from his companion follows, and I see something tossed at my feet. The jingle of coins is unmistakable.

Placated, my attacker loosens his grip. A mistake I will make him pay for. Instinct takes over, and before I can think not to, I ram my elbow into his gut with all my strength. Doubling over, he stumbles as I whip out of his grasp.

"You goddamn son of a bitch!" I scream, slapping him repeatedly.

Suddenly, a new pair of arms wrap around my waist and lift me clear off the ground as if I weigh nothing.

"Hey!" I gasp in protest but not before a wet crunching sound makes my gut roil. Craning around, I see the younger brother pull his fist away from the bloody pulp that used to be my attacker's nose.

Bursting into the tepid daylight, Dark and Brooding sets me on my feet.

"Find yer escort and be gone. Now," he says, his voice an anvil, blunt and immovable.

Dizzy and frantic, I grip my aching shoulder and stare dumbfounded as he runs across the churchyard. My mouth falls open. Two shaggy horses stand at a hitching post in what should be the parking lot. Beyond that, matted woods extend in every direction. Neither structure, nor fence, nor road is visible through the greenery.

The edges of my vision wobble. "What the fuck is going on?"

Content to toy with the trees, the wind doesn't answer. There's no time to process the impossibility of what I'm seeing as the fair brother runs past, blood-splattered and smiling. He nods in acknowledgment before springing onto the horse his brother readied for him. They're leaving.

"Wait!" I cry, too desperate for rational thought. "Where are you going?"

"Dwyn Blair." Free from the dim church, the teen's fair cheeks glow pink with exertion, his hair a pale ginger mane around his head. "Our father be freeborn with land o'er yon mountains." He points in what I think is west.

Over the mountains. "Is it near Bala?"

"Aye," he says.

The dark brother barks something as the horses prance and snort impatiently. He wants to leave—now—and there's no time to think.

And it's in that moment of stillness that I see it.

Just beyond the tree line, a tiny, nebulous blue light appears over the shoulder of Dark and Brooding.

The *ellylldan*. With unnatural certainty, I know what to do.

"Take me with you," I say. "My sister lives in Bala. That's where I'm traveling."

The brothers exchange a speaking glance.

"Shall not yer companions wonder after ye?" the older brother reasons.

I worry about Mrs. Jones, if there ever was a Mrs. Jones, but am not about to walk back to the village alone after what just happened. "I'm alone."

Taken aback, the men look at each other again.

I swallow, not wanting to reveal too much but sensing they won't help if I don't explain. "Look. My things have gone missing, and the person I was trying to find isn't here," I say as calmly as possible, though I'm still struggling to breathe with the adrenaline pumping through me. "I don't have any money with me, but you can have my watch as payment." I hold up my wrist. It's a nice watch but not overly expensive or sentimental. "Please."

Just then, a strangled roar erupts from inside the church. We turn. My attacker stumbles into the yard, knife in hand, gore smearing his ruined face from brow to neck. A violent spray of Welsh pours out of his mouth as he starts toward us.

The red brother reaches down to me. "Milady?"

I don't need to be asked twice. Grabbing his hand, I let myself be hauled into the saddle behind him. My arms barely slide around the stranger's waist before he kicks the horse into a gallop toward the woods.

Clouds sift the milky sunlight as we emerge from the trees after riding hard for what feels like an hour. In front of us, the moorlands stretch away like the monstrous surf of an emerald-and-auburn sea. Dizzy and sore from galloping, I watch the world go by in a blur. My mind is no less tangled. I cannot explain the changes to St. Melangell's church any more than I can explain everyone's bizarre dress and speech. Is it possible that I'm hallucinating this vividly for this long? Or can I truly be somewhere so remote that modern clothes and language aren't readily used? Some sort of elaborate hoax? Nothing seems possible, and that thought alone makes my insides turn over and over and over.

"Can we stop for a minute?" I say into the strawberry-blonde's ear.

With a nod, he pulls the horse up and gives a loud whistle. "In need o' a rest, are ye?"

"If it's safe."

"Oh, aye. I could use a spot to drink myself," he says.

Having turned around at the whistle, the dark-haired brother rides close enough for me to see that his long nose is slightly hooked, his heavily lashed eyes the exact shade of a mourning dove's wing. If his mouth wasn't twisted into such a nasty scowl, he'd be handsome.

Shivering with cold and probably shock, I slide off the horse as a single, icy raindrop splashes my cheek. My legs wobble a bit as I work to steady my breathing. The younger brother dismounts after me and pulls a leather pouch from his saddle bag.

"Milady," he says, offering it to me first.

My throat aches with thirst. Trying not to think of germs, I upend the odd canteen into my mouth. The tang of wine shocks my taste buds, which had been expecting water. I manage to swallow before coughing against my arm.

"Thank you," I wheeze and take another pull before handing it back.

"'Tis good, I trow," he says before knocking back his own mouthful.

"Yep."

Capping the canteen, he wipes a forearm over his face, smearing the still-damp splatters of blood across his chin. "Pray, what be ye called?"

I blink, cursing myself silently. In all the chaos, I never even told them my name or asked theirs. What am I doing here?

"Meg. Meg Quinn." Another raindrop lands on my cheek as the wind rises, nipping through my sweater. Cold seeps through my body until my fingertips ache with it. "And you?"

With his ruddy hair splayed like a halo, the young man smiles wide enough for me to see that one of his bottom teeth is missing. "Madoc ap Cai, yer servant." He gestures toward the man with the bow who hasn't moved. "Yon *gafr* be my brother, Steffan."

Steffan looks up at the sound of his name. Without changing his expression, he retrieves something from his own saddle bag and tosses it to Madoc.

"I would present Mistress Meg Quinn," Madoc says, handing me what looks like a hunk of beef jerky.

Steffan dips his chin a fraction and turns away.

"I don't think your brother's very happy about me being here," I say, sniffing the dried meat.

"Steffan be"— Madoc grunts and makes an all-encompassing gesture with his hand— "Steffan," he says through a mouthful of the dried meat. "'Tis naught to do with ye."

I can't help but find his gooseberry-green eyes sincere. I let my gaze slide over to Steffan as he tends his horse. Remembering the accusing way he looked at me in the church, I say, "I'm not so sure about that."

"Nottsashurabootthat? What means this?" Madoc asks.

"A nottsa—oh, nothing," I amend and take bite of the meat. It's gamey and salty, sucking even more moisture from my mouth, but the protein is welcome, so I keep chewing.

"Do you stop at St. Melangell's often?" I ask after finally swallowing.

Madoc stuffs the remaining meat in his mouth and nods. "Aye. We travel to market in Llanrhaeadr-ym-Mochnant since—"

"Whence have ye come?" demands a not-so-good-natured voice from behind me.

I turn to find Steffan alarmingly close. The disparity between the delicate color of his eyes and their vicious expression does something to my pulse.

Madoc steps closer. "God's bones, man, have ye nay shame to ask her such? And ye say I have a dog's manners, do ye? I think not."

Steffan keeps his eyes trained on me.

I look between the two, not quite understanding their exchange, before answering. "I already told you. I walked from Llangynog."

"Afore that. Whence do yer kin hail?"

I cross my arms. I still don't think I'm in immediate danger —at least not from these two—but revealing too much information seems unwise. On the other hand, I'm in no position to make demands. So, the truth, but not quite.

"My mother was born in Cardiff, and my father was born in Pennsylvania but grew up with his grandmother in Ireland before coming back to the States. So, I'm an American with Welsh and Irish parents."

"American?" Madoc repeats and grabs the horse's reins before it can wander off. "I ne'er heard o' that commote."

I crane around to look at him but find nothing to say. The facade of my disbelief rumbles, chips.

Steffan frowns. "What part o' *Iwerddon*?"

"I don't speak Welsh."

His scowl deepens. "Ireland."

"County Clare," I choke out. "Now if you'll excuse me," I say, addressing an issue I could no longer put off, "I need to use the bathroom."

Madoc inclines his head. "A bath? Now?"

"No. I need a few minutes of privacy to … relieve myself."

Madoc's face lights with understanding, and he points to a small outcropping of stone about twenty feet away. "Ye can have a piss o'er yonder."

The spitting rain morphs into a steady drizzle as I pick my way around the mossy pile of rocks. I'm embarrassed and trembling violently, so it's a chore not to fall or pee on myself. But I'll be damned before I make things worse. If that's even possible. Part of me wonders if I should escape—head back to the church somehow or even toward Llangynog. But a deeper sense knows it would be jumping out of the frying pan and straight into the fire.

After struggling with my wet jeans, I trudge back to where both men sit astride their horses, faceless and menacing with their hoods pulled tight against the rain. Water rolls off their wool-and-leather clothing in glassy beads.

I can't hold back full-body shiver. "Is Bala much farther?"

"Aye, a bit," says Madoc as he hefts me up behind him.

Clenching my teeth to stop the chattering, I try—and fail— to be grateful for his honesty. Long past reserve, I press myself against Madoc's back for warmth as Steffan pulls alongside us. When his heavy cloak falls across my shoulders, I flinch at the unexpected weight and knock it into the muddy grass.

"Shit." I slide off after the garment, landing hard.

"*Beth sy'n digwydd?*" says Madoc, looking back for me.

Words refuse to form as I hand the hooded cape up to Steffan. Rain drips into my eyes, and the fabric is still warm from his body heat. It's all I can do not to press my face into the cloth.

With an expertly raised eyebrow, Steffan takes his cloak, brushes off the flecks of mud, and gestures for me to turn around.

"I'm f-f-fine," I stutter, unable to keep my teeth from chattering.

Belatedly, Madoc joins in. "Ye be welcome to use my mantle, milady."

"I don't n-n-need anything."

"Turn around." Like a deep current that leaves little disturbance along the surface, Steffan's quiet voice belies the force beneath.

I pause, hating to show these strangers any further weakness. But desire for warmth wins out over pride, and I turn, letting him wrap the heavy cape around me. I nearly moan as I press my hands and face into the warm fabric, nearly dizzy with relief. Closing my eyes, I inhale. Wool, woodsmoke, sweat, and some underlying sweetness waft up from the garment like steam.

Madoc clears his throat.

"Thank you," I say and struggle back onto the horse. Pulling the hood tight around my face, I link my arms around Madoc. The last thing I see for a good long while is Steffan's wide back riding away from me.

CHAPTER 4
BALA

Traveling by horseback on a stormy afternoon is not the ideal time for conversation. Madoc doesn't agree. As the rain thins to a blustery mist, he chatters like a magpie, needing no more encouragement than the occasional "mmhmm" I utter from between his shoulder blades. His accent is still so prominent that most of what he says is unintelligible to me, but I glean that he has several younger siblings and hates sheep. Then he sings. Momentarily grateful for my ignorance, I tuck my head and ignore him. Steffan remains impressively silent.

What feels like hours later, I look up. We're descending into a valley. Twilight-soaked woods clot around us, obscuring my view, as I listen to the sounds of evening and catch my breath. Even my fatigue and fear can't blot out the wild beauty of this place.

"Are we close?" I dare to ask. The sense that I should be able to see or hear the city by now persists like an itch.

Madoc points at a clump of trees. "Aye. 'Tis yonder. Have ye ne'er been?"

Without answering, I stare over his shoulder, hardly daring to blink, until the branches peel away and Lake Bala comes into view.

Flecks of waning daylight skip across the black water, pointing my gaze toward a jumble of twinkling lights at its head. Skeins of white smoke spiral into the darkening sky. In that exact moment, I understand that either the city is on fire or something is terribly, terribly wrong. Electric light doesn't move like that.

The panic I've dammed behind a levy of disbelief sprays out from the cracks. Gulping air, I replay the events of the day, trying to make sense out of the nonsensical. Then I remember what Reverend Fitzwilliam said about the rood screen in the church, and my heart crawls into my mouth.

"Fifteenth century," I wheeze, forcing the words past my chapped lips.

"Milady?" Madoc asks, interrupting himself.

I can't respond. Looking over, I study Madoc and Steffan as closely as the coming dark allows, trying to place their clothing and weapons, given my limited knowledge of medieval art. The process leaves me dizzy, as if I'm suddenly free falling, tumbling end over end, with nothing to grasp but the string of a broken balloon. Trying not to hyperventilate, I make a clumsy attempt at prayer as we merge onto a muddy road. Well-used and triple the width of the mountain track we've been following, the road's empty of travelers until we round a final bend and Bala springs up ahead.

I suck in another tight breath. Structures made of wattle, daub, and timber form a clear perimeter, but without a fortified wall, the city seems little more than a collection of gingerbread houses alight with candles. Shapes start to appear out of the low light, and after crossing a crowded bridge, we fall into line behind several lumbering wagons. Panic roars through me, but with nowhere to go, I freeze, no better than a terrified rabbit. At the mouth of the city, soldiers wander about, their chainmail flashing in the torchlight as they check cargo.

"Keep yer head down, aye? Whatever ye do, do nay speak," Madoc whispers. If I wasn't already petrified, the tension in his voice would have made me so. Clearly, here is something else to fear.

With a garbled command, a metal-laden man hails us to stop. Steffan obeys. The soldier speaks again, louder this time. Steffan's reply slides out in a hiss. Whatever is said ignites the damp air around us. I hold my breath. Animosity simmers between the men until the soldier gives a yowling laugh and shoves a gloved hand into Steffan's saddlebag. Finding nothing of interest but Steffan's wine carrier, the soldier helps himself to a deep swig and turns his attention to Madoc and me. He doesn't return the canteen.

The already hard muscles of Madoc's back go rigid, but neither brother protests the intrusion. After the fight I witnessed at the church, it's difficult to imagine what kind of threat keeps them muzzled, but clearly, this soldier does. As the man approaches to search Madoc's things, I glance over, curious.

A mistake.

The bearded soldier leers up at me, his face split into a lascivious grin. I turn away, feeling instead of seeing his hand on my thigh. I jerk back, but Madoc's free arm whips around holding me in place. My stomach roils, and it takes every speck of self-control I have not to fling the soldier's hand from me like a tarantula. Furious and scared, I close my eyes like a child who believes the monster will disappear.

Seconds later he does, laughing at my discomfort, his point

clear. We start moving again, and I peek around the folds of my hood as a wide dirt street opens before us. Sewage perfumes the air, and dozens of people dressed for *The Canterbury Tales* dart through the street. As my heartbeat thrums in my ears, I know with shocking, crystalline clarity that I won't find my sister here.

That I won't find her *now*.

We stop just in time. Fear and shock rocket through me as I slide out of the saddle and retch in the street. No one looks twice as I turn inside out.

"Greensick from the road, milady?" Madoc asks calmly when I regain my feet.

"You could say that." I wipe my mouth with a shaking hand. "Who was that man? What did he want?"

Madoc makes a derisive sound as he ties off the horse. "*Saeson* dogs," he says, though his voice is pitched low. "Ye need not be affrighted."

I stare at his shifting expression in the torchlight, willing him to confess the lie, but neither of us say anything. Behind him, Steffan clears his throat. Taking this as his cue, Madoc steps close.

"I would take yer trinket to market afore curfew, milady." He opens his hand, unabashed.

"Right," I mutter and hand over my watch. I should thank him for the escort, but knowing I've come all this way for nothing freezes the words in my mouth.

Madoc tucks the prize into his leather vest and steps back with a grand bow. "Shall I escort ye to yer good-brother's on the way?"

Shit.

"Uh, I'd like to rest a few minutes. I'm not feeling very well," I say, which is more than true. Cold sweat springs out of my already muddy palms. I wipe them on my jeans, frantic.

"Goon about yer task, Madoc." Steffan's voice rumbles from the shadows as he tends to the horses. He makes a dismissive gesture in my direction. "I shall see to this."

Despite being indebted to them, I bristle at being referred to as *this*.

"'Tis warmer inside," Steffan says and points to the busy establishment behind us.

"You don't need to bother. I'll be fine."

He raises an eyebrow and looks straight at me. Through me.

My cheeks flush against the cold air. He's calling my bluff, and it's a problem.

"Pray, come along, milady. I shall help ye find yer kin," Madoc petitions.

Pinned between Steffan's shrewd stare and Madoc's pleading words, I do the only thing I can. I stall.

"Thank you," I say to Madoc and give him the best smile I can conjure while queasy. "But I'll find my way. I'd like to go inside and warm up first."

"As ye please, milady." Madoc's eyes tighten, but he bows deeply before stalking through the mired streets. He doesn't spare his brother a glance.

I turn to find Steffan waiting in the busy doorway. With my mind on fire, I gather my nerve, pull the cape tight around my shoulders to hide my clothing, and follow Mr. Dark and Brooding into the light.

If it was difficult to see outside, it's only slightly less so inside. Hay covers the floor of the large room where wooden tables crowded with people take up most of the space. There's a bar at the far end and too many sconces and table candles rendering the air smoky and dense.

"Do not stray." Steffan's voice is a gravelly hiss near my ear. I flinch when he takes my elbow but don't pull away when he guides us to a free bench near the door, his grip firm but gentle. My skin is so cold I can feel the heat of his hand through the cloak. Next to us, a pair of ripe-smelling men hunch over some kind of game and speak in loud, sporadic bursts of Welsh, which, along with the hypnotic flicker of the wall sconces, leaves me completely disoriented.

The feeling reminds me of our last trip as a family of four. Clad in braces and first bikinis, Meredith and I giggled as we backed into the ocean. While the surf crashed against our adolescent thighs, making our faces sticky with salt, the sand shifted beneath my feet. Before I could even scream, I went under. The water was only a few feet deep, but as the swell swept over my face, I'd no idea which way was up.

Folding my hands to keep them from trembling, I try to think. I have no supplies, don't know the way, and need to get back over the mountain as quickly as possible without being seen. My insides start to roll, and I swallow hard as my mouth waters.

Steffan, who hasn't taken his pale eyes off me, waves his hand, and seconds later, a plump woman in a wool dress of ambiguous color materializes with two mugs of what smells like piss.

"Do ye know where to find yer sister?" Steffan asks after taking a long pull of the dubious liquid.

I chew my bottom lip but can't muster the mental clarity to lie. "No." The truth lands between us, heavy with meaning. "But I'll find my way. I just needed to warm up for a minute."

Steffan's breaks his gaze to contemplate his mug, the

muscles of his jaw clenched. "What trade has yer good-brother?"

My mind stumbles over the words for several long seconds before understanding. "He's a ... I don't know what you call it here. Someone who gives medicine to people when they're sick?" The explanation comes out as a question, and I want to kick myself. I doubt the title of pharmacist would mean anything to him.

Steffan furrows his thick brows, drums his long fingers on his mug. "The apothecary be at the end o' the street afore the church."

I nod. "I should, uh, be on my way then." Setting my untouched beverage on the bench, I stand, careful not to bump into anyone. "Thanks."

With unsteady hands, I unclasp the cloak and hold it out to him. Steffan's powder gray eyes shift between the dense material and my denim-clad legs. Over his shoulder, I catch the look of a woman across the room, her mouth open like a fish.

He waves the cloak off and takes another long pull from his mug. "Pray, give my greeting to Master Padrig," he says, pale eyes meeting mine. "'Tis unexpected for certes to hear o' his marrying again, seeing as I spoke to his bride o' many years on St. Dafydd's Day."

The blood congeals in my veins. He knows I'm lying.

"Yes, it was ... sudden," I say and nearly run for the door. I don't need to look back to know Steffan is watching me. I can feel it.

Night has settled in quickly, draping the sky with her own star-flecked mantle as I re-clasp Steffan's cloak around my neck. Too grateful for the cover to feel guilty, I sink into the hood and look around. There's clearly no point in going anywhere except directly back to that damn tree, but between the darkness and my lack of provisions, I need to get creative. Ducking between the horses, I yank the remaining wineskin off Madoc's saddle and shove it under my sweater before rifling through the saddlebag for anything else that might help.

I gasp when the blade bites into my flesh. Whipping my hand out of the bag, I press my fingers to my mouth. The hot, metallic taste of blood does nothing to quell my quaking stomach. A ginger inspection reveals two of them are sliced across the tips, but the cuts aren't deep. I ball my hand into a fist and reach into the bag with the uninjured one, slowly this time. Feeling the blade, I move down to the smooth hilt and pull out a dagger.

"Thank you, Baby Jesus for thick socks," I mumble, tucking the unsheathed knife into my boot. I have no idea how to wield the weapon but feel safer nonetheless.

At that moment, a large group rides past, causing the thick-bodied horses to shift their weight and neigh. Weak torchlight glints off the riders' armor, and I know just enough about Welsh history to gather the military men are English. One of them guffaws, and Madoc's horse jerks its head. I scuttle out of the way as the last horseman passes by. I freeze. It's the soldier from the gate. His gaze skims over me without interest as I slink back into the shadows. It's difficult to hear with my heart thundering in my ears, but when the street goes relatively quiet, I peek out. Up ahead, on the far side of the crossroads, looms the ghost of a steeple.

A church—now that could be useful. Maybe I can claim sanctuary and stay until morning? It's worth the chance. Decided, I dart into the street, hugging the dark as much as possible. The church looms just ahead, but I have to traverse the crossroads to get there. Only a few silhouettes move among the shadows now as I start forward.

Stars burst in my vision as a blow comes from behind. Hot

pain shoots through my skull. Staggering, I cry out and fall to the ground, catching myself hard on my open hands. Someone yanks me back by my braid, clamping a rough hand over my mouth. I try to bite, but my attacker presses his fingers together and drags me away as the wineskin slips from under my sweater and bursts in the street. If anyone sees me, they melt away into the night.

Scratching at the arms that hold me, I flail violently, but the man moves his hand from my mouth to around my neck and pulls. Helpless, I dip in with my fingernails as the breath is choked out of me. Terror pulses through me with every heartbeat as I'm pulled deeper into the darkness of a side street.

Suddenly, I'm on the ground, gasping.

Coughing and gagging, I look up and find exactly what I feared—the soldier from the gate. I lunge for the dagger in my boot, but I'm too slow. Knocking my arm away, the man shoves me to my back and forces his weight on me, crushing the breath from my lungs. Packed earth and rocks dig into my shoulder blades as I fight to breathe, to free myself, but pain can't pierce the screaming alarms in my head as his hard length presses against my thigh. Panicked that I'll suffocate, I gasp while another voice reasons that if I stop breathing, I won't get raped. At least I won't notice.

"Give us a kiss, wench," the soldier slurs, using one hand to grab my jaw while the other grips my throat. This frees my arms just enough to reach up and rake my nails across his exposed face. He roars.

"Whore!" the man spits and smashes his fist into my cheek.

Pain radiates across my cheek, and I moan, the world spinning. I start to drift, going slack against the nausea blooming in my gut. No, no, no, no, I think as he starts ripping at my jeans, his forearm now at my neck, pushing.

This is it.

The thought appears just as I hear the sick punch of flesh being torn. I wonder if it's mine as something hot and slippery splatters my face. Then the weight on my chest and neck disappears, and my lungs balloon without my consent. My eyes flutter open. A dark face peers into mine, shadow against shadow. Then the world wavers and everything goes black.

CHAPTER 5
DWYN BLAIR

I'm dead. It's the only logical explanation for why the sulfurous stench of the alley has been replaced by a heady mixture of woodsmoke and hay. I assumed the afterlife would smell more delicate—like hyacinth or vanilla. A vague hope. Instead of music or endless silence, there's only a faint clanking sound in the distance.

Wait. That can't be right.

I sit up. Pain radiates across my skull and shoots down my back. "Ow," I hear myself say, easing back to a soft surface. I reach toward my pounding head just as small, cold fingers clamp around my own. My eyes fly open, and I jerk away from the unknown touch.

A girl stumbles back, her long, pale hair fluttering out from behind her shoulders like wings. Eyes wide, she points first to her face and then to mine before shaking her head and disappearing into the darkness. Breathing in shaky gasps, it feels like my blood will burst my veins, it's pumping so hard. The girl doesn't return.

Trembling, I strain to make out my surroundings. Gray light seeps in around a small, shuttered window, but nothing else is visible beyond the simple bed I'm on and a strange candlestick flickering on a nearby table. The firelight wobbles against the pallid walls, making me feel faint. Clearly, I'm out of the alley, but where am I? And with whom?

Struggling to stay calm, I take inventory of myself—my face feels swollen and tight, my hands and back scraped and bruised. Everything aches but only dully.

It could be worse.

My mind snaps to a memory of the soldier's blubbery lips curled back in a snarl. With a shudder, I wrap my battered arms around myself, the cool rub of naked flesh coming as another shock. I'm bare under the heavy woolen blanket, and dread pools in my belly all over again.

"Be not affrighted," says a voice, rolling out of the dark like quiet thunder. "Nay harm shall come to ye here." A woman wearing a gray wool gown wades into the shallow pool of light near the table. Black hair curls out from under her white cap, and an earthen bowl sits in the crook of each arm.

I pull the blanket tighter, my cheeks burning. "Where am I?"

The woman's eyes go wide at my voice, but she remasters her expression and moves to the edge of my cot, skirts swishing. I tense. Holding my face with her shiny, serious eyes, she sits with care. "Dwyn Blair."

"I don't understand."

She sets the bowls next to me. "My husband's farm. 'Tis but a few hours ride from Bala."

I close my eyes as unshed tears burn my throat. I've been beaten, nearly raped, and gotten myself even farther from St. Melangell's. My mind whirls, but I need answers. Now.

"Who are you?" I ask.

"Angharad gwraig Cai ap Hywel. Pray, come by here, now. Let me fetch this off ye." She reaches for me.

I flinch away. "How did I get here?"

Undeterred, she gently takes hold of my chin and pulls something from my cheekbone. I look down, and my stomach heaves. A leech squirms in the first bowl, its slimy body gorged on my blood.

Forcing my gaze from the writhing thing, I ask again, "How did I get here?"

Angharad's lips tighten. "Steffan and Madoc brought ye. 'Tis nay wonder ye cannot recall much," she says and picks up the other bowl.

I lean away.

"Be still. This shall not cause ye pain," she says, clearly having enough of my resistance, and smears a garlic-smelling paste around my eye socket and into the scratches down my back.

I sit still while the news and the salve sink in. Madoc and Steffan brought me here in the night, which given the thread of light I noticed around a shuddered window, had come and gone. So much time lost. I groan, knowing I'll never forgive myself for disappearing on Meredith like this. There's a good chance she won't either. I have precious few responsibilities to worry about back in the States—I made sure of that before agreeing to spend several months abroad—but every day spent here is one more to explain. But how can I explain the impossible?

Finished with her ministrations, Angharad gathers the bowls and stands. "Yer breeches and shirt shall be washed, though they be damaged. There be spare garments for ye."

Now that my eyes have adjusted, I take in my surroundings for the first time. The wood floor's strewn with hay, and the small bed I'm on boasts a straw-stuffed mattress with a heavy wool blanket. Two others just like it line the opposite wall. A modestly carved trunk rests in a corner with a tidy pile of clothes on top.

"Thank you," I manage, unable to look at her.

"Gwenhwyfar shall bring ye some *cawl* to break yer fast." With that, she disappears through a small doorway in the whitewashed wall, the tired flames swaying with her departure.

I put my head in my hands. I want nothing more than to roll over and drift back into oblivion, but my stinging wounds prove a tiresome reminder of all that has happened. At least, all that seems to have happened. Gingerly, I swing around and place my feet on the cold, prickly floor. Dragging the blanket with me, I shuffle to the chest. There's a linen slip, a long-sleeved green tunic with a full-skirted brown overdress, a pair of knit stockings that tie above the knee, leather slippers, and a white cap like the one Angharad wore.

The slip, stockings, and shoes are easy enough. I'm not about to put a strange hat on my already filthy hair, so I ignore that. The dresses are another matter. Once I get both tunic and gown over my head, the laces prove a struggle.

"Fuuuuuuck," I hiss as the towheaded girl reappears in the doorway.

In one arm, she holds yet another basin, in the other, a loaf of bread. Thank God.

"Hello," I greet for lack of anything better to say and flop my aching arms down like a frustrated child. "Would you help me with this?"

If this is Gwenhwyfar, her name quite outsteps her. Barely out of girlhood and truly petite, the top of her snowy head just clears my chin, and her enormous eyes leave a petite nose, mouth, and chin little option but to cower. Crossing the room, she sets the bowl and bread on the table before looking back at me. Feathery hair drifts down to her waist.

"You look a lot like Madoc," I say.

She stands there, filling up the cell with her unnerving silence.

"Is he your brother?"

Still silent, her jadeite eyes sweep over my predicament before she starts adjusting the neckline and sleeves of the dress, making the green tunic less visible in some places and more prominent in others, before lacing up the front of the heavy woolen gown.

"You don't understand a word I'm saying, do you?"

She doesn't answer, but when she finally looks up, a web of unspoken questions stretches between us.

"You wouldn't believe me if I told you."

Inclining her head, Gwenhwyfar searches my face before pointing to the table. After pantomiming what I guessed was washing and eating, she points toward the doorway. When I nod, she reaches into the pocket of her apron and pulls out a small wooden spoon. The simply hewn utensil shines in the candlelight before she sets it down and scurries out the door.

Comforted by Gwenhwyfar's brief appearance, I focus on the table. The basin brims with water, and I sink my hands in. Freezing cold, the water shocks me awake as I splash my face again and again until my cheeks sting with something other than pain. After rebraiding my hair, I attend to the other item. What appeared to be a round of bread is actually a bowl brimming with stew. My mouth waters as I take a timid bite. Warm and dense, the soup tastes wonderful. I can't identify a single ingredient and don't care as I eat every salty, earthy mouthful.

Now dressed and fed and as clean as I'm likely to get, I consider the doorway. I believe what Angharad said about not being harmed here, but my heart bounces against my ribs nonetheless as I listen. From somewhere below, voices rise up on the backs of heat and light, drawing me in and terrifying me in turn.

With a steeling breath, I step over the threshold—and right

into a pair of scrawny, black-haired boys. I gasp and nearly topple over the railing of the landing I've just stepped onto.

"Holy shit," I gasp as they spring up like marionettes. Chattering loudly in Welsh, they stampede down the narrow staircase to my left, trampling each other as they go. Gripping onto the railing for dear life, I will myself not to slide to the floor and have a proper cry.

"Be ye well, milady?" Madoc's tawny hair crests the stairs. Holding a candle in one hand and stuffing something crumbly in his mouth with the other, he stands over me, looking concerned. "Did the wee lads affright ye?"

"Hello, Madoc," I manage and straightened up.

The only thing changed is his hair, now the color of rust and slicked back. Droplets of water drip onto the floor when he bows. I give an awkward curtsy but make no attempt to smile. Swollen and sore, my skin pulls tight against my bones, and pain starts to make itself known. Madoc steps close, openly studying my face. I lean away without meaning to, the back of my head throbbing.

"Be not abashed, milady. Ye still be most fair." His eyes shine like sea glass in the candlelight. He starts to say more when a voice booms from below.

With an exaggerated flourish, Madoc rolls his eyes and steps aside. Clutching the railing, I descend the stairs into a spacious, dimly lit room with a stone floor, large hearth, shuttered windows, and a wooden door. Polished chests and stools loiter in corners and reflect the firelight like obsidian. The most striking feature is a brightly colored tapestry hanging on the far wall, beneath which lays the biggest, mangiest dog I've ever seen.

A half-dozen pairs of eyes regard me from either side of a long, wooden table. Angharad, Gwenhwyfar, the little boys who scared the shit out of me, and Steffan remain seated as a barrel-chested older man steps forward. I dip into a curtsy this time but not before getting a look at the man. Fair and sharp-nosed with a forked beard, he's obviously Madoc and Gwenhwyfar's father. The twin boys—a fact I see clearly now—resemble Angharad, as does Steffan, though she hardly looks old enough to have a grown son.

"Ah, here be the wench who stirs a bit o' trouble," says the man as he looks me over. His voice is gruff, his gaze penetrating but not frightening. The air around him practically glows with mischievous good humor like his son.

"Apparently," I say.

The man arches a bushy eyebrow at me as the corner of his mouth twitches. "I be Cai ap Hywel o' Dwyn Blair. 'Tis good to see ye nay longer abed after yer ... affright." His stance remains easy, but the edge in his voice clips through the pretense. He clearly knows all about my *affright*.

"I can think of a few other words for it," I add.

He chuckles. "Ha! 'Tis a spirited one, for certes!"

Sucking in my cheeks, I curse my big mouth and try to play along. "Thank you for your hospitality."

"Well, Mistress Meg Quinn o' America," says Cai, stepping closer, "ye be welcome at my hearth whilst ye recover."

A forced exhale hisses past Angharad's teeth as she stands and begins clearing the table. Cai grimaces. Not sure what to make of this, I pull my attention away from the dispersing family and wonder what else Steffan and Madoc have said about me.

"That's very kind," I say, "but I was hoping to be on my way as soon as possible."

Cai shoots me a meaningful look down the bridge of his long nose. "Aye, I understand yer wish to make haste and see yer kin, but methinks ye would be wise to avoid Bala for a time. Our sheriff be an inquiring man."

I meet his frank stare. "I see."

And I do. Whoever fought the soldier likely caused trouble for themself, and while my presence here might implicate the family, showing up in Bala could draw even more unwanted attention. Of course, I'm not going back to Bala, but explaining this is out of the question. Having no answer at all, I simply nod.

Seemingly satisfied, Cai issues a sharp bow first to me and then to his wife, who refuses to look at him, before swinging open the front door. A dull patch of morning light falls on the floor like a rug as the damp air blows across my face. I shiver. One after the other, Cai, Madoc, and the twins leave the house until only Steffan remains, emerging from the corner like a shadow.

My eyes find his gray stare as if compelled. He looks larger than I remember in the enclosed space, and though his dress and appearance are mostly unchanged, I track new details. A pale scar arcs across his left cheek. His unbound hair curls at his collarbone. His mouth, no longer pressed thin in annoyance, is quite wide. It hits me. He's beautiful as a jagged cliff—brutal and desolate. He holds my stare for a heartbeat before giving a solemn nod and closing the door behind him with a loud *snick*.

Angharad is at my elbow in a heartbeat.

"Can ye work, or shall ye return abed?" While still polite, a new, unexpected dislike crackles around her tone. Over Angharad's shoulder, Gwenhwyfar stoops to give the massive dog a companionable scratch before she disappears through a small side door next to the tapestry.

"Oh. I ..." Though sore and unsettled, I'm not physically damaged and sense there's only one acceptable answer. "Work?"

The word comes out in a squeak, and I clear my throat.

She opens a trunk against the wall. Her movement jostles a sling on her back I hadn't noticed, and its occupant lets out a cry of protest. I start at the unexpected noise, which sounds very much like the yelp of a kitten.

"Methinks ye shall be too sore to churn the butter just yet," Angharad says and thrusts what look like a pair of large hairbrushes toward me. She gestures to a basket near a stool by the hearth. "The wool be just there."

The mysterious yelp escalates into a piercing yowl as Angharad sits down at the spinning wheel and proceeds to bring a tiny baby around to face her. Within seconds, she's unfastened her gown to expose one swollen breast and dried-rose nipple to the grunting babe.

Dropping my eyes to the archaic tools in my hands, I sink onto the stool, my body flush with embarrassment. What the hell am I doing here?

After the child is sated and a brief tutorial from Angharad, I spend an inordinate amount of time scraping raw wool back and forth between the paddles. All is quiet but for the fairytale whir of the spinning wheel and the crackling fire. Occasionally, Angharad glances down at the baby now strapped to her front, and twice I catch Gwenhwyfar casting furtive looks at me as she scuttles around the house. I've accomplished next to nothing before my muscles burn with fatigue. My cuts sting, and a monstrous headache pounds behind my eyes.

But worst of all are my thoughts. I'm starting to imagine the nightmare unfolding at home, and my pulse spikes at every new scenario.

Mrs. Jones or Meredith will have contacted the police by now. I'm sure of it. Which causes another problem. When I get back—I refuse to think of it as if— I'll have to concoct a story about where I've been. Because the truth, if that's what this is, will land me in a psych ward.

Looking around the room, I'm not completely sure I don't belong in one. Then one thought of a hospital snakes into another and another, until memories of Mom come pouring out.

December had not been cold, but as I stood in the doorway of her hospital room, I started to shiver. A sweet, putrid smell filled the tiny space, and I swallowed against a gag. Somehow knowing I was there, she turned toward me, smiling. My breath rushed out of my lungs like air from a balloon. It was close. Unable to speak, I walked over and leaned against the bed. She'd always been a thin woman, but the cancer had eaten her from the inside out until all that remained was a gaunt shell, so insubstantial I hesitated to touch her, fearing she'd crumble like ash. She opened her mouth to speak. I tried to shush her, to reassure her, but she wouldn't be silenced.

"Be brave, my pearl," she whispered. "Go back to her. Make it right. For me."

The paddles slip to the floor with a clatter. My ring.

Angharad's head snaps up. Her amber eyes cut between me and the tools at my feet. "Be something amiss?"

"Where are my things?"

"Things?"

"My clothes. I'd like to see them."

Her face sours. "Can it not wait?"

I shake my head. Nausea swirls in my gut again. "No."

She gives an exasperated sigh but stops the wheel and eases herself up. "Come."

I follow without picking up the paddles.

Though the wool dress is remarkably warm, the gray air pinches my face and hands as I swing my head around to get a look at the place. Perched atop a hill, the large timber-and-plaster house stares down out of shuttered eyes and a checkerboard face. A crude chimney pokes through the dense thatch and seeps smoke like the lit end of a cigarette. Skiffs of sunlight slant in from the east, and all around us, the smells of smoke and moss and manure hang in the air like mist. The world is silent save for the wind, the birds, the distant churn of water, and the surf of my own breath.

Following the slope of the land, we walk a good fifty yards down to the tree-lined bank of a swollen river. Water rushes by, jumping and foaming, snatching at everything it passes with greedy hands. I don't like the look of it. I pulled Meredith from a creek once. Looking back, we hadn't been in real danger, but I can still feel the slick rocks under my hands. The sting of the frigid water. My heart jumps like a netted fish at the memory.

When our destination comes into view, I gape. On a level spot near a clump of boulders sits a large cauldron. Bubbling and spewing steam, it looks like a bloated, black egg on a nest of kindling. Gwenhwyfar, with her flushed cheeks and sweat-darkened temples, plays the part of a weird sister well as she stirs the pot with a long paddle. The enormous dog sits at her heels, a familiar if ever there was one.

"Double, double, toil and trouble," I mutter.

Ignoring me, Angharad gives a soft whistle, and the dog's head snaps up. Gwenhwyfar looks first at her companion and then toward us, her liquid eyes locking onto Angharad as the older woman speaks in Welsh. I watch as the girl looks from Angharad to the pot of simmering water.

I dig my nails into my palms, imagining the soft white orbs of my inheritance bubbling away. Pointing, I ask, "Can I help with that?"

Angharad waves her hand in a dismissive gesture that reminds me of Mrs. Jones, just as the baby shifts in the sling. With a gurgling cry, the infant draws her attention. Angharad starts for the house without looking back. I'm not sure why she's soured to my presence after her attentive care, but I feel freer in her absence.

Turning to Gwenhwyfar I try, unsuccessfully, to smile without wincing. The tiny blonde's eyes widen farther, but she offers me the paddle when I reach for it.

"Thank you," I say, careful to avoid the scalding water.

Despite the monumental hospitality I've been shown, the truth is plain: I didn't know these people or what my ring could do for them financially. Quite a lot, I'd guess. Knowing I'll need to find it without being seen, I lean over the bubbling pot and stir. Steam swirls around my face, and within minutes, I'm sweating through the linen slip.

"Is it done?" I ask, pulling the paddle free. "How do you take it out?" My miming skills are laughable, but she nods before pointing to reed baskets on the ground and then a nearby outcropping of rocks.

"Got it." Okay, this is fine. I snatch up one of the large baskets while Gwenhwyfar smothers the fire.

Next comes the difficult task of transferring the soaking clothes from the scalding water to the baskets. My arms feel like jelly as I haul a load to the rocks, only to gape in awe as Gwenhwyfar grabs the blistering cloth with her bare hands and proceeds to wring the water from each piece before laying them across the stones. With glaring ineptitude, I grit my teeth and do my best. When my jeans finally come into sight, I grab them up and slip a scorched hand into each pocket.

Nothing. It's gone.

Instantly, my throat burns as I blink back tears.

Enough of that. I get back to the chore. After the last shirt is spread out, I run back to the cauldron and peer in. Steam drifts up from the glassy edges, but nothing remains except the wavering reflection of my battered face. Shocked at my appearance, I don't notice the other head gazing in the water with me until it speaks.

"I would that I had gutted that Saxon whoreson."

My head snaps up.

Madoc stands across from me, his young face twisted in anger. "Ye should ne'er have been on yer own, milady."

I stare at him, incredulous. "What did you say?"

He blinks, looking uncharacteristically abashed. "Pray, forgive the curses. 'Tis only that I—"

"No. The other part," I say, my ring momentarily forgotten.

"The other part?"

"What did you just say about someone getting gutted?" I nearly gag on the last word.

Madoc, looking relieved, pushes hair out of his eyes. In contrast to my morning spent mostly indoors, the ginger-haired teen has the grimy, disheveled look of a man doing hard physical labor.

"Oh, do not fret. He deserved a knife in the back long afore he smote ye." He spits on the ground.

I absorb this slowly, stupidly. "The soldier's dead?"

Madoc nods.

"Who ... who killed him?"

"Steffan. After the fool let ye wander off," he adds, kicking a stone.

Steffan. With a deep breath, I close my eyes and make myself remember the alley. The dark face hovering over mine. The soothing, unintelligible, half-recalled words spoken against my ear. The strong arms that carried me away from that place of pain and fear.

A feeling, slick as a dagger, slides between my ribs, touching my heart. It takes me a moment to name it. When I do, a new understanding of myself drifts over me, quiet and cold as snow. Regret. I regret not being the one to drive the blade into my attacker's back. And I do not regret that he's dead. Exhaustion crashes over me, sudden as a rogue wave, and I blink my eyes open only to realize Madoc is still talking.

His voice drifts into my consciousness as if from far away. "Be ye ill, milady?"

I study his face. The freckles straddling his long nose and broad cheekbones quite match my own, and I think how nice it would've been to have a little brother like Madoc.

"Just tired. Very tired," I admit, noticing absently that Gwenhwyfar is already halfway up the hill, the waist-high hound by her side.

Madoc offers his arm. "Shall I take ye back?"

All I can do is nod. Linked at the elbow with Madoc, I push all thoughts of Steffan aside and cast a despairing look around. Shame surges through me. I've lost my mother's ring. Her parting gift, my emotional anchor, is now flotsam adrift in the wilds, free to be claimed by anyone who happens upon it. Like me.

Stripped to their linen shirts and woolen trousers, the men arrive a short time later for the evening meal, the tang of sweat announcing their approach like a foreshadowing fog. Noise and energy fly off Cai and Madoc like sparks as they enter the house. Quieter but nearly smiling, Steffan follows the little boys inside. He looks up, and our eyes pull at each other, magnetic. I see two men when I look at him now: A taciturn farmer who resents my presence, and behind him, shadowy and indistinct, a second man. A man who killed another to save my life.

Breaking our gaze, Steffan closes the door, and something in my chest tightens, ratcheting up. I press my palms to the cool wall at my back as the room vacuum seals around me.

Not now, not now, not now.

Everyone jostles companionably into place around the long table while Angharad and Gwenhwyfar set bowls of stew, bread the color of almonds, and gooey, white cheese on the table. Hunger twists my gut, stealing attention away from my tightening throat as I force myself to join the group. Movement darts across my vision, and I recoil violently, an image of the soldier's fist flashing before me. Stumbling, I land hard on the hearthstone, banging my elbow, just as heat laps at my face. Before I can blink, hands like steel wrap around my arms and yank me away from the intense heat.

Dizzy and gulping air, I blink to clear my vision only to see Cai's outstretched hand hanging in the air, his eyes wide with dismay. Madoc has literally leapt onto the table, spilling ale everywhere. The rest are staring. Slowly, I turn to find Steffan crouching right in front of me. He's so close I can see the red glint of his facial hair, smell the mint and hops on his breath. Moving slowly, he peels his fingers from my arms and eases away.

"I'm s-sorry," I stutter. Blood rushes to my cheeks as mortification swiftly takes the place of my panic. "I don't know what happened," I lie.

To my surprise, it's Angharad who swoops forward.

"'Tis a crack on yon stone. Will ye not smooth it down on the morrow, Steffan?" she says, helping me to my feet.

Cai drops his hand, the corners of his eyes tight with concern.

"Pray, forgive me, mistress. Would ye honor our table?" His voice is steady, his movements careful now as he gestures to the seat to his left.

Coming back into myself, I nod and wobble to my place. The food is blessed, and everyone starts in as if nothing out of the ordinary has happened. I hold still for several more moments, grounding myself in the scents, textures, sounds, and sights of the table. These people. This house. When my brain finally believes my body is safe, hunger overrules any lingering unease. I nibbled at the bread then the cheese in between long drinks of the malty, spicy ale. Next to me, Gwenhwyfar's hearty appetite calms my nerves as the food settles in my belly.

I haven't had a panic attack in years but am no stranger to them. Meredith slept curled around my back for months after the car accident with Dad. My own human dreamcatcher. She'd wake me from my nightmares, hushing my screams so Mom wouldn't hear them. We were fifteen then. Over the next seven years, the flashbacks have faded. Until now.

No one objects when I excuse myself just after the table is cleared.

"*Nos da,* Mistress Meg," Cai says from his place near the hearth. "May the blessings o' the Virgin and *y Tylwyth Teg* be on ye."

Not sure what to make of the sentiment, I nod my thanks and trudge upstairs. I can't bring myself to meet a single eye.

In the loft bedroom, a pile of straw and blankets has been laid just inside the door. Gwenhwyfar's apron is sprawled across it. Already feeling guilty about invading the family's limited space, I move the apron back to the main bed and curl up on the straw myself. As muffled strains of familial chatter drift up from below, I bite down on my fist to keep from sobbing aloud. Only after the corner of my blanket is soaked with tears do I fall asleep to the scent of wet wool, my sister's name on my lips.

CHAPTER 6

THE LADY OF THE LAKE

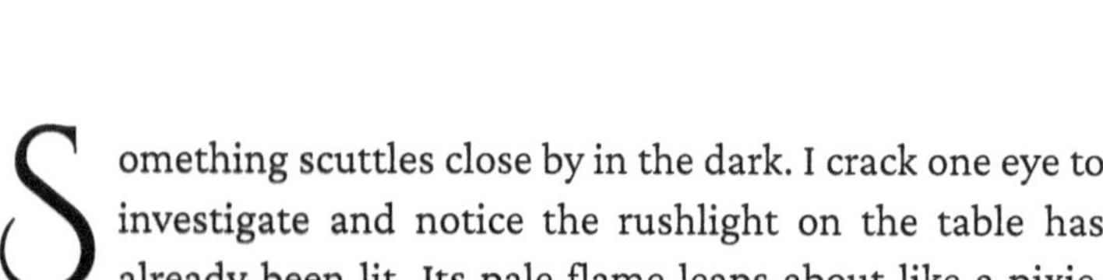

Something scuttles close by in the dark. I crack one eye to investigate and notice the rushlight on the table has already been lit. Its pale flame leaps about like a pixie, casting just enough light for me to see the twins crouched by my head like affectionate puppies.

"Hello," I croak.

With squeals of delight and terror, they jump up in unison and run from the room, their bodies bouncing off one another like Peter Pan and his shadow.

Blinking slowly, I roll onto my back. My stomach sloshes unpleasantly, my head feels the size of Canada, and the fresh scabs on my back itch. Staring up at the thatched ceiling, I let the obvious wash over me—it wasn't a dream. Overwhelmed, I lay very still and consider the possibilities, but nothing makes sense. One moment I was chasing a rabbit, and the next ...

A hysterical cackle bursts from my lips. "I fell down a rabbit hole."

Without warning, Meredith fills my mind's eye. Huge with child, she lays on her tiled kitchen floor sobbing. Her soft caramel hair swirls around her head as if she were underwater, the knuckles of her hand bone-pale against the black phone. As quickly as it arrived, the vision disappears. I bite my lip hard enough to draw blood and sit up.

I'm no stranger to these types of visions; my twin's passions and distresses are nearly as intimate as my own. But questions I've never dreamed of now crowd forward. If I'm truly in the past, how can I possibly see something happening in the distant future? To someone who hasn't been born yet? There are no answers, but I'm now certain of three things: Meredith cut her hair, she wears Mom's engagement ring on her right hand, and she desperately needs me to get back.

"Can ye fetch eggs?"

I look up from the ladle I'm scrubbing with vinegar in time to see Angharad slice off the tasseled roots of a leek. She works her way up the stalk with precision any chef would admire. all while staring at me, one dark eyebrow cocked.

After choking down a bowl of motley porridge for breakfast, I'd followed the women into the small prep kitchen off the main room while the men headed outside again. Gwenhwyfar, who had yet to speak in my presence, sits in the corner, her bony elbows protruding from a bowl of dough. She doesn't look up.

"Yes," I say decisively, though I have my doubts, and wipe my hands on my apron. Picking up a small basket nearby, I look to Angharad for further instructions. None are offered. Okay then. It's like that still. "Which one is the hen house?"

A slick, black curl falls across Angharad's eyes as she glances up again from her chopping. With a practiced move, she tucks it back into her cap, brandishing the knife as she does.

"The one with hens," she says and brings the knife down with a bang.

Biting my cheeks to keep my mouth shut, I leave through the tiny back door and stalk across the tangled remains of a vegetable bed. I suck in the cool air again and again to keep my emotions in check. It's a fact I'm still in no condition to make the journey to St. Melangell's on foot. And it doesn't take a genius to know staying in the good graces of this family is essential to getting home, dragon of a matriarch or not. So, I will smile at whatever bullshit the lady of the house dishes out for as long as possible. Which I really hope isn't much longer.

Reaching the edge of the garden, I pause, listening. Ever since passing through or whatever happened to me, the quiet of this world has hung over me, smothering and inescapable. But each moment reveals a new sound held in the silence: bleating, lowing, and stamping beasts; insects drumming their wings against the breeze; wood groaning under the weight of work; sloshing water and jangling metal, all blending into an organic symphony. The wind tangles its fingers in my hair, and I sigh, feeling oddly calmer than I have in a long while.

With new resolve, I look at the smattering of outbuildings and animal pens. Fortunately, the "one with hens" proves obvious. All mortar and thatch and fence, the coop accommodates a dozen or more chickens bobbing their elastic heads for worms. Carefully, I open the gate and squeeze inside. Chickens squawk at the intrusion and cluster around my ankles looking for feed. A rooster struts around the perimeter but makes no move toward me, thank God.

"Shoo!" Shuffling forward, I duck inside the coop. Feathers, straw, and shit dominate the tiny space. "Lovely," I hiss, breathing through my mouth.

I scan the ground first, gingerly moving clumps of straw until I spot one.

"Aha!" I cry and scoop up the tiny, speckled jewel. Emboldened by success, I dart my sore hands under unsuspecting tailfeathers and am rewarded with nine warm eggs. Filthy but triumphant, I emerge with my spoils just as a new sound draws my attention.

A voice, deep and dense as the ground beneath my feet, rises in song. I don't understand the words, but the essence of the music rings through my bones. As if compelled by the Pied Piper himself, I leave the coop and follow the sound until I reach the fields. Plots of land stretch away from the big house like a massive, brown cape, which ends near the tree line where a second, smaller version of the big house sits. In the middle of the center field, three figures maneuver an ox and plow up and down each lane. Their pace is sloth-like, and I feel my own limited patience tested within moments. But it's the view that has me distracted.

Cai, Madoc, and Steffan are shirtless. Even from a distance, I can tell despite their varying builds and ages, all three are lean and muscled, their bodies sculpted from a lifetime of hard work. But it's the dusting of black hair across Steffan's glistening chest that has my belly heating. And he's *singing*. I don't know what I expected, but it wasn't the sight of gruff, grumpy Steffan with his head thrown back in song, his shoulders flexed. He hits a low note that has my bones humming in return, my spine a tuning fork to his deep baritone.

When a shout breaks into my revelry, I flinch, heat rushing to my cheeks. Madoc is waving my way with embarrassing enthusiasm. His hair glows like a matchstick against his pale torso and the vivid land behind him. Flustered at being caught staring, I raise my hand in a quick greeting before hurrying away. Behind me, the rough breeze jumps and snatches away the last strains of Steffan's song, even as it echoes through me.

Fleeing like a child caught spying, I tuck my head against the sudden wind only to smack straight into Gwenhwyfar. Milk from the bucket she's carrying sloshes onto our feet.

"Oh, God. Sorry. Didn't see you there," I ramble, lifting one foot to shake milk from it. Before I can blink, my other foot shoots out from under me, and I land hard on my ass, the basket of eggs still clutched against my chest.

Gwenhwyfar stares from between the folds of her platinum hair, her mouth and eyes round as a carp's. Splattered in chicken shit, mud, and what smells like goat milk, I throw my head back and laugh. I'm tired, bruised, and filthy. Laughter wheezes out of me until tears run from my eyes and my sides ache. When I'm finally able to breathe, I rub my watering eyes with the back of my hand and look up. Having set down the buckets, Gwenhwyfar reaches for me, a small smile tugging at the corners of her mouth. Feeling much better for the release, I shift the unbroken eggs and link my fingers through hers.

"Thanks," I say, shaking off what mud I can. "I'm not usually quite this much of a hot mess. Though I guess that's debatable."

The tiny teen wipes her hands in the dewy grass before picking up the milk pails and starting past me without a word.

"Wait," I say, laying a hand on her arm. "Why won't you talk to me?"

She cocks her head, eyebrows scrunched.

"Will you talk to me?" I ask again doing my best to communicate through gesture.

Gwenhwyfar's eyes light with understanding. Setting down a pail, she touches her ear then her mouth and shakes her head.

All the obvious signs fall into place with a tidy *click*, and I feel very obtuse. She's deaf and possibly mute. And while she might read lips in her native language, she most certainly doesn't understand English. I nod to her that I understand.

"Can I help with that?" I ask and move to take one of the buckets from her.

Instantly, irritation flares in her face as she jerks the milk pail from my reach. Setting both her burdens down, the previously demure girl gestures wildly as a string of guttural sounds fly from her mouth.

Taken aback, I hold up my hands.

"Whoa, I was just trying to be nice," I say, despite her deafness.

Gwenhwyfar continues to move her lips at me sometimes silently, sometimes forming sounds like a radio signal going in and out of focus. Her cheeks are bright with color, her green eyes shiny with unshed tears.

Suddenly, I understand my blunder.

"I get it, don't do that," I sputter, trying to use my hands to communicate. "Believe me, I know you're very capable and don't need my help. No one needs my help around here. I didn't mean to offend you."

Flushed and huffing, Gwenhwyfar's reserve gradually returns with her silence.

"Friends?" I asked after a moment, gesturing between us and smiling.

She doesn't respond, but her expression softens a bit before she turns toward the house, both milk pails securely in hand. With nothing else to do, I follow.

Angharad receives the eggs without interest before sweeping me into the vegetable patch with her. Despite her pendulum swings between hospitality and hostility, I enjoy the time outside and spend the rest of the morning on my hands and knees clearing away winter debris. As we work, cool air numbs my nose, and the spicy, wet smell of green things wafts around us until I find myself humming with contentment.

"Ye have a good hand with the herbs," Angharad concedes.

"My father liked to garden," I say, running my fingers through the dense soil. "He taught me."

"And yer mother? Was she not one for the gardening?"

I ignore the clenching in my chest and yank a prickly bramble out by the roots. "She delivered babies."

Angharad cocks an eyebrow in interest. "A midwife, eh? Be yers a large commote?"

I deflected questions at breakfast by claiming America was the name of my village in Ireland. After all, there was a decent chance that I did, in fact, have relatives there now. Whenever now happened to be.

Sitting back on my haunches, I flex my sore hands. "Yes. Very large in fact."

"And yer kin?"

Kin. Family. The question hangs in the air between us, a bubble of mixed meaning waiting to be burst. I have no idea how to answer this other than the unusual truth.

Leaning forward, I rip out another irksome plant and toss it aside.

"They're dead." I spit the words as if they can hurt her instead of me. "Last time I saw my sister, she was living in Bala. But ..." I stretch the word out not knowing how to lie. "But that was a long time ago. I don't know how to find her now."

Angharad crosses herself without irony.

Swallowing around the knot in my throat, I rub my sore hands. Caked with dirt and ragged-nailed, I barely recognized them as mine.

Angharad takes one of my hands and turns it over in her own. "Fine as a lady's."

It's not a compliment. I pull my hand free. "I'm no lady."

She sets her dark eyes on me then, assessing. Judging. "What be ye, then?"

Something in her voice gives me pause. What is she getting at? I meet her stare. "Just a lost girl trying to get back home."

Pinching her lips in distrust, she continues to look at me like I'm a fox scouting a chicken coop. And I've had about enough.

"Okay, here's the thing," I say and stand. "I don't know what I've done to make you dislike me, but I didn't get attacked on purpose. And I am very grateful for your help. Truly. But I'd just as soon be on my way too, so if there's something you'd like to say to me, please just say it already."

Angharad's fierce little frame stares up at me, dirt smearing her face like war paint. "I shall return yer plain speech. What plot have ye on my husband's sons?"

"Plot?" I repeat, hoping I misunderstood.

"Methinks ye know my meaning."

I stare, incredulous. I don't know what I was expecting her to say but it wasn't that. "I have no idea what you're talking about, but I certainly do not have a plot against your family or anyone else for that matter."

"Nay? Then tell me true: Why be a fair *Gwyddeles* journeyin' through the woods alone? Be yer maidenhead even whole?"

My mouth falls open. "I. Am. Lost. And my 'maidenhead' is none of your concern."

"'Tis my concern if ye mean to lure away one o' my men."

"Lure away?" I parrot and throw my arms in the air. "Of all the ridiculous—"

Just then the twins, whose names I learned are Ieuan and Iolo, come barreling up to the garden fence. An empty slops bucket swings violently between them as they talk excitedly at the same time. Their likeness is staggering. Even Meredith and I never looked so similar.

The thought of my twin triggers an ache near my tailbone.

It radiates across my right hip and down into my thigh. I clench my jaw: Meredith's sciatic. It's far from the first ghost symptom I've experienced, but feeling her across *time* makes no sense. Part of me wants to hold the sensation tight and push back my own thoughts through whatever strange connection we still have. But to what end? Wallowing in our mutual discomfort won't get me back. Instead, I focus on the scents and sights of the world around me before pulling my mind away from hers.

Angharad barks a reply that sends the boys bolting. She gathers her things and heads for the kitchen door. "Our kin arrive in three days' time for Lady's Day. There be much to do."

"I'm not trying to take anyone away from you, mistress. I want to leave as much as you want me gone."

Angharad turns. Regards me. "We have lost many good men o' late to their own foolishness. I cannot lose ours to a *pwca*. Stay clear o' the lads if ye have nay wish to aggrieve me."

With that, she leaves me standing among the leeks and cabbages, quaking with annoyance and the seed of an idea.

I spend the remainder of the day learning to churn butter and card wool properly, redoing the sections I mangled the morning before. Angharad makes no mention of our conversation in the garden, but her distrust crackles around me like static. It's exhausting, so when the evening meal is finally cleared away, I excuse myself, ready for sleep.

"Shall ye not stay a bit?" Madoc's voice drips with disappointment.

I cut a look to Angharad. Already seated by the hearth, nursing the baby, her black eyes meet mine. The fierce warning they hold falls in stark contrast to the tender scene of the sleeping infant snuggled against the soft ridge of her breast. Milk dribbles from the corner of the baby's puckered mouth, its tiny fingers curled into a fist.

"I don't think so," I say, my smile polite.

"Come now, Mistress Meg Quinn," Cai pipes up. "Stay for the tale." My host runs a hand through his bushy hair and refills his tankard with weak ale. "'Tis a good one," he adds before sinking into the chair by his wife, either oblivious or indifferent to her irritation.

Clinging to the remains of my tattered nerves, I suck in my lips, nod, and head for the hearth, where Gwenhwyfar is snuggled against the dog. The massive animal lifts its shaggy head at my approach, yellow eyes watching me longer than seems natural. Being completely obvious, Madoc pushes the twins off the bench with all the compassion of an older sibling and gestures for me to join him.

Shit. There's no way to decline, so I smile tightly and perch on the edge an arm's length away from him—putting me directly across from Steffan. Leaning against the adjacent wall, he cleans his fingernails with the tip of a knife. He doesn't look up, but I can feel his presence like an exposed wire against my skin.

After a long drink and a brief belch, Cai claps his hands together signaling for our attention.

"*Amser maith yn ôl,*" he begins.

Madoc slides down the bench. "Shall I translate?"

His breath smells of ale and onions, but his lopsided grin really is infectious. I nod.

"Long ago, nigh *Myddfai,*" Madoc says, "there lived a widow who sent her only child, a son, to graze their cattle near the Black Mountain. One day, whilst the youth walked along the banks o' *Llyn y Fan Fach,* he saw a young woman on the surface o' the lake, using the water as a glass."

Here, Cai pauses for effect, staring at each audience member in turn.

"The lady be so sheen," translates Madoc, "that the young man became entranced and offered her his meal o' barley bread.

But she refused him, saying, 'Hard baked be yer bread. 'Tis not easy to catch me!' Then she disappeared into the lake.

"The lovesick youth returned home and told the strange tale to his mother. Being wise, the mother told her son that the maiden would return if she desired him and to take unbaked dough on the morrow. Listening to his mother, he met the dawn at the lake. Once again, the fair woman appeared but refused his second gift, saying, 'Unbaked be yer bread, I shall not have ye!' And under the water again she went.

"Disappointed, the young man went home and told his mother the tale. She encouraged her son to try one last time and to offer half-baked bread to the lady o' the lake. On the third day, when the sheen lass appeared, she accepted the bread and stayed on the land with the young man. She called herself Nelferch, and the youth begged her to marry him. Nelferch agreed but warned that the marriage would only be binding if he did not strike her—"

Someone lets loose a thunderous fart, and the little boys erupt into giggles—which immediately causes the culprit to fart again.

"*Hisht*," Angharad pokes the closest boy with her foot, which does nothing but elicit yet another fart.

I bite my lip and wheeze, trying not to laugh. Madoc covers his face, and Steffan's grim expression is twisted in a smirk. Even Angharad struggles to keep a straight face as she scolds the boys back into silence.

Stifling his own laughter, Cai continues. "*Tri ergyd diachos.*"

"Three blows without care," says Madoc, still stifling a chuckle. "For then she must leave him. Just as the young man agreed, the lady loosed herself and dove back into the lake. Overwrought with grief, the young man made to cast himself after his beloved. But afore he could leap from the rocks, he heard a loud voice call, 'Forebear, rash youth!'

"The young man turned toward the voice and saw a hoary-headed mountain o' a man standing with not one but two beautiful women. The youth be sore affrighted until the old man spoke, saying that he would consent to the union if the young man could tell him which one o' his twin daughters be the object of the youth's affection.

"So alike were these ladies that the young man despaired until one maiden thrust her foot forward exposing the laces o' her sandal. Having gazed longingly on the woman afore, the young man understood and went forward to choose her.

"'Ye have chosen well,' said the old man. 'Be to her a loving husband, and I shall give her a dowry o' as many sheep, cattle, goats, swine, and horses as she can count without drawing breath. But ne'er forget, that she and her dowry shall return to me upon the third causeless blow.'

"Overjoyed, the young man agreed and the two were wed in the fairy ring. Then the lady o' the lake counted by fives until her breath failed, and the full number o' livestock came out o' the lake. The father and the other twin vanished, and the young couple settled at a place called Esgair Llaethdy, where they lived happily for several years, and Nelferch bore three strong sons.

"When the first son be still small, the farmer and his wife were expected at a cousin's wedding some distance off, but she refused to leave. The farmer tapped his wife, saying, 'Go! Go!' Nelferch replied, 'Ye do not see what I see, for if we had left afore now, our child would have sickened from the heat. Ye, husband, have struck me the first blow without care.'

"Then the lady bore her second babe, and the family attended the christening o' the cousin's child. In the midst o' the celebration, Nelferch wept. Again, the farmer tapped his wife and said, 'Hush! Hush!' to which she replied, 'Ye do not see what I see. I cry for the great sorrow that shall befall them. Ye, husband, have struck me the second causeless blow.'

"Another son be brought forth, and soon the day came when the family attended the funeral o' the babe at whose christening the second blow had been cast. During the ceremony, the lady o' the lake laughed gaily. Ashamed, the farmer touched her arm saying, 'Do not laugh!'

"The lady replied, 'Ye do not see what I see. I laugh for the babe shall suffer nay more, but ye ha' struck the third blow without cause, and our marriage be ended.' She walked away from her husband, and though she ne'er quickened her pace, he could not catch her."

Cai and Madoc continued to speak, but I heard nothing over the ringing in my ears. A strange woman, a twin, appeared out of a lake with knowledge of the future—and she went back. She went *back*.

My hands shake with excitement. If I really had traveled into the past through a tree, perhaps other landmarks, like bodies of water, held similar powers.

If so, then folk stories like this one could be based in truth.

But what did the three strikes mean? And how would I know such a place if I found one? And where, or when, would it lead?

Overcome with wonder, my attention drifts once again to the twins who, having grown bored with the tale, have cornered a cricket. Like a pair of puppies, they herd the insect in circles. Hell-bent on survival, the wily bug finds a suitable niche in the wall and fixes itself there just beyond reach. The boys soon tire of the game and turn their attention back to the tale. From the corner of my eye, I watch the cricket emerge, leg by leg, and leap toward the kitchen.

Hurry, I think in solidarity with the creature. *Find a way out.*

CHAPTER 7
A VISITATION

Over another gut-loosening breakfast of Angharad's porridge and hostility, Cai presents me with a welcome, if unintentional, gift.

"Though ye do seem gentle born, mistress, methinks ye have mettle for more than distaff chores," he says while wiping crumbs from his beard. "What say ye?"

"Yes," I blurt, my mind scrambling for purchase. "Horses. I know a bit about horses." This is surprisingly true, though it's been many years since Meredith and I haunted our neighbor's stables. *Stay as close to the truth as possible. Survive.*

Cai claps at his own cleverness and pushes back from the table, the chair dragging with a screech. "O' course ye do. Come."

With the household's attention heavy on my back, I stand quickly, pull on a borrowed cloak, and follow Cai out into the wind. I can't help but admire the view, even as my hands tingle with cold. Early morning light stamps the sky with lilac clouds while some kind of songbird riots in the still, black trees. The air smells of wet wood, manure, and smoke. I inhale it, swallowing the beauty whole. A tiny bolt of anxiety shakes loose from my heart with a clatter as I breathe easier. But there's no time to examine the feeling.

Apparently, stables haven't changed much in several hundred years because I recognize the simple rectangular structure with an attached paddock as soon as it comes into view. When we enter, a horse whickers, reminding me of my purpose here. Escape.

"Now," says Cai, handing me a large bristle brush. "Tend to Hen Wyneb and Fychan here. I shall send Madoc anon to help with the feeding and watering." With no other instruction or introduction to the horses, the master of the estate strides off into the morning mist, whistling.

Well then. The horses flick their tails dispassionately as I stand in the dim light of the doorway. Stables really haven't changed much. One side of the wide center aisle holds two horse stalls; the other contains a loft where hay hangs over the door below like a mustache. Staring at what I assume is the tack room, the idea planted by Angharad's warning the day before, ridiculous as it was, takes shape. Stepping up to the stall door, I hold out a hand for the dappled gray to smell. He snorts warm air against my palm. Next door, the amber horse flaps his velvety lips at me and stomps, impatient for a meal.

"You know what?" I say, scratching the soft underside of the gray's chin. His thick whiskers tickle my palm as I look back at the tack room door, wondering. "It could work."

"What could work, milady?" Madoc's bright voice snaps the quiet in two.

I whip around to see him saunter in, his usual precocious smile in place and a large key dangling from his hand.

Bingo.

"I was just trying to convince your friend here to let me brush him so I could give him some extra feed." I turn my attention back to the gray horse.

"Be a good lad." Madoc makes a clicking sound at the beast, reaching across me to unlatch the gate. For a second, his gaze flicks to my mouth.

"Thank you." I move cautiously into the stall. Sweeping the brush over the animal's heavy muscles, I focus on my chore until the click of a lock draws my attention. Madoc has opened the tack room.

My idea stretches skyward, expanding. I swallowed, steadying my voice. "How can you find anything in there? It's so dark."

Madoc reappears in the dark doorway, holding a bucket of oats and a pitchfork. "'Tis nay great feat. I could find my way round this land blind, for certes." He hands me the bucket. "Half for each," he instructs before launching the pitchfork, and then himself, into the hayloft.

I go about my task, chewing my bottom lip. Find his way in the dark, could he? When both horses are fed, I set down the pail and take a deep breath. Part of me recoils from what I'm about to do, but I can't think of another way and rationalize that although Madoc is young, he's only a few years younger than me and undoubtedly considered a man by now. Conjuring my most alluring voice, I aim a smile at Madoc. "I'd like to see you try sometime. Find your way in the dark, that is."

A pile of yellow-green hay tumbles out of the loft. Madoc follows. Flakes of the stuff cling to his clothes as he stands in front of me, breathless, pitchfork in hand.

"I could show ye whatever ye wish, milady." He steps closer.

Well, that was easy. I lower my gaze. "Please. Call me Meg. We're friends, aren't we?"

"'Tis time." Steffan's gravelly voice booms through the door.

Madoc jerks at the sound before leveling a scathing look at his brother. Without greeting, Steffan approaches, carrying two buckets of water. Setting one down, he reaches for the latch.

"I'll take those," I say.

Steffan wrinkles his brow at me but hands each pail over the low door. The water is heavier than the feed, but I manage to fill the trough between the stalls while the men hiss at each other in Welsh. When I glance up, Madoc's nostrils are flared. Steffan remains expressionless.

"Pray, forgive our haste, mistress, but 'tis plowing season," says Steffan, still staring at Madoc. "There be much to do, and Cymry skies be as fickle," his gray eyes sweep across me, through me, "as the attentions o' *y ellyll*."

It's the most I've ever heard him say and was clearly an insult, though I don't quite understand how.

With a snort, Madoc flings hay into the stalls and stalks back to the dark confines of the storage room. Steffan gestures for the empty buckets. As I heft them over the stall door, our cold fingers brush. My breath catches. He doesn't move away. Staring, silence hangs between us, crowded as a Christmas tree with things unsaid.

Frowning, Steffan's lips part as if he's going to speak just as Madoc emerges with a huge wooden yoke resting across his big shoulders.

"Yer servant, milady," Madoc says in a sulking tone, and heads for the fields.

As if spooked, Steffan retreats into the tack room. What the hell, I think and shimmy out of the stall, careful to latch it behind me. Now it's Steffan who emerges laden with heavy leather harnesses. Closing the tack room door, he plucks the key from its lock. I expect him to leave without acknowledging me as I grip the empty buckets. Instead, he steps directly into my path.

"Ye would do well to remember that Madoc be young and rash. He thinks not afore he acts."

Wondering just how much he heard, I scramble to Madoc's —and my own—defense. "He's kind and artless. Unlike you."

"Aye. See that ye forget it not," Steffan warns and tucks the key to my departure firmly in his belt.

Flustered with frustration and whatever the hell is going on with Steffan, I finish brushing the horses and head for the house. Before I reach the stoop, a crash sounds from within, followed by the high-pitched wail of a baby. The door swings open, and I jump back, barely missing being smacked. Angharad stomps out, holding one of the twins by his ear. Her cheeks burn red, and from the boy's mouth runs an unending string of Welsh. I gawk as Angharad marches the child up to a nearby tree and yanks down his pants, baring the boy's skinny buttocks. My mouth hangs open as the boy, still talking, wraps his arms around the trunk and his mother swats his backside with a switch. Hard.

For a moment, I don't move, shocked. Meredith and I got into some serious trouble a time or three, and I carry an early memory of getting swatted on the backside by my mother's palm for stealing a handful of mints from a convenience store. But I've never seen anything like this. The boy finally stops talking in exchange for small grunting noises through his teeth. Trim pink welts rise in strips across his fair flesh.

Don't do it, don't do it, don't, I chant in my head at the exact moment the child gives in and sobs.

"Stop it," I holler.

Angharad casts her livid gaze back at me and gives the boy a final smack before looking back at him. Speaking in a low voice, she pulls up his breeches. The boy's rumpled black head nods solemnly as he sniffles against his mother's chest. With a pat to his shoulder, Angharad sends him shuffling into the house, where the baby is still crying. Then, hands planted on her hips, she faces me.

"He's just a little boy," I say determined to hold my ground. "I can't imagine what he's done to deserve being hit like that. It's … it's cruel."

I half expect her to come after me with the switch. What I don't expect is for her to double over and laugh.

"Ye cannot imagine, as ye say, mistress?" Angharad straightens up but can't keep the amusement from her face. "I shall tell ye, then. Iolo hath been throwin' his tinker horse after being told to stop. Again. Now my best bowl be broke, the babe's awake, and the day's eggs ruined." She shakes her head in exasperation. "I know not who yer kinsmen be," she says, "but among the Cymry such foolishness earns a thrashing."

"I understand the need for discipline. I do. But beating a child with a stick is—"

A snarl rips the air. Angharad and I turn as Gwenhwyfar's giant dog tears out the front door and makes a dash for the tree line, his hell-hound bellows ringing out as he bounds through the underbrush. Gwenhwyfar appears in the doorway, the red-faced infant clutched in her reedy arms. The girl's keen eyes train toward the swaying ferns. Rushing forward, she presses the baby into Angharad's care before charging after the berserk animal.

"*Aros!*" Angharad calls after them, her voice useless.

I drop the buckets and run, trailing the pale whip of Gwenhwyfar's braid through the woods until it comes to a stop at the base of a delicately budding tree near the river. Baying like a fiend, the dog's front paws stretch six feet up the trunk and scratch at the dangling white robes of a man. With a screech, the man scrambles higher trying to get away from the creature's bared teeth.

I stop next to Gwenhwyfar, who notes my presence with a nod before approaching the animal.

"Be careful," I caution out of habit.

The man looks down just as Gwenhwyfar lays a hand on the beast. Turning, the dog licks his mistress's face and moves away with her coaxing. Calling out in Welsh, the stranger's insistent voice grows angry as Gwenhwyfar leads her four-legged companion home without a backward glance. Once they're out of sight, the man swings free from the tree with an awkward lurch.

"The girl can't hear or speak," I say. "The dog is her protector. She didn't mean any harm."

He startles at my voice and stares. I'm getting used to this. While different people have certainly had different reactions to my strangeness, the look the robed man casts my way is nothing short of hostile. I glance in the direction of the house.

"Mayhap not, but the same cannot be said for that devilish wolfhound." Trapped between a hiss and a whistle, the man's voice makes the hair on my neck rise.

"Good dogs are like that. Are you hurt?" I ask as he steps into focus.

Slight and spindly, the man's billowing robes and scant, fly-away hair give him the overall appearance of a dandelion plume. Both of his top front teeth are missing, which accounts for the whistling noise, and while he must be my age or older, his bearing is oddly juvenile. Except for his eyes. Large, clear, and a perfect shade of cerulean, they're beautiful and betray a sharp intelligence trolling beneath.

"Nay, but I have lost Horace." He adjusts a bag slung across his back. "Did ye see which way he ran?" the man asks before tromping off, calling for his friend.

"Afraid not," I say and turn toward the house. I haven't the slightest intention of traipsing through the woods with that character.

Suddenly, the man breaks into a run.

"Horace!" he calls and is rewarded with a loud bray.

The animal call catches me so off guard I stupidly crash through the bracken after the man to see confirm what I think I heard. Yep. Catching up, I find the stranger petting and cooing over a large, speckled mule. Horace, apparently, is an ass.

"Pray, forgive me, mistress," the man says before stepping much too close. "Horace hath been my sole companion o' late." He bows to me then, the movement causing his tonsured head to wink like a cycloptic eye. "Brother Gwyn ap Twm o' Cymer Abbey, yer servant. I am on my way to Bala from Valle Crucis. It has been some time since I encountered another soul."

I fight the urge to lean away. "There's nothing to forgive. I'm Meg Quinn."

Brother Gwyn smiles his gummy smile. "The girl be yer … sister?"

"No." I pause, unsure what to say. "I'm a guest at her family's home."

He nods as if this explains my unnatural presence before raising his thin eyebrows in expectation. I just smile back, hoping to deflate his curiosity.

No luck.

"Whence do ye hail, mistress? Forgive me, but ye do seem a stranger here. I do not have occasion to speak to outsiders over much and am curious about the world beyond our mountains."

I sigh. "Ireland," I say "I'm also traveling on. I'll be leaving here soon."

Brother Gwyn nods again with unnecessary enthusiasm. "I see."

Wondering what exactly the monk thinks he sees, I step back and turn in the direction of Dwyn Blair. "Well, I need to be going now."

Still gripping Horace's reins, Brother Gwyn bows again. "O' course. I shall not hinder ye, though I wonder; would the mute girl's family welcome a man o' the cloth to their table?"

I have no right to answer for Master Cai and am certain Angharad will have my head for doing so, but the monk's silken tone makes it clear there's only one acceptable answer.

"Certainly," I hear myself say and turn, the white hobgoblin and his steed tight on my heels.

The baby still hasn't stopped crying when we arrive at the house. Frazzled and reeking of shit and milk, Angharad welcomes Brother Gwyn with all the graciousness of a mother grizzly before stomping back to the kitchen, where Gwenhwyfar is trying to calm the dog. The creature hasn't stopped whining since Brother Gwyn and Horace entered the yard. With the men still in the fields, that leaves me to stable the beast and entertain the new guest. Awesome. After fetching Brother Gwyn a cup of ale, we sit in front of a banked fire as the infant's wailing escalates to a jagged shriek.

He runs a pink hand over his face. "'Tis nay wonder Saturn devoured his young."

My glance snags on the monk. He smiles. My mind immediately conjures Goya's nightmarish painting on the subject: the muddy, base palette, the frenzied eyes and gaping maw of a jealous god, red with his son's blood. I've never been one of those women who fawned over babies, and my head aches from the noise. But I have no interest in probing a mind that would reach for such a sentiment.

When the crying finally subsided, Brother Gwyn clears his throat.

"Shall the master be in soon?" he asks, sniffing at his untouched ale.

"I'm afraid I don't know. I'm sorry you've been left with only me," I say because it's the truth and also to fill time. "It's been an ... unpredictable morning. I'm not as familiar with the work that needs to be done here."

Brother Gwyn latches onto this confession with surprising

interest. "Aye, the same oft be true o' me, mistress." He leans forward. "I confess I have not the skill o' my brothers in husbandry, so Horace and I travel and deliver messages for the abbey. 'Tis a task o' great importance, which I be pleased to undertake, for certes." He pauses here, choosing his words with care. "But there be little comfort in travel and less thanks for our trouble." He spreads his palms with unconvincing nonchalance. "Such be the life o' the cloth."

I've already seen enough intensity from this man to doubt he takes being slighted well. But I nod and stare into the smoldering fire, willing the rest of the family to arrive. After a time, they do. The twins appear in the doorway first. Windblown and cherry-cheeked, the animated pair skid to a stop when they see the monk.

"*Bore da,*" Brother Gwyn greets. "Blessings to ye."

The boy on the left chuckles. His straight-faced brother elbows him in the ribs. Looking at them closely, I recognized the more serious boy as Iolo.

"*Bore da,*" Iolo says before showing me an embarrassed smile.

The second twin bows to their guest before pushing his brother and bolting for the kitchen. Iolo follows, albeit with a limp. Feeling rather pleased by the silent exchange with Iolo, I stand when Cai, Madoc, and Steffan enter the room.

"You have a guest, milord." I gesture to the robed man. "Brother Gwyn ap Twm."

If the news surprises Cai, he doesn't show it. Stepping forward, the older man's powerful frame dwarfs the newcomer, who looks like nothing so much as a pale shadow. Introductions and pleasantries are made before Angharad appears from the kitchen, signaling the start of the midday meal. Like well-trained school children, we file into our seats.

Scooting down from my usual place near Cai, I can't decide

which is worse: another meal of mystery pottage or the waves of awkward tension rolling through the room. Both are enough to make a person seasick, though I'm not sure why the monk's appearance should upset the family's rhythm so much. Surely his presence, sudden as it was, is more customary than mine? With my appetite squelched, I push the food around and let my thoughts tumble through one flawed escape plan after another.

"Pray, tell us o' yerself, Mistress Meg." Brother Gwyn's voice pierces the comforting drone of Welsh.

I stamp down the flair of panic as all eyes swivel to me.

"There isn't much to tell," I say and nibble the inside edge of the bread bowl.

"Come now, o' course there be," Brother Gwyn insists with a toothless grin.

I offer a tight, apologetic smile still hoping to sidestep the conversation. "I'm afraid not."

"Then I must insist," presses the monk.

What the fuck is this about? Struggling to keep my face in check, I bite my cheeks, thinking Horace the Ass might be less obstinate than his owner.

"Aye, mistress," Angharad chimes in. "Tell us a tale from yer country."

Everyone is looking at me, except for Gwenhwyfar, who sways gently in her seat to some internal rhythm. I sit dumbstruck. What on earth can I tell them? That I'm excellent at ordering takeout, breaking in running shoes, discussing post-impressionist female painters, and provoking oncology nurses in a country that won't be discovered by Western Europeans for another ninety years?

"If milady shall permit me to say so, she hath a fair way with horses," says Madoc. The tips of his ears glow like embers in the dim room, and I can almost feel the spike in Angharad's irritation.

I press my lips into a rigid line and scramble for an idea. Shit.

"Aye, 'tis true," booms Cai as if this were a credit to himself.

Desperate to stem the tide of conversation, I blurt, "I'm an artist," only to be met with a bevy of quizzical looks. "I can draw."

Madoc's head juts forward in disbelief. "A bow?"

Seven pairs of eyes examine my feeble frame. Oh for God's sake. "No. I mean I can use"—my eyes dart around the room for inspiration—"charcoal to copy an image," I say hoping to be understood.

Again, expressions range from questioning to outright hostile. This isn't going as planned, and I don't have anything else to talk about, especially since I can't figure out why the monk is so set on it.

"I'll show you." Pushing away from the table, I approach the grate in search of an instrument. Carefully, I nudge a half-burnt stick out of the fire. After scraping the scorched tip to a point, I blow the fine ash back into the low flames as they lick the sides of their stone prison. No one says a word as I set my hand to the first work I've done since Mom died.

"There." After a few minutes, I step back from a silhouetted sketch of Gwenhwyfar on the hearthstone. It's a rough sketch, the likeness unsatisfactory to me, but my body hums with the act of creating. One by one, my companions peer at the drawing, and I know I've done enough to get my point across. Cai smiles, letting out a low whistle. Angharad backs away as if I've conjured a snake. Gwenhwyfar stares at the dark lines and shadows of her face for a long time before a quiet smile plucks at her pink lips.

"I must say, 'tis a cunning trick." Brother Gwyn's voice slides out in an unexpected hiss. "From a cunning charmer."

His tone sends alarm bells through my system. Confused, I

look up from the sketch to find his cornflower eyes slicing through me. The room is silent. Everyone holds still, as if any sudden movement will trap them in a quagmire of my creation. I look around, confused. I don't know what I've done, but something is very wrong.

Angharad speaks first.

"The girl be naught but a guest here, per the laws o' hospitality, brother," she says, obviously trying to distance the family from me.

Brother Gwyn holds up his hands. The gesture of peace disturbs me more than the family's silence.

"For certes," he says and turns back to the table.

Everyone follows, eyes cast away from me. Everyone but Steffan. With a probing look, his ashen eyes ask the question no one else bothered to: How did you learn such a skill? There's a softness to his expression I've never seen before. It unnerves me more than his guarded glares every have.

We finish the meal in a fog of silence pierced only by the occasional belch from one of the twins. When the trenchers have been scraped clean, Cai rises.

"*Gorau amheuthun, chwant bwyd,*" he says, smiling a smile that doesn't reach his eyes.

"Aye, Master Cai," agrees Brother Gwyn. "I thank ye for yer hospitality, but methinks I shall make ready to leave. I have pressing news to tell my abbot. Mayhap the mute girl would care to fetch Horace?"

Unhearing, Gwenhwyfar remains at the far end of the table with the baby tucked into the crook of her arm like a football.

"Pardons, Brother," says Angharad. "But I be in need o' her to gather the goats. She hath a way with the beasts, ye see. Madoc shall aid ye."

Busy baiting the twins into kicking one another under the table, Madoc's head snaps up at his name. "Aye, Brother."

"For certes, I have nay wish to trouble ye, mistress," the monk says, though his pursed lips tell a different story.

Switching to Welsh, Cai gathers the men around the hearth while Iolo and Ieuan dart outside, leaving the door ajar. A cold draft skitters through the room as Angharad lays a hand on Gwenhwyfar's shoulder before mouthing words in front of the girl's face. The white-hair waif nods, transfers the baby to its mother, and disappears into the green yard, soundless as a ghost.

Overburdened with pewter mugs and curiosity, I stand on the threshold to the kitchen and peer over my shoulder. Brother Gwyn stares outside, his bulbous eyes following Gwenhwyfar. As he does, the tip of his tongue presses out between his missing teeth like a snake tasting the air for prey. Overlooking the monk's oddities is one thing—but the predatory gesture is something else entirely. Revulsion and understanding rise in my throat just as Steffan steps forward. Closing the main door, Steffan turns to look at the monk, and his lean, severe face is nothing but a mask of cold, brutal warning. Brother Gwyn's eyes track up to Steffan's. The monk's entire countenance shifts instantaneously to open, wide-eyed curiosity. He even smiles before turning sharply toward Cai. The change is complete and eerie.

A noise of disgust escapes me, drawing Steffan's attention. Our gazes snag and hold. Even in the flickering light, his pale eyes have gone cold and flat. Deadly. One, two, three heartbeats pass before he nods in acknowledgment and turns to the hearth. Behind me, the great wolfhound's ragged claws scratch against the door, and I know the beast isn't the only member of the household ready to sink their fangs into the monk.

CHAPTER 8

THE STORM

"This." Steffan holds up the nut-brown cap of a mushroom. "'Tis what we be after."

The morning dawned unusually warm and muggy, perfect for foraging wild mushrooms, according to Angharad. So, after a sleepless night with the baby, she was ready to delegate chores. Anxious to become more familiar with my surroundings, I offered to go. The fact that I couldn't tell which woodland fungi would kill you and which wouldn't presented a problem—until Steffan volunteered to take me. If a chair had turned sentient and spoken on my behalf, no one would have been more shocked.

It's nearly warm out, and Steffan has rolled his shirtsleeves, exposing long, pale forearms. Trying to ignore the map of blue veins under a dusting of dark hair, I force my attention to the frumpy little fungus.

"What's it called?" I ask.

Steffan twirls the spongy stem between his fingers. The movement causes the corded muscles under his skin to shift and flex. My traitorous mouth goes dry as I pull my eyes back to the mushroom.

"*Cén fáth a bhfuil tú anseco?*"

"Of course it is. What is it with the Welsh and horrendously long words?"

A hollow scoff comes from Steffan, as if he were a gourd being tapped.

I bristle. "Have I said something amusing?"

His mouth flattens. "Trust me, mistress. I be not amused."

My hackles rise with an irritation I don't completely understand but am too tired to fight. "Good. Then we agree on that. Not a single fucking thing about this situation is amusing."

I expect him to meet my attitude, but instead, the outburst seems to calm him.

He just tucks the mushroom in the satchel on the ground between us before fixing his unsmiling eyes on me. "I spoke not o' the *madarchen*, but o' ye, Ellyll."

I raise my eyebrows at him. "I wasn't lying about not speaking Welsh. If you have something to say to me, say it plainly please."

"I did. In the *Gaeilge*."

My stomach plummets. Mom never learned Welsh, but my father had known enough Irish Gaelic to stumble through long distance phone conversations with his grandmother in County Clare. So having claimed to be from Ireland myself, I should at least be able to recognize the language.

I clear my throat and look away. "Your accent is confusing."

If Steffan has anything to say to this, he keeps it to himself as we settle into a pattern of Hunt, Find, and Make Sure It Won't Kill Everyone. Eventually, I break off on my own but continue to check my specimens against his.

By noon, the first unfiltered sunlight I've seen in days seeps through the canopy. All around us, the frothy, green ferns and budding trees gather the light greedily, balling it up until a haze descends that makes the air stick in my lungs. Sweat trickles between my breasts and under my arms as I stretch my aching muscles.

"I think I need to sit down," I say, wiping my forehead.

We've been silent so long my voice startles a mouse from under the bracken. Steffan straightens up as well. His dark curls are plastered and shining around his face, his neck and forearms damp with sweat. With a nod, he starts back toward the horse we hobbled in a nearby meadow. Sinking onto a large, flat stone, I close my eyes and might have fallen asleep sitting up if not for a sharp, nutty smell drifting across my face.

"Bread," I breathe and open my eyes. Steffan is crouching right in front of me, holding out the dark, grainy offering. I take the bread and swallow when his calloused fingers brush mine.

"Thank you," I force out.

To my surprise, he sits next to me with his own crust before pulling a hunk of cheese from his vest. He's so close I can smell the salty tang of his sweat mingled with the earthy bread and damp meadow around us. Using the dagger at his waist, Steffan carves off a large slice of cheese and offers it to me. My stomach growls, and I don't hesitate to pluck the gooey gift from the knife before folding it into the oat bread. Goat, thyme, salt, and something floral fills my mouth as I bite down. The brackish flavors are unlike anything I've ever tasted, and I groan in delight.

"This cheese is amazing," I say through a mouthful.

Steffan takes an enormous bite of his own cheese sandwich in agreement.

Normally, I'd prefer a silent companion, but something about Steffan's perpetual quiet around me sits like a canker sore I can't keep from biting.

"So," I say after another mouthful, "are you going to tell me what you said earlier?"

Steffan continues eating, unbothered by me. Once finished,

he dusts off his hands and takes a long pull from the kidney-shaped water skin. Handing the leather container to me, he says, "'Tis o' nay matter."

I drink deeply, despite the bitter edge to the thin ale. "It matters to me."

"Why?" He looks at me openly now, so I look back. Droplets of sweat bead together over his brow before dripping down his temple into the slick hair curling above his ear, which is surprisingly delicate looking. Almost elfin.

Focus.

I clear my throat. "Because you said it was about me. And unlike the rest of your family, you don't say much, so I assume that when you do, it's important."

His eyes tighten as if I'm a wall he's trying to see through. "Why do ye not speak the *Gaeilge?*"

I feign innocence with a shrug and finish my snack. "I only learned a little when I was young," I say before glancing around for mushrooms I know aren't there. "How did you learn?"

Steffan's attention follows me, heavy as a hand on my neck. "I served as a bowman for Richard II."

My thoughts spin around this new nugget of information. When had King Richard II lived? What did that have to do with Ireland now? Unable to remember anything useful, I throw a low blow to change the subject. "I see. Is that where you got your scar?"

It works. As if suddenly remembering its existence, Steffan traces the jagged, white line that runs from his earlobe to his chin. His jaw clenches.

"Aye." The word drops like a lid, sealing off the conversation.

Steffan walks off, the green ferns murmuring against his boots.

"Do we have enough yet?" I ask, dumping another apron full of fungi into the bulging satchel.

It's well into the afternoon by now, and every inch of my body aches. After working our way through a particularly dense patch of forest, Steffan and I circled back around and were once again near the meadow where we'd left the horse.

With a curt nod, Steffan buckles the flap.

I heave a sigh of relief, running sore hands over my face, too tired to care if I'm smeared with dirt. "Finally."

Steffan gives a soft grunt before hefting our spoils across his wide shoulders.

In an instant, I see red as heat rushes through my limbs at his patronizing tone. My face burns with embarrassment at his condescension before I feel the constant simmer of fear explode under my skin at Steffan's disdain. How dare he judge me? Think poorly of me? I'm on my feet before I know what I'm doing.

"Hey," I say, jabbing a finger in his direction. "I know you think I'm a pampered idiot, and that's fine. Maybe I am here. But you don't know me. You have no idea who I am or what I've been through, so save your growling for someone else."

I stalk off.

When I finally burst through the moss-encrusted trees and into the clearing where we started, the horse whinnies at my intrusion. Still vibrating with the force of my outburst, I plop down and wrap my arms around my knees, feeling no bigger than the ants trickling under the grass. Each blade shivers as the tiny, Herculean insects pass by, and I wonder about my presence in the world.

Will my being here, now, affect my own time? I've never given much thought to wild, hypothetical ideas like the butterfly effect, but what if such possibilities exist and my very presence in this time changed history? But if that's possible, how am I still able to feel Meredith? Does all of time and space exist at once, or is my awareness of her nothing more than the pain of a phantom limb? Closing my eyes, I lose my breath at the magnitude of these questions. At the damage I've already caused and will continue to cause if I don't get home.

I sense more than hear his approach. Despite his size, the man moves like a shadow. He stops just behind me, the salty, spicy tang of his sweat announcing his presence more than anything.

"I meant ye no offense, Ellyll. I know well what ye be. I see you."

His voice breaks an eerie stillness all around us I hadn't noticed until it's gone. I lift my head. We'd spent much of the day in silence, but the soupy air was filled with noise from the woods. Until now. As if in response to the thought, thunder rumbles in the distance.

Tilting my head up, I find Steffan staring over my head at something in the distance, his severe face grim.

"We've tarried too long," he says.

I follow his gaze. Flat-bottomed clouds billow and spread as we watch, mounting into a massive, indigo anvil. The clearing hums with energy until another roll of thunder unfurls over the landscape, louder this time. Even as we walk, the wind picks up, the sky darkening.

"How much time do we have?" I ask.

But Steffan's already gone, strapping our supplies and goods to the horse as fast as possible.

"Right," I breathe and run after him to help.

The creature dances and knickers as Steffan swings into the saddle before helping me up behind him. Pressed against his broad, hard back for the second time today, I cinch my arms around him, and he spurs the horse forward. Our double burden makes a true gallop difficult, so we canter along the edge of the meadow until my sides ache. The smell of rain rises up, mingling with Steffan's scents of leather and sweat and spice as the world rattles around us. Then, with one punch of lightning, everything shifts. Wind rushes across our backs, pelting us with debris as thunder slaps the sky. Rain heaves itself out of the clouds in icy sheets, and we're soaked within seconds. Flashes of blue light illuminate our path as darkness swallows the land.

"Hold fast!" Steffan hollers over the roar of the rain, and I obey, tightening my grip as the horse breaks into a gallop. I gasp and squeeze my eyes shut against the dizzying assault of branches, wind, and rain. On and on we ride through the storm until Steffan pulls the horse up short without warning.

I opened my eyes to blackness. Squinting against the rain, I wait for my vision to clear while trying in vain to keep the water out of my face. Slowly, I make out the ash-gray silhouettes of endless trees in the stormy gloom.

"Why are we stopping?" I yell.

Steffan just reaches around to help me slide off as another bolt of lightning flashes overhead. The muddy ground rushes up, and I cling to the stirrup for support as thunder crackles. Steffan dismounts before leaning down until his warm breath mists against my ear.

"'Tis not safe to go on. There be naught to do but wait and

pray it eases." Without another word, he holds tight to the nervous horse's reins and heads deeper into the woods.

I'm left standing alone in the driving rain, my mouth agape.

"Are you crazy?" I yell.

If he responds, I hear nothing, the roar of the storm swallowing up both.

With the horse lashed securely between two stout trees, Steffan strides back to me. His pale face glides through the dark like a specter, disembodied in the gloom.

I fling my arms in frustration. Anger feels better than fear, so I let it flow. "What are we supposed to do now? Curl up like rats against rocks? Is that your brilliant idea?"

Again, he leans close until his breath is hot against my ear. "We shall not be against rocks," he shouts.

Taking my arm, Steffan turns me toward his intended sanctuary, pointing. Not five feet away from us, a massive oak tree squats in the dark, its tangled canopy swaying violently in the wind. Blood pounds in my ears as I take in the slick, black roots pushing up through the ferns like tentacles, the cavernous hole in its truck.

I whip out of his grasp and stare at what I can still see of his face through the rain. "Are you insane? I thought we were trying not to die!"

Steffan grabs my elbow again, his touch firm but not biting. "'Tis fair dry! There be taller trees about to draw the lightning."

"I'm not getting in that thing!" I scream as a deafening clap of thunder rings out. The rain redoubles its onslaught.

"Aye, ye be!" His deep voice is barely audible, but I feel the finality of his statement in my bones. My gut. He's going to make me.

I look at the jagged opening in the trunk, and the wave of panic crashes down. My pulse thunders like the sky, my heart beating so hard I can taste it. "I can't. You don't understand. No!"

Steffan's strong fingers wrap around my arms as memories of traveling through the yew well up like bile. The searing heat, the crushing pressure, the white panic courses through me all over again. He pulls, and I dig in my heels like a spooked animal.

"Let go!" I cry, thrashing against him.

Pressing me against his chest, Steffan lifts me clear off my feet before forcing me into the hollow of the tree. Blackness engulfs me as I flail against the cold, ragged wood now surrounding me. I can't breathe.

"No, no, no. Please. Please, Steffan," I beg against his chest.

Murmuring in Welsh, his voice calm and steady and gentle, Steffan pulls himself in across from me, shutting out the storm with his back. The darkness is complete. Cold mud cakes my feet and hands, my ribs ache, and my sodden gown hangs heavy and limp, weighing me down.

Gasping for breath, I wait for the heat and pressure. For the burning and nausea. The light. But nothing happens.

After several long moments, I open my eyes.

Just a tree trunk. Just a storm. Just a man crouched next to me, a shadow in the darkness.

I swallow hard. Blink against the flashes of light still visible through the tight canopy above us.

"I'm sorry. I just ... How long will it last?" I ask over the rhythmic pounding of rain.

Now isn't the time to explain my panic, even if I could.

"Long enough." His voice is low and dense but not unkind.

Shaken but steadier, I settle into our cramped shelter. Steffan all but melts into the wood, his back still blocking the worst of the rain and wind. At every crack of thunder, I jump, our knees bumping until he slips back out into the storm.

"Where are you going?" I cry, unable to hide my fear.

Steffan's hard mouth and strong chin, the only parts of his face not hidden by his hood, appear. "To guard the horse."

"From what?"

"Anything that be o' a mind to eat it." Thunder punctuates the last word.

Then he's gone, and a gust of wind slams into my face.

Cradling my head in my arms, I slide down into the space left behind and shake.

Deep in the night, the storm passes. I must nod off at some point because I wake with a start to discover Steffan back in the tree trunk and snoring softly. In the glinting starlight, our knees press together in a row of awkward hillocks.

Stiff and aching with cold, I shift. Steffan jerks awake immediately. Our glassy eyes meet in the shadows, and a shiver that has nothing to do with the cold bursts down my spine.

"How did you find me?" I blurt.

My voice rasps as breath fills the space between us like a puff of smoke. I don't have to explain what I mean.

Steffan blinks. It's the slow, measuring blink of a cat.

"The wineskin," he says.

I swallow hard. My palms start to sweat despite the cold as I remember: the smooth leather sliding against my belly, the scent of wine and fear blooming together in the night, the stench of the hand clamped over my mouth.

"You followed me?" It's not really a question.

He hesitates before clicking his tongue, as if deciding how much to say. "I thought mayhap ye would thieve a horse."

A chuff of laughter trips over my cold, chapped lips. "If only I'd been that s-smart," I chatter. From cold or adrenaline letdown, I can't tell. "We'd both be better off if I had."

Steffan says nothing.

I absorb his silent agreement and press on. "And then?"

He shifts slightly then, and I can just make out the hard plains of his face in the thin moonlight. He's staring at me, his eyes flecks of obsidian in the night. "I saw."

I press my torn nails into my palms and swallow.

"Why bother helping me? You weren't happy about it the first time." The words come out more accusation than question, but I don't hide the bitterness. The surprise.

He doesn't flinch away from me. "I had to."

"Others wouldn't have. Didn't."

"My reasons be my own, but I do not regret aiding ye, if that be yer concern. And I be not *others*." His deep voice rises over the lingering wind as he scans my face. "Sleep, Ellyll. Gather yer strength. I shall keep watch till the morrow."

"I know," I say and close my eyes again, never doubting I was safe.

Something crawls across my hand. Jerking awake, the prickle of tiny legs dissolves into a more substantial sensation as I whack my knuckles against the frigid trunk.

"Ow!" I complain, holding my fist to my chest. When the

wet leaves next to me rustle, I bolt out of the trunk and straight into six inches of mud.

"God damn son of a bitch," I seethe.

Nearby, someone chuckles. Turning, I find Steffan leaning against the horse's flank. Without further greeting, he reaches into the saddle bag and tosses something to me. I grab the hunk of salted meat out of the gray air.

"We leave once ye break yer fast," says Steffan before going back to picking at his teeth with a small twig.

Clearly our kumbaya moment the night before has passed. I want coffee and a pastry, I can't turn my head to the right without my neck cramping, and some insect has bitten the hell out of my hands.

"Stupid, ass-freezing, bug-infested ..." I complain through a mouthful of leathery meat and look around.

A film of cement-colored clouds has strapped down the damp air, promising a cool day ahead. I can't tell what time it is but guess just past dawn by the chattering birds. Hunger takes over then, and I chew until my jaw aches and my thoughts turn to the day ahead. So much so that I start when Steffan touches my shoulder.

"Mistress," Steffan greets formally and offers the wineskin. He's as rumpled and filthy as I surely am but manages to wear it like the trees around us, natural and starkly beautiful. The thought unnerves me. I take a long drink before handing it back, the liquid welcome on my rough throat and empty stomach. "I need a few minutes of privacy before we go."

Steffan points into the mist. "Do not lose sight o' the horse."

Wiping my hands on the already destroyed dress, I march off. The ground is both sticky and slick, suctioning to one foot and then sliding out from under the other. Carefully, I walk in a straight line and duck around the first large tree I come to. Misty woods stretch all around me and my heart twitches at the gloomy expanse. After relieving myself, I carefully follow my own tracks back to the hollow oak, nearly running into the horse for my efforts.

Steffan isn't there.

Thinking he's followed nature's call as well, I snuggle against the horse and wait. And wait. And wait.

"Steffan?"

Nothing but the chatter of birds sounds among the mostly barren trees.

"Very funny," I say, louder this time. "I get it. Don't wander off into the fucking forest." Still no answer.

Fear strokes my neck, but I push it away and awkwardly haul myself into the saddle. This is not the time for games. The old horse twitches his ears at me before taking another mouthful or soggy greenery.

"Where's Mr. Dark and Brooding, huh?" I coo, giving him plenty of rein. "Go find him. Find Steffan."

The amber beast snorts, shakes his head, and starts picking his way through the cindery trees.

"Steffan," I call as the horse plods along. Cold, hungry, and now without my guide, anxiety twists in my belly.

I let the animal go where he wants, a sketchy plan at best, but I don't dwell on it. A niggling sensation inches across my skin, as if I'm being watched. I strain to ignore it, even as my torso grows hot with panic, my ears straining for any sound.

"Steffan?" I whisper. "Ste—"

I scream as a hand reaches from behind a tree and grabs the horse's bridle. The beast skitters sideways before chuffing in pleasure as Steffan steps into view.

I, on the other hand, come unglued.

"What the hell is wrong with you?" I hiss, my fear and anger sizzling like water on a hot griddle. "Do not lose sight o' the horse," I mimic his voice. "You should listen to your own advice!" I dismount in a huff.

"*Hisht*, woman" he says, unmoved.

"I will not—"

"Ye shall affright it," he whispers and turns my head to follow his gaze.

I gasp at the bizarre sight before me. Releasing me, he ties off the horse before creeping through the tangled branches. Understanding the need for quiet, I shadow Steffan's steps until we're just a few yards from the creature.

Grazing among the tender grass, the potbellied animal is more Shetland pony than glamorous steed, its white mane hanging almost to the ground full of burs. My fingers ache for pencil and paper as I stare at the single spike protruding from the homely beast's forehead. Blunt and knotted, the horn looks more useful for foraging among tree roots than battling an enemy, but its presence is undeniable.

"Holy shit," I breathe. If my view of reality wasn't already in shreds, this would have done it handily. As the beast lazily swishes its tail at bothersome insects, new light falls across every myth I never believed in. Too soon, Steffan taps my shoulder, and we creep back to the horse.

"Was that what I think it was?" I ask as Steffan pulls me into the saddle behind him.

"And what be that?" He rebounds the question, turning the horse toward what I assume is the direction of Dwyn Blair, though how he can tell, I'll never know.

Both grateful for and leery of Steffan's warmth, I try not to lean too close. "If I didn't know better, I'd say it was a unicorn."

"Why should ye know better than to call a creature by its name?"

"Because they don't exist. I suppose you have mermaids off the coast and dryads in the—trees." I close my mouth, struck by the sudden possibility of anything. Everything. Who am I to say what is or is not possible?

Steffan clicks his tongue at the horse before echoing my thoughts. "Who be we to say what almighty God can create, Ellyll?"

I bite the inside of my cheek, unable to counter that particular logic. "Why do you call me that?" I ask after a moment. "You know my name."

Steffan looks back at me over his shoulder. Deep auburn eyelashes frame irises the color of fog. "'Tis not for who ye be that I name ye. 'Tis for what."

CHAPTER 9

LADY DAY

Steffan lets out a sharp whistle as we ride into the yard. The goats scatter at the intrusion, bleating. The ruckus brings Angharad from the house, the baby strapped to her chest. Though it's still early morning, her face is flushed and damp with sweat, her apron covered in flour. She looks exhausted.

"We feared the horse had gone lame," she says by way of greeting. "Or been carried off." Her tone made it clear as Waterford the horse's disappearance hadn't been the true concern.

"'Twas naught but the storm." Steffan spoke mildly, but the heavy muscles of his shoulders bunched under my hands. Even he seemed to resent her assumption.

"'Twas a queer thing how it blew in o' a sudden, for certes," she says as if I'd conjured the rain.

Sliding off the horse, my sympathy and patience as raw as my thighs, I face my hostess. "Oh, I don't know. I personally had a wonderful time freezing my ass off all night in a wet, insect-infested tree trunk just waiting to get struck by lightning or attacked by a wolf."

Angharad's eyebrows shoot up as Steffan makes a strangled

sound that might be a laugh or a cough. She opens her mouth to retort but is cut off as squeals of glee erupt from the direction of the chicken coop. Two dark heads and one fair one tear down the hill, converging on us like ants to a picnic. The twins prattle unintelligibly as Steffan ruffles each of their inky heads before kissing Gwenhwyfar's pale cheek. One of the boys—Ieuan, I think—darts his head around Steffan to stare at me. I stick out my tongue and go cross-eyed at him. He rewards me with a radiant smile.

After a moment, Angharad clears her throat.

"Be ye well?" she asks Steffan, her tone gentler.

The whisper of a smile touches his mouth as he nods and unstraps the saddlebags. He presents the bundle of fungi to Angharad as if it was a queen's ransom. "For ye, madam."

She accepts our hard-earned gatherings with nothing more than a satisfied nod, and I roll my eyes.

"Cai be in yon field. He would that ye speak with him afore ye break yer fast. There be plenty o' *cawl* inside." Bag in hands, she walks off with the children scampering behind like yin and yang ducklings.

I let out a noisy breath. *Sorry* nearly slips off my tongue, but I hold it back. I'm not sorry. Not for what I said and certainly not for events outside my control. Snatching the horse's reins off the ground, I glance at Steffan. He's already staring. His dark, wavy hair sticks out in wild tangles, and the skin under his eyes is bruised with fatigue. The thick amber whiskers covering his jaw and neck only add to his brutal demeanor, but his face looks softer too. As if the hinges holding each feature in place loosened. I wait for him to say something. Anything. To acknowledge the last twenty-four hours or the crackling energy still singing between us. But he remains ever silent before turning sharply and heading for the fields.

Once in the stables, I manage to corral and unsaddle the horse before sliding to the ground. Hunger and fatigue rub like a pair of hot stones in my stomach and do nothing to clear my head. I've been here for days and haven't gathered a single supply. Have no solid plan for getting back to the yew. To Meredith. Tears burn in my throat as I wipe my face and inhale long, deep breaths. I'm convinced Angharad will notice if I take so much as a flint, but I have to try anyway. Soon.

"Enough whining, Quinn," I say and get up.

Moving toward the wide door, I give the ground a peevish kick. A lump of mud skids a few feet and shatters against the stable wall. Enjoying the release, I take aim at a larger clot in the doorway and swing my foot. The Rodinesque mass of mud arches impressively through the air before slamming into the heavy bosoms of a woman standing just outside. Stumbling backward, her eyes go owl-wide. Black goop covers her torso.

I slap a hand over my mouth and rush forward. "Shit. I'm so sorry. Are you hurt?"

The woman just stares at me, her round eyes bulging as she forces an overdue breath in and out of her lungs. Her companions—two teen girls and a younger boy, all strangers to me—stand frozen off to one side. Their heads swing between us.

"I was just—" I start. "I didn't see you there."

One of the girls rushes forward. Chestnut-haired and buxom, she looks close to Madoc's age. Carefully avoiding the woman's besmirched cleavage, she brushes at the mud.

"I'm sorry," I repeat, my ears hot with embarrassment.

Recovered from her shock, the thick woman surveys herself and proceeds to berate me in a string of fiery Welsh that needs no interpretation. Startled into action, the freckled boy and thin-faced girl with hair the color of dried leaves move to help, but the woman flails her arms at them before turning toward a new man approaching. Tall and wiry with graying hair, he stops next to the ranting woman, his chin rumpled into a frown.

"It was an accident," I try to explain when his eyes find mine.

Like serene, blue pools amidst craggy terrain, the man's eyes twinkle as his long face breaks into a grin, and he howls with laughter. The teenagers chortle along until the woman, who I suspect is their mother, shouts again. Needing no more encouragement, all three of them bolt.

I bite my cheeks to keep from smiling.

"Is there anything I can do?" I offer, stepping forward. I suspect these people are the relatives Angharad told me about, but there was really no telling. Besides, my tolerance for shock seems to expand hourly.

"Methinks ye have done enough, mistress."

At the sound of Cai's voice behind me, I turn. He strolls around the stables. Stripped of his doublet, Cai surveys the scene, his face ruddy from work.

"As usual," I add.

Chuckling, the master of Dwyn Blair stretches a hand toward me.

"Mistress Meg be my fair guest, a traveler from across the sea in need o' honest Cymry hospitality," he says before pointing to the couple. "My good cousin, Indeg, and her husband Yestin. Though ye seem to have met!" he sputters, unable to hold a serious face any longer.

Yestin keeps laughing before taking off his own hood and mopping down his wife.

"I really didn't mean to," I say, relieved that at least the men aren't angry. From the look Indeg levels at me, she feels no such relief.

"Do not fret, lass," chuckles Yestin. "'Tis not the first time my bride hath greeted the morn in a gown o' filth."

Indeg smacks him on the shoulder. Her pale skin is flushed scarlet under the remaining flecks of mud. "So says the man who fell in a pigsty and pissed himself the night o' our hand-fasting."

"Aye, well," admits Yestin in a sheepish tone. "'Twas grand mead, nay?"

Cai puts a hand on each of his cousins' shoulders. "Indeed. And ye," he addresses me, "Madoc shall be rare pleased ye did not faerie away his brother."

"Contrary to popular belief, I am not trying to steal anyone away," I say crossing my arms. *Just a horse and some food*, I add silently. Each of them looks at me in confusion before turning back to each other. I sigh. It's what they normally do when I say something untranslatable.

"Come now. Angharad shall fetch ye ale and a pot to clean in." Cai lumbers toward the house, expecting to be followed.

I have my doubts about Angharad fetching me anything, but Indeg is eager for an appropriate welcome and darts after Cai like a quail seeking shelter. With an exaggerated exhale, I wipe my hands on the ruined dress as an unpleasant scent wafts up. It only takes a moment to realize it's me. I reek and feel about ready to sell my soul for a long, hot shower and a toothbrush.

Ignoring me, Yestin turns to the neglected horse and wagon standing a few yards away. "Off with ye now, mistress. And send yon lads to me, aye?"

At that moment, a cocktail of raised voices issues from the house. Yestin cocks an eyebrow at me. I shrug.

"Maybe I can help instead?" I offer. The prospect of food and drink notwithstanding, I'm not ready to face the drama inside.

Yestin stares at me, openly taking my measure, before giving a nod.

"Hold fast to the old cunny," he instructs as he unhitches the sweaty horse from the wagon. Wondering if that's a term of endearment or insult, I tightened my grip on the bridle just in time for the horse's answer. With a jerk of her newly freed head, the mare snaps at my arm.

"Hey!" I whip out of reach, but she swings around again, slobbery lips flapping over two rows of burnt-marshmallow teeth. I slap her nose away once then twice before the fiend shakes her head, snorts, and stands still.

Yestin's blue eyes dance with approval. "'Tis how ye must handle all feisty bitches," he advises with a wink before leading the mare toward the stable. "Best take the food in and be done with it, girl."

Waffling between inspired and offended by such advice, I crawl into the wagon. After a brief scan around, I shove a wedge of hard cheese and a leek down the front of my dress before filling my arms with the remaining blocks of fermented dairy and a loaf of dark bread that makes saliva pool in my mouth.

"Time for your big girl pants," I tell myself and head for the house.

I enter through the kitchen, hoping the myriad smells will mask the briny stench coming from my diminutive cleavage. If I've learned anything about the past, it's that modern people have lost their sense of smell. And possibly for good reason. While nothing here—now—holds a fragrance beyond its own merit, the scents of smoke, candle wax, shit, drying herbs, sap, yeast, grass, rain, animal, dirt, and sweat permeate every aspect of life. Banking on this, I set the basket of goods on the small prep table.

Gwenhwyfar's standing in the corner, her platinum hair swinging dangerously close to a tub of cream she's skimming with what looks like a scallop shell. The two new girls sit at the table with a mug of ale between them. They nod to me before looking at each other with a speaking glance—a clear signal that my strange speech and dubious backstory have been explained. Too anxious to hide my contraband, I ignore them and hurry toward the main room. Angharad materializes in the doorway like a phantom.

"Here," she says and thrusts the baby into my arms.

"Oh, really I can't ..."

"Ye can," my hostess admonishes, skirting around me.

"But I'm filthy."

Angharad just shoots me a look of exasperation, her pretty eyebrows arching.

"Take her with ye while ye wash up," she says before barking orders at the girls sitting.

Too tired to check myself, I scowl at her back and mumble a foul curse. So, with mud in my hair and a wedge of cheese going soft in my bodice, I face the bundle in my arms; a pair of stone blue eyes regard me from between a thatch of black hair and a begonia-blossom mouth. Ripples gurgle through the baby's impossibly small back, and my own insides growl empathetically.

"What's her name?" I call realizing it's rather terrible I don't already know.

Angharad stops mid-sentence.

"Branwen," she says with the first tepid smile she's shown me in days before seizing the butter churn.

Following the apricot glow of the fire, I stray into the empty room, pleased not to be churning butter at least.

"Hello, Branwen. I'm Meg," I whisper as if sharing a great secret. "I'm going to be an aunt to a little bean like you soon. Two of them, actually. It's kind of a big deal."

In response to my revelation, Branwen blinks, thrusts her tongue out several times, and pees through her swaddling.

"Shit," I hiss as warm urine runs through my fingers and drips on the floor. Pressing Branwen to my chest with one hand, I grab the hem of my skirt and hoist it high to soak up the mess. Now wet and squashed, the irritated baby kicks, and the leek shoots out from its hiding place, hitting the floor between my feet with a dull thump. I swear in earnest this time, stooping again to grab the whiskery vegetable, just as a pair of tall, black boots step away from the shadowed wall.

Looking up, my heart bounces like a dropped ball.

Steffan. Watching me.

I freeze as he walks closer, right up to me, his eyes making a slow path from the stolen leek, to my exposed thighs, to the baby in my arms, and finally to my face. A muscle feathers in his clenched jaw.

Neither of us move. My heart thuds against my ribs as I wait for him to say something. To chastise me or alert Angharad. Anything. Instead, what might be humor flickers through his pale eyes as he reaches down and scoops Branwen from my arms. My skirts drop, covering the contraband and my legs— the latter of which have started to tremble. Cradling his wet infant sister in one arm, Steffan picks up a steaming mug from the table and hands it to me, an amused smile twisting his lips.

"Drink this and wash, Ellyll. Ye shall be in need o' yer strength this eve," he says before turning away, his attention fully focused on the wet baby pressed against his chest.

ours pass after the incident with Steffan, but I can't relax. Even after washing, changing, and a celebratory meal of oat bread, buttered leeks, cheese, fish stew, and custards made with honey and ginger, I feel skittish as a harassed house cat. If it had been anyone else, I would assume they hadn't noticed. But not him. I know he saw everything and likely guessed what I was up to. So why hadn't he said anything? Was he trying to protect me? Or only waiting for the right moment to expose me? All evening my neck flames with shame, despite telling myself I don't care what he thinks of me. But my body knows better, betraying me.

Finally, when the food is cleared away, everyone gathers around the hearth where Madoc, looking even more pleased with himself than usual, starts playing a small, wing-shaped harp with astounding skill. The combination of his mischievous demeanor and the spritely music he creates strikes me in the chest. It's delightful. With Gwenhwyfar sitting beside him, her hand perched on his strumming shoulder like a pale bird, I wonder if she feels the music.

Out of nowhere, Cai starts singing along. Immediately, the twins leap up, spinning around the room, arms linked, their faces wild. As Madoc plays and the family sings and dances, I find myself grinning. Deeply, genuinely smiling. Despite the constant churn of anxiety and my desire to get home, the scene before me is infectious. Charming. Having no outside source of entertainment, these steely people are adept at amusing themselves and do so without reserve. Even Steffan and Angharad clap along, eyes sparkling.

The music speeds up to a rollicking frenzy, Madoc fulling focused on his instrument.

Noticing my smile, Yestin swings a tankard in my direction, spilling most of his ale on the rushes spread out for the day. "Come now girl, ha' a drink and a dance!"

"No thank you. Really," I say, fending off the zealous offering from my seat against the wall.

Laughing at my rebuff, Yestin grabs his dark-haired daughter and twirls her in a brisk, if unsteady, jig before releasing her to the twins, who scramble to get hold of their pretty cousin's hands. Content to haunt the edges of the scene, I sway to the music until the younger, blonder daughter plops down next to me. Branwen is nestled in the crook of the girl's arm, and I smile politely at the invasion. Then she leans over and says something I can't hear.

"Pardon me?" I ask.

Her eyes sweep the room. She scoots right next to me. "'Tis true? The Irish—be they comin' to aid his cause?"

"I don't know," I say, the truth easy for once. I have no idea who or what she's talking about but decide the more information I have, the better. If the girl wants to gossip about local events, I'm not going to stop her. I might even discover something useful.

"I've been traveling, so perhaps I missed the news. What have you heard?" I prompt.

Again, she glances around. Whatever it is, she doesn't want to be discovered talking about it. "They say that Lord Glyndwr hath called on the Irish to join the revolt."

My mouth falls open. "Wait. Did you say Glyndwr? Owain Glyndwr?" My voice carries over the music.

Madoc's hand drops like a stone, scraping the harp strings. Steffan and Cai stop singing. A loaded silence floods the room.

"Be there word o' Lord Glyndwr? Be he raiding again?" Madoc says, as wide-eyed as a baby owl.

Angharad shoots me a withering look before turning to Madoc. "Be nay concern o' ours."

I swallow my questions, choking on their implications as Cai shifts in his chair. "I have heard that his lordship—"

"I hath no stomach for such talk," Angharad interrupts.

Cai regards his wife before placing a big-boned hand on her shoulder. It's a tender, soothing gesture if I ever saw one.

"My wife be affrighted o' what this tide may bring. And justly so, but I do not believe ye mean us harm," he says, looking straight at me. "The house o' Cai ap Hywel holds Lord Owain ap Gruffudd to be its true sovereign—though Bolingbroke mayhap sees it differently," he adds with a chuckle.

"Be not a jest." Angharad stands brusquely and retrieves Branwen from my bench mate's care. The girl's cheeks flush red as she darts away from me, caught out.

"Shall be a bloody mess afore the end," Angharad says, her voice low and hard.

"'Tis a bloody mess now, for certes," Yestin says, his wavering gaze turning to his son, who's been mostly quiet. "Though some things be worthy o' blood."

The boy sits with Steffan, shadowing his every move.

"Pray, let us talk nay more o' blood," Indeg says from her place next to Angharad. "Play another, Madoc."

Sullen-faced, Madoc strums a chord on the harp as everyone falls back into step with forced enthusiasm. Still seated against the wall, I fold my shaking hands in my lap and think about the last time I heard the name Owain Glyndwr.

Mrs. Jones had left me in the lounge to look around while she got ready. Hanging on the crowded wall of photos was a thin-framed picture of a handsome young man with jet hair. He looked close to my age and was making a goofy face at the camera.

"I see you've found my cheeky Dai," said Mrs. Jones as she emerged from the stairwell. "I took that last summer whilst on holiday in Machynlleth."

I smiled at the affection in her voice.

"What's that?" I asked, struck by the unusual object in the photo. Next to the young man, a pointed slab of gray slate thrust upward from the ground like a huge subterranean sword. A circular seal stared down from the top of the stone like a golden eye.

"That's the Owain Glyndwr Memorial. Just marked the six hundredth anniversary of his revolt a few years past, we did."

"Revolt against what?"

Scandalized, Mrs. Jones clicked her tongue. "Why the English, love. Did your mum never tell you about such things?"

"She was really little when she left," I defended.

Mrs. Jones made a gallant attempt to organize her face. "Well, Glyndwr was a Cymry baron who led an uprising for more than a decade against mad old Bolingbroke." Taking in my confused expression, she added, "You know, King Henry the IV, the one who went doolally up top." She twirled her index finger at her head.

"You mean like Shakespeare's King Henry IV?" I asked.

Mrs. Jones smiled and bobbed her head approvingly. "Wasn't successful o' course and made life more the miserable I'm sure, but it was a bold stand whilst it lasted."

"Holy shit," I breathe. I am somewhere—no—*somewhen* at the turn of the fifteenth century in the middle of a country just past the precipice of a war they are going to lose.

"Mistress?" A voice breaks into my thoughts.

Looking up, I find the older cousin holding out a mug to me.

A swag of dark hair slips over her shoulder as she offers a kewpie doll smile.

"On second thought, I think a drink is in order," I say and drain the cup as the music speeds up again, racing to the beat of my blood.

CHAPTER 10
SAVE YERSELF

The tip of my nose is numb. I press it with my index finger just to be sure. Yep. Numb. As I scrunch up my face, I have the unfortunate realization the cold air isn't to blame. Losing track of my thought, I stare into the mug in my hand. The contents wrinkle, and my stomach does the same.

"I'm going to be sick," I announce to no one in particular and grab the first container I see before my insides turn themselves out.

A barking laugh pierces the alcoholic haze as the wave of nausea peaks and ebbs. I close my eyes, the world wobbling, and set down the ruined container with a groan. The soft hum of voices and music echo around me. Through me.

"I have seen babes keep their mead better," says Cai, amused.

"Aye." Yestin's voice slides out in a tangled slur. "Reminds me o' the time the lad got into the ale. 'Twas nigh past my knee and pissed," he sniggers, slapping his bony thigh with glee. The noises ricochet around the room, too confusing to keep track of.

"Be nay wonder who he takes after," adds a woman's voice. Indeg?

I lift my head a fraction, eyes focusing.

"Bah. Get us another drink, cow." Yestin grabs his wife's wrist and pulls her into a rough kiss.

In return, Indeg jerks out of his grasp with just enough effort to leave question as to whether or not this exchange is teasing. "Leave off, ye great oaf, or ye shall walk home."

Mead! That's the word. Blasted honey-tasting stuff was a quick balm but turned my brains to cotton, my stomach a heaving sea.

"I think I should go to bed," I say slowly and focus on Cai.

Pink cheeked and glassy eyed himself, the lord looks me up and down.

"O' course, Mistress Meg. May the blessing o' our Lady be on ye," comes the gravelly reply. Then his wavering double image cracks a grin and winks at me.

I close one eye, hoping the second Cai will disappear. It does. I'm just sober enough to know I'm good and truly plastered, I ask in mock offense, "Are you laughing at me, milord?"

Throwing back his great blond head, Cai laughs outright.

"May Jesu strike me down if I have offended ye!" he shouts before striding over to where I still sit propped at the table. He leans in close then. Close enough to see the worn furrows of skin around his bright eyes. As if we're co-conspirators, he gives me yet another playful wink and whispers, "Cai ap Hywel would ne'er wish to displease a member o' the Fair Family."

"The Fair Family? Do you mean—"

"Another, mistress?" Angharad appears at my elbow and shoves a full mug of mead right under my nose.

I can't turn away fast enough. My stomach roils at the too-sweet smell. "No, thank you," I manage with a forced swallow.

Water, some distance rational part of my brain thinks. I need water and bread and sleep. "I'm going to bed."

"Shall I escort ye?" Angharad's small hand bites into my arm as she hauls me off the bench.

I gain my feet without the room spinning and take a few steps before trying to shake her off. She doesn't let go.

"I've got it," I say through clenched teeth.

"Got what?" Madoc pipes up from his place in front of the fireplace where he and Ieuan lay dozing against the dog. Looking around, I see the fire's been banked and the family lay in comfortable heaps all about, talking or dozing.

Beyond manners, I wrench away from Angharad's grasp. My face still tingles, but a stomach devoid of alcohol is rapidly improving my sobriety.

"I've got this," I say gesturing toward myself.

"O' course ye have," Madoc say. "Ne'er did I hear o' a pissed *Tylwyth Teg*."

At his words, a feeling of déjà vu penetrates my drunkenness, though I can't identify the source. Where have I heard that word before?

"*Byddwch yn dawel*," commands Steffan, coming out of his chair against the wall. With one big hand, he cradles a swaddled and silent Branwen against his chest.

"Stop bloody telling me what to do," Madoc shoots back, more than a little drunk himself.

Disturbed by the noise, the great wolfhound rolls over and gets up, shaking itself before facing the door, ears perked up. Ieuan's head flops on the floor with a gentle thud. Steffan just holds a hand up for quiet seconds before a sharp knock sounds at the door.

Those still awake freeze. The sleeping stir awake.

Cai, raking a hand through his hair, calls out in Welsh, and although I don't understand the sharp reply, the looks exchanged around me say enough.

Trouble is at the door.

"Aye, milord," calls Cai, stepping up to unlatch the door, hands loose at his sides. Ready.

As he does, the familial groups bunch together. Only Steffan, Angharad, and I stand on our own.

Several men blow in with the dank night air. The heavy clinking of mail announces them as English garrison soldiers—the same kind we saw in Bala. My heart thuds at the memory, and ice runs through my veins. After they file in, a final man ducks under the lintel and unfolds himself into the firelight. And keeps unfolding. Atop his towering height sits a long nose, sleek jaw, and winged ears that give him the overall appearance of a dignified weasel. Despite these oddities, the stranger's dark eyes flash like spinning coins and rest on each of us in turn, the authority in them unmistakable.

"Ichabod, Ichabod Crane," I hum under my breath.

Cai bows deeply. "A blessed Lady Day to ye, milord. Will ye and yer men take some mead?"

The tall man flicks his hand in dismissal and walks the room, trailing his gloved fingers over things as if to check for dust. His fur-lined cloak swings to the rhythm of each heavy step. No one moves.

"Pray, milord, if I may ask, to what do we owe the honor o' yer company?" Cai's normal, jovial tone has gone brittle.

The man doesn't respond but stops in front of the tapestry. Next to me, Angharad gives a breathy gasp. Though small and simplistic compared to the masterpieces I've seen in textbooks, the tapestry is treasured. I've watched Angharad use her hem to tenderly wipe soot from its edges and scold the boys for playing too near it.

Leaning close, the tall man runs a possessive hand over the intricate vegetal design not unlike the carvings on St. Melangell's rood screen.

"What a shame for such finery to languish in squalor," he says in a reedy voice, his tone flat and bored. Then he gestures to the closest man-at-arms. Immediately, the soldier steps forward and rips the tapestry from the wall.

A collective hiss seeps from every mouth as Angharad clutches my arm, this time in what I can only guess is panic and rage. I glance over, and her anguished expression sends another wave of nausea rolling through me, this time from fear.

"Do ye not agree, Master Cai?" asks the man as if concurring on the weather.

The proud, kind, jolly master of Dwyn Blair's face bends into an unfamiliar expression: quiet fury. But Cai's voice betrays nothing as he speaks. "Milord hath grand taste. That tapestry, 'twas my father's and his father's afore him."

Somewhere in the room, knuckles pop.

"Aye. That I do, though I would not hath ye feel used, for certes." The powerful guest circles the room again, like a dog preparing to rest. "A tale then, in exchange. Six nights past, a man-at-arms be found dead in Bala. Stabbed in the back. Thrice." He holds up three fingers as if we're toddlers. "A shopkeeper found him the next morn. Stepped out for a piss and fell over the corpse."

A whimper leaks out of the chestnut-haired cousin crouched near Madoc by the hearth.

The man comes to a stop and peers down into Cai's face. "'Tis unfortunate, aye?"

"Aye," Cai offers without backing away. "Most unfortunate."

The scarecrow-like man straightens to his full, considerable height. "I be glad to hear o' yer sympathy since the dead be nephew to Lord Reynold de Grey. The family be most aggrieved and seeks repayment. They hath tasked me with finding the source of this ... injustice."

Every mouth in the room swallows its breath.

"Your *sons*," the powerful man drawls, "be seen ridin' for the woods in great haste that night. I hope naught be amiss?"

I hold my breath. Every instinct in me commands retreat—that this man, whoever he is, poses truly terrible danger.

But Cai only smiles. "My sons had nay wish to break curfew, milord," he says. "Jesu forfend Cymry wolves be left to roam in the dark."

A corner of the tall man's mouth twists upward. "Indeed."

In a spasm of action, Angharad lets go of my arm and my stomach drops. "'Twas the girl that sent the lads home in such haste."

Every eye in the room flicks to her and then to me. To my horror, I feel faint. Buzzing erupts in my ears as several people begin talking at once.

"By the laws o' hospitality—" booms Cai.

"—some ruffian—" interrupts Madoc.

"The lads had nay part—" says Angharad.

The tall man holds up his gloved hands, black as oil, and an agitated silence once again takes hold of the room. He points to Angharad. "What have ye to say woman?"

My hostess, the person responsible for both the care of my wounds and my harassment, turns from me. "The girl be set upon near High Street, milord, but claims she saw naught o' her attacker. My husband's sons found her and brought her to my care."

The spindly man's eyes bore into Angharad. To her credit, she artfully plays the part of meek, concerned wife and does not meet his stare. I nearly chuckle. If only he could see her claws.

But then, the tall man's attention swings to me, and my damned knees wobble. *Don't you dare faint.*

"Pray tell mistress," the man croons. "What misfortune hath befallen ye?"

"A bloody Saxon, 'tis what." Madoc's voice, full of righteous fury, slices across the room. "Tried to ravish her, he did."

I close my eyes, willing my young defender to shut up. Apparently sharing my sentiment, Cai makes a low, thrumming sound in his throat. A clear warning to his son.

The man merely glances at Madoc's livid face before chuckling. "Tried? 'Tis difficult to accuse a man o' an act he did not accomplish."

His laughs grow into big, juicy guffaws. A few of the soldiers crammed by the doorway snicker.

My blood pressure surges, eliminating the dizziness, and the words are out of my mouth before I can think of a better plan. "Yes, he did."

Shadows from the dying fire fall across the man's finely cut face, rendering it a terrible, hollow-eyed mask. "And what be that, mistress? Exactly. Pray, speak with care, as ye seem a stranger here."

"He raped me," I lie as anger overrides my fear. "I was ashamed to tell the lady." And I was, though I hadn't realized the truth until that moment. While the solider hadn't technically violated me, the memory of his abuse ached like a yellowing bruise I had no wish to ever speak of again.

The man's shoulders hunch as he leans forward, a cat about to pounce. "And then?"

He's close enough to smell now and stinks of cloves.

I let the half-truths slip past my tongue like breath. "I don't know. After he—he let me go. It was dark, so I crawled down a back street until I saw a crowd." I force myself not to look at Steffan then, even as his clear gray eyes fill my memory. "I remember seeing a lantern and several faces. I called out but don't remember anything after that until I woke up here."

The man, whose identity I still don't know, purses his lips in thought before moving toward the hearth. People slide away from him like water to a hull.

"Do ye believe this *ruffian*, this *bloody Saxon* to be our king's murdered man?" he asks, kicking at a stray ember. It shatters against the stone walls with a hiss.

Cai, who's still standing closest catches my eye, a silent plea in them. I don't dare acknowledge him.

"No," I say, praying my voice sounds steadier than it feels, the mead still singing through my head, which has started to ache. "He wasn't dressed like them." I point to the soldiers. "I don't know who he was or what happened to him."

And I'm glad he's dead. The thought flairs in my mind, but I just stare straight ahead. I can feel the man regarding me but am not prepared for the jolt of fear that rocks me as he grabs the fireplace poker and jams it into the blistering coals.

"I have ne'er heard yer speech afore," he comments. "Whence do ye hale?"

My head starts to swim again. Shit, shit, shit.

"I'm from— I'm looking—" I stammer.

"The *Gwyddeles* be searchin' for her kin." Steffan's voice rolls through the room as he hands the baby to Gwenhwyfar, whose white head I barely see crouched by the stairs to the loft. He takes a step forward but no more. "She hath no desire to anger ye, Sheriff."

With the poker still in hand, the man—the sheriff—swivels slowly as if savoring the movement. "Captain Blaidd. Still obliging the wenches, I see."

Steffan is taller than most men I've seen in this time, easily six feet or more, but even he has to raise his chin to look the sheriff in the face. "Only as they wish."

I can't see my interrogator's expression, but a palpable rage slips off him like water, filling the room. "Aye. To their own end."

Rekindled, the fire crackles and spits, flaring to life.

With deceptive casualness, the sheriff raises the poker to eye level. Everyone moves at once, some stepping forward, while others jump back. We all freeze when he throws the blistering metal against the hearthstone with a violent *clang.*

Turning on his heels, the rangy man strides to where the men-at-arms stand at attention. Cai's family tapestry hangs limply over one of their shoulder's.

"I thank ye for yer hospitality, Master Cai," the sheriff spits at no one in particular. But when he turns, he has eyes only for Steffan. "'Twas most informative."

Wrenching open the door himself, the lawman disappears into the night.

Hours after the soldiers leave, it's easier than I expect to sneak out. Everyone is on edge and eager to disperse. As the fire in the big house burns low, the muffled sounds of fitful sleep emanate from the bodies slumped around the room. I simply grab a cloak and leave.

I need to speak with Steffan. Tonight.

A yellow half-moon hangs mid-sky and does little to light my path. Past the fields near the tree line, Steffan and Madoc's cabin looms out of the dark with the suddenness of a picture book popup. Quaint and foreboding, the thatched roof and gently smoking chimney are straight out of a fairytale. I'm frightened and dizzy, with no clue what to say or what's about to happen, but stubbornness has me creeping steadily forward. Between the sheriff's interrogation and walking across the fields, the last of my drunkenness has burned away, but I still feel lightheaded.

I nearly fall backward when the dark door of the cottage swings wide. I freeze, a rabbit caught in a snare.

Steffan fills the moonlit doorway. Bow drawn and shirtless, he looks more war god than man, his hair falling over unblinking eyes, every muscle rigid. I can do nothing but stare. I should be terrified. Some deep, primal part of my brain knows this. Instead, every ounce of tension melts down my body as a profound feeling of peace falls over me. I've been dirty, hungry, cold, sore, tired, terrified, and angry for nearly a week, but as my eyes take in Steffan, dangerous and dark in the doorway, the air changes.

I exhale long and hard, as if I've been holding my breath for years.

He lowers the lethal weapon, carefully releasing the tension on the bow. "Ye should not be here."

"You have no idea," I say, careful to keep my voice low. "But I have to talk to you." I stop, flustered by more than his words. I force my eyes away from the broad plains of his chest and shoulders to his face. "The sheriff—what will he do?"

Steffan tips the mighty bow upright, again making it more wizard's staff than instrument of death. "Sheriff Godfrey Holloway's hatred o' me hath naught to do with ye."

"That's not what I asked, and you know it."

The seed of a smile touches his wide mouth. "Nay, 'twas not."

I cross my arms against both the cold and his stubbornness. "You know exactly what I mean."

No longer smiling, Steffan dips his head in acknowledgment but holds his silence.

Fine. I don't have time to play his games, so I'll say what I came to say. "Then at least let me say I'm sorry. For everything. I never meant for any of this to happen, and I know I'd be dead by now if not for you. So, thank you for saving my life."

Face flaming with embarrassment and a heat I don't want to think about, I turn to go.

Steffan grabs my shoulder. Looking back, I note the clean, blunt tips of his fingers before he snatches them away. As if he didn't mean to touch me at all.

"Abide," he whispers, voice gravelly before retreating into the dark cabin.

I peer after him, hardly daring to breathe. Silent as a shadow, Steffan moves through the dark room, past the sleeping forms of Madoc and his young cousin, until he reaches the farthest corner where, seemingly from the air, he retrieves a small pouch and crosses back to me. This time, Steffan steps into the night air and closes the door behind him with a soft *snick*. He's so close now I tip my head back to see his face. Overhead, stars whittle away at the sky, his curls a dark corona around his face.

He presses the object into my hands. "Take this."

A cream-colored hilt protrudes from a simple leather sheath no bigger than my hand. Carefully, I draw the blade. Moonlight kicks my reflection back as I touch the slick steel where an engraving runs down the spine.

"It's beautiful," I say, sheathing the blade, "but I can't accept this. I—"

Steffan presses a single long finger to my lips. I go perfectly still. Wind ruffles his hair as he stares down at me, for once his eyes black against his pale face. He drops his hand, but the feel of it remains. A stamp. An imprint.

"I shall not always be there to protect ye. Learn to save yerself, Ellyll."

I back away, clutching the knife to my chest. He watches me until I break into a run, no better than a startled rabbit fleeing. I don't stop until I'm all the way back to the house, lungs, lips, and mind ablaze.

CHAPTER 11

THE DRAGON'S THROAT

I open my eyes, fully awake, but can't identify what roused me. Looking around, I watch sooty light seep in around the water-tight shutters and spread across the chamber. Gwenhwyfar is snoring softly from the bed, her childlike form a small mound in the dark. The cousins sleep on another pile of sweet straw and blankets on the floor. My head throbs, and I close my eyes. Wisps of some ominous dream float around the edges of my memory, but each time my mind reaches for them, the images slip away.

Then a distant shout punctures the morning stillness. I sit up. The shout comes again, followed by the heavy beating of hooves, and I know.

Steffan is gone.

The household springs to life: bare feet slap against stone floors; wooden doors slam on their hinges; frightened, breathless exclamations fill the air. Wearing only my shift, I leap up and rush onto the landing in time to see a half-dressed Cai bolt out the front door with Yestin and Angharad on his heels. Near the hearth, Indeg fights to keep hold of the twins. The boys, thrashing like spooked cats, yowl in protest at their captivity.

Blood rushes to my face despite the icy railing under my hands, and before I know what I've decided, I'm hurtling down the steps toward the door.

I race through the mists, shoeless and shivering, to catch up with the others. Each panicky breath leads the way in frosty puffs. Halfway through the last field, I skid to a stop and gasp as my heart pounds impossibly faster.

Yanked from its hinges, the door to the cabin hangs open like a flap of torn flesh. I stare as Madoc stumbles through the doorway and into his father's chest. Urgent Welsh breaks through the sharp chorus of birdsong, and I start moving again, both terrified and fascinated by the bright stain across Madoc's face.

As I approach, Cai guides Madoc to the ground. Blood and mucus run unchecked down his chin and chest as Angharad looks for further wounds. Shouts stab my ears as Yestin ducks into the cabin. What could have been seconds or hours later, he reemerges with the trembling but unharmed young cousin under his arm.

"What happened?" I interrupt, unable to stand not knowing.

Heads snap toward me as if I've just materialized into existence. In a way, I have.

"Sheriff Holloway's men," Madoc switches into English, his voice hoarse. "I fought back, but the ungrateful whoreson broke my goddamn nose!"

Apparently reassured by Madoc's cursing, Angharad grabs the feature in question and pulls, setting the bones with a crunch.

Madoc howls. "God's bloody nails, woman, have ye nay gentleness?"

She doesn't bother answering, just hands him a rag to stanch the bleeding.

"'Twas Steffan who struck ye?" Cai asks.

Madoc gives a weak nod. "I had my dagger on a man-at-arms, but Steffan freed himself from them and hit me! 'Twas the only struggle the milksop made."

Kneeling in the mud next to his son, Cai places a hand behind Madoc's head. "He would not have ye share his fate, *coch.*"

"What will they do to him?" I'm trembling violently, but from cold or fear, I don't know.

Before anyone can answer, Angharad grabs me.

"This misfortune be yer doing!" she cries and sinks her fingernails into the soft underside of my arm.

"Stop!" Madoc protests, struggling to his feet.

"Yer brother hath been taken, and ye defend this *pwca* still?" Angharad jabs an accusing finger in my face. "Open yer eyes, man—she be our ruin!"

I want to slap her hand away. To squeeze her flesh in return and shake my own reality into the woman. But I can't because she's right. I am their ruin.

"Enough!" bellows Cai before pulling Angharad by the shoulders, breaking her grip on me.

Stumbling back, my mind whirls like a top as tiny, crescent-shaped tracks flare along my skin.

Cai holds Angharad to his chest. "He could have done nay different, *cariad,* and ye know it well."

Angharad doesn't protest being held, but her baleful stare tells me she does not count my honor worth Steffan's life. I'm not sure I disagree.

"I shall get him back," says Madoc. Having pinched his nose to stem the bleeding, his words come out garbled and comedic despite their gravity.

"And turn yer sire's land to forfeit?" scoffs Yestin, looking bedraggled and angry as a wet cat. "Nay. Steffan hath made his choice. There be naught to do but pay the debt owed against the Saxon's life."

Madoc spits a mouthful of blood on the ground. "There shall be naught left to forfeit if we do."

I grind my teeth to keep them from chattering and straighten my shoulders.

"How much?" I say it loud enough that every head turns toward me, each face grim and drawn. It's an answer all its own.

Cai lets go of Angharad. "Too much."

And for the first time since I've met him, the master of Dwyn Blair lowers his gaze to the ground.

"And if you don't pay?" I push, needing to know.

Angharad's face goes from livid to cold as the sky. "Steffan be condemned to irons. Or worse."

I stagger as guilt punctures my chest, twisting into my abdomen like a snarl of roots. "I have to go."

"Aye," Angharad agrees. "Anon."

"Nay," says Madoc.

Cai looks at his wife with unreasonable tenderness. "Turning the girl out does nay honor to Steffan's sacrifice."

Angharad lifts her chin. "I too love him well. Doubt it not, husband, but Yestin be right. Steffan hath made his choice." She points toward the big house. "'Tis time we made ours."

With my heart pounding and my mouth so dry I can barely swallow, I look back. Gwenhwyfar stands in the distance, weeping, her downy hair tangled around her neck. Farther back, the other girls clutch at the twins while Indeg comes last, her stout arms full of a crying Branwen. Like grim statues, they line the path to my departure.

Tears glaze my eyes as I turn and stride past them all.

I hobble through the house on muddy feet. Clumsy with cold, I wash my stinging extremities in the water basin and retrieve my clothes from Gwenhwyfar's trunk as quickly as possible. After nearly a week in long, layered dresses, the snug denim and porous sweater leave me feeling cold and exposed. I now know that even one night in the open without adequate warmth, shelter, and supplies is miserable at best and lethal at worst. And with only a vague notion of which way to go, I have more than one night ahead of me.

Listening for the family's approach, I pull Steffan's dagger from under the straw. My first impulse is to leave the gleaming gift behind. I have no right to it.

Then I think about Steffan. About his sacrifice. About his command to save myself.

I secure the dagger around my waist. The pressure of the sheath against my back proves a small comfort in the midst of epic chaos. I take a breath to steady myself as a patch of white flashes over my shoulder, and I turn. Deceptively frail looking in her shift and muddy feet, Gwenhwyfar stands in the doorway, holding out her cloak to me.

I shake my head. "No."

Her enormous eyes narrow, and she tries to fling the mantle across my shoulders. I dodge the offering and catch her wrist, pulling her close.

"Thank you for trying, but I can't," I say, determined to communicate. "Angharad might kill me," I add and point toward the fields.

Wilting slightly, Gwenhwyfar chews her bottom lip before darting out of the room, reappearing moments later holding what looks like a carefully wrapped loaf of bread and a small wineskin. The roots of guilt thrust deeper still, twisting.

"Thank you," I say, curtsying deeply before accepting the bundle. Refusing this gift would be suicide.

Gwenhwyfar cocks her head then. Fidgets. I know in that moment if I ever get the chance, I'll draw her impish face for the rest of my life. Throat tightening mutinously, I kiss her cheek and move to leave when she presses something into my palm. I freeze and stare at Gwenhwyfar as the flush on her cheeks deepens to a blazing shame. It's all the admission I need, but it doesn't matter after everything they've done for me. Suffered because of me. Just like always.

Tucking my mother's ring back into the pocket of my jeans, I offer Gwenhwyfar a forgiving smile and a lie.

"Everything is going to be fine," I say and leave.

I'm at the base of the stairs when shouting erupts again outside.

"Here we go," I say, squaring my shoulders, and open the heavy door.

Bare-legged, muddy, night shirt streaked with blood, Cai and Angharad stand nose to nose, hissing at each other like a pair of pit vipers. The rest of the family has scattered. Cai straightens when he sees me and switches to English, his face red with emotion.

"Mistress Meg, I shall escort ye to Bala once we have broken our fast. Angharad?"

Angharad bristles at the command in his voice and stalks past me, stopping just short of the door. Black curls blow across her handsome face, and the front of her shift is wet with leaking breast milk. The faintly sour smell hits me in the face.

"I do not wish ye ill will, Meg Quinn. I never have." Her voice crashes through the air. "But I do wish ye gone."

I see the exhaustion and worry etched around her eyes and try not to resent her. "Thank you for your help. I'm sorry."

Unbowed, Angharad nods before disappearing inside.

"Come." Cai gently takes my elbow and points me toward the stable. "Tend to the horses, lass. I shall be with ye anon."

"No. Absolutely not," I say as Madoc slams around the stable, making the horses snort nervously. I snatch a saddle bag from his grasp. "You can't leave them."

"She shall not drive ye off in this manner," Madoc seethes, grabs it back. Flecks of dried blood cling to the ginger stubble along his jaw. His eyes are already bruising brilliantly.

"She isn't driving me off. I should have left days ago," I argue.

He frowns. "I shall not be caught."

"Yes, you will, and I won't be responsible for this family losing another person."

"Nor shall ye," Madoc says before entering the stall to ready the horse.

Growing frantic, I ball my hands into fists and try to think. What would make him stay? There's no getting around his emotions. Even in this short time of knowing him, it's clear that Madoc is a creature of feeling before anything else. Appealing to his reason won't work, but perhaps if I fingered his guilt …

I follow him into the stall, determined to make my point. "Are you so stupid that you think they'll just let you walk out of there? Do you even know what will happen?"

Pulling the saddle cinch taut, Madoc wrinkles his face as if smelling something rancid. "Godfrey Holloway could not find his own arse with—"

I poke a finger in his chest. "You'll either get killed outright or arrested. And then what? Do you think Iolo and Ieuan are ready to replace you and Steffan? Do you want your father to work himself into his grave, or should Gwenhwyfar work the land until Angharad marries her off?"

Madoc stops.

Neither of us move. Then his confidence cracks and flakes away like dried mud, and I press harder. He cannot follow me.

"If you take him by force," I press, "neither of you can come home. And then what?"

The horse shakes its head, causing the bridle to jingle merrily against our silence.

"Find a way to pay the debt," I say. "It's the only way."

Madoc gives a stuffy sniff and pins me with an uncharacteristically serious stare, his jade green eyes bloodshot and wild. "Go ye to Bala, then?"

"Yes." I know what he really means but as usual don't know quite how else to respond. "To stay. My sister is still expecting me," I say truthfully.

A sudden look of determination crosses Madoc's face before he darts in for a kiss. His bloody lips catch the corner of my mouth as I pull away, stumbling backward into the wall just as Cai thunders through the door.

"Madoc," he barks before taking hold of the startled horse's reins. "Be a good man and oversee yer cousins' departure whilst I escort Mistress Meg to her kinsmen."

I wipe my face and stare at the damp hay under my feet. I do not move until Madoc's protests have ceased and his stomping footsteps disappear. Incandescent with mortification, I look up and meet Cai's sea-glass gaze, so like his son's.

Now fully dressed, he arches a bushy eyebrow before handing me an oatcake. "Make haste, fair one. There be nay time to squander."

Cai says little on our canter through the woods, but before the blood orange sun has cleared the tree tops, he's folded us in with a convoy of merchants on the deeply rutted main road. The men chat amicably with him and say nothing about my presence—a small, much-needed mercy.

Now, we lumber across the wide, creaking bridge at a cadaverous pace. Sweat trickles from under my arms while questions roll around my brain, clinking like marbles. As the crisp air gives way to the fug of smoke and sewage, I focus on breathing through my mouth and not making eye contact. I'm successful on both accounts until the bottleneck opens out into the city. Cautiously, I glance around Cai's shoulder. Deprived of night's forgiving cover, every imperfection of thatch and mortar is on display, along with a dizzying array of unvarnished, grizzled humanity. I pull back into the cloak.

As we make our way down the high street, a teenage girl with sunny hair draws my eye. Selling eggs from a stall, her profile is smooth and fine-boned as a cameo. Then she turns, revealing a motley web of burn scars that run from her cheek, down her neck, and into her bodice. The girl's pale eyes flick up as we pass, catching my stare. Before I can blink, a cart rolls by, sweeping away her Janus face.

"Whoa," says Cai, pulling the horse up in front of a tidy shop.

A chimney juts up from the roof like an apple stem, and a large, amber cat stretches languidly across the threshold. It's tidy and charming, and I'm mute with terror. I slide off the horse, wondering who the current apothecary of Bala really is, since it certainly isn't my brother-in-law like I've claimed. My mind whirls with no answer in sight except to stall and deflect.

Cai dismounts and unstraps my supplies from the saddle.

"Shall we greet yer kin?" he says, gesturing to the door.

I open my mouth to protest, to lie, and release a stuttering sequence of half-formed sentences my teenage self would be embarrassed by. "You see, I haven't ... They aren't—"

Thrusting the bundle into my arms, Cai claps his hands in front of my face as if to scare the hiccups from me.

"Enough," he says with uncharacteristic gravity. Running a hand through his bushy hair, Cai looks down the ridge of his long nose at me. "So now, the truth."

My breathing goes shallow, and I clear my throat hard before speaking. "The truth is too strange to tell," I whisper, but hold his gaze, willing him to believe me. "But I haven't lied to you about who I am or that I'm trying to get home to my sister. And I will do everything I can to repay your kindness to me."

Even as I say the words, the promise settles in my core like a warm drink and steadies me. Cai regards me for a long moment like the stranger I am, and I realize that despite his genial and gregarious manner, he never forgot.

"I accept yer word, Mistress Meg. 'Twas an honor to aid ye." He bows and, upon straightening, casts a withering look down the street. English men-at-arms cluster near the market stalls, their presence blatant and menacing. "We do not all hold ye to blame, girl. The twisting o' our fates began long afore ye arrived." With an anxious smile, his robust voice dwindles to a trickle. "Be ye still in need?"

A violent longing for my own father's comfort and counsel knifes through me. I have missed him every day since he died but maybe never more so than in this moment. But I see the price of the offer on Cai's haggard face and shake my head. The price of my presence has already been far too high.

"No, milord," I say. "Thank you."

He nods, the forks of his beard quivering. "So be it. Now, 'tis time I attend to a few taxing affairs."

Cai swings into the saddle with surprising grace and reins the horse around to face me.

"May the Blessed Virgin and the Fair Family guide ye," he says before disappearing into the crowded street.

Frozen with indecision, I watch the town's inhabitants from under the protective canopy of Cai's oversized cloak—his final gift. Intent on their business, no one notices me. So, I wait, weighing my options.

Leaning against the mystery apothecary's shop wall, I watch until a wagon full of barrels rolls past, laboriously making its way back toward the city entrance. A wiry boy sits on the back, his feet dangling treacherously close to the wheels. I close my eyes and imagine running after it, leaping aboard like a stowaway on a train, offering the child a smile before slipping into the unseen spaces of my way home. But all I can feel is the warmth of Steffan's fingertip against my mouth, the amusement in Cai's laugh, the curious tilt of Gwenhwyfar's pallid head.

If I leave now, I'm sentencing them to suffering. Maybe even death.

With the past week's memories still tingling on my flesh, I turn away from the wagon and dart into the busy street, deeper down the dragon's throat.

CHAPTER 12

FOR BLOOD AND GOLD

I almost don't recognize him. Slumped forward against the wooden stocks, Steffan's elegant hands and head protrude grotesquely from the slats, even as his long legs brace against the pillars, every heavy muscle taut. Mud mars his clothes, and fresh blood leaks from the corner of his mouth, a crimson ribbon.

This is my fault.

The thought strikes like an arrow, and I lose my breath at the enormity of the situation. Putting my hands on my knees to steady myself, I don't notice the girl until it's too late. I look up just as a clump of dung and mud crumble against Steffan's shoulder.

"Stop it!" I scream and run at her.

Small and grubby as a rat, the child darts back into the horde, accompanied by a spatter of chuckles.

I turn back to Steffan. "Are you all right?"

It's a stupid question, but I don't know what else to say. Shame at my role in putting him here twists my gut, and I can hardly look at him.

Unable to look up, Steffan turns his head sideways. Splinters from the weathered wood riddle his neck. "Be gone, Ellyll. Ye do me nay good here."

At his stubbornness, resolve solidifies like a stone in my hand. I stand defensively in front of him. "I've come to pay the debt."

"Go home," he rasps.

"I can't," I say over my shoulder, not wanting to look away from the crowd. "Angharad threw me out."

Steffan makes an exasperated noise. "Bloody hell, woman, will ye look at me."

I turn as he spits out blood before raising his eyes just enough to meet mine. His face is streaked with dirt and blood, but his gray eyes, limbed with a nimbus of gold I never noticed, focus on me with preternatural force. They are no longer soft.

"Not my home," he says. "Go back whence ye came—wherever that may be."

"I told you where I'm from."

"Did ye now?" His words sweep through me like a ghost.

He knows. Of course he does. Knows I'm not just a strange, lost girl attacked by an English soldier but something else altogether.

I shake my head against the questions clamoring for utterance and speak the only one that matters right now. "Where do I find the sheriff?"

Steffan presses his lips into a vicious line.

"You can't stop me," I warn, "so you might as well help."

He says nothing.

"Fine." My hackles rise, and I whirl to look for someone to approach. People dart across my path like roaches, and the thought of engaging anyone sends fear boiling up in my chest, fresh and hot. But after several deep breaths, I shout, "Can anyone—"

"Silence," Steffan hisses.

"—tell me where to find Sheriff Holloway?"

Several sets of eyes slide my way.

I meet each one even as fear spikes through my body, but nobody speaks up. "I'm looking for—"

"At yon end o' High Street," someone calls.

I turn toward the voice. A shriveled woman looks back at me from across the square. She points with a lank arm toward a large building at the far end of the street. Sporting glass windows, a polished wood frame with white plaster walls, and a severely pitched roof, the structure juts out like a manic brownstone.

"Thank you," I call.

The woman nods and, turning aside, reveals two wispy children behind her. The boy and girl watch me with big, empty eyes, and I find myself moving forward, pulling Gwenhwyfar's gift of bread from my sack, holding it out in a feeble attempt at compassion. Their hands fall on the food with the frantic want of fledglings.

"Slow down. You'll get sick," I caution in vain as the children swallow fist-sized clumps of bread. When more than half the loaf is gone, they retreat behind their mother's skirts and press the heel of the bread into her hands. The woman stares at me, her watery eyes more suspicious than anything, but I'm already backing away. Other hungry faces follow.

"'Twas a foolish kindness," Steffan says when I reach his side.

"Like you don't know anything about that," I quip and look toward the sheriff's house.

He clenches his fists against his bindings. "Pray, do not go."

"I have a plan."

"Piss on yer plan and get yerself away." His voice pitches higher with desperation.

"In case you haven't noticed, I'm trying to help you," I shoot back.

A irritated snarl slips from behind Steffan's bared teeth. "Ye do not understand!"

I lean into his face, tired of his protests. "Then explain it to me, for Christ's sake!"

His jerky movements rattle the stocks. "Do ye not see that Holloway be a man who takes what he wants, when he wants it?"

The fear already clutching at my stomach squeezes tighter. "I'm not blind," I say, balling my own hands into fists. "But you saved my life. Twice. Don't I have the right to save yours?"

Once more, Steffan lifts his eyes to mine. The beseeching fear I see there nearly undoes every bit of courage I've managed to rally.

"There be more to the tale than I can tell now. Ye must know —I took something the sheriff craved once. Something dear to him. He would do the same to me. I beseech ye, lady. Leave. Now."

The cold terror in his eyes strikes deep, and it takes every ounce of courage I have not to do exactly as Steffan asks. To turn on my heels and flee this place now. Instead, I wipe the blood from his bottom lip with my thumb, quieting him as he did me only last night.

"I'll come back for you," I say and hurry away.

Steffan's roar of protest propels me forward like a wind at my back.

For several long moments, I consider an oddly placed square of glass, fitted waist high in the massive door. The window isn't large enough to let in light and doesn't appear to be on hinges. Deciding it doesn't matter, I pull Cai's cloak tight around me to cover my clothing and knock. Almost immediately, a white smudge appears behind the wobbly glass, and the door creaks open. My focus drops several feet.

"Well?" asks a markedly short man. Dressed in a beautiful, black velvet vest and shocking green tights, the man scowls up at me from underneath a rusty mustache.

"Greetings. I'm here to see the sheriff," I manage.

His mouth drops open at my voice. Of course. I expect this reaction now and keep my own expression firmly in place. As his large, brown eyes travel up and down the length of my person, I wonder if he ever gets tired of people looking at him oddly too.

The man clears his throat, eyes round with surprise, and asks in a gruff voice, "On what business?"

Oh God, oh God, oh God, here I go. "I need to speak with him about the man in the stocks."

"Who be it, Pawl?" comes a languid voice from inside.

I stiffen at the sound.

"'Tis naught but a queer wench," replies Pawl, who starts to close the door on me.

"It's Meg Quinn, milord," I shout over the little man's head, pressing my hand to the door. "I've come to pay Steffan ap Cai's debt."

From some unseen niche, the legs of a chair scrape against stone.

"Show her in," commands the disembodied voice.

Pawl rolls his eyes but ushers me inside before shoving the door closed. I look around the dim, lavish room and force myself to keep breathing. Colorful rugs sprawl across the stone floor and anchor the intricately carved furnishings, which include a crowded bookcase and a cabinet full of trinkets. On the far wall hangs Master Cai's ancestral tapestry, and my fists clench at the sight. Despite the mild weather and large windows, a hot flame leaps and hisses in the hearth of this thieves' cave.

"Good morrow, mistress," the sheriff greets as he pulls his staggering height into the room from an adjacent doorway. "'Tis a pleasure to see ye again."

I curtsy, knowing better than to trust my venomous tongue.

"Sit." He gestures toward the cushioned chairs by the fire.

"I prefer to stand, milord."

A smile, slow as molasses, spreads across his narrow face.

"Mayhap a cup o' wine?" He grabs an enameled pitcher from a side table without waiting for my answer.

"No thank you."

Godfrey Holloway cocks an eyebrow, salutes me with the cup, and drinks the wine himself. Irritated with his charade of civility, I pull my mother's ring from my pocket and hold it up. Every instinct is screaming to get this over with and get the hell out.

"How much of the debt will this cover?" The twin pearls and solid gold gleam in the firelight.

The sheriff's eyes flash. "Pawl," he calls to his man still lingering by the door. "Fetch Master Juda. I would that he attests to the value o' the lady's gift."

Grumbling, Pawl bows to his employer and leaves. Goosebumps race up my arms as the front door latch clicks.

"Pray tell, mistress, how did ye acquire such a bauble?" the sheriff asks, ducking his head for a closer look. "A lover's boon, mayhap?"

I palm the ring, pressing it against my chest, and straighten my spine. "It was my mother's. I want it used to free Steffan ap Cai, or I'll throw it in the lake."

Holloway drums a ringed finger on the cup and smirks. "Such spirit. And that tongue! Some men admire that in a woman. Alas, 'tis a shame he would deceive ye so."

After a long pause, I bite. "Deceive me how?"

The sheriff smiles in earnest this time and takes another drink, clearly amused at knowing something I don't. As if this was a great feat. "What kind o' man, I wonder, sends a woman to barter for his freedom—to give up something dear to her—without even revealing his name?"

I'm unwilling to take the bait a second time and so stand there, choking on my desire to know what he means, if anything. For all I know, he's lying to distract me. Fortunately, the sheriff appears to be the kind of man who loves to hear his own voice.

"The mighty Steffan *Blaidd* be naught but the landless son o' a bastard Englishman." He smacks his lips, setting down the wine with satisfaction.

I raise an eyebrow in mimicry. Displeasure darkens the sheriff's face like the sudden shadow of a cloud.

"I'm sorry to disappoint you," I say, matching his nonchalant tone to cover my surprise. "But who he is, exactly, or what he owns doesn't interest me. What does interest me is that he's being unjustly held by you for helping me after I was attacked by some sack of shit man who was not who you think he was."

He reaches me in one step. My head snaps back with the force of his slap.

"Mind yer tongue, shrew," Sheriff Holloway bellows in my face, showing honest emotion for once. "That sack o' shite, 'twas the king's man, nephew to a great lord." He rips the ring from my grasp and slips it into the tasseled leather pouch at his waist. "And I be king in this place."

Staggering but still on my feet, I manage to speak through the mineral tang of blood in my mouth. "Will it be enough?"

"'Tis a start," he says, smoothing his hair. "Unless the lady hath another gift to bestow?"

Before I can move, the door eases open as if blown by the wind.

"Who—" Sheriff Holloway snarls, when something flies past my head, striking him. I flinch as wetness splatters my cheek, like droplets flicked from a paintbrush.

I look back just as dark blood spurts from the lawman's neck. He pitches forward like a scarecrow cut down from its perch, his long body hitting the floor with a sickening smack. I freeze, unable to even turn to see who threw the knife now grotesquely protruding from the man's collarbone. He barely twitches as blood seeps across the stone floor, the ruby red stain expanding at an unnerving pace.

"Get the keys!" comes the stifled hiss of a familiar voice.

Dread races through me as I clamp my mouth shut to keep from vomiting and pull my eyes from the gore at my feet. Madoc is crouched in the doorway, white-faced and sweating.

My breath rushes out in a terrified hiss.

"What have you done?" I ask, still unable to move. "He took the ring. He was going to let Steffan go," I protest as Madoc hurries toward me and kicks the sheriff in the face, knocking him unconscious.

"Aye, he took the ring," he says bending to retrieve the stock keys from the sheriff's belt. "And he would have taken a good deal more afore refusin' to release Steffan." Madoc's eyes rest on my inflamed cheek before he jerks the knife free from its victim and grabs my elbow.

"Wait," I say, pulling free.

"We must make haste," Madoc urges.

I crouch, determined not to look at the gash or the tortured face above it. Reaching into the blood-soaked pouch, I pull out a handful of coins. Twin pearls push up amid the garish cash. My hands shake as I stuff the ring in one pocket, the money in another. Barely able to breathe, I wipe the blood off my face and follow Madoc out the door.

We stride toward the stocks, dodging merchants and live-stock as we go. Madoc pulls up his hood and gestures for me to do the same.

"Keep yer head down," he advises as we step into the crowded square. "And by God's bones, do not run."

My breath comes in terrified gasps as I follow his lead. Exhaling hard, I wipe my nose as if to eradicate the smell of blood and feel an odd sympathy for Lot's wife; it's nearly impossible to focus forward when ruin looms behind you. Steffan comes into view as the first flurry of voices break out behind us.

"*Brawd*," greets Madoc.

Steffan glares at us, his gaze shifting between Madoc and me, his lips white with anger.

"What the devil be ye about, man?" he snarls as Madoc produced the sheriff's keys.

"Hurry," I urge, my voice as unsteady as my pulse.

With eyes both defiant and pleading, Madoc holds his brother's stare. With what I imagine is a vicious Welsh curse, Steffan looks away, ending the silent conversation.

Madoc works each key until the massive padlock clicks, ringing out like the toll of a bell just as a voice shouts from behind. Without looking back, Madoc and I lift the top portion of the restraint enough for Steffan to slip his head and wrists out.

"Take her. Ye know where to meet," says Steffan.

Without so much as a glance, he backs away and slaps the

rump of a nearby goat, sending it running and bleating into the gathering crowd.

"*Mynd ymlaen!*" Steffan shouts before pushing over a barrel of ale and darting away.

Unable to control myself any longer, I glance over my shoulder to see two English soldiers coming down the street at a run. Adrenaline sings through my blood as my heart thrashes.

Away. We have to get away now.

"This way," Madoc says, grabbing my hand. Still walking fast, we turn down an alley and nearly stumble over Pawl.

"Oy! *Pisho bant!*" Pawl bellows up at us and adjusts himself before his button eyes light upon the keys in Madoc's hand. Then at my face. Fuck.

Madoc's lightning-fast left hook knocks him to the ground with an audible crunch.

"Run!" gasps Madoc, sprinting back into the street.

"Wait!" I holler after him. "You said not to run," I accuse, stumbling.

He grabs my hand again, yanking me behind him. "Damn what I said!"

Saving my breath, I dash after him through the sludge at the edge of the street, oblivious to anything but the shouts behind us and my heart beating like a kettle drum in my ears. Around carts, over animals, and through stalls, Madoc whips across the crowded street like a gale leaving a trail of frothy destruction in his wake. He's making a scene, some calculating part of my brain thinks. He's going to get us caught.

"Stop!" I cry, skidding to a halt. Attempting to comply, Madoc slides through the mud and lands soundly on his ass before flipping over and dashing back to me.

"Nay, milady," he says reaching for my hand. "Make haste."

"Shut up for a second and listen to me," I insist, "We have to slow down. Stop making a scene," I wheeze, trying to speak through the stitch in my side.

Feeling as dizzy as Alice in a hedge maze, I look around until a familiar face stands out among the throng. Drawn by a gravitational pull I can't explain, it's my turn to yank Madoc along.

"This way." My voice leaves no room for argument.

Grumbling and reluctant, Madoc follows.

To her eternal credit, the egg girl's nut-brown eyes only widened at our approach. She makes no move to turn away or call for aid. She just watches us approach, the unburned half of her face unruffled. Lovely.

"Buy her eggs," I instruct Madoc, pulling both our hoods down.

Madoc shakes his head in disbelief, snatching at his cover.

"Leave it down and buy the goddamn eggs," I say through clenched teeth and whip my hair out of its braid. It unfurls over my shoulder, long and shining like a copper flag.

Understanding my intent, Madoc speaks in Welsh to the girl, who obligingly offers her basket to us for inspection. I make a show of pondering the eggs while Madoc mimes around for the leather pouch at his waist. When the first group of men-at-arms run by, my stomach turns over, and I pray very sincerely that I don't piss myself. Clearly the sheriff's body has been found.

I quickly pull two coins from my pocket and offer them to the girl.

"Ask her how many these will buy," I say to Madoc.

"The lot," she replies in a beautiful—modern—British accent before handing me an egg.

The egg slips from my fingers and smashes against the street.

"What did you say?" I breathe, as if my terrified mind has tricked me.

She only smiles, her expression knowing. "You heard me."

"Who are you?" I ask, dumbfounded.

"Dilys," she says, turning her head to watch as more armed men run by. The livid, ropelike scars snaking down her neck stand out with the movement.

"We must be away afore they close the bridge," Madoc whines. A dog awaiting its master's command could not have squirmed more.

But I'm unable to care about anything besides the strange girl in front of me. I grab her hand. "Where did you come from? Please."

Dilys locks her brown tourmaline eyes on mine as she slips the basket full of eggs over my arm. Taking the coins, she releases herself from my grip. "From the fairy ring."

I gasp as if kicked in the chest. Everything blurs, shouts erupt all around, and Madoc yanks me backward out of my confusion. Disoriented, I stumble after him until the world rights itself as abruptly as it went sideways. I drop the basket and break into a sprint. The last thing I see over my shoulder is the glossy, maize-colored yokes bleeding into the mud. Dilys is gone.

I press my face against the cool, dewy grass, unable to go any farther. Blood beats behind my eyes, sweat drips from every pore, my sides pinch. Running for your life is not for the faint of heart. When the dizziness finally passes, I look up and am greeted by the soles of Madoc's boots. They protrude from the greenery along the creek bed where we finally come to a stop. The soldiers are nowhere in sight.

"Are you alive?" I wheeze.

Madoc's face, pink as a cherry blossom, emerges from the deep grass. "Aye," he says, his eyes bright with something more like excitement than fear. "And ye?"

"No." I crawl forward and sink my face in the stream. Shocked and mollified by the icy bubbles, I sit up and let the droplets fall where they may.

"How will we find Steffan?" I ask, looking over my shoulder once again. We managed to lose them in the melee, but if the soldiers decided to chase us, it wouldn't take them long to catch up.

Madoc doesn't answer. Now on his feet, he shakes himself like a dog and begins walking in circles, poking at the underbrush.

"What are you doing?" I ask.

"Aha!" he says before pulling a saddlebag from the depths of a rotten tree stump. Then like a spooked deer, he freezes before rushing to me. Hauling me up, he points to a particularly large, frothy clump of ferns. "Hide yerself."

"What? Why?" I pull away.

Madoc rakes a hand through his hair in a distinctly Cai-like gesture. "I be off to retrieve our mount. The damned beast hath wandered off, and I do not know if the soldiers shall give chase again."

"You brought the horse?" I gape. "Never mind." Of course he rode here. It's the only way he could have gotten to Bala so fast.

Madoc nods, nudging me toward the underbrush. "Be swift now, milady."

"I want to come with you," I protest.

"Nay." He speaks sharply, his normally chipper voice strained. "I shall not see ye in peril again."

The success of my flirtatious manipulations sting like a wasp, and I drop my gaze as Madoc's already flushed cheeks deepen to crimson. "All right. But what if Steffan needs our help?"

He compresses his lips at my second mention of Steffan and thrusts the saddlebag into my arms. "I have already aided my brother more than he wishes. Now go."

He bounds off, red hair flashing like the tail of a fox between the trees.

I swear under my breath at the collective pigheadedness of men and pull Cai's cloak tight against the gloom. Crawling under the ferns, I lean against a fallen tree trunk and do my best to find a position that is both comfortable and well hidden. In spite of everything that just happened, when the greenery cocooning me stops quivering, my thoughts turn to Dilys.

I have no doubt the burned girl in the square is from another time like me. A traveler. But the longer I mull over the possible circumstances of her presence, the more one question niggles at me: why didn't she go back? Chill bumps rise on my arms as I consider, for the first time really, the possibility that the yew tree—the passage—only goes one way.

"That can't be right," I breathe just before a hand appears over my shoulder.

Slamming his palm against my protest, the attacker cuts off my noise and pins me under him. My heart lurches as a large, solid, very male body pins me to the ground. A stone digs into my back, and I arch into the body above me, eyes wide, scream poised in my throat. The emerald fronds flutter over us as Steffan glares down at me, his face livid with warning.

Then I hear them. Still a way off, the soldiers move through the forest with the stealth-less swagger of paid men, the swish of their swords cutting through the undergrowth.

The urge to flee like a flushed pheasant blazes up in my chest. *Stay, stay, stay.* I close my eyes. Clinging to the dark like a child imagining herself invisible, I suck in one shallow breath after another. Each holds the spicy scents of leaf mold, Steffan, and my own acrid fear. Finally, the jumbled noise of the soldiers peaks and then fades back into the forest. Several more minutes tick by before Steffan rolls his heavy body to the side, carrying me with him.

I ease off the rock with a hiss of pain, trying hard not to let my traitorous body notice we're still pressed together from chest to knees.

Scooting me to clear ground, Steffan cautiously braces himself with one arm and peers over the greenery. He's clutching a dagger I've never seen. The generous blade is clean, but something dark and sticky smears the base of the hilt where the pale metal twists into a double-stranded braid.

I look away.

Dipping back down, Steffan motions me farther onto my side. Still hardly daring to breathe, I shiver as he reaches for my back. He holds my stare, waiting, until I give a nod. He gently pushes up my cloak and sweater, exposing my back to the damp air. He doesn't touch me, but I hear the sharp exhale as he eases the cloth back down.

"'Tis bruised and scratched but will heal." His voice is so low I hardly heard him. "Pray, forgive me."

Still on my side, I look up at him now, our bodies still pressed tight, not moving. I swear his soft, gray eyes flash. Darken. But he doesn't so much as blink.

"Just add it to the list of debts I owe you."

With a slight shift, he's crouching over me now like an avenging beast, his jagged face full of questions. I open my mouth to explain when he looks up abruptly.

I tense.

"Madoc," Steffan greets his brother lightly, as if neither have murdered for the other's sake. Or mine.

Pushing myself up, I follow Steffan's gaze as Madoc emerges

from behind a large alder tree. In one hand, he carries a knife the length of my forearm; in the other, a quiver of arrows and the two-toned staff of an unstrung yew bow.

"I had nay desire to hear ye pine like a milksop after her," Madoc teases before tossing the long weapon. Steffan sits up, catching it deftly, but his movement reveals my disheveled sweater and cloak.

Suddenly feeling guilty for something I haven't done, I straighten my clothes.

"I bruised my back hiding," I half-lie, already anticipating Madoc's jealousy.

Madoc thrusts a quiver of arrows into his brother's hands with more force than necessary and sits on his heels. He twirls the dagger restlessly, not looking at me.

"Did you find the horse?" I ask, still whispering.

Madoc shakes his head. "The fool beast hath spooked or been stolen. 'Tis well I hid the weapons afore hobbling him."

"'Tis for the best," says Steffan, slipping a quiver full of arrows over his head. "We must go canny."

I nod as we all stand. Except for the wind and the chirrup of birds, all is quiet.

No longer daring to speak, we gather our meager supplies and flee farther into the forest, cowering like prey in the grass.

CHAPTER 13

RED DRAGON

Clouds flash pink with silent lightning overhead as we settle into a stand of young birch for the night. Far in the distance, wolves howl as a breeze trips through our fireless camp, sending the bleached trunks swaying like a swarm of ghosts. I shiver.

"Blasted midges," Madoc grumbles, swatting at the air around his head.

Crouched next to him, Steffan merely blows at the cloud of tiny insects and adjusts the arrow notched in his bow.

Madoc makes an irritated gesture at his brother. "Jesu forfend ye be bitten. The damned things must have nay taste for *Sais* blood."

Steffan doesn't respond.

Exhausted and determined to banish all thoughts of the havoc we left behind, I ease myself down into the dense moss and watch the sky.

"Do you think it will rain?" I ask. The memory of being caught in the storm with Steffan is still fresh, and I have no wish to repeat the experience.

"Nay," says Steffan.

"Aye," insists Madoc.

"Never mind," I say, putting my hands up. "Forget I asked." The last thing I need is a contrary diatribe from either man. It doesn't matter anyway. I huddle deeper into my cloak.

We'd been silent much of the day out of necessity and had yet to recount our separate stories of escape or hash out a plan for what came next. Still, it would have to wait. I squeeze my eyes shut, wanting nothing more than to forget the blood-spattered face of the enraged sheriff. But there's no forgetting. No escaping what we've done.

"What do we do now?" I ask.

There's a long pause. Even though Steffan and Madoc's faces lay in shadow, I can tell they're looking at each other.

After several beats, Steffan sighs. "We make for Glyndyfrdwy afore dawn."

Madoc's Cheshire grin splits the dark.

"What is that?" I ask, wondering if it will take us closer to—or farther from—St. Melangell's church and the yew tree.

"Lord Glyndwr's estate," chirps Madoc. "'Tis the seat o' the baron's forces and nay more than hard day's walk east."

I ignore Madoc's jubilation and turn on Steffan. "Why go there?"

"To join the revolt." His answer rolls out of the dark like a mid-ocean swell.

I shoot to my feet. "Have you both lost your minds?"

"*Hisht.*" Both men shush in unison.

"What in the hell kind of plan is that?" I hiss, ignoring them.

"The best one we have," says Steffan.

"Pray, listen, milady," Madoc pleads. "When all o' Cymru joins under Glyndwr's standard, Bolingbroke shall have nay chance."

"I thought the idea was *not* to get ourselves killed."

"We be outlawed under the English." Steffan stands up, and his voice rises with him. "If the sheriff's men have not yet visited the crown's wrath on our kin, they soon shall, and we three shall be killed upon sight."

I quiet myself at these grim words. Of course. Without the three of us to punish, blood payments for the soldier—and now the sheriff—will be extracted from Steffan and Madoc's family.

"Putting Glyndwr on the throne be our only chance," Steffan finishes, voice so, so weary.

The agitation rushes out of me, and I sit down hard. Madoc sidles up, leaning so close his musty breath warms my ear.

"Do not be affrighted. Glyndyfrdwy be a vast estate with men-at-arms. 'Tis not so grand as Sycharth, they say, but soon —" Madoc's voice quickens. "Soon, Lord Glyndwr shall be our rightful prince instead o' that bloody Saxon. Ye shall see."

No, I think bleakly, unable to look at him. *You will. You will see your countrymen slaughtered. You will see the last Welsh uprising end in defeat. If you survive.*

And there isn't a damn thing I can do.

Smothered by the weight of such knowledge, I slide away from him. Despite the bone-deep fatigue tugging at my limbs, I know sleep will be impossible. "I'll take first watch."

"There be no need, milady—" Madoc starts.

"Yes, there is," I interrupt.

"Let her be," says Steffan from his place among the ferns, his bow and dagger still in hand. His gaze wanders my way. "Wake me when ye would sleep."

"Why ye?" Madoc challenges.

"For God's sake, I'll wake up whoever I fucking feel like waking, okay?" I bark. Neither man moves as my words fade into the faint gossiping of the trees.

Madoc sinks to the ground with a disgruntled heave. "As ye wish."

Taking hold of my dagger, I lean against a narrow trunk, forcing my attention toward the wide woods. An owl hoots in the sooty canopy as leaves click against each other in the wind. Soon, night presses in, deepening, and takes hold of my thoughts.

Trying to release Steffan legally had been the right thing to do. I knew that, though the knowledge proved little comfort.

Once again, I'd made a mess of everything.

Once again, I'd failed to get home.

Despair rises in my throat like bile. Gulping the cold air in long, shuddering breaths, I look around and freeze. Something is glistening near Steffan's head. My pulse spikes as I squint into the dark. Two shiny points squint back and then blink.

Steffan is looking at me. Letting the panic drain away, I stay quiet until the heavy breathing of sleep radiates from Madoc.

"He told me your real name," I whisper. There's no need for preamble.

"Aye?"

"And that you're the landless son of a bastard Englishman and not Cai's son."

A rough chuckle blooms in the shadows. The corners of my lips tip up at the rare sound, only to fall again.

"I told him it didn't matter who you were. He didn't like that," I say, remembering the sting of the sheriff's hand across my cheek.

"'Twas not yer fault," says Steffan, his voice once again serious. "Would that I had stopped ye from goin'."

Against the night, Steffan's no more than a large, gray shadow against the night. But I remember this morning clearly—can see him struggling against the stocks, face white with fury, fists clenched and impotent.

I turn my head as if to escape the memory. "You couldn't have stopped me. And someone had to try."

"Not ye."

I look back at him. "Why not?"

"Because losing something precious 'tis not the same as letting it go, Ellyll. Methinks ye know this well." His words slide across the ground and lap against me like a gentle tide, beckoning me deeper.

Part of me wants to wade in. To sink from sight. But I'm still tethered to the shore of my past—the future—so I back away from his meaning like a coward.

"Cai isn't your father then?" I ask.

Madoc picks that moment to stir. Rolling onto his back, he lets out a series of small snorts before turning over again. A long time passes before Steffan speaks.

"My sire be called Hugh Goch. As the half Cymry bastard o' an English nobleman, he claimed no family name but made his trade as a brewer. Whilst on the road, he stopped at the inn o' my grandsire. He took one look at my mother and ne'er left," he says with a smile in his voice. "After he died, Cai married my mother and brought us to Dwyn Blair. Madoc be born that leaf-fall and shall inherit the land. Holloway spoke true o' that."

"I see," I say as several lingering questions are answered. "And ... Gwenhwyfar?" I hesitate to say her name out loud, as if doing so will curse the sweet girl with the misfortune I brought her brothers.

"Mother died in childbed with her. A sickly babe from the first and ne'er spoke, though she be sharp and kind and strong. The twins and babe belong to Angharad, Cai's second wife."

As the complicated web of relationships I'd been thrust into untangle themselves, so does the fact that Steffan and I have something vital in common.

"Then you're an orphan too," I say. Then sadness clenches my throat, making words impossible.

"Aye," he says and closes his eyes, disappearing into the night.

Terrified of what the morning will bring, I sit in silence until the shifting shadows announce the end of my vigil. I can't stay awake any longer. Stiff and cold and losing the battle to fatigue, I struggle to my feet and lay a hand on Steffan's shoulder. His eyes open at once. Without a sound, he eases himself up as I descend to the ground to sleep, envying the wild animals their dense hides and uncomplicated existences.

I'm standing next to the car this time. The air metallic and smoking, the smells of burning rubber and blood everywhere. From outside, the jagged remains of a busted windshield, metal twisted all around, I watch myself regain consciousness. Watch as I wipe glass and blood from my face. Watch myself look over at Dad and scream.

"Milady!" an urgent voice calls against my ear.

I open my eyes on a gasp. Madoc's kneeling over me, his cabbage-green stare full of concern. All too familiar with the dream, I push myself up on shaking hands and look around. The forest floor remains dark, but bands of lavender and indigo show through the thin gaps in the trees. Birds trill in the gloom as dawn approaches.

"Be ye well?" Madoc asks, his voice tight with worry.

"I'm fine," I lie, knowing I probably screamed in my sleep.

Madoc helps me to my feet. "Here." He hands me a crust of bread and the wine skin. "'Tis not much but shall keep yer belly from gnawing at yer back."

Feeling my stomach do exactly that, I take the small meal.

I'm too queasy to eat but know I'll need something in my body later. "Thank you."

Madoc gives me a pained smile, and I look at him closely. Dark bruises rim his bloodshot eyes, and his nose appears even more swollen. Beyond that, his entire body is rigid with tension.

I touch his arm. "And you?" I ask. "I mean, yesterday was …"

I let go and gesture uselessly with my hands. An image of the blood spurting from the sheriff's neck flashes through my mind before I can push it away.

"Worse than the arsehole o' a dead dog," he supplies, his colorful vulgarity more reassuring than anything.

"Exactly," I agree. "And if I hadn't been so stupid as to think—"

"Forgive me," he cuts in. "I did not kill the whoreson afore he struck ye. I failed ye a second time, milady."

His open, freckled face hardens as he runs a gentle finger down my aching cheek. The fresh bruise throbs under his touch. I know I should say something, anything, to squelch Madoc's misguided affection, but the words refuse to come. I don't want to hurt him more when he's so obviously a mess.

"Thank you" is all I can manage, and I step back.

Madoc nods and turns away, only to reveal Steffan. Remote and solitary as an oak, he stands perfectly still among the slender birches, watching us.

We move swiftly through the predawn light. Mist swirls around our feet, and a delicate cloud of breath marks each step. With little food or sleep, it doesn't take long for my mind to grow as numb as my fingers. We travel for what feels like miles before the forest cracks open and we spill out onto a high, grassy plain. In the distance, a river weaves through the landscape like a vein of silver, kicking back the pink light seeping over the horizon.

"We must keep west o' the river and make haste if we would

reach Glyndyfrdwy by nightfall," Steffan says. It's the first time he's spoken since our conversation last night, and my pulse jumps at the sound.

"Shall we hunt?" asks Madoc. "'Tis not possible to go so long with naught to eat."

Steffan's bearded jaw flexes as if straining to keep his words caged.

"Could we gather something? Are there any edible plants nearby?" I suggest, not really knowing if this is possible but wanting to avoid an argument.

Before either man can answer, Madoc lets out a low, brassy whistle and points over our heads. "By St. George—*edrych ar hynny!*"

I crane my neck to follow his gaze—to the most astounding sight in a week of wonders. Stretched across the violet peak of the heavens is a massive comet, its tail rippling out like a kite.

"Wow." I glance over to see Steffan staring at the apparition in awe.

As devout as his brother is profane, Steffan crosses himself before turning to me. "Do ye know what it be?"

The expectation in his voice surprises me, openly revealing what we both know—I am not from somewhere else entirely. I nod and look at the comet again, its beauty undiminished by explanation. "It's called a comet. It's a ..." I struggle for a description they won't reject. Failing, I tell the truth. "It's a giant ball of crumbling ice hurtling through outer space."

"Ice, my arse." Madoc chuffs. "'Tis a sign in fire." His tired eyes glint. Steffan makes a disparaging noise in his throat. Ignoring his brother, Madoc points to the tail. "Do ye not see it then?"

"See what?" I ask.

Madoc leans in then, his lips nearly brushing my ear. "Look there."

I obey as Steffan fills the gap on my other side, wedging me between them. Staring at the apparition in the sky, I let my vision blur until the illusion of talons, wings, and a forked tongue become visible in the red stardust.

"Hold shit, it looks like a dragon," I blurt. Steffan crosses himself again.

"Aye. *Y Ddraig Goch*—the Red Dragon. 'Tis said to foretell the rise o' Cymru." Madoc's voice is unusually soft with reverence before he lets out a dangerous, joyous whoop.

Not bothering to shush his brother, Steffan stares up, moving his lips silently. I suspect he's praying but, for what, time will tell.

It's midday by the time we make it to the *Afon Dyfrdwy,* or River Dee as Madoc translates, to fill our dry wine skins. Steffan refuses to hunt, despite Madoc's insistence that the late sheriff's arm is not long enough to pursue them into Glyndwr's lands, which are controlled by rebels. Apparently, the river was the boundary line.

"Be ye willing to take such a risk for yer stomach?" Steffan asks his little brother as we rest by the swiftly running water.

Madoc's gaze slides toward me before he shifts into Welsh. Rather than being perturbed at the exclusion, I welcome the moment of privacy and slip downstream. The time to care about normal hygiene habits has long since passed, but there is one thing I can't reconcile myself to: the unseemly tickle of underarm hair. In spite of the extraordinary, dangerous events of the last twenty-four hours, I am anxious to wash and shave. Or maybe, I muse, pushing my way through a clump of newly budding willow branches, it is precisely because of these strange events that doing something normal feels paramount.

Carefully, I pick my way along the riverbank until a cluster of smooth stones at the water's edge comes into view. It's a perfect spot to wash. Rain-free for the second day in a row, the sun-ripened smells of algae and mud spring up to greet me as iridescent dragonflies dart over the water. Watching them hover and glide, their wings opalescent in the mellow light, I feel a shift deep inside. A subterranean tremor I recognize as understanding.

"Well, I'll be damned," I breathe.

Meredith was right. Wales is in my blood. Even now, I can't deny the echo of home this wild landscape rings through my bones. I still don't particularly like the cold and wet. I doubt I ever will, but the treacherous green expanses and mercurial skies loosen a door inside me I didn't know was rusted shut. But more than anything, my fingers itch to capture the land-scape around me, and for the first time in nearly a year, sadness doesn't stamp out the yearning.

Wearing a true smile, I unfasten the cloak and slip out of my bulky sweater. Having not bothered with my tattered bra yesterday—had it truly only been one day?—I press the garment to my breasts and draw my knife.

Steffan emerges from the shrubbery on my right, silent and swift as a panther.

I jerk, dropping the blade on the pebbled shore. "Will you *stop* doing that?" I seethe when I see who it is. "You're going to give me a heart attack one of these days. Now if you don't mind, I'm washing."

Steffan doesn't move. He doesn't turn away but stares pointedly at the ground. I square my shoulders and, taking great pleasure in his uncharacteristic discomfort, pick up the dagger. I refuse to act as exposed as I feel.

"Pray, forgive me." His voice is a ragged whisper that goes straight to my gut.

"Do you need something?" I ask, wincing at the gravel in my own voice.

In answer, Steffan approaches a nearby stone and sits down. He doesn't so much as glance at me but rests his hands on his knees and stares out at the water. I wait for him to speak. When he doesn't, I wet the blade and watch him from the corner of my eye. Chestnut curls spring out wildly around his head, softening the prominent lines of his nose, cheekbones, and chin. His heavy brows are furrowed, and I can tell by the tension in his bearded jaw that his lips are pressed into their characteristic stubborn line. His ferocious beauty lances through me, so painful it edges into pleasure. Gritting my teeth against my body's reaction, I face the river.

"I would have the truth from ye," he says finally. "All o' it."

Frustration coats the desire, stifling it. Of course he wants what I can't give. I cover my unease with a jaded laugh. "No. You wouldn't."

"Ye be mistaken," he says and looks fully at me. His dove eyes roam my face, my neck, but no farther, though he swallows hard with the effort. "What be yer name?"

I meet his stare and bristle at the accusation even as the naked skin of my shoulders and back flushes. "Megan Alice Quinn," I answer, overemphasizing each name. "I didn't lie to you."

"Do ye think me a fool?" He stands. Steps forward. "The Fates' thread runs betwixt us now. We have shed blood for blood, and I shall have the truth from your lips. Who be yer people?"

The magnitude of his words settles around us, deep and heavy as a snow drift. Looking up into this face, I don't have it in me to lie.

"They're gone," I choke.

Steffan crouches now, close enough for me to see that the tips of his black lashes are russet like the hair along his jaw. "And yer sister?"

I swallow hard. The truth then. Or as much of it as I can. "She might be alive. I ... I don't really know. But we left each other a long time ago out of anger." Chin trembling, I work to calm myself and look out across the water. "I came here to ... to mend things between us. Try, at least, for our mother's sake. It was her—" I balk, still not used to the past tense. "It was her dying wish. Now I'm lost. I've ruined everything all over again, and I don't even know if I can get home. Ever."

Speaking more truth than I have in days, I feel an unseen burden lighten.

Steffan must sense it too, as the tension leaves him as well. He believes me. "If you did not mean to come to ... this place, then why have ye?"

I meet his pale, smoky stare, feel the heat from his body against my bare neck, and the words bubble up without my consent. "I think I've come for you."

Steffan's head snaps back as if I've struck him. nostrils flared, he says, "And Madoc?"

Shocked by what I said, I lower my head. "I never meant—"

"Aye, ye did."

My own temper rises, no matter how just the accusation. "I was trying to get away and leave you all in peace. I didn't want to be stuck here two hours, let alone a week. I was trying to go home. That's all."

Steffan seethes, unconvinced, but he doesn't accuse me further. "Shall ye still leave then?"

His voice is flat and cold now. Unreadable.

Timid sunshine peeks through the trees, and the stubble covering his jaw glints red. His color is high, his eyes glassy, and

I become more and more aware of how vulnerable I am here. Now.

Yet, the shiver in my stomach isn't one of fear. Not. At. All.

"Yes," I answer, pulling my eyes away from him.

"When?" he asks, his voice once again gentle.

"As soon as I can. *If* I can." My voice shakes with the last part. I've barely begun to admit such a thing to myself, but seeing the Dilys girl in Bala fractured my hope. I still have to try, but to what end, I know longer know.

Steffan nods, accepting the ambiguity.

"We shall eat well at Lord Glyndwr's table. Until then …" He produces a handful of berries from within his jerkin. A peace offering, no doubt.

I take them. Mortified by my inability to contribute, I fully intend to offer the tiny morsels to Madoc, but Steffan, likely guessing my intent, stands over me until I pop the berries into my mouth. He continued to stare until I bite down and swallow the bitter pulp, scowling at him as I do so. Satisfied, he turns to go, still carefully keeping his gaze to my face. Cringing at the taste, I turn back to the river and lift the knife to finally accomplish what I came here to do.

Steffan's hand clamps over mine.

"Hey. Let go," I say, jerking away.

Instead of obeying this time, his other arm grabs my shoulder to steady us. More angry than afraid, I whirl my head to confront him and am shocked to see unveiled fear in his eyes.

"What be ye about, woman?" he demands in a husky voice.

Belatedly, it occurs to me that Steffan has never seen a woman shave.

"It's all right," I explain, softening. "Where I'm from, women shave off the hair under their arms."

Steffan's eyebrows rise in surprise.

"Why?" he blurts the question before regaining his composure and backs away, frowning.

"Well …" Since I don't actually know, I answer for myself. "It makes me feel cleaner. And smell better. It's nice to have smooth skin. Like on your face, but I've never tried it with one of these." I ramble, holding up the dagger. Irritated with my discomposure, I turn back to my task.

Once again, slowly this time, Steffan comes up behind me.

"This way," he says. Positioning himself against my bare back, he raises my left arm, and guides the blade in my right hand to tender flesh.

I hold my breath, not daring to move as Steffan carefully— so carefully—scrapes the razor-sharp blade against my skin. The intimacy throttles me. His hands are steady, seemingly unfazed by our closeness, except for the slight rasp of his breathing by my ear. A deep, burning flush seeps through me, staining my pale skin pink as the smells of leather, wool, and salt waft off him. The bite of wine on his breath caresses my cheek, and my breathing hitches again.

I don't dare to move or speak as he finishes and then switches sides, the rough pads of his fingers scraping along my wrist as he lifts my right arm. Once again, he gently shaves the bristles from my skin, pausing only to dip the blade in the icy water, a move that presses him to my bare back. His clothing rasps against my flesh, and I don't know whether I want to arch into it or pull away. Neither. Both.

When Steffan finishes, I finally look over my shoulder at him. I don't even know what I feel, but something in my face has his expression softening, even as his eyes grow black, his pupils blown wide. He clears his throat.

"I have nay wish to see ye injured again. I could not bear it," he says in a voice deeper than I've ever heard. Then he's gone, stalking back through the trees before I can respond.

Shaken, I put away the dagger and slip back into my sweater. I scrub my face with the cold water, determined to dispel the smoldering in my stomach. Turning to go, I notice Steffan's footprints in the spongy grass. As if compelled, I step in his tracks just as a thought springs up.

Mind yourself, Meg.

Mind yourself. My father said that whenever I helped him in the garden. Despite her skill at ushering newborns into the world, Mom could kill a cactus. Dad, however, had been raised by his Irish grandmother and inherited Granny Quinn's affection for good whiskey and roses, an appreciation I shared. The week before I caused the accident that killed my father, I asked him how he never pricked himself on the thorns.

"It's simple, Muffin," he said with a wry smile and ruffled my hair. "The big thorns are easy to see, so they're easy to avoid. It's the tiny, unexpected ones right under the petals that you have to watch out for. They'll get you every time if you don't mind yourself."

Deliberately stepping out of Steffan's footprints, I move up the bank and ignore the drops of blood welling up from my heart like a pricked finger.

The wind roars. Steadily gaining strength since midday, it whips my hair into a tangled mass and blows across my ears, filling me with its mournful howl until I feel certain that if I opened my mouth, I could hear the sea. We stay away from the rutted roads, picking our way along the riverbank instead. Steffan leads the way, while Madoc guards our backs. I try not to think about the unspoken implication of this and focus solely on putting one foot in front of the other. I will keep up or die trying.

We speak little. Even if there was something to say, the lack of food and sleep is taking its toll. As lengthening shadows change from deep green to charcoal, I stumble several times, exhausted and nauseous with hunger. Even Madoc's jaunty whistle dwindles to silence. So, it's no small token of grace that we do, in fact, reach Glyndyfrdwy just after nightfall. The icy wind kicks hard against our backs, carrying with it the threat of a storm as the compound comes into view. I gasp at the sight, and my breath tastes both of fear at what might come and relief at the prospect of shelter.

Seated on a hill and ablaze with torches, the great, many-storied manor house stands out against the stars like a beacon. From our position just inside the tree line, I see red-and-gold standards snapping back and forth like flames above the huge, spiked wall surrounding the estate.

"Make nay move for yer weapons, or 'tis all for naught," Steffan says pointedly to Madoc.

Ignoring the advice, Madoc grips his dagger and glances over. "Best cover yerself."

"Best not kill anyone," I say through cracked lips, already making sure I'm well hidden under the cloak.

"I shall try." Madoc's voice is completely unironic.

At Steffan's signal, we walk into the open, arms loose at our sides. My heart thumps in my ears as the front gates loom closer and closer. Between the waxing moon and the firelight, we're easy to see—and shoot—if we're being watched. And from the look of the perches on either side of the entrance, we most certainly are.

As if in answer to the thought, a voice hails us from atop the bulwark. We stop. With exaggerated slowness, Steffan cups his hands around his mouth and shouts above the wind. I try to read his expression for signs of danger but should know better. Steffan's face remains impassive, his hands loose and open until a booming voice cut through the wind like a foghorn.

Madoc and Steffan tense.

Shit, shit, shit, my brain chants unhelpfully.

Madoc pulls his knife, and my stomach drops when a small door inside the massive gate cracks open. Steffan's arms fall to his sides, deadly still. Afraid I might vomit from the anxiety at any moment, I relax a fraction when a lone figure appears.

Then I notice the battle axe in his hand, and my blood goes cold with dread.

Taller and wider than either of my companions, the man crosses the moat's bridge with the ambling confidence of a bear. I draw my puny weapon and firm up my stance, even as Steffan catches hold of my elbow.

"*Cymru am byth!*" the man hollers as he closes the distance between us.

I can't move as the black-bearded beast of a man walks right up to Steffan and glares down at him. Next to me, Madoc brandishes his dagger and unleashes a string of Welsh that is no doubt profane. Twisting, the big man catches Madoc's wrist with ease and barks a reply.

I nearly jump out of my body when Steffan throws back his head and laughs.

The Goliath's face splits with a grin of his own as he shrugs off Madoc's weight and wraps Steffan in a back-pounding hug. Steffan and the man speak in the easy, garrulous manner of old friends before turning to Madoc and me, both standing there gaping in shock.

"May I present," Steffan says in English, "Mistress Meg Quinn and my brother, Madoc ap Cai." He points to us before gesturing back to the giant. "Captain Arthur Vaughn ap Huw."

"*Croeso i Glyndyfrdwy,*" Arthur says, his thick arms flung

wide with beneficence, "in the name o' my Lord Glyndwr, the rightful prince o' Cymru. Come, let us be inside afore this bitch o' a storm bares down on us."

He swings the addorsed head of the ax over his shoulder and ambles back toward the gate. Steffan follows without hesitation. Though still confused, it's all the reassurance I need to get out of the elements. Next to me, Madoc fumes at being the butt of a joke, but I pay him no mind as we trudge over the bridge and through the small door in the gate. I sway under the eyes of so many, and when the door within the door swings closed behind us, my muscles go limp with release.

CHAPTER 14
SAPPHIRES AND BLOOD

I open my eyes to darkness with no memory of falling asleep. A faint glow emanates from somewhere behind me, and I roll over. Whiffs of smoke linger in the air, giving the space a comforting, spicy smell, rather like coffee.

"Good eve to ye, mistress," greets a soft voice.

I blink and curl my fists into the heavy blanket on me realizing that I am—once again—half naked in an unfamiliar room with a stranger. This was becoming an unfortunate habit.

"Hello," I croak and look around.

Like Gwenhwyfar's tiny cell at Dwyn Blair, the walls and floor of this space are made of wood and plaster, with a single slit window high in the wall. The floor is covered with fresh-smelling rushes, and a large, bright sconce hangs near the door. Standing underneath it is a young woman. She smiles. Solid yet spry, she darts forward and hovers near me. Energy purrs around her like the beat of a hummingbird's wings.

"Yer possessions," she says, pointing to a low table next to the bed. The gold coins, my ring, and Steffan's dagger rest in plain sight.

"Thank you," I say, more than a little amazed at their presence. Then my stomach growls, knotting painfully, and the young woman is by my side in an instant, holding out a steaming bowl.

"Drink," she says.

Saliva pools in my mouth at the herbaceous, oniony scent of the broth, and I drink deeply. Only after I've drained the bowl do I bother to recall the previous night.

Once inside the palisades, Arthur Vaughn had swept us through the busy bailey, up and across another moated bridge, and into a cavernous hall where mugs of strong ale and leek-filled pastries were pressed into our hands. I remembered a fire blazing in the center of the crowded room, warming me. Paying little attention to my surroundings, I ate and drank until I thought I would be sick, and then I drank again and laid my head on the table like a lush. I must have dozed off then because, the next thing I knew, the trailing sleeve of a deep blue gown passed in front of my face. The vivid color and the scent of sandalwood washed over me at the same time, entwining, and I drifted back under, pondering the smell of sapphires.

Now, tucked into bed and feeling more fortified than I have in days, I put the strange memory away.

"Thank you," I say again and hand the bowl back.

Then this sprite of a woman says something truly shocking. "Does mistress desire a bath?"

I nearly fall out of bed. A bath! Ranking right up there with toilet paper and coffee, hot water and soap sound no less than life altering. "Oh, you have no idea. Yes. Please, yes. And call me Meg."

She raises one eyebrow with impressive flexibility. If this is in response to my words or my accent or my informality, I don't know or care. She isn't the first or the last to find me shocking, but at least I'd be clean when the rest of the household inevitably gapes and points.

"Follow me," the girl says and starts toward the door of the small chamber.

More than eager, I fling myself out of bed, grabbing at the woolen blanket.

"How should I ..." I let the question hang.

"Do not fret, mistress—"

"Meg."

The girl inhales at this detail. "Mistress Meg," she amends, "what men remain in the manor be banished to the hall below. Come."

With nothing to do but trust the pixie woman, I slip my mother's ring on before shoving the coins and Steffan's dagger between the straw-filled mattress and polished bed frame. It's a shoddy hiding place but probably won't be discovered unless someone's actively searching. The girl has the good grace to feign ignorance. Quickly securing the blanket under my arms, I nod my readiness and follow her down a narrow corridor.

Everything in the sparsely lit hallway is made of wood: floors, walls, ceiling. Not for the first time, I wonder how in the world everything doesn't always burn down now. Then I remember that sometimes it does.

"Where are we going?" I ask as we round a second dark corner.

"To the Arglwyddes," she chirps.

"The what?"

"The who," she corrects. We stop outside a large door with twin sconces flickering on either side. The heat casts enough light for me to see my guide more clearly. Everything about her is warm and buttery, from her large, slanted eyes to the wisps of hair peeking out from under a white cap.

"What's your name?"

She blinks at the question. "Efa." Dipping into a perfunctory curtsy, she moves to go. "I shall fetch ye back for the meal, Mistress Meg."

"Wait. What meal? Aren't you coming with me?"

Efa turns back. "The eve meal."

Now it's my turn to blink in surprise. "I slept all night *and* all day?"

"Mistress Meg hath slept *two* nights and days." A kind smile brushes Efa's bowtie mouth. "And yon room holds ladies enough to attend ye," she says, gesturing to the door behind me. With a nod, she skitters back down the corridor and into the dark.

Two days.

Holy shit, I swear silently at the loss of time even as my body and mind register how necessary the rest was. I turn back to the door and shake out my shoulders like a boxer before squaring them against the newest unknown.

"You can do this, Quinn. Just play the part," I ramble under my breath. Trembling slightly, I knock. Immediately, the door swings wide, and the scent of sandalwood rolls over me like the surf carrying a voice on its back.

"Come in," commands the sapphire lady.

I obey.

Upon entering the large, perfumed room, a pretty girl with cinnamon hair and a dress the color of bluebells whisks me into a corner. Behind a dressing screen, she eyes me with a mixture of scorn and curiosity before handing me a sliver of soap. It smells strongly of lye and heather. The scent makes my head swim, and I hope I'll be free to eat again soon. I curtsy awkwardly, and with a wordless rustle of skirts, the girl moves back to her end of the room. I don't need to be invited twice and slide into the narrow, metal tub.

I let the steaming water go tepid before bothering to move. I don't know when I'll have the chance to bathe again and am in no hurry to get out of this tub. Now, with the slick weight of my hair against my shoulders, I lift my hands into the torchlight. The wrinkled fingertips and small, calloused palms looked skeletal in the shifting light. But not weak. I roll my hands into fists as more than filth sloughs off my being. The grief and insecurity and shame and anxiety—I can feel them. All still there, and present, but quieter now. Less important against the things I've faced and survived. Lowering my hands, I tense and relax each hardening muscle group in turn, feeling more embedded in my limbs than I have since before the accident with Dad. Since before Mom told us about the cancer.

When Mom told us, Meredith slid off the old corduroy couch and lay at Mom's feet. I watched as my sister curled around the still invisible swell of her pregnancy and sobbed. I didn't cry. I just sat there as my body turned hollow, a functioning, soulless shell left behind to carry out the details of my mother's dying. Alone.

Slow deaths are like that. At first, the agony is muted by hope then by the opportunity to fight it. To make final declarations of love. But we lost Dad in an instant, and not a single day passes that I don't wish I could go back and tell him exactly how much I loved him. How completely I adored him. And yet, seeing the alternative, I'm grateful he was spared the undignified work of dying piece by piece the way Mom did.

I shiver, pushing the past—the future—away, and slide down until submerged. Faint murmurings echo through the hammered metal tub and remind me of a hollow tree. Of rain pounding against its sides.

Of Steffan crouched across from me in the dark, his big body between me and the roaring storm. His eyes in the dark.

I sit up with a gasp, my body burning for more than air.

"Oh," I say to the wobbling figure in front of me as I wipe the water from my eyes. "You came back."

"Aye, Mistress Meg," says Efa, her presence already an unexpected comfort. "Shall we begin?"

Then I notice the rough cloth she holds in one hand and the wicked-toothed comb in the other. I nod, dreading the next part, and step from the tub, my body still timorous and raw despite the inner clarity. Wrapping me up, Efa proceeds to rub the water from my skin. I've never been overly modest, but being towel dried by a stranger sets my jaw on edge. Efa's businesslike manner helps though, and I quickly get over my embarrassment and slip into the garments she's brought with her. The clothes fit perfectly. I run my hands over the finely woven wool as the linen shift swishes pleasantly around my legs. The pale yellow kirtle and dusty-blue overgown make a striking combination, and I find myself wishing for a mirror. Stockings tied off above my knees and leather slippers finish the outfit.

"Yer hair be a grand color," Efa says. "Rather like dark sap."

"Maple," I say without thinking. "My mother always said it was the color of maple." It feels surprisingly good to speak of her as I crouch so Efa can slide the last hairpin into place. Gingerly, I touch my head to get an idea of what the hairstyle looks like. The top half winds around in an intricate braid crowning my head, while the rest falls down my back in damp waves.

Efa circles me, an artist inspecting her handiwork. Satisfied, she widens her eyes in a meaningful expression before glancing toward the far end of the room.

"Right," I say and, with a steeling breath, step around the screen.

The lilting strains of a harp lead me across the tapestry-lined room toward a small, stone fireplace where the Arglwyddes—the Lady of Glyndyfrdwy—sits ensconced with her entourage. Their unintelligible conversations hang together like the drone of cicadas. The women fall silent at my approach, leaving only the fire in the great hearth to hiss and snap out my greeting. I bite the inside of my cheek.

"That be better." The Arglwyddes speaks in the slow, easy manner of people with power as she stands and advances on me.

I drop into a deep curtsy and stay there for good measure despite the trembling of my still fatigued muscles.

"Save yer fair manners for the men, girl. I would speak plainly with ye."

The corners of my mouth curve as I rise. She's surprisingly plump for the time, her access to food no doubt a sign of her privilege. Her graying hair is pulled away from a broad, handsome face with bright eyes and ruddy cheeks. She wears her candor as plainly as the emerald gown and gold rings that bedeck every finger. I like her immediately. Whether or not she likes me is an entirely different matter.

"They call ye Meg Quinn," she says. It's not a question.

"Yes, milady."

She doesn't try to hide her shock. "'Tis true, ye do have the strangest of tongues." Her eyes remain wide open, calculating. "Who be yer people?"

Here we go again, I think with trepidation and take a deep breath of the spiced air. "I came from my family's home in Ireland to find my sister," I begin. "She left to marry a man from Bala and I have news for her of ... of our mother." I swallow. "But she is lost to me and I do not know where to find her."

The grand lady purses her lips. "And yer companions?" She pause slightly before the last word. Drawing it out. I'm not sure what her interest is, but my senses start to tingle with wariness.

"They are good men who helped me when I was in need. I owe them my life." I hope she recognizes the truth when she hears it.

"Indeed. And have they left a bloody trail leading to my lord husband's door?"

I will myself to hold her bold stare. "Yes. But it is my fault."

Over the tip of her button nose, Lady Glyndwr fixes her blue-green eyes on me. "Do ye think, Meg Quinn, that yer men be the first to take their revenge on an Englishman?"

I clear my throat, realizing she already knows everything there is to tell and was likely just testing me. "No, milady."

"Or mayhap ye believe 'tis only the English who spill needless blood?"

I don't have to close my eyes to see Godfrey Holloway's contorted, blood-smeared face. I shake my head again. "No, milady."

"Be it only sanctuary ye seek?"

Sanctuary. Yes, I wished for sanctuary, and so much more. "For myself, yes. Though my companions wish to aide your lord husband."

A wry smile causes the corners of her eyes to pleat. She steps closer and I have to look down to maintain eye contact. For all her imposing magnitude, the woman is quite the shape of a tea kettle.

"And ye? What do ye seek?"

"To go home."

"I trow," she says, taking hold of my hand, "that since ye have come all this way," she gestures around us, "ye must stay for a time." She drops my fingers, strolling back to her cushioned chair. "'Tis wise, Meg Quinn, to remember these be dangerous times."

Despite her pleasant tone, the Arglwyddes' meaning is clear.

"Thank you, milady," I choke out.

She puckers her lips with satisfaction and nods, as if trapping me on her estate is indeed a gift.

Mouth pinched, I dip into another curtsy before Efa's already familiar hand slips under my elbow and guides me back.

"Sit whilst I fetch ye a trencher." Efa points to a bench near the back of the great hall before darting away.

I sit and look around discreetly. Long trestle tables run in neat rows on either side of the massive firepit that dominates the space, over which I can just make out the high table stretched across the front of the room. Red-and-gold banners ripple down from the soot-blackened ceiling, and kitchen urchins scurry like roaches to clear away what remains of the meal. Though early in the evening, several dozen men and women mill about in various states of inebriation. In one corner, someone bursts into song. In another, a sonorous belch is released.

Fascinated, I peer through the fire and watch the bodies shift and distort as if moving within the flames themselves. Then I see a figure that must be the lord of the hall and nearly laugh. Set apart by a purple mantle and a thin, golden band encircling his brow, Owain Glyndwr's receding blond hair and forked beard cause him to resemble a powerful, dignified billy goat more than the mythic lion splashed across his crest.

"More eels," says Efa, plopping down a stale bread bowl and mug in front of me. Her tone tells me everything I need to know about the offering.

"That's him, isn't it?" I ask, pulling my gaze from the king beyond the fire.

She nods without asking who I mean.

"Meg!" A brassy voice hails from inside the crowd. I turn just as Madoc stumbles into view. Pushing several people aside, he successfully focuses all nearby attention on himself—and then me.

"Shit," I swear softly and lower my head.

"I feared ye would stay abed forever!" He lurches onto the bench across from me. "Did I tell ye not? 'Tis so, so grand." The plumes of alcohol surrounding him are damn near visible.

"Hello, Madoc," I say and sneak a look at him.

Despite his drunkenness and the unwanted attention, it's nice to see a friendly face. I smile before taking a sip of the murky stew in front of me. It is intolerably briny. But my stomach rumbles again, so I slurp another spoonful before remembering some shred of manners.

"Efa," I say, "this is Madoc. Madoc, this is Efa."

Efa dips politely. Madoc's either too drunk to notice or doesn't care.

"Christ on the bloody cross—ye look a proper lady!" he curses, belatedly noticing the change to my appearance.

Efa clears her throat and addresses me as if Madoc hasn't spoken. "Do ye have further need o' me, Mistress Meg?"

I shake my head, wiping a hand across my mouth like a messy child. She's gone before I can thank her for everything. Unable to eat any more of the fishy soup, I take several long pulls of ale and turn to Madoc. "What have you been up to?"

Leaning precariously on his elbow, he glances toward the ceiling without altering his expression of sloppy bliss.

Right.

Get your head back in the game, I tell myself. "I mean, what have you been doing since we arrived?"

"Oh, aye." Madoc sits up. His eyes shine with such excitement I half expect him to crow. "Lord Glyndwr's scribe himself bid us welcome. Then we ate and slept, though not so long as ye, and once the snows ease, we shall begin training." He stifles a burp. "I shall be a spearman, ye see."

Once I absorbed that fountain of information—snow, damn it—I bite my tongue against the questions ping-ponging through my head and ask the most pressing. "Are we free to leave?"

Madoc frowns so hard his lower lip protrudes. He looks younger than ever. "Leave? We just arrived, and ye cannot go back to Bala, aye?"

I sigh. "Yes but—"

"Nay," says a deep voice behind me.

My breath snags in my throat. I glance back just enough to glimpse Steffan standing behind my left shoulder, blocking my view with his wide shoulders. He's wearing some sort of dark tunic, but I look away without finding his face.

"I was afraid of that," I say as he slides onto the bench next to me.

Madoc frowns harder. "Hath Aunt Marred not bid ye welcome, then?"

"Aunt?" My eyes go wide in shock.

The bench creaks under Steffan's weight as he shifts uncomfortably. "Lady Glyndwr and my father share a sire."

I scrunch up my face, not understanding how such a thing is possible until I remember our conversation in the woods. Steffan's grandfather had been an English nobleman, his father an unacknowledged bastard. So, the lady must be a legitimate daughter.

"Does she know?" I ask.

"O' course she knows," interjects Madoc. "The woman may have been born a *Saesnes*, but she be our Arglwyddes now. She be nay fool."

Agreeing with Madoc on that point, I turn to face Steffan and fall mute.

He's shaved. For the first time since I saw him in that church, I can see clearly the contours of his face. The pale scar snaking across his angular jaw, the gentle slope of his mouth, the tiny mole near the corner of his chin. The long, smooth column of his neck. Such harsh, unforgiving beauty.

My hand rises to touch him, pulled by a string I can't control. Our eyes meet.

"Ellyll," Steffan warns just as something bangs behind us.

I jerk at the noise, my raised hand knocking my ale into the rushes at our feet. Craning around to look, we watch the great door to the hall swing wide. A flurry of bright snow rushes in, along with a band of grim-looking men.

The room goes silent as the dead.

"Who are they?" I ask no one in particular as the group cuts a path through the room and gathers in front of the high table. A dark, tightly-coiled man dressed in rough leathers and furs mounts the steps with confidence and leans in to speak privately with Lord Glyndwr.

"'Tis General Rhys Gethin and his spearmen," Madoc says with breathless awe. He gains his feet, swaying.

Steffan makes a low rumbling noise. I glance over. Judging from the squint of his eyes and the tension in his jaw, I can guess he knows more about these men than he's letting on. Then raised voices bring my attention back to the dais, where the one called Rhys Gethin gives a sharp whistle.

Immediately, two more spearmen enter the hall, marching a third man between them. Bound and without a cloak, the third man shivers violently as he's thrust to his knees in front of Lord Glyndwr. Despite the prisoner's ragged appearance, his clothes look nearly as fine as Glyndwr's. Flanked by the surly spearman, the two noblemen exchange words. The crowd presses in closer, frenetic energy thrumming through the space, barring my view. Not for the first time, my lack of Welsh weighs on me.

"What's going on?" I hiss at Steffan.

He doesn't look away from the tableau. "Our lord be passing judgment."

"Judgment on what?" I crane to see just as the prisoner lurches to his feet, his voice wild with pleading.

Rhys Gethin simply steps toward him, the movement so fast, so subtle, I don't understand what's happening until the general steps away and the prisoner sinks to his knees. My hands fly to my face, but it's too late. I've already seen the dead man's head droop against his chest like a rose overburdened with dew, already seen the arterial blood gush down his chest. Pool around him.

It's too much after the sheriff. Too much blood. Too soon.

Blindly, I turn away and find Steffan's firm shoulder next to me. I don't think. I just press my forehead against it, not caring what it means. A big, long-fingered hand finds the back of my head and holds me gently in place until the scrape of boots against stone is gone and the great doors bang shut once again.

"'Tis over," he says, deep voice a gentle rumble against my hair.

With a fortifying breath, I look to where two servants are already removing the soiled rushes.

"Why did he kill him like that?" I ask, my voice as thin as the blood on the stone floor.

No one answers, so I glance over at Madoc, who's staring at the gore, unblinking.

"'Twas a *bradwr*," he says. "A traitor."

Pulling myself together, I glance from Madoc to Steffan for explanation.

"'Tis not only the English we must fight now," Steffan explains, "but any Cymry who would betray the revolt." His eyes turn to flecks of steel beneath his long, straight lashes.

I grip the table for support as understanding presses down on my head.

Betray the cause, and you're dead. A doomed cause. A cause that had already, and would continue to, shed innocent blood in vain. *Stay with them and you die. Try and stop them and you die.*

"I'm going to my room," I announce, feeling sick.

Madoc reaches for my elbow. "I shall escort ye."

"I'll be fine. I remember the way," I say, in no mood for company after all that's happened.

Steffan steps closer then, but doesn't touch me, though I can still feel the echo of his hand against my head. "Ye should not go alone. Just because we be among our people does not mean we be among friends."

"Captain Blaidd?" a cracking, adolescent voice interjects.

Madoc turns aside to reveal a wiry boy of maybe twelve dressed in the Glyndwr livery.

"Aye?" says Steffan, before the boy begins speaking in Welsh.

Captain? What else did I miss while sleeping?

Steffan gives a faint nod, and the boy scampers away.

"Do not leave her side," Steffan admonishes Madoc before walking away. He doesn't so much as glance at me.

Pleased for once to oblige his brother, Madoc links elbows with me, his wavering stare the only remaining sign of intoxication. I hate to admit it, but searching for my room alone with half the manor drunk doesn't seem like a good idea after all— even if I'm holding up my escort.

"Come on then," I say and lead Madoc toward the stairs, away from the small crowd still hovering around the scent of death like a murder of crows.

Several wrong turns later, Madoc and I stumble upon a vaguely familiar hallway. Guttering sconces give off an acrid smell, and I feel an unexpected longing for the aromatic wood fires of Dwyn Blair.

If it's still there. The thought jabs like a voodoo needle, and my stomach does yet another flip.

"I think it's this way," I say more to distract myself than anything.

Madoc just stifles a yawn in response as we ease our way along the dimly lit passage. I'm not tired after my long sleep, just weakened and need time alone to think. Staying here isn't an option. Neither, apparently is leaving. And the idea of escaping the compound only to traipse through war-torn wilderness makes my skin prickle with cold sweat. But there's something else—something worse. Out of every sour wisp of smoke or drifting shadow, my mind conjures Steffan: his stern face and elegant hands, the way he cradled Branwen's head against his chest, the bright bark of his rare laugh. My desire feels nothing short of traitorous.

Distracted and with Madoc still in tow, I round the last corner and trip over someone. Righting myself, I start to apologize before squeaking softly in shock. Standing with his hands pressed against the wall, a man has a woman pinned in front of him, her skirts up around her waist. Thrusting away, they don't even look at us.

Suddenly alert, Madoc barks something unintelligible in Welsh at them. I elbow him in the ribs and rush us past the couple as fast as I can move. Demonstrating a typical lack of restraint, Madoc bellows, either in outrage or amusement I can't quite tell, until I shove him through what I hope is the right door and bolt it behind us.

Smelling of damp hay and illuminated only by the dim glow of a burned-down rush light, the room is dark and quiet. We wait, but no ominous sounds of occupancy come from the inky corners.

"'Tis yer cell, aye?" Madoc loudly whispers. Clearly, he's still too buzzed to regulate his volume. Great.

"That's one way to put it," I say while my eyes adjust. The room is indeed empty and looks identical to the one I woke up in, but there's only one way to be sure. I tiptoe to the low bed and slide my hand between the mattress and the frame. Coins clink, and I swear happily. Then my hand brushes the familiar folds of Cai's cloak, and I pull everything onto the floor in a heap.

"I can't believe it's all still here," I say, incredulous. I'm ready to talk about anything besides the scene we interrupted, and this is as good as any.

The woman in the hall picks that exact moment to climax. Enthusiastically.

I cringe at the sound even as my blood heats, my mind treacherously picturing Steffan's face flushed with pleasure, head thrown back exposing his neck to my lips, my teeth ...

"God's bones, wench, shut yer—" Madoc shouts.

"Hush," I say. "Don't draw their attention." I sit on the bed to loop the dagger hilt through the belt of the dress. "They'll be gone soon anyway."

Please, please, please let them go away so he can leave.

Even in the thin light, Madoc's ears glow ginger-pink. He shifts uncomfortably. "I regret ye had to see that."

"Me too, but they're the least of our concerns right now," I say, really not wanting to talk about it.

I have no doubt the sound of the woman's exposed flesh slapping against the wall is just as vivid for Madoc as it is for me. The last thing he needs is encouragement. I owe Madoc my life and am grateful for his friendship and company, but the way he's looking at me sends ripples of discomfort across my skin. The exact opposite of his half brother, and I feel awful about it, even as I know the body simply wants who it wants sometimes.

I clear my throat and stand up. "Thanks for helping me find my way," I half-shout for the benefit of our hallway companions. "But you'd better go get some rest in case you start training tomorrow. You wouldn't want to spear anyone."

If I could physically kick my own ass in this moment, I would.

The bad joke falls flat as Madoc nods. "For certes."

He opens his mouth as if to say more, stops, turns curtly toward the door, stops again, and then spins back around.

Here we go. My stomach sinks.

"I did not think to give ye this yet, but I would that ye had a trinket o' my own to add to yer treasures." The words come out in a rush of ale-soaked breath as he steps close and pulls something from inside his vest. Nervously, he thrusts it into my hands.

I look down and feel my heart come to an utter stop. Smooth and finely carved, the handle of the tiny spoon has been fashioned into a blossom. My mind jumps back to Mrs. Jones and her collection of love spoons.

Guilt squeezes my heart, and I think I might be sick.

"It's beautiful," I manage and mean it.

"Took damned near two days," he admits without shame. "I'd rather be sparing in yon snow then sitting on my arse, but 'twas a pleasure to make it for ye."

"Madoc, I can't accept this," I say and hold the token of affection out to him.

Injury sweeps over his flushed face with the severity of a slap.

I backpedal. "It's wonderful, and I appreciate it more than you know, but ... well ..."

I don't want you. The words stick in my throat, and I swallow them whole like a coward.

"I don't have anything to give you." It's not a complete lie. And far from the truth.

Upset and flustered, Madoc grabs my hands too hard. The

spoon bites into my palm. "Milady Meg. I would that ye knew—"

"Thank you." I pull away harshly and place the spoon onto the cloak. "I think you should get back to the hall now."

He steps closer, hunger rolling off him like water. I can almost smell it. He takes my hand again, gently this time. It feels warm and strong and calloused and utterly wrong. Not dangerous—but not welcome either.

I stare at the floor. "I'm tired, Madoc."

The awkward moment expands around us, sucking all the air from the room. When there is no space left for misunderstanding, he releases my hand.

"As ye say." His voice is hoarse with emotion and drink.

I don't move or speak, caught between wanting him to go and hating that I've hurt his feelings. Finally, his footsteps reach the door.

"Milady?" Madoc ask softly.

I look at him then but say nothing.

"'Twas not as I expected. Killing a man."

"I'm so sorry, Madoc." My cheeks burn shame, and my tightly held shoulders droop. "God, if only you know how fast I'd take everything back if I could," I say, knowing the words mean nothing against all that's happened.

He nods and opens the door, his eyes glassy. The passageway is empty.

"'Tis how we differ, for I would do it a thousand times over, ye see. For ye." Then with a last sharp look, he's gone.

"That's what scares me," I say and bolt the door behind him.

CHAPTER 15

BIRDS OF A FEATHER

"Hungry?" asks Madoc through a mouthful of porridge.

"Nope," I say and push my trencher toward him. The mound of oats wobble, and I lose what little appetite I brought to the table. Which is a shame because I definitely need to eat more. Somehow not suffering from a hangover, Madoc nods in thanks and tucks into his second helping, leaving me to brood in peace.

Yesterday's faint sense of well-being disappeared with the night. I'd paced my room for hours without getting any closer to a plan for getting back to the yew. Quite the opposite. The more I thrashed at the strands of my snare, the more entangled I became. When I finally did fall into a restless sleep, I was plagued by nightmares. Over and again, I watched the corpse of Sheriff Holloway engorge, the brutal neck wound gape obscenely, Meredith's children being born from the bloody slit of my enemy's throat as I stood by, futile and inept. I woke up sticky with sweat, only to be dressed quickly and hustled to the great hall by Efa, whose only instruction was not to leave the bailey. As if I was stupid enough to try. Not yet anyway.

Only when Madoc reaches the bottom of the bowl does he register my dark mood.

"Be ye well, milady?" he asks. His voice is gentle, and for once, he doesn't try to touch me.

I blink and straighten up. "I'm all right. Just didn't sleep well."

He wipes his mouth, surveying my face. "Goat's milk."

"Pardon me?" I gape.

"Warm goat's milk be good for sleep. Have ye not tried it?"

I clamp my teeth. The mere mention of warm, animal-scented dairy products makes me want to gag. "Tempting, but I'm sure I'll sleep better tonight."

"'Tis nay bother, for certes. I shall see to it this eve." He laces his fingers behind his head and gives me a magnanimous smile.

I chuckle in spite of everything. "Of course you will."

"What boon hath my brother vowed now?" Steffan's deep voice fills the air as he steps up to the table. Fresh from a morning wash, Steffan's hair slides back from his face like a seal's pelt. The tips cling to his neck in slick curls, and I have to restrain myself from leaning in to smell him.

"The key to perfect sleep," I joke to cover the jump in my pulse.

"Goat's milk," Steffan says and sits next to me, his trencher heavy with porridge and leeks.

I wrinkle my face in disgust. "Not you too."

Madoc gives me a puzzled look, but any response is cut off by the heralding clang of a page boy's bell. Madoc springs off the bench.

"I beg yer leave, milady. Brother," he says formally before dashing out the great door as if Christmas morning awaited. Other men follow, hurriedly finishing their meals as they go. I can hear their clomping boots and noisy chatter as they descend the ramp that leads from the manor house down into the fortified bailey below.

I give Steffan a questioning look.

"Arms training," he replies.

"Do you have to go too?"

"Aye." He goes on eating.

Having no legitimate reason to stay, I drum my fingers and stand. "Well, I'll leave you to your meal."

"Eat." Steffan slides his mug of ale over to me. "Ye be in need o' the strength, and it shall help settle yer *bol*," he says while tearing at the soft inside of his trencher and holding out the least-soggy part of bread. The part I usually eat.

I sit back down and take the offerings. "Thank you."

After several sips of the crisp, spicy ale and bites of bread, I do start to feel better, and we finish eating in comfortable silence. As I brush crumbs from my skirts, I notice the amber-and-blond longbow resting against the table.

I gesture toward it. "Madoc seems excited to start his training. Are you?"

Steffan drains the last of our shared ale and places it on the table between us. "I find nay joy in killing men."

Taken aback by this blunt statement, I watch Steffan closely, doing my best to be objective. His face is striking, though not classically handsome; his nose is too long, his eyes too close set. But his waving chestnut hair is lovely, his broad back and long limbs strong. And it's all too easy to imagine his clear eyes and wide mouth twisting from tenderness to vicious cruelty and back again. There's no doubt—Steffan Blaidd is a dangerous man, more than capable of violence. But then I picture his beautiful hands clasped in prayer, remember the way he clucked and cooed to the farm animals, and realize a blind man could see the truth: Steffan is gentle.

"I know." I lay my hand on his arm.

He looks at me, gaze sharp with warning, even as I see the heat gather in his eyes. The same heat from the riverbank. I pull away.

"'Tis an honor to serve my lord and Cymru," he says, reaching for his bow. Then he leans close and, in a voice just for me, adds, "But by God, I do hate it."

As if to mock him, the clang of steel drifts into the hall, chased by men's shouts and laughter. Steffan is a warrior by necessity, but I wonder suddenly who he would be elsewhere.

"What does bring you joy?" I ask, not ready to let him leave.

Steffan blinks in surprise, and I wonder if he's ever been asked such a thing. Deliberate as always, he lets several moments tick by before answering. "Tending the land. Song. Chapel. Ale. Walking among the trees. I would that I knew more o' the world, but a man needs not much to be at peace."

His honesty touches me, and I think about how he sang while plowing the fields. Not for the first time, I wonder why he doesn't already have a farm and a family of his own.

He looks at me then, his expression earnest. "And ye, Ellyll? What would please ye?"

A million things sprang to mind: toilets, coffee, takeout, antibiotics, cars, suffrage, books, jeans, museums, running water, birth control, central heating, mass printing, pencils, waste management, hospitals, electric light, ice cream …

"To be home," I say, pausing for a moment over the last word. I meant to say, "with my sister," but choose the idea of a true home of my own at the last second. Glancing up, I find myself pinned by Steffan's smoky stare. Heat surges through my solar plexus, and I scoot off the bench away from him.

Steffan's reserve falls back into place like the portcullis outside. "Good day, mistress."

We dip our heads in a formal gesture and turn away, but the

growing intimacy of our conversations linger like a perfume that follows me.

I'm nearly to the stairs when Steffan's seldom raised voice echoes through the hall. Startled, I spin around. The remaining men leave their meals and join him by the doors, longbows hanging over their shoulders. I blink, both surprised and not surprised at all. It seems the peaceful Steffan is raising an army of archers.

I soon learn the ever-present potage, breads, and fish stews are on account of Lent, so other than being willing to sell my soul for a bowl of Thai curry, a cappuccino, and a chocolate donut, the following few days are oddly enjoyable. Each morning begins with an aggressive grooming from Efa before she retreats to her regular responsibilities. Her attention smacks of duty, but I don't mind. A sharp mind and bubbling humor lurk beneath the obliging manner, and I like her better for it.

Madoc and Steffan are mostly absent from the great hall. Now surrounded by old friends and new comrades, they spend most of their time down in the bailey among the military men and their families. Whether this is by accident or design, I can't say. But my time is my own, and I'm grateful for that. Having nothing better to do, I stuff myself with eel stew and leek pies at every opportunity, explore the dank confines of the manor like a wayward mouse, and find ways to entertain myself. Most days, this involves avoiding chapel, steering clear of Lady Glyndwr and her ladies, and ferreting out sturdy bits of charcoal. I've taken to drawing on the stone hearths. I doubt this earns me any love from the scullery maids, but it keeps the pendulum swings of panic at bay. Soot-stained and cagey, I linger in the perpetual shadows of natural light, always carrying the uneasy sense of a mouse with a cat close behind.

On the evening of the third night, I meet my cat. After yet another solitary meal, I am just leaving the great hall when a voice arrests my attention like a shepherd's hook.

"Be ye the *Saesnes* conjurer?" asks a reedy voice.

I turn to find a boy of twelve or thirteen staring at me. Gangly and fine-boned with floppy, dark hair and gleaming boots, he's clearly highborn, though unfamiliar to me. And he's leaning heavily against the wall. Odd.

"I don't know what you mean by that," I answer, measuring my words. Accepting my identity as an English-speaking outsider—a Saxon—is one thing. Being labeled a conjurer seems like a horse of an entirely different color.

His large eyes widened farther, a now familiar reaction to my voice, but instead of explaining himself, he simply says, "Milord."

I raise an eyebrow in question. "Milord ... what?"

The boy shakes an errant strand of hair from his face and makes a production of clearing his throat. With the arrogant certainty of a child, he says, "Ye must call me milord."

Mentally, I fold my arms and count to ten. "Very well. But I still don't understand your question. Milord."

Clearly unused to my tone, the young man clears his throat again. "Be ye the wench who casts soot faces on the stone?"

I look at him quizzically for a few moments before grasping his meaning. "Oh. Yes, that would be me. I can clean them off if it's a problem."

"What do ye call it?" His voice is a ragged murmur now, and he takes several eager steps forward.

"Are you all right?" I ask, ignoring the question.

Closer now, it's clear that, despite the boy's well-groomed appearance, he's unwell. The fine, brightly colored clothes hang from his shoulders and make his pale flesh appear waxy. Shadows encircle his eyes. No child should look that tired.

In answer, he hunches over as a cough takes him. Covering the space between us in two strides, I grab his arms and brace him against myself. He jerks away wildly, clinging to the wall until the wheezing subsides.

"What do ye call it?" he persists.

"Sketching," I answer. My voice curt with worry. "Drawing. You need to sit down. Is your mother here?"

"Sketching. Drawing." After clearing his throat, he rolls the words around as if positioning a peppermint candy in his cheek.

"Did you hear me?"

He waves me off before wiping away the cold sweat beading along his upper lip. "My mother be dead. I killed her in childbed. What do ye call yerself?"

Too stunned to be annoyed, I answer. "My name's Meg Quinn. What's yours? Milord."

His eyes go big with surprise and lifts his chin. "Dafydd ab Owain ap—" His voice cracks. "Gruffudd Fychan," he concludes before scowling at me as if his voice changing is somehow my fault.

I bite my cheek to keep from smiling. "Well, Milord Dafydd, was that all you wanted?"

The boy's haughty mask slips just enough to reveal naked yearning on his lovely, ill face. "I would that you teach me to sketch," he gestures into the air as if drawing, "As ye do," he confesses in a rush of breath. "'Tis different from the scribes. Be like life," he adds with unjaded feeling.

Struck dumb with surprise, I merely nod. "Okay."

"Okay?" he repeats in the halting, mimicking way people often do when trying to understand me.

"Yes, milord. I will teach you to draw."

A bucktoothed grin splits his freckled face. Fighting against another cough, he says, "Meet me at the mew on the morrow after terce."

"Here. Let me help you back."

"Nay," he snaps, the grandeur returning to his voice. "Ye shall not speak o' this," he commands before retreating back the way he came.

I have the feeling I've just made a terrible mistake but can't help smiling all the way back to my room.

"Psst. Psst."

I stop. The sound came from close by.

Ignoring my cold fingers and dirty feet, gifts from my first trip down into the bailey, I turn a slow circle and spy a tuft of black hair poking out from behind a large wooden shed. The structure, which has a heavy door and several closely slatted windows, hardly looks big enough for a drawing space. As I approach, a staccato chorus of bird calls erupts from inside, making me wonder if my pupil could have possibly picked a worse place to meet.

"Ye be late," Dafydd greets when I round the back of what I suppose is a mew. Glaring at me, his brandy brown eyes and upturned nose make him look more like a disgruntled Christmas elf than a young prince.

"You didn't tell me what a mew is," I say squatting next to him.

He frowned deeply. "Have ye nay mews in—whence do ye hail?"

"Ireland," I lie.

Dafydd's oddly colored eyes narrow. "Ye do not. I had a nurse from *Iwerddon*. Ye be naught like her."

There's no point in arguing. "Why did you want to meet here?"

"'Tis what I wish to sketch," he says and gestures behind us.

Grateful for the distraction, I look at the strange shanty. Considered it. "Well, it isn't very exciting but could be a good subject for studying light and shadow."

"*Paid â bod yn dwp,*" he says in exasperation. "The falcon."

A scream from the now identified bird makes me jump just as a heavily scarred hand rounds the corner behind Dafydd. I squawk in alarm as the appendage grabs my student by the collar and hauls him backward.

Dafydd shrieks.

"Hey!" I yell and scramble after him. A wiry, middle-aged man wearing a leather vest, stout boots, and a floppy cap holds Dafydd by the scruff of his neck as he snarls down at the boy in Welsh.

"Stop it," I scold, stepping into view. "You're hurting him."

My appearance distracts the man long enough for Dafydd to land a solid kick to his shins. Completely unfazed, the man's stare swings between me and his wriggling captive.

"This what ye be about little lord bastard?" the man says as he let go of Dafydd. "The *pwca* wench?"

Before Dafydd can respond, he doubles over coughing.

"See what you've done," I say as if the fit is entirely the man's fault.

Still coughing, Dafydd takes a swing at the man. "She be mine and—*cough*—ye cannot speak to me so!"

"Aye, I can, *bach,*" the man says while calmly deflecting the boy's scrappy kicks and punches. "Ye best stop now, boy, and be gone. Me babes be molting, aye?"

Dafydd won't be calmed. "I may be—*cough, cough*—a bastard, but ye be naught but—*cough*—a falconer."

The man roars with laughter.

"Stop it!" I shout again and pull Dafydd away to face me. "Hold up your arms."

Dafydd gives me a baleful look before hacking into his sleeve. His face is bright red and starting to go purple.

"I mean it. Hold them up now. Like this." I demonstrate.

Curiosity gets the best of him, and he raises them begrudgingly.

"Good. Higher. Now close your mouth and breathe through your nose." Again, I demonstrate. I'm not sure this will work but saw my mother do something similar in the maternity ward with hyperventilating spouses. So it's worth a try.

Dafydd does his best to copy me and, within a few moments, is breathing easier. His coloring eases, his freckles like black stars in a pale sky. He continues to clear his throat, but the worst has passed.

Reassured that he's not going to die or vomit at my feet, I turn to the falconer who has gone quiet but lingers close by.

"I am not his," I clarify. "I'm teaching him to draw. Do you know a quiet place we could go?"

"I told ye to hold yer tongue," Dafydd whines.

The falconer chuffs a laugh again, his eyes fixed on Dafydd. "Be that what the lads call it now, lord bastard? Drawing?" The man turns to me. "He be a wee bit o' a green stripling for a swive," he says before coming close enough for me to notice with a start that he doesn't have any eyebrows or lashes. "But I be not."

He flashes a rotting smile before grabbing a handful of my ass.

Fear and outrage shoot down my spine as I jerk out of his reach. "That's *not* what I meant," I shout as white-hot rage explodes inside me. "And what the *hell* is the matter with you people anyway? Since the moment I set foot in this country I have been grabbed, hit, chased, insulted, ogled, told where to go and what to do, and I'm fucking sick of it!" I scream directly into the man's face. "So, if you ever touch me again, I will shove my dagger so far up your ass no one will ever find it."

The last words come out in a hiss, and I feel the release of anger all the way to my toes.

The falconer's expression morphs from lecherous glee to shock to something like admiration. The man actually lets out a low whistle. "By God's bloody nails, the wench hath a tongue as loose as a whore's cunny."

I'm tempted to throttle the man. My face must reveal as much because he steps back and smiles. The bastard actually smiles.

"*Mae'n ddrwg gen i,* mistress—Rhodri Moel means ye nay harm. I thought ye be offering, 'tis all," he says and scratches his smooth cheek before gesturing toward Dafydd.

The boy's still standing with his hands over his head, his eyes round as buttons.

"What ye be wanting with yon boy then?" Rhodri asks.

Blood pumps hot and fast through my chest as I inhale deeply to get control of my voice.

"I'm going to teach him how to ... well, how to make the likeness of something on a smooth surface. Like an illumination," I explain as calmly as possible. "I need sharp, blackened sticks and flat stones." I think quickly. "And somewhere quiet to go. Master Dafydd wishes to keep his lessons private." I lift my chin with more confidence than I feel and stare at the hairless falconer. "Will you help me?"

The skin above the falconer's right eye crinkles upward—if he had an eyebrow, he'd be arching it at me.

"Aye. Rhodri Moel be yer man," he says and gives me a jack-o'-lantern smile.

CHAPTER 16
OMNIA VINCIT AMOR

Early spring in the desert southwest is glorious. Mild and fresh, the frequent sunshine warms your skin one minute before the wind, thick with pollen, gives you goosebumps the next. Thorny mesquite trees sprout nests like tiny haystack hats while green-trunked palo verde trees unfurl their buttery blooms. Everywhere, the earth is warming, yawning, stretching toward the still-tempered sun.

Wales holds no such loveliness this morning. The late spring snow stripped all but the hardiest new growth from the trees, leaving gelatinous mud and near constant mists in exchange. Efa, me, and what feels like every other serving woman in the compound are on our way down to the river to do the wash. Apparently one of the massive laundry cauldrons cracked, and all available hands are being culled to help. After the eventful day of lessons with Dafydd, I went to bed feeling accomplished and was pleased when Efa asked if I wanted to help this morning. While the company and activity are comforting, what I'm really after is a better understanding of the estate.

Overburdened with a basket of foul-smelling shirts, I walk

with exaggerated caution. I have no desire to go sprawling or be any dirtier. As we near the bank, the already cool air grows colder still. Low, cement-colored clouds roll across the sky, mirroring the frothy river below. I wish this particular chore could wait until the ground dried a bit, but when I voice this thought, the woman next to Efa rebuffs me sharply. Robust and red-faced, she looks like an angry apple and punctuates her thought with an aggressive hand gesture that makes Efa's little mouth drop open. I watch the feisty woman with a kind of admiration. At least the washer lady has the guts to say what she thinks to my face.

Once we settle onto a rocky portion of shore, I follow Efa in scrubbing, rinsing, and literally beating the dirt from the clothing. My muscles ache with the effort but do not tire as easily as they did at Dwyn Blair. I feel a bit proud of myself and invigorated by the work. It isn't long though before a ripple of murmurs reach me, and I become aware of being watched.

"Am I doing something wrong?" My hands sting from the lye soap and the frigid water, but I don't dare stop or complain.

"Nay," Efa says.

I glance down the bank and see one of the angry apple lady's minions giggle before averting her eyes. She's a curvy, freckled girl with a pretty smile, chapped hands, and looks about Gwenhwyfar's age.

"I'm not blind, Efa. Or an idiot. Is it the accent thing?"

Efa stands and snaps a clean shirt in the wind before saying in an even voice, "They wonder if ye play whore to the brothers one at a time or together."

I choke on my own spit and drop a clean shift in the dirt.

"What?" I wheeze. I don't know what I expected to hear, but it wasn't that.

Efa shushes me, snatching up the garment. "'Tis nay wonder."

"'Tis certainly a wonder to me," I hiss, my face contorting in outrage. "Not that it's anyone's business *what* I do or *who* I do it with, but I've hardly seen either of them since we arrived."

Efa opens her mouth to speak, but I'm not finished.

"And"—I punctuate the word by snatching up another filthy shirt—"I may not have had my skirts up since getting here, but plenty of other people have. So who are they to accuse me?"

A smile tugs on Efa's lips, even as she shakes her head in exasperation. "Forsooth, ye do not understand. Yer speech be strange. Ye carry yerself as a born lady yet prefer the company o' serving wenches and men," she says, wringing out the twice cleaned linen. "Ye do not keep the church." She pauses, waiting for me to object. When I shrug, she folds the wet fabric and lays it in her basket. "Nor do ye claim a husband, even a dead one, though ye be well on in years."

I swallow the 'well on in years' part and rock back on my heels. At the moment I do, in fact, feel much older than my twenty-two years. After a moment's consideration, I scoff, voice dripping with sarcasm. "Of course. I'm not a maiden or noble lady or a nun or a peasant, so I must be a whore, right?"

Efa turns to me, her tawny eyes serious but without judgment. "So 'tis true?"

I snort and grab another cloth.

"No. 'Tis not true," I say and sink my hands into the gut-wrenching cold.

Scrubbing hard at what appears to be blood stains, I think of my mother's years in the hospital, my sister's kindergarten classroom, my own university education and art. Even Mrs. Jones and Reverend Fitzwilliam come to mind, not to mention the countless other female professionals I've encountered in my life, and I feel a gutting flood of sorrow for the bright young woman next to me.

After a time, I say gently, "There will be more for us some-day. So much more than this. I wish you could see it."

I look at her then and will her to believe it. Perhaps even the dream of such a distant future will do Efa some good. It's all I can offer.

Efa gives me a peculiar, piercing look but says nothing. We finish our work in silence before loading up our now doubly heavy burdens for the trip back to the manor. Struggling under the weight of the wet laundry, we're nearly to the gatehouse when Efa stops short.

"*Twpsyn,*" she says in exasperation.

"What?"

She makes a hissing sound and turns back toward the river. "I left the soap."

The angry apple lady, whose name I don't know, rounds on us at the word 'soap.' I suspected she spoke English, but she banters hotly with Efa in Welsh and refuses to look at me.

"I'll go back," I cut in.

Efa shakes her head. "Nay, mistress."

"I can't carry as much as you can. Take some of mine, and I'll catch up."

"I would go with ye," Efa argues.

The girl who laughed at me says something, and everyone chuckles again before moving toward the compound.

I shoot a nasty glare at their backs. "Efa," I say, gently. "I'm just going to get the soap and will meet you at the bailey."

She tucks her bottom lip over the top, considering. "As it pleases ye," she says with an exhale and redoubles her grip on the basket. "Make haste."

I trot back to the riverbank before she can say another word.

The errant soap is a bright spot in the leaf mold. Not wanting to touch the stinging lye more than necessary, I pick up the bar and gingerly wrap it in my apron. Overhead, a bird trills in the clammy cold, sharp and melodic in turn. I close my eyes and listen, savoring the crisp scent of unsullied earth and the quaking quiet of the breeze. Despite the much-needed provisions of the estate, I miss the freedom and solitude of the woods. I look around, but there's no question of slipping away. I might be alone outside the walls but am also without supplies or any notion of which direction to take. Nor am I foolish enough to think my absence would go unnoticed for long. And untrue or not, leaving will mark me as a threat.

No, I have to go back. What I don't have to do is rush.

Where are you?

My eyes fly open. The high, smooth voice clips the quiet like shears, but I don't need to whirl around to know I'm still alone. I would recognize that voice anywhere. Because it's my voice, only sweeter. More honey than whiskey.

Meredith.

I still didn't understand how we remain connected across time, but once again, her call is undeniable. I think ferociously back to her, *Here. I'm here. Wait for me.*

At that moment, a delicate, rattling meow breaks through the bird songs. Animals abound all over the manor, but the pathetic little cry is so incongruous with the surroundings that I crane my neck in search of the source.

There. Something moves high up in a tree not fifty feet upriver from me. I can't see it clearly but know the ruckus came from that direction.

"Hello there," I call softly and follow the cries until a kitten comes into view. Tar black with a bottlebrush coat, the tiny feline thrashes and mews from its precarious position out on a limb.

"Well, you've gotten yourself into a pickle, haven't you? I feel you, kitty." When I step forward, a girl comes into view.

Already well into the tree, her fox-red hair falls in a tangle down her back. She holds very still and calls gently to the creature, but the kitten, sensing a game, scampers farther and farther out onto the branch. The young girl follows doggedly, until the limb bends at a treacherous angle over the water.

I start moving faster. "Hey! You there! Don't move!"

Suddenly uncertain of its footing, the little feline screeches. Creeping closer, the girl lets go with one hand, reaching toward her prize. When she falls, the child hits the water with a vicious slap and slips under.

Her tiny, disembodied hands thrash at the surface like fish on a line.

The kitten disappears in the dark water.

Fear grabs my throat, strangling my voice as I scream "Hold on!" even as my numb legs propel me forward. "Please God, please God, please," I pray and swear together as I sprint to the edge of the bank and leap into the river.

The frigid water punches my chest and gut, instantly saturating my gown. Panicked and struggling for breath, I wave numb arms under the muddy surface as the current carries me downstream, the silky swirl of red hair always bobbing just out of reach. Every inch of me aches, and I can't think, can't breathe. Only instinct shoves me forward.

The girl. Get the girl.

My lungs are screaming. My foot hits something solid, and I push off, launching forward. My fingers sink into a snarl of hair, and I yank the child's face above water. Her head lolls against my neck as water splashes us both in the face.

I can't tell if she's breathing.

Carried on the back of the river, we drift downstream until a large stone jutting up from the riverbed strikes my back. Pain stabs through me, but momentarily anchored, I plant my feet and push us out of the central current. My thoughts churn in time with the water as I grab frantically at exposed roots along the bank. Once, twice, three times, I miss until I finally catch hold and pull with all my strength only to fall back into the frothing eddy, my palm shredded.

True terror shoots through me—I can't get us out.

My teeth chatter as I hoist the girl farther up my shoulder and draw in a painful breath. Only then do I scream. It's a pathetic, shallow noise.

Louder. I have to be louder.

Fighting the chatter of my teeth, I draw a burning breath and scream and scream and scream until, all at once, voices surround us. Hands tug and lift until the river finally—*finally*—falls away and the world starts to go dark.

"Release her, Ellyll. That's it. Let go, *cariad*," assures a mahogany voice, and at the sound, I know we're safe.

I open eyes I don't remember closing to find myself lying on the ground, caked in wet wool. Several men kneel nearby. One has the little girl propped up next to me, her head tipped forward like a discarded marionette's.

"She n-needs to b-breathe." I heave myself onto all fours, but a hand holds me back. "Let-t go," I stammer, and the hand obeys.

Crawling forward, I get the child onto her back and start CPR. Overcome with the task of forcing air into the small husk, the world around me goes unnoticed until the delicate bones under my palms heave as water and bile sputter out of the girl's mouth. Eyes like two river stones fly open, wide and shocked, before her pale, oval face crumples into a howl. More arms sweep in to lift the girl as she spits and sobs. On the tail of the girl's cry, a woman screams.

As if in a dream, I watch as a flash of red hair and green skirts tear down the steep embankment toward us. After reaching the girl and grasping her face, the woman looks over to where I sit slumped in the mud. She stares at me for a long time before turning away. Only then does my brain register that she's pregnant as a full moon.

That's when the shaking begins. It starts in my hands, moving up my limbs and across my body like a quake, causing my teeth to chatter. Pain, like a bone-deep ache, snakes through me until my stomach tightens, hard as a knot, and I curl into myself, useless against the shaking.

The hum of the activity around me wavers in and out of focus.

Sleep. I just want to sleep.

I don't look up—can't look up—when he scoops me into his arms. His salt, leather, spice scent mixes with the reeking mud, but soothing heat radiates from his chest as he presses me to him. But Steffan's breaths come fast and hard as if he's struggling, running even, and I feel myself jostled about for a long time until more hands are pinching and pulling at my clothes. Voices jump and roll in Welsh, and I want to resist, to speak, but can't find the strength.

Dark. The world is going dark again, when a sudden shock of cold air across my skin is replaced by soft, smothering warmth. Large hands knead my own, and I hear myself hiss in pain.

But the hands don't stop.

Then a new voice like steel barks a command, and all goes quiet. Somewhere close by, a fire crackles and spits, but no other sound remains. So, I lay there, slowly coming back into myself. My limbs still sting, but the ache in my gut has loosened enough for me to breathe more easily.

In, out. In, out. In, out.

A long time seems to pass before he speaks. "By the rood, if ye e'er do that again, I shall drown ye myself."

I blink open my eyes and find Steffan's face inches from mine. Firelight halos his russet curls, casting his frowning mouth and hawk nose in shadow. His gray eyes are dark and unreadable. He does not lean away.

"I'll try to remember that," I say, my voice thin but steady.

Lifting a big, calloused hand, Steffan brushes my wet hair away from my face and tucks it gently behind my ear, his fingers barely grazing the soft skin there before he stands and moves to the foot of my cot.

We stare at each other, unblinking as he reaches for me again, slow enough for me to pull away if I wish. When I don't, he slips his hands under the huge fur covering me and takes hold of my feet. I flinch but don't pull away. He waits, long fingers cupping my heels. I have no idea what's about to happen but feel the brush of his fingers all the way in my core and brace myself. I nod, and Steffan rubs my feet. Kneading my heals, the arches of my feet, my toes, forcing blood into the still too cold flesh. It burns, but I don't pull away, biting my lip instead to trap the moans of pain and pleasure threatening to escape at his insistent touch.

"Forgive me," he says, voice like gravel.

Not entirely lucid, I look down my body to where he stands and ask, "For touching me?"

Steffan pauses, his face severe before he slides his strong hands over my arches and up to my ankles, my calves, massaging as he goes. Only then do I become fully aware of my nakedness under the animal skin—and of the possibility that Steffan has seen me that way. Heat of a different kind spreads through my belly and thighs, chasing away the cold faster than any fire.

Behind my head, a door swings open and strikes the wall with a crack.

"Why in the name o' bloody Christ did ye let her go alone?" Madoc howls, stalking into the room.

"'Tis not yer concern." Efa's voice cracks like a whip from behind him.

"Aye, 'tis!" Madoc hisses back at her.

"Hello," I say, hoping to shut everyone up. It works.

Madoc drops down next to me on the stool Steffan was on. "Ye be nigh on blue, my Meg," he observes with a dramatic sigh and takes my hand. "What the Devil be ye thinking? Ye could have been killed."

"I suppose ye have ne'er done a foolhardy thing afore?" Efa chastises Madoc. She nudges in front of him, a steaming bowl cradled in her hands. "Here, Mistress Meg, drink this. Slow, slow," she says, cradling my neck in her hand as I lift my head to the bowl.

"Thank you. I'm fine." And I am, mostly. The liquid burns as it slides down, but the remaining cramps loosen immediately. I'm still cold and sore and suspect I will be for a while, but the shaking has stopped.

Having carefully removed his hands from me, Steffan stands up. "Keep her warm. Mistress Viviane shall return once the child be tended."

Both Madoc and Efa start, having not noticed him there.

Who is Viviane? And the little girl. Was she all right? I open my mouth to ask, but Efa only guides the broth back to my lips.

"Soon," she croons at me. "For now, drink."

Despite my questions, the warm liquid is welcome.

"'Tis fortunate ye found her, brother," Madoc says. "What brought ye so nigh the river?"

Even through the hypothermic fog, I note the challenge in Madoc's voice. Lifting my gaze, I flinch at his expression. He displays his jealousy like bone China in a glass hutch for all the see.

Steffan moves toward the door, and I swear I can feel his absence like the moon sliding behind a cloud. Only when he's across the small room does he speak, his tone perfectly even against Madoc's accusation. "Arthur Vaughn sent a group o' us to scout new training grounds. Her screams reached us at the hillock below the gatehouse."

"'Tis the child who be fortunate," interjects Efa, bless her. "Pray, good sirs, leave us now that Mistress Meg may wash and rest." She speaks with such submissive formality that the underlying message of *get out* hardly seems impolite. Both men obey, and I smile faintly at her deft handling of them.

When the door shuts and we're alone in the small cell, Efa patiently rinses my limbs and hair with warm water before coaxing one burning mouthful of broth after another into me until the bowl is empty. Finally, with my stomach sloshing pleasantly and my body clean and warm, I'm allowed to curl into myself and close my eyes. As I do, unexpected tears leak down my cheeks. It's been a long time since anyone showed me such care. I think my heart might break from the sweetness.

"What troubles ye, Mistress Meg?" Efa asks at my tears.

I shrug, not ready to confess how pathetic I truly am.

"I'm sorry I lost the soap." The apology falls from my mouth as my consciousness drifts down into sleep.

Just before the faint glow of the room goes black, I almost think I hear Efa whisper, "Damn the soap."

"Ye be the first Saxon I have nay desire to gut," says a lilting voice right as I tip my goblet back.

I suck in a mouthful of wine. Eyes watering, I cough against the arm of my new green-and-gold dress until my lungs clear. When I finally look up from wheezing, a woman with hair so red it glints blue in places and eyes gold as a tiger's stares back at me, grinning. The mother from the river. Taller than me by several inches and heavy with child, her mighty breasts strain against the neckline of her fine, red gown. But her most striking feature by far is the delicate spray of freckles that covers her from forehead to cleavage.

I dab my face with the damp sleeve.

"Sorry about that" is all I manage to say, gesturing to the droplets of wine I sprayed across her dress.

She brushes the moisture off the top of her stomach as if dusting a shelf. "There be nay harm. If my husband does not lose his drink on me afore vespers, my son shall piss himself and blame his sister," she says in a matter-of-fact Irish brogue. "Who—thanks be to ye—still be mine."

I look down at the now empty cup in my hand.

"I tried to reach her faster, but the water—it..." I trail off, shaking myself. The memory of the girl's gap-toothed mouth spewing water is uncomfortably fresh. I saw it in my dreams the night before after Efa got me back to my own room.

The woman's catlike eyes swim as she grabs my shoulders and gives each cheek and then my mouth a firm kiss before wrapping me in a hug. I jump and bumble against the casual affection and her protruding stomach, but she holds me to her tightly. She smells faintly of lavender.

Once released, I clear my throat. "Is she well then?"

The woman smiles without bothering to wipe the tears from her cheeks. "Aye, hale as the day she be born and cried as loud," she laughs. "I be Niassa O'Cuinn," she says and curtsies.

I curtsy back, though after the kiss this feels like silly formality. "Meg Quinn."

Still smiling, Niassa grabs my hand and tucks it through her arm. "I know. Come, Meg Quinn. Ye shall join us for the bard."

"Thank you, but—"

"'Tis ye who must be thanked," she says and turns, splitting the crowd with her girth like a hull through water.

Pulled behind in her wake, I spy an almost-red-not-quite-blond head bobbing along the opposite wall, and my stomach drops. Madoc. This hunt and hide game has to stop. I need to tell him how I feel. More precisely, how I don't feel. I've put off the unpleasant task long enough, though the thought of confronting him directly still feels like planning to shoot a songbird. Or so I tell myself as I down the dredges of my wine and follow Niassa.

Trestle tables and benches have been moved aside, exposing great heaps of dubious-looking hay. I curl my lip at what might lurk beneath, but couples and families lounge in the stacks unconcerned as Niassa tows me through the smoke to the far end of the high table where a large black-haired man is wrestling with a pair of children. The boy and girl squeal with laughter, darting under the straw before being dragged out again. Sprigs of hay stick out all over them like quills.

"Beasts, all o' ye," Niassa scolds over the chatter.

Captain Arthur Vaughn faces us with both children hefted in the air, the girl clinging to his back while the boy swings from his massive arm. "Ah! My lover returns." Arthur plops the children into the straw without ceremony and reaches for Niassa. "Did ye fetch another flagon like a good wench?"

"Nay," she says and moves into his arms like the sea into a cove as the children tangle themselves in her skirts.

Quite without warning, my heart folds in on itself.

The captain kisses Niassa deeply before ducking to her mountainous stomach and pressing his face against it.

"Kill any English dogs, my son? Bed any wenches? Nay? Well, if ye must tend yer crops and play with yer babes, so be it. The night be young!" He pats the great bulge with affection.

Laughing, Niassa shoves him away before turning to the boy and girl climbing her legs.

Feeling alone and awkward, I hover on the edge of their familial bliss until Arthur catches sight of me.

Standing with his fists planted on his hips, he looks like an oversized, bearded Pan. "Be this the *gwraig annwn?*"

Niassa plucks straw from her son's hair. "Aye, milord."

Not sure what I've been called—there's really no telling by now—I curtsy.

He looks me over. Knowing the attention is born from curiosity and not threat only helps a little. My skin prickles.

"What be ye called again?" he asks finally.

I pull myself tall and find the river girl's round, hazel eyes staring out of Arthur's rugged face. My mind stills with the realization. "Meg Quinn, milord."

The big man leans in close. The bite of wine is strong on his breath, though not unpleasant. "And what boon would ye have o' me?"

A boon? Pride and unease flair hot in my chest. There's no end to things I could use to get back home, but the idea of demanding payment for saving a life?

"I don't want anything from you," I say and mean it.

He straightens up, bushy eyebrows raised. "Then ye must take the eternal thanks o' Arthur Vaughn ap Huw and that," he says in a deep, dramatic tone, "be a fair gift indeed, for the life o' my wee girl be worth more than naught."

With that, he bows so low the back of his furry hand brushes the floor.

Flustered, I stare in the empty cup I'm somehow still holding. "You should thank the archers, really. They saved your daughter. If they hadn't heard me calling ..."

I stop, suddenly wanting another glass of wine very badly.

"Aye," Arthur says, his voice knowing. "'Tis as ye say."

"Thank God, not men," says a voice over my shoulder.

Arthur's gaze shifts, and he smiles. My breath hitches as Steffan steps past me to greet his friend. I haven't seen him since he left the healing room, the feel of his hands still warm on my calves, and suddenly I feel shy. I always say too much to him and feel the sting of embarrassment after each new encounter.

"That I do, *Blaidd,* though I be o' a mind to thank the *pwca* as well," Arthur says and winks at me.

"As be I," Niassa interjects as she rejoins the group with her young son straddling her stomach, a thumb vacuum-sealed between his lips. Niassa greets Steffan with a kiss before turning to the girl behind her.

Crooning in what I think is Gaeilge, she nudges the child forward. Freshly washed and sporting a large scratch across her nose, the little girl shuffles toward me with her hands clasped together. Tousled red hair the same shade as her mother's frames her face like scarlet petals.

"Hello," I say, kneeling. "I'm Meg. What's your name?"

The girl looks back to her mother for reassurance before answering. "Fiona."

"That's a beautiful name," I say, not sure how to proceed.

The girl's chin quivers, but she holds her head up bravely. "It died."

I blink at the unexpected statement before remembering the cat. "I know. I'm sorry about that."

She nods, sniffling. "Mama says I shall have another if I swear on Christ's holy cross not to leave the bailey or she shall hide me."

I bite my cheeks to keep from smiling, careful not to look up at Steffan. "Yes, well, don't worry. I was told about the same thing."

Her wobbling little pink lips tip up at the corners. Then she darts forward and presses yet another kiss to my cheek before launching herself into the nearest haybale to hide.

"Will she be all right?" I ask Niassa, who has somehow conjured a fresh cup of wine for me while still holding the boy.

"Aye. She be off to find another o' the bitch cat's litter. Sweet Jesu, aide me," she sighs. "Now, let us sit. My feet be the size o' blood sausages."

Something is off. Niassa jabbers cheerfully as we nestle into a stack of rushes, but I can't help but notice several long looks passing between her and Arthur before he takes up a position along the wall by Steffan and several other men. Sipping the spicy wine, I scan the room. Lord Glyndwr and several other high-ranking nobles whose faces I've come to recognize are conspicuously absent. Men-at-arms no longer carouse merrily but are standing at attention in pairs along the walls.

"Has something happened?" I ask in a low voice.

Still smiling, Niassa glances toward Arthur and Steffan, who stand with their heads bent together, their jaws tight as if conferring about something.

"Aye," she answers but offers nothing more.

Since arriving here, I've been primarily concerned with my own well-being and adjustment, but the sudden shift in mood reminds me that a war is about to begin in earnest. A war the people around me, sheltering me, befriending me, will lose. Attempting to push the unease aside, I turn toward the high table and notice an elegant old man with a face like bark and long, white hair standing near the Arglwyddes, who looks resplendent in an emerald gown. A handsome teen boy with dark hair perches on a stool at the old man's feet, tuning what looks like a rectangular violin with a neck strap. Before I can ask anything, the boy strikes a chord across the unusual instrument with his bow, and the room falls into a hush.

"Who is that?" I ask as a surprisingly loud and mesmerizing voice escapes the old man's mouth.

"Gruffudd Llwyd, the Lord Glyndwr's bard," explains Niassa as the old man and young boy speak and play in turn, weaving their instruments together in a beautiful tapestry of sound.

I nod. Though I've become familiar with a few words and phrases, understanding the song is far from me. But the sonorous quality to the bard's voice takes me back to Cai's story of *llyn y fan fach*—the Lady of the Lake. Pondering the twisting, blurred lines between fact and folklore, my mind returns to Dilys, the girl in Bala. She claimed to have come from a fairy ring, but if that was true, then why hadn't she gone back?

After meeting her, I'd assumed the portal must only go one way and she couldn't go back to her own time. But looking around the hall, I wonder for the first time since crossing over through the yew tree if she chose to stay. Two weeks ago, I wouldn't have believed such a thing. That anyone in their right mind would ever just abandon an entire life. An entire time. At the thought, my heart quivers and shame flushes my cheeks. To even think of such a thing makes me more of a monster than my sister already believes I am, and I drink deeply to cover the thought that she might just be right.

Many unintelligible verses later, Niassa nudges me with her elbow, careful not to disturb the sticky-cheeked boy asleep on her chest. "I would ask ye a question."

Blinking back into myself, I turn to face her and the flushed toddler pressed to her. I nod.

"The men say ye pressed the water from Fiona and breathed yer life into her. Whence did ye learn such cunning healing?"

I pause, cautious. "It's not really healing."

Niassa purses her full lips. "I do not understand."

I inhale and think about how to explain. "I mean, yes, I kept her heart beating and helped push the water out of her lungs, but anyone can learn how."

The last thing I want is for people to associate me with an unexplainable rescue. It doesn't take a medieval historian to know that letting people draw their own conclusions about a woman performing what looked like a medical miracle in the fifteenth century isn't a good idea. While I may not feel in imminent danger here, being accused of witchcraft could change that real quick.

Niassa leans closer. "Pray, do not be affrighted to answer true—be it cunning?"

I nearly choke on my wine again. Shit.

"No. No, it's science. Medicine," I say, searching for a word that will be understood. But I know what she means. To those who don't practice it, medicine might as well be magic, even in the twenty-first century.

"Teach me?" Her golden eyes darken to amber in the firelight.

"I can try." I don't want to think what introducing CPR several hundred years early will do to medical history, but the idea of helping save lives is a needed ember of hope.

Satisfied, Niassa nods. "Who gave ye such knowledge?"

I pause, having not expected the question. "My mother."

Speaking about her is like flexing an atrophied muscle, excruciating but necessary. I wonder if it will ever get easier.

"A rare healer was she?"

My mother loved her work as a labor and delivery nurse and continued bringing babies into the world until the cancer prevented it. The idea of Meredith struggling to birth not one but two children without her or me—

"She was," I say, throat tight. I feel Niassa watching me, though I can't bring myself to look at her.

"Be she dead, then?"

Dead. My mother is dead. Just like my father. The blunt, strangely curative words seep in between my jagged edges, soothing them somehow. I nod.

"'Tis a hard thing." She speaks gently, but there's nothing gentle in her cat eyes as they hold mine without fear.

"It is. Thank you," I say to my strange new friend.

Niassa flashes her charmingly crooked teeth. Shifting to ease the ache in my lower back, I feel the sheath of Steffan's dagger bump the floor. Both it and Madoc's spoon survived my trip into the river, and I can't tell yet if it's a miracle or a curse. "Now can I ask you something?"

"Aye."

"Do you—whoa does that hurt?" I blurt as a bizarre lump protrudes and retracts several times from the side of Niassa's swollen abdomen.

Crooning nonsensical noises to sooth the stirring boy, Niassa nods. "Aye, a bit when the end be nigh and there be nay room for either o' ye," she says. "But not in the beginning. 'Tis like feathers brushing yer insides then."

"Oh, that wasn't what I—" The lump resurfaces and then disappears again like the cresting back of a marine mammal. "I meant to ask, can you read Latin?" I ask, refocusing my thoughts even as I continue to stare at Niassa's belly.

Her eyebrows lift in surprise. "A bit. Can ye not?"

Shaking my head, I draw the dagger Steffan gave me and hold it out to her.

Niassa's freckled nose twitches as she bends over the steel in the flickering light. "A fine blade, that. How did ye come by it?"

"It was a gift."

Niassa peers at the weapon. "Can ye not ask the gift-giver?"

I shake my head.

With her face screwed up in childlike concentration, she

sounds out each word with much effort. Finally she looks up, triumphant. "I cannot understand this here, but methinks it reads: Love covers all things, let us too yield to love."

A green-tinged feeling as sharp and small as a shard of glass pricks behind my chest. "Conquers," I say and sheath the blade. "Love conquers all, let us too yield to love."

A curious, lopsided grin stretches across Niassa's face. "There now, ye can read it, and ye have an admirer, for certes," she teases. "The *rua* lad, mayhap?"

I shake my head, assuming she means Madoc. "It wasn't made for me. I just wondered. Thank you."

Niassa arches a ruddy eyebrow, saying nothing. I close my eyes and try to refocus on the bard and the music, but it's no use. Only the lines of the ancient poem and the questions they raise echo through me like the roar of the sea through a shell.

CHAPTER 17

WITCH

Winter has finally cracked. The cold remains, but as I step outside, the morning smells of sap as well as frost. Sunshine leaks through the clouds in long, creamy bands hinting at warmer days to come. I'm glad to see it. The bailey, however, resembles nothing so much as a soggy anthill as I descend from the manor house. Servants and nobles alike swarm through the ankle-deep mud while the din of mock battle hangs overhead like an audible fog.

The archers have already gone to the shooting range, but I find myself staring as the men-at-arms jab, slash, punch, dodge, and generally pretend to murder one another. Maneuvering around a dirty crust of snow, my attention snags on a ruddy figure off to one side. I turn just as Madoc knocks a spearman flat. Caught high across the chest with a heavy wooden sword, the man clutches at his probably broken clavicle and is slow to get up. Madoc smiles, a boy winning at a man's game.

I have to tell him. And soon.

Instead, I turn toward yet another fool's errand.

Across the yard, a gaggle of servant girls make their way

toward the outer wall. Picking up my skirts, I keep my head down and run after them, dodging dubious puddles and carts of hens as I go. The group is almost to the gate when the girl closest to me looks back. Small and round with a delicate face and large ears, I have a sudden recollection of *The Tale of Mrs. Tittlemouse*. The idea of the girl sprouting whiskers and a rodent tale makes me smile outright. She does not smile back. Instead, her eyes go wide as she pedals backward into her companions, toppling them all to the ground.

"Are you hurt?" I ask, reaching to help.

The girl cowers as if I've struck her and pulls away.

"Get back, witch," comes a harsh rebuke.

I look over and encounter the most magnificent face I've ever seen. Large, wide-set violet eyes stare out of a porcelain face framed by wisps of hair as black as tar. The young woman's lush lips curl back in a snarl, deepening the cleft in her chin.

I hold up white-flag hands. "Whoa. I was just trying to help."

Pulling themselves off the ground, the girls squawk and cluster together as the stunning woman inserts herself between us. Then she spits at me feet. Frozen, I watch each tiny foam bubble burst and dissolve into the dirt before responding.

"I don't know what your problem is, but I didn't do anything wrong," I say through clenched teeth and meet her amethyst stare.

"'Tis nay what ye do, but what ye be, *Saesnes. Cer o'ma!*" she says and flicks her hand as if shooing a stray dog.

I'm too stunned to move as she leads the girls away. All around us, bystanders gape. Embarrassed and angry, I glare back until every last one turns away. Clenching my hands to hide their shaking, I walk the rest of the way to the main gate, chin high. I don't know who she is or what I've done to piss her off, but she can fuck off. I have somewhere to be.

"Captain Arthur Vaughn has a message for Captain Steffan Blaidd," I lie to the guard at the Judas gate.

A big man with sandy hair and the smashed nose of a boxer, he doesn't move except to lift his eyes. I follow his gaze. Atop the barricades stand men holding razor-sharp points of steel that flash, kicking sunlight into my face. The threat is abundantly clear. The expressionless guard casually brings his eyes back to mine.

My stomach quakes at the insinuation, but I nod. With an understanding reached, he unbolts the small door within a door, and I step through.

The archery range sits a good way east from the compound, and I'm glad of the distance. I need time to think and clear my head of anger. Moving carefully through the frosty grass, I replay the confrontation over and over again in my mind.

Witch.

There's no doubt I've been called as much and more since passing through the yew, but this attack felt weirdly personal. And dangerous. I have no memory of the woman, I'm sure of that. I'm equally certain we know one another. Kicking pebbles from the path, I flip through my memories of the last week to no avail. I can't place her, and each failed attempt hones the edge of my frustration.

When the training grounds jut into view, I force my attention back to the task at hand. Just ahead, the great expanse of rolling earth bottlenecks and sinks inward, forming a huge, three-sided basin roughly the length of a football field. Whether manmade or organic, I can't tell, but an eerie energy pervades the place, and I slow my step. Just inside the mouth of the little vale, a large company of bowman stand with their backs to me. Each man's shadow stretches behind him, creating an army of Gemini.

I find Steffan easily. Standing apart from the line, he holds the stave of his bow out like a baton, ready to conduct a grisly symphony. The hood of his cowl is pushed back, and he's pulled his hair into a low tail. Against the sea of dead grass, Steffan's profile stands out pale and sharp as a stone crag.

I stare, barely daring to breathe. The shape of his skull, the slant of his shoulders, the ice-white shock of his hands; I commit it all to memory. When his voice rises in command, the men take aim. He calls a second time, and arrows rip the air with a wicked *thwish* and pepper a group of targets barely visible in the distance.

Dad would have loved this, I think. The thought springs up, quick and benign as a cricket. I shake my head as if to fling the unbidden idea from myself. Neither it nor the tightening in my belly will do me any good now. Determined to remain unnoticed, I creep closer, only to trip.

I hit the ground with a hard *oof* and bite my lip as an ominous whistle rushes overhead. Blood touches my tongue just as a roar unlike anything I've ever heard erupts from Steffan. The sounds jangle my bones, and I can only guess that I was almost shot. My heart beats hard in my ears until the silence rings louder still. I lift my head.

Every last man has turned toward me.

Bows are lowered, though several still hold nocked arrows. Many faces are familiar by now, though I don't know many names, and understand that most of these men, including Steffan, are bound together by blood—either the sharing or the spilling of it.

I watch from the ground as Steffan approaches a thin man nearby, whose own face is sickly pale. Steffan says something to the man, who gives a curt nod before setting down his bow and squaring his shoulders to Steffan. When Steffan punches him in the face, it's my turn to howl. The thin man staggers a little under the force but keeps his feet and makes no move to defend himself.

"Stop!" I cry, but Steffan either doesn't hear me or doesn't care. I scramble up.

After striking the archer twice more, Steffan gently claps the man on the shoulder and hands back his bow before facing me. Blood, either his or the archer's, drips from his knuckles.

"*Bore da,* Mistress Meg," he calls. Like a bird alighting with perfect stillness after frantic flight, his voice is perfectly calm, giving away nothing.

"You shouldn't have done that," I snap at him.

His eyes flash, never leaving my face. "I would say the same o' ye."

Looking away, Steffan speaks to another man close to him, and that man starts barking commands. The bowmen obediently dribble down the vale to retrieve their precious ammunition. For the hundredth time that day, I wonder what the hell I'm doing here as Steffan's long strides eat up the distance between us. He looks furious.

"Why be ye so far afield?" he hisses once we're close enough to speak in normal tones. "Do ye not know—" he bites off his own question as he yanks out the arrow embedded in the ground not two feet from where we stand. He holds it up for me to see, his face livid with accusation and ...fear. Steffan is raging with fear.

I stare at the inert thing in his elegant hand, nothing more than wood and metal, feathers and string. Torn grass falls from the deadly head, and I have a gory flash of my flesh doing the same, blood dripping from the arrow's wicked tip. Steffan hurls the weapon away from us.

There's nothing to say. Shielding my eyes from the strengthening sunlight, I look up at him. His lips are white with anger, his smoky eyes flashing.

"Will he be all right?" I ask, nodding toward the man Steffan just bloodied for my foolishness.

"Aye. Tomos hath been careless with his aim afore. 'Twas not yer doing alone," he says as if sensing my own guilt at the man's punishment.

Stewing in my shame, I freeze when Steffan's rough, warm thumb runs across my bottom lip. The touch is a scrape that has desire coiling deep in my body. When he pulls back, I see his thumb is scarlet.

"Ye be bleeding."

I suck in my lips as if I can lick his touch into my mouth, which has suddenly gone dry.

"So are you," I accuse.

Steffan gives his split knuckles a negligent glance before cocking his head. "Why have ye come, Ellyll?"

His words echo our conversation in the woods by the river, and the back of my neck flushes at the memory of my bare skin exposed to him, the feel of his hands around my wrists.

"To give this back." Fumbling, I unhook the dagger from my belt and push it toward him. "I know what it says now. It must be precious to you, and if I have to leave in a hurry ... here."

Steffan looks from me to the weapon and back again, his face unreadable.

"Please," I push the word against his silence. "Take it. I don't want to be responsible for you losing something that was obviously made with care." I stumble on the last word, an awkward child flinching away from the word love.

Steffan accepts the knife and turns it over tenderly as if it were made of glass. Just then, an annoyed-sounding voice reaches us from below. We turn to find the man Steffan spoke to gesturing for his return.

I step away. "I'll go. I just didn't know when I'd see you again so ..."

Steffan doesn't touch me, though his long fingers reach out, staying my retreat.

"Abide," he says before walking away, the clank of his buckle shield marking each step.

Pleasure spreads through me like the hit of a drug. I close my eyes to steady myself and inhale deeply once, twice, three times. When I open them, Steffan is coming back to me as the men pair off to spar.

"I shall escort ye back." It isn't a question.

Even as I crave his company, the assumption that I need help chafes. "You don't have to. I didn't come to be a nuisance."

"What be a nuisance?" he asks, falling in next to me.

"Something that continually causes trouble." An ironic chuckle bubbles up with the words, and I can't help laughing at myself.

Bright and sudden as a shooting star, Steffan laughs, and I think my heart skips at the sound.

"Then I have ne'er met a woman more o' a nuisance then ye," he says, amusement thickening his accent.

I smile, knowing full well the casual word doesn't begin to describe the extent of my ruinous presence. "I don't doubt it. But I can manage a walk on my own, you know."

"Aye, I do know." His voice is sober again as he tucks the dagger into his leather belt.

Recognizing the escort for what it truly is, I shut up, and we fall in step together. When the archery range drops out of sight, Steffan says in a voice I have never heard from the quiet archer. "The dagger belonged to my wife."

I suck in a jagged breath as the attachment already pricking my heart drives deeper, like a thorn into flesh.

Steffan looks over at the sound of my inhale. I have no idea what he sees in my face, but he presses on quickly. "Hafgan had hair like new butter and kind eyes."

I stop, hold up a hand. "You don't have to explain anything."

But he doesn't stop, and I think perhaps he needs to tell the story more than I need to hear it. So, I close my mouth and listen, no matter how it feels.

"I thought the wanting o' her to be love, and so I took her as my wife as soon as could be managed, the consequences be damned," he says with surprising candor.

I open my mouth only to clamp it shut. I have no claim on this man, no right to a single comment. In fact, I've brought nothing but devastation to his life and am still planning to abandon him at the first opportunity. So instead of indulging the jab of jealousy, I look over at the self-contained hero of a man at my side and picture him as a lust-crazed youth trailing after a girl with pretty hair and flirtatious eyes. The image is so reassuring that I grin.

Steffan, being himself, frowns. "'Tis a jest to ye?"

I drop the smile. "No. No, it's not that. I was just thinking that some things—like young men chasing pretty girls—never really change."

The ghost of a smile brushes Steffan's mouth as he drums the fingers of his uninjured hand against his thigh. Suddenly, I have a realization that makes the ground tilt beneath me. He's nervous. Either to be alone with me or to be telling this story. Both make my heart squeeze a little tighter, jabbing pain or not.

"What happened to her?" I ask gently and start walking again.

"We were children together." His words unfurl between us, a herald of trust.

I press my lips tight, not wanting to know but determined to listen.

"I had just returned from my fostering with Cai's uncle near Llanfyllin. Angharad arranged the match, and though I had not seen Hafgan in years, I was not opposed. She had been a stubborn, headstrong child but merry and strong." He continued to drum his fingers. "Her father be a mercer in Bala still. Hafgan seemed pleased, though Jesu knows I had naught to offer, save a strong back."

The heart-thorn ache deepens and spreads at his words, the most I've ever heard him speak. About another woman. His wife.

"But the match did not please all." He says matter-of-factly, voice riddled with tension. "Though she was not highborn, Godfrey Holloway courted her beauty in my absence."

My head snaps around, and Steffan meets my gaze as the connection clinks into place.

"She spurned his court, and we wed with haste and spent the spring together afore King Richard's call to arms."

I hold my breath, already guessing what he'll say next, my heart aching for him.

"She died," he whispers, stops, clears his throat. "She and … and the babe in childbed. Her pains came too soon, and 'twas nay way to turn the child. Her kin buried them afore my return."

The last sentence is choked out, and while I don't have to imagine the pain of not being able to say goodbye to a beloved, at least I was able to mourn my father properly. To have a spouse and child buried without even knowing? The shock must have been unspeakable. No wonder Steffan has so few words for this brutal world.

"Did you name the child?" I ask gently, hoping it's the right thing to say.

His face pinches, but he nods and glances at me. "Aye. 'Twas a girl. They named her Elen," he says, voice breaking on his daughter's name even as the hint of a smile touches his lips.

For some hurts, there are no words of comfort, and so I offer him none. Instead, I reach out and boldly lace my hand through his and wait. Steffan squeezes our fingers together and doesn't let go. As we walk in silence, the wind rises through the trees with a hiss, drowning out all but the most robust bird songs. It whips loose strands of hair into my face and causes my skirts to billow around my legs, but I don't mind. As always, Steffan's mere presence both electrifies and soothes me.

Too soon, we crest a small ridge overlooking the estate. Below us, the massive timber house rises over the fortified compound and the river, which weaves away among the newly budding trees and kicks back the sunlight in blinding white smudges. Sheep bleat in the distance, and the clean woodland smells of wet bark and moss give way to smoke and manure and humans. At the sight, Steffan pulls away, and I curl my hand around the memory of his touch.

For the second time, he holds out the bone-handled dagger to me. "I know well what it says, Megan. I would that ye keep it."

It's the first time he's said my full name, and the sound rings through my body like a gong. Grappling with the burden and the blessing of his gift and the story behind it, I take back the weapon. I curl my fingers around it greedily as if it's a part of him. And I suppose it is.

"I'm sorry you lost them. Truly. I know what it is to lose people you love. And I'm sorry for getting you into this mess. For ... for everything," I say, praying he'll understand all the ways I mean it.

With an unfathomable look on his beautiful face, Steffan nods before turning to go back.

I take a step toward the compound when an idea seizes me. "Wait."

He looks back at me.

"Will you teach me how to use this?" I ask, holding up the dagger.

Shadows fall across Steffan's face, his eyes turning to flecks of iron. "Nay harm shall come to ye again whilst I be nigh. I swear it."

He says it with the quiet fortitude of a man who knows exactly what he's promising. And I have never felt smaller. Despite everything that's happened, everything I've done, Steffan would continue to defend me. And now I'm asking him for more.

"I know," I say and lift my chin. "And I'm grateful, but you were right—I have to save myself. I'm asking you to show me how."

Steffan scratches at his jaw before pinning me with a wary stare. "I shall not be gentle. If ye take up arms, ye must learn it well, or ye be naught but a danger to yerself."

Relieved and terrified that he didn't say no, I meet his challenge. "I think you'll find me to be an excellent student."

Apparently satisfied, Steffan looks up as if admiring the chalky scrawl of clouds before turning away.

"Is that a yes? When? Where?" I call.

"Do not fret, Ellyll. I shall find ye," he says without looking back and disappears from view.

I haven't made it more than a few feet inside the gates before little Gwilym, Niassa's son, trots across my path, pantsless, and squealing with glee. His tiny penis bobs joyfully as he runs from his mother who stalks her son with the singular intent of a lioness.

"Gwilym!" I call, choking back a laugh. "Gwilym!"

The toddler's head swings around at the sound of his name causing him to tip sideways and stumble. Now sitting bare-assed in the dirt, the thrill of freedom crumbles into a wail of despair. Niassa pounces, gathering her son into her arms amid a thunderstorm of Gaeilge that I have no desire to be on the receiving end of.

"I didn't mean to startle him," I say by way of greeting as I approach.

Niassa flashes me a broad smile. Today her long braid hangs loose over one shoulder like a fat, russet snake. "I be glad ye did. 'Tis hard to catch the wee beastie when I be so far gone."

The wee beastie in question is once again smiling and sitting astride his mother's belly, curled into her, his little backside covered by her arm.

"Well, you can always count on me to make small children cry, I guess."

Niassa laughs outright at my awkwardness before glancing toward the gate. "Be ye expected elsewhere?"

Fast as a rip current, the uncanny understanding of where I've been flows between us. As it so often did now, part of me longs to confess everything, but I hold back. "No."

Niassa purses her lips but doesn't pry. "Come then. Ye shall keep with us today."

After this morning's rebuff from the beautiful woman and her ducklings, Niassa's friendly invitation is welcome. So, I set off with them across the bailey, fervently hoping the dark smear on Gwilym's salt-white thighs is only mud.

The whirlwind of Niassa's morning includes locating Gwilym's breeches; removing a mysterious sticky substance from Fiona's hair; eating an impressive amount of cheese, bread, and small beer; locating a particular herb good for pregnancy in the massive kitchen gardens; and mending Arthur's stockings. That's how I found myself, once again, in Lady Glyndwr's solar, though the lady herself was absent.

"How have ye not learned afore now?" Niassa clicks her tongue at the tangle of yarn in my lap.

I lift my needles for inspection. "Luck?"

Flabbergasted by my inability to complete a single stitch,

Niassa makes it her mission to remedy this shortcoming. Immediately. She scrunches up her face in annoyance and corrects my hand position. Sticking my tongue out at her elicits a giggle from Gwilym. Despite Niassa's attempts to shoo him off, the toddler loiters around his mother's skirts in a perpetual search for attention or food, whichever is most readily available. I turn back to my knit stitch but don't accomplish much. My mind is elsewhere.

"Do travelers still come to Glyndyfrdwy?" I ask, hoping to sound casual.

"Aye, though not so often. A group o' Oxford scholars arrived a few days afore ye, and a lone monk arrived at prime today. Why do ye ask?"

I shift in my cushioned chair. "There was a woman in the yard this morning that I didn't recognize, and I wondered—"

"Owww!" bawls Gwilym from a corner of the festooned chamber that he finally wandered off to. Given her girth, Niassa moves with unnatural speed through the room. Retrieved for the second time that day, a tear-streaked Gwilym holds up a finger for examination. Much kissing and murmuring ensues until Niassa plops her son at her feet, conjures a crust of bread from thin air, and resumes knitting.

"Well," she says, looking at me expectantly as if she never moved, "what be she like then, this woman?"

"Oh. Um, beautiful, actually. And mean. Black hair and light eyes?" I say vaguely as if the siren's snarl didn't stain my memory.

"Viviane ferch Gruffudd Llwyd." She says the name as if discussing a prize horse that bites, and her expression pickles.

Given Niassa's tone, I see no point in being vague. "Is she always such a bitch?"

Laughter, loud and honest, shoots from Niassa's red mouth. "Jesu, what did the *bean-sidhe* say to ye?"

"I don't know exactly, but spitting at my feet is easily understood."

The rhythmic scrape and click of Niassa's needles ceases and then starts again, faster, her annoyance clear.

"Don't worry," I quip. "She missed."

"Fie," Niassa says, her mouth tight. "For all Mistress Viviane's beauty and wit, there be nay love lost betwixt her and anyone without a mortal wound."

This strikes me as more than a little odd. "What does that mean?"

"Just as I say. The girl pays mind to nary a soul except when they be needing her services."

"Services, huh?" I waggle my eyebrows.

"'Tis not as ye think," Niassa chuckles. "Though more than a few lads have gotten themselves walloped on purpose for the chance to shed their breeches in her chamber. Most find her sheen face to be nay match for her sharp knives and sharper tongue."

Even more confused, I put out a hand to stop Niassa's incessant knitting. "I don't understand. Who is she?"

With her head cocked like a tawny tom cat, Niassa regards me. "Do ye not remember? 'Twas Mistress Viviane who aided ye and Fiona after the river. For all her venom and youth, she be a fine healer. 'Tis good fortune our lord keeps her father on as bard."

The river. Snippets of a voice surface in my mind along with a pair of ungentle hands, and I understand. Almost.

"But what does she have against me?"

Niassa takes the measure of me from under her copper lashes and leans close. "Efa."

Standing in the center of my darkened room, I want nothing more than to sink into the cold wood floor, but Efa is having none of it. She doesn't say anything at my appearance. She doesn't need to. Her eyes, raking down the mud-splattered dress and back up to my face, say everything.

"I know. My apologies. I'll clean it myself." I didn't realize until Niassa pointed it out, just how disheveled my trip to the archery range made me.

Efa sucks in her cheeks at the suggestion before brusquely spinning me around. She yanks at the laces in silence, irritation rolling off her tiny frame. I tip my eyes to the ceiling and decide now is as good a time as any to jump into the fire. She's already angry, so why not poke the bear a bit more?

"I met a friend of yours this morning," I say.

Silence.

I squeeze my eyes shut and leap. "Is there a reason you didn't tell me that Mistress Viviane hates me?"

Efa's ever-nimble fingers slip before she recovers the errant cord. "'Twas nay need to distress ye o'er naught."

I look over my shoulder at her, my eyebrows raised in question. "Naught? You think having the bard's daughter and resident healer as an enemy is naught?"

Her small mouth puckers as she continues to work.

"Can you at least tell me why?" I press.

Efa peels the muddy outer gown off me. "'Tis well known that Mistress Viviane hath nay love for Saxons," she says, avoiding my gaze.

"I can understand that, but Niassa thought you had something to do with it … ” I let the statement trail off, hoping Efa will fill in the blank, but she just sets about removing my muddy shoes. Patiently determined, I hold still until she finishes and looks up at me.

"Does Mistress Viviane's regard matter so?" Efa asks, her usually brisk voice wary.

"I don't care what she thinks of me personally," I say and sit down to peel off my wet stockings. "It just—it worries me," I admit. "She's important here. Powerful even, in her own way. I can't afford enemies like that." Certainly not with my chances of escape already so slim. If someone as prominent as Lady Viviane actively works against me, I can kiss any chance of getting back to the yew tree before open warfare breaks out and then …

I shake my head to clear the thought from taking root. It can't.

"Ye prefer yer foes be fools then?" Efa asks, gathering my soiled clothes.

I give a weak smile at her joke. "Yes, actually. Don't you? And leave the clothes. I'll scrub them with the water here and let them dry overnight. I promise to be presentable tomorrow."

Efa scrunches her nose in debate before acquiescing and setting the clothes on the cot. She's dropped some of her perfunctory manners since the river, but when she looks back from the doorway, her tidy, intelligent face holds an expression I've never seen. For a moment, our eyes meet across the little cell, and she's no longer Efa the servant girl or even Efa the friend. In that moment, she is Efa the woman.

"Ye would be wise to avoid Mistress Viviane, but pay her venom nay mind. I be fond o' ye, Mistress Meg, but naught more. Viviane misplaces her jealousy."

Then, without any sign of deference, she leaves me to sit in the silence of my own blind stupidity.

CHAPTER 18

EASTERTIDE

"Mistress Meg." Efa shakes my shoulder.

"I'm awake," I lie in a rasping voice and roll out of her reach. The room is dark, and I've been dreaming of Meredith again: a kaleidoscope montage of linked hands, biting words, hushed laughter. Skinned feelings and dirty knees covered over by kisses. Clinging to the strands of my vision, I drift back under the filmy veil of sleep.

Efa strips away the blanket without warning. Cold air rushes over me. "Come now. Lord and Lady Glyndwr expect the household this morn."

Shivering and irritated, I sit up and rub my eyes.

Efa lights the tiny rushlight on the low table and pulls an oatcake from her apron. The flickering light tosses shadows against the walls like black petals. "Eat. Ye shall need more than mulled wine afore terce."

I'm not hungry but nibble obediently as Efa helps me into my now clean, if ripening, blue-and-yellow dress. Several blustery, dripping days have passed, and the entire estate smells of damp hay, mold, and too many people. Unwilling to be drenched outside, I spent much of the time with Dafydd. To my amazement, the lecherous falconer Rhodri Moel made good on his word and procured a place for me to teach. The drafty, stinking cupboard wasn't ideal, but it had good light and we were never disturbed. With my attention split between a tempestuous student and Niassa's domestic sphere, I had yet to think of a way out of the estate and grew more anxious by the day.

After splashing my face with water and squatting over the chamber pot as privately as possible, I felt more awake. A mistake, I realize, when Efa starts combing my tangled hair and I long for oblivion once again.

"You know," I grump as my head snaps back. "You don't have to do this anymore."

Efa remains quiet. We haven't spoken again of her relationship with Viviane, but the restraint isn't uncomfortable. I'm content to know the source of Viviane's dislike; Efa trusts I won't judge or betray her confidence. It's enough for us both. That doesn't mean I need her constant grooming and hovering.

"You really shouldn't—ow—waste your time. I'm sure you have—ow—better things to do than my hair."

Efa makes a humming sound in the back of her throat that I've become rather adept at interpreting.

"See." I whirl to face her. "I appreciate you waking me up and the food, but I can manage the rest."

Efa presses her lips thin in annoyance. "Mistress Meg would look her best, nay?"

"Mistress Meg isn't going to look her best no matter what you do," I say and dodge Efa's grasp.

Planting her hands on her hips, Efa makes another exasperated noise before leveling me with a look. "Aye, there be much and more to look after, but none so much as ye."

Her frank words sting. Even after the river, after all I've

survived and contributed, does she still think me so weak? Do they all?

"Don't worry," I say with icy emphasis. "I am perfectly aware of the numerous things I'm incapable of doing here. But brushing my own hair is not one of them."

"I meant nay offense," Efa says in slow, formal tones.

"Then what did you mean?" I ask, struggling to check my temper.

For the first time since we met, Efa squirms, unsure of where to focus her energy.

And I understand. Heat floods my cheeks, and I feel so stupid for not realizing it before now. "Oh." The word slips out as I lose my breath. "You've been told to watch me, right? To spy on me."

Efa's chin remains high even as pink stains her neck and cheekbones.

"What have you told them?" I demand, crossing my arms in a vain attempt to hide my hurt. Had I really thought she offered me assistance and company because she cared?

"I have given my mistress naught but a true account o' yer time here," she says without apology.

Silence, thick and spiked, expands between us as the racket of early morning rises up from below, curling under the door like smoke.

"And what truth is that?" I ask, struggling to keep my voice flat. Unfeeling. "Is when I eat and sleep and use the privy so important to the Arglwyddes?"

Efa squares her narrow shoulders, a pixie ready for a battle. "As commanded, I have told milady what I trow: that I do not find ye to be anyone," she pauses, gathering her words, "or anything that would harm milord's campaign."

Her words and their meaning puncture the animosity

billowing in my chest. Any*thing*. My hurt drops away, only to be replaced by shock.

"I don't know what you think I am, exactly, but I didn't come here on purpose, Efa," I say. "I'm just a girl who is somewhere she's not supposed to be, and I want to go home."

To her eternal credit, the young maid comes straight out with the question everyone, including Steffan, has danced around since my arrival. "Be ye o' the Fair Folk, then? *Y Tylwyth Teg?*"

Fair Folk. Each reference to the simple words comes flooding back with new understanding. I shouldn't be shocked. It makes as much sense as anything else. After all, I went back in time almost six hundred years and appeared out of an ancient tree so, truth be told, who knew what I was? Perhaps that's where all legends and fairy tales come from. Travelers like me.

I meet her curious stare, wishing momentarily that she could peer straight into my mind and see. "No. Not exactly. But I'm from farther away than you can imagine."

It's as close to the truth as I dare venture.

Efa's browned-butter eyes go wide before her face relaxes, and she pulls something from her apron pocket. An egg, dappled and streaked with blue, lays in her hand.

A shaky breath slips out. "Is that an Easter egg?"

"There be nay new stockings this Eastertide on account o' the rebellion," she says by way of changing the subject, "but a *ŵy Pasg*—'tis a gift betwixt friends." She hands me the egg. "*Pasg Hapus,* Meg Quinn. 'Twas ne'er my wish to grieve ye."

The smooth, cool shell leaves the shadow of a stain on my palm. Deeply moved, my voice wobbles when I speak the unfamiliar words back to her. "*Pasg Hapus.* Efa."

I haven't made many friends over the years. Grieving, volatile, guilt-ridden teenagers can be dangerous—I could never pull my edges together well enough to fool anyone at school, even into college. It was as if everyone saw me for the bomb I was. Am. A few brave souls tried: fellow art students, a date or two, one professor and, later, Mom's oncology nurses. But no one really stuck. Now both Niassa and Efa have befriended me, but I've been alone for so long I hardly know what to do. Luckily, they do.

"Now, as it would please ye." She gestures for me to turn around and sit on the bed. "I shall go gentle ... and show ye how to style it yerself on the morrow."

Efa's words haven't changed, but her tone tells me we've entered a new space. A place of understanding and respect that is no small thing. I sit and grit my teeth.

It's a long, crowded descent into the bailey for the Easter service, but when dawn finally arrives, it does indeed cut. Spears of gold and pink slice into the indigo sky as nearly everyone in the compound huddles between the stagnant puddles of rainwater, earthbound. Fortified by mulled cider and the press of both noble and common bodies, I do my best to hum along with the hymns. From his elevated position on a makeshift platform, the priest leading us seems younger than me and sweats profusely despite the cold. But he looks over the crowd with genuine affection, and I know any surprise I find in his reverence speaks more of me than of him.

The priest wipes his high forehead and begins intoning in Latin when a familiar energy creeps across my skin, heavy as a hand on my neck. I close my eyes and force myself not to look around for the source of the unnerving energy, instead swaying to the soothing cadence of the priest's voice. But when something brushes my ear, I start, nearly dropping my spiced wine. Glancing over, I find Efa's face pressed close.

"Does *y Goch* know? Who ye truly be?" she asks.

I follow her gaze with my eyes. Madoc stands at the edge of the crowd, watching me with unnerving intensity. Next to him, Steffan bows his head in solemn piety. A believer, that one, and I can't help but admire him for it. His curling mess of hair has been pulled into a tight knot at the base of his skull, exposing the bold lines of his face. From this angle, I notice that his ears stick out ever so slightly, and my chest warms at the sight. He stares as intently at the ground as Madoc does at me.

I smile politely at Madoc before looking away and shrug. If Madoc suspects the true depth of my strangeness, he isn't deterred by it.

"And *y Du?*"

It's perfectly reasonably that Steffan never believed the half-baked story I told about being from Ireland to explain myself, but did he really think me inhuman? After a few shallow breaths, I give Efa an almost imperceptible nod. She leans away.

We continue our merry greeting of the sun until it's well free of the horizon. All around the bailey, whitewashed walls glare bright against their rain-darkened roofs, and when the bell tolls the prime hour, Lord Glyndwr's splendidly dressed family and entourage enter the small chapel. I turn away planning to follow Efa who, as a servant, won't go inside, when a well-known mass bumps into my back and grabs my arms.

"*Pasg Hapus! Cáisc Shona Duit!*" Niassa greets before kissing my cheeks.

I smile as Fiona and Gwilym greet me with hugs to my legs.

"Happy Easter," I say to them.

"Ye must join us." Niassa says, leaving little room for refusal.

I glance back at Efa, who gives me an amused smile. With a pleading look, I allow Niassa's tide to carry me to the mouth of the chapel, over which sits a small, circular window. A few weeks ago, I might have passed it by without a second thought. But today, against the ubiquitous green-gray backdrop of this curious world and its common squalor, the colors are startling. Panes of Madonna blue and cherry red wink down like a god's eye, and I understand how grandiose displays of stone and glass awed people into devotion and submission. As I follow Niassa inside, Efa's egg bumps rhythmically against my hip. Suspended in a small purse at my waist, the gift nestles against Madoc's spoon and balances the weight of Steffan's dagger. I make a fist around my mother's ring and, for the first time in a while, feel fearfully, wonderfully anchored.

An hour later, we spill out of the chapel in a clump of aching legs and bellies. I lift my face to the wind, seeking relief from smell of incense and bodies, before looking around. Across the yard, Efa leans against the dovecote, the picture of patience.

"I be off to feed these wee beasties and myself afore we collapse right here in the mire." Niassa appears at my back, her face pinched with irritation and hunger. "Shall we?"

"I'll be along in a few minutes," I say, rumpling Fiona's hair as she tries to free herself from her brother's sticky grasp. "Fresh air first, then food."

Niassa nods and herds the children off through the crowd. I smile and make my way to Efa, who straightens at my approach.

"Shall ye be in need o' me, Mistress Meg?"

"No more than usual. Aren't you going to the feast?"

"Aye. In time."

My interest piques. After the fasting of Lent, Efa is as anxious as anyone to fill her belly with something other than porridge and eel stew and isn't likely to miss the hearty meal I keep being promised.

"Are you feeling well?" I furrow my brow and look at her carefully. Her eyes are shadowed, and she seems thinner than usual. I could kick myself for not noticing before now.

Suddenly aware of my attention, Efa gives me a dutiful smile. "Aye," she says before adding. "I have an errand to run is all. Shall ye join me in the kitchen gardens on the morrow? It will be nice to quiet down after all this pomp, aye?"

The offer is a diversion, but I nod yes.

"*Pasg Hapus!*"

The shout explodes from behind me at the exact moment a pair of thick fingers clamp over my eyes. I screech, nearly jumping out of my shoes. The prankster laughs and kisses my ear. There is only one person here who would do such a thing.

"Madoc!" I yell and twist away.

Wearing red breeches and a gold tunic, Madoc grins at me like a little sun.

"Good morrow, fair lady," he greets with a cheeky smile.

I shake my head but chuckle through the panicked racing of my heart. "You're a pain in the ass sometimes. You know that, don't you?"

Charming in his predictability, Madoc bows as if this is a great compliment. I smile, not unhappy to see him, and turn back to Efa, but she's already gone.

"I be famished," proclaims Madoc. "I shall eat mutton pie and honey cakes and drink a cask of ale, and then I shall be fit for the sparring. Ye shall come and watch, aye? 'Tis a grand day, for certes."

"Maybe not for your sparring opponent. Where have you been lately? Hiding from the rain?"

"Here and about." Madoc gestures broadly. "Only Saxon dogs be afeared o' a wee bit o' rain."

"I'll try and remember that," I say dryly and shiver when the unmistakable tingling of being watched creeps up my spine for the second time this morning. I crane around.

"Be something amiss, milady?" Madoc asks

"No," I say, uncertain.

People mill about the yard, but no one looks our way. Unable to pinpoint the source of my unease, I stamp down my angst as Steffan emerges from a cluster of archers and starts toward us. He looks exceptionally surly this morning, but the sight of him drives the last shiver of eeriness away and replaces it with another kind altogether.

"You really should try not to look so happy," I quip.

One corner of his mouth curls up in amusement before he addresses Madoc in Welsh, something he doesn't normally do in my presence. Madoc answers before turning to me.

"Milady," he says and drops into a bow so low I see the freckles on the back of his neck where the ginger hair falls away. Upon straightening up, he grabs my hand and kisses it.

Enough, I think sharply.

"You don't need to do that," I say and pull my hand away. "And I'm not a lady. Yours or anyone else's." My voice is too harsh, and the awkward moment distends around us like a bubble until Madoc bursts it with a quick, forced smile.

"Okay. Meg," he says, imitating my voice. He leaves without so much as an incline of his head.

Swearing silently, I roll my eyes toward the pale bowl of the sky before meeting Steffan's long, measuring stare.

"*Pasg Hapus.*" Steffan speaks softly as if the now familiar greeting is personal. He doesn't touch me or even lean close, but the energy around his body sings to mine and somehow I know he feels it as well.

"*Pasg Hapus.* Happy Easter. I'm trying, you know."

Steffan gives the faintest nod, gray eyes clear and bright and sad, before following his brother. As their dark and bright heads move off, I'm tempted to throw rocks at the brothers' infuriating backs but settle for the next best thing. I stomp off to find Niassa and finally stuff myself with food.

It's the faintest sound imaginable. No more than the whine of a fingernail over glass. But it's there. The sound skitters down my bones as I lie still in the dark, small hours of night and listen, not breathing. When the sound comes again, the feeling of being watched from this morning in the bailey returns with force, and I'm wide awake.

Someone is following me.

I clench my fists, straining to hear. Sure enough, the noise gains strength until it comes to a stop outside my chamber. Silence fills the air like a noxious gas, and my body goes hot with adrenaline. I ease myself up and look through the pitch black toward the table where I know my dagger rests. Heart jackhammering against my ribs, I wonder if I can reach it in time and know with deadly certainty that whoever is outside my door is wondering the same thing.

Tensed to leap off the bed, I jerk as the whine starts again, this time moving past my room. When the twisting hallway gulps down the noise, I leap off the bed like a child avoiding the monster beneath and snatch up the weapon. Sweating and shaking, I crouch in the shadows clutching the unsheathed blade to my chest. The smell of the steel and my own bitter sweat keeps me awake until flakes of gray light leak through the tiny shutters.

When Steffan fetches me just after dawn, I'm ready.

CHAPTER 19
HIRAETH

Low clouds hang in rumpled heaps across the dim sky and do nothing to cool the blood pounding in my fingertips. Steffan smiles and raises his weapon.

"Again," he commands.

"Merciless bastard," I pant.

He lunges, testing my deflection. "Aye. Though I warned ye I would not be gentle."

I'm tired from my sleepless night but didn't mention the strange sounds to Steffan. The longer I stand in the open air of morning, the more I suspect imagining the whole thing. Even if I didn't imagine it, there's no proof. And no harm done. Viviane, however unlikely, is an easy target for my paranoia, but accusing the person who prevented me from dying of hypothermic shock seems like a poor repayment. Her relationship with Efa might complicate the matter, but it certainly doesn't mean she's stalking me through the halls at night. The idea is ridiculous, really.

Steffan and I have only been working about an hour, but sweat drips into my eyes, ridges of new blisters burn my palms, and every muscle in my body is already quivering with fatigue.

But I keep at it. Again and again, our wooden daggers meet with a cold crack. Knowing that Steffan uses next to no strength against me, I throw all of mine into every move until I finally overcompensate. Quick as a lizard, he grabs my wrist, pulls it behind me, and presses his training blade to my side.

"Again." Heat and the musky scent of a man radiate off him like an aura, and my stomach does a traitorous flop at his proximity—even if it means I fake died in battle.

I shake out of his grasp with an exasperated noise. Besting him isn't remotely possible. I know that. But it doesn't stop me from wanting the satisfaction of besting him at something just once. Fueled by a picture of Steffan on his back facing my sword, beautiful and ruined, I ignore my screaming muscles and lift the wooden dagger. "Ready."

Steffan takes in my frustration with a sweeping glance and straightens up. "Remember, Ellyll, they shall think to take ye swiftly."

I blink. "Who?"

"Any who seek to harm ye." He lets the mock weapon swing in his grasp. "They shall see naught but a thin, wan, sad maid. A Saxon wench to be conquered."

I stagger back as his words hit their mark, fresh irritation leaping up with my own shame.

"Is that what you see? What you think of me?" Even as I say it, I know I have been all of those things—still am, perhaps—but the idea that I resemble the person I was two weeks ago strikes me as absurd. I barely remember her and wonder bitterly if everyone else still sees only my vulnerabilities. While I know such weaknesses are ever-present, I can't help but feel like so much more now. Here. Not only in my body, which has been pushed and tested, but in my mind and heart too. But perhaps I've been a fool for thinking so.

"Mistake me not," says Steffan kindly as if reading the frustration on my face. "'Tis wise to hide yer strength. The unseen enemy be a hard one to vanquish. The Cymry know this well. We have not beaten back generations o' our enemies by our might and our mountains alone," he pauses, gesturing around us. "But by our wits. Ye must do the same."

I search his eyes for sarcasm. Finding none, I once again lift the weapon. "I am all of those things. I might always be. That doesn't mean I'm weak."

The corners of Steffan's eyes crinkle, and he gives a faint nod of approval.

"Show me," he challenges.

Trying only to defend myself, I dodge two of Steffan's jabs before pretending to stumble over a stone. He steps forward to take advantage of my perceived mistake, and as he does, I ram my left elbow into his gut. He doubles over, and I press the mock blade to his throat.

Panting and hyper-aware of every sensation, I feel for the first time like the animal I am. The exact color of the sky, the sound of my breath, the smell of Steffan's skin are suddenly magnified and radiant. I like it.

From under his lashes, Steffan looks up at me and smiles. "Well done, Megan."

I smile back and step away as Steffan gestures toward the manor wall.

"Come. Let us break our fast," he says, rubbing his middle.

Sore, hungry, and terribly in need of another bath, I plop down in the dirt while Steffan retrieves a flagon and three cold meat pies from within the folds of his cloak on the ground. Handing me one, he sits comfortably next to me and crosses his long legs. He doesn't even have the decency to be out of breath. Reminded of the day we hunted mushrooms together, I push sweaty strands of hair from my face and take the drink he offers. The ale is cold and welcome.

"Breakfast of champions," I say and hand it back.

Taking turns with the thin beer, we eat and drink in silence. After a time, Steffan disposes of his crumbs next to a mouse hole in the wall and clears his throat. "Have ye more lessons with milord Dafydd then?"

I whip around to face him. "Who told you about that?"

The corner of Steffan's mouth twitches. "A featherless bird."

I make a face. "I should have known that bald, old goat couldn't be trusted to keep his mouth shut."

Steffan flashes a sharp grin. "That be nay way to speak o' my kinsman."

My mouth hangs open. "Your kinsman?"

"Aye. Rhodri Moel be cousin to my mother's half sister's husband," he says in all seriousness.

I laugh outright, and it feels good to see the amusement mirrored on Steffan's face. "Well, that explains it. I should have known."

"Blood be thick, nay?"

My smile freezes in place. Cracks as I think of Meredith. Of all the times I've found enjoyment here, and then thought of the agony she must be going through. Shame burns in my chest.

"It is," I say quietly, twirling the wooden dagger.

Sensing something amiss, Steffan backs off and places the omnipresent yew bow between us.

Gently, I run a finger over the gorgeous two-toned wood. "Why is it colored like this?"

"The best bow wood hath two parts—heartwood and sapwood," he says, gesturing to the different colors.

Unsure of where this is going, I lean in and listen. There's no point thinking about my twin now, so I focus on his words.

"After every storm, part o' the young tree hardens deep inside to form the heartwood." Steffan points to the dark belly of the bow. "'Tis strong. Powerful. But heartwood alone does not a bow make." This time, he trails his finger down the blond back of the stave. "Ye must have the soft sapwood, or the bow shall snap." Then he looks straight at me. Into me. "'Tis the scars o' the old bound together with the suppleness o' the new that make the arrow fly."

I shift my gaze to the sky, afraid he'll see the profound effect of his words on my transparent face. I clear my throat.

"Thanks for the lesson," I say and hand the training dagger to him.

With a nod, Steffan pulls back into himself and stands. Then his wide mouth twitches in thought. He extends his hand toward me, gray eyes glinting. "Pray, I would show ye something afore ye go."

I ignore his hand and push myself off the ground. "All right," I say after dusting the dirt from my skirts. "Where to?"

He gives a little bow before gathering up his things. "'Tis but yonder."

Steffan starts off. Shaking slightly with fatigue and anticipation, I follow.

When we round the back of the multi-storied manor house, I gaze up in surprise. A massive chimney covers most of the wall. Made of large stones cobbled together, it resembles a playground climbing wall, minus the bright colors and smooth edges. At the top, the slate roof kisses the chimney offering a perch for the not-so-faint of heart.

"Have ye strength left for a bit o' climbing?"

I gape at him. "Seriously?"

Steffan folds his arms. "I do not understand seriously."

I close my mouth and rephrase the question. "Do you expect me to climb that?"

He shifts his weight as if only now considering the possibility of a problem. "'Tis not so difficult—the children play at it. Place yer hands and feet as I say and do not fall."

"Of course," I mutter, examining the vertical gauntlet. "Why didn't I think of that?"

Steffan, either not understanding my sarcasm or choosing to ignore it, rubs dirt on his hands and gestures for me to approach the chimney.

Unwilling to be defeated, I grab the back hem of my dress, pull it between my legs, and tuck it firmly into my belt, making a billowing pair of pants. Steffan raises his thick eyebrows in surprise.

"You're mad if you think I'm doing this in a skirt."

I do not, in fact, die. When Steffan finally hauls me onto the roof, I press my back to the shingles and gasp. Vivid as a paint slick, the colors spill in every direction, mingling in the shadows, only to reemerge at the ragged hem of the sky. Every shade of green is present: emerald, sage, olive, pine, jade, and lime, all amidst cinnamon tree trunks and jagged outcroppings of gray stone polished silver in the morning light. Alder trees lining the riverbed sway recklessly in the wind, but Steffan crouches next to me as casual as a bird on a wire.

"Wow. Is this what you wanted to show me?" I ask, pushing strands of hair from my eyes.

"Aye. And to say that I know why ye must go."

Startled, I throw Steffan a questioning look.

To explain, he sweeps his arm across the glorious view. "I too could not depart from the place that feeds my blood. I have suffered the *hiraeth* once afore. I shall not again. Nor shall I wish it on another."

Taking in his meaning, I think about Tucson for the first time in a long while. There is no doubt I miss the weight of the desert sun. The smell of the sepia earth. The violent sunsets. But as I watch Steffan drink in the sight of his homeland, I know the longings I feel don't touch his marrow-deep tie to this place.

"Thank you for showing me this, but you're wrong," I say.

Steffan turns toward me, his face unreadable.

"Not that I don't miss ... where I come from," I say carefully. "I do. It's very comfortable and life is much easier there in many ways. But that's not why I need to leave." I pause, weighing exactly what and how much to say. "I made a promise that I need to keep. Going back—it isn't about me."

I shiver as the memory of my mother's wasted hand squeezing mine stings like a fresh cut. Even from the grave, she's depending on me to make things right. To mend the rift between me and Meredith and be there for the babies when she can't.

Steffan lays his big hand over mine, unknowingly banishing the memory. "I did not mean to sadden ye."

"I'm not sad, exactly," I say and know it for the truth even as I say the words.

"Ye have been. I see when it takes ye unawares."

I go very still at the idea of Steffan watching me so closely. My skin warms against his, and I stupidly savor the feel of his skin while I can. "That's true. But now ... well, I'm more home-sick than anything."

"Homesick." He repeats the word, narrowing his eyes in thought.

"Oh, it means—"

"Sick with longing for one's home. *Hiraeth*," he finishes.

I meet Steffan's rain-cloud eyes and release my breath as his fingers lace through mine. "Exactly."

We don't smile but turn back to the view and sit peacefully side by side until a hailing voice from below breaks the air. Steffan presses his lips into a thin line before stepping over me to the edge.

I still can't decipher much Welsh, but the repeated call stands out clearly. Blaidd.

As Steffan and the unseen voice speak, his guarded expression turns grim. Whatever news the stranger brought isn't good. Immediately, my thoughts turn to the people in the bailey below. They are not just dates in a history book, not figures carved from wood or stone but breathing, smiling, bleeding humans, all unknowingly doomed by their place in history. My singular concerns shrivel in the light of so many lives in danger. And I don't know how to help them or if I even have the right to try.

When Steffan comes back, I look up at him framed by the sky. "Why do they call you that?"

He stares back for a long time, and I realize I've gotten used to his long silences. When he finally speaks, his voice is rough and low. "In battle, a man must become a thing other than himself if he would remain a man at all."

I let his words sink in, ponder them. Dad had fought briefly in the last year of the Vietnam War and, being both red-headed and of Irish decent, had been deemed Mac on sight by his platoon. He didn't talk about being a soldier much, and I'd been too young to understand why. Until the accident, anyway. Then at the ripe age of fifteen, I discovered for myself the irony of trauma; only by experiencing it ourselves are we then capable of understanding it in others. We just don't want to anymore.

"And what do you become?" I ask.

Now it's Steffan's turn to look away. "A wolf."

I don't need to see his face to know the name fits.

"Good," I say, surprising us both.

Steffan swings around, his mouth grim. "Naught but harm comes when men abandon themselves to the beast within, Ellyll. Remember that." Then, like the great beast he's named for, he shakes himself and sighs. He offers a small smile to lighten the mood. "Ye did well today."

I grin back broadly. "I told you I would."

That tugs a half grin from his lips. "That ye did. I shall not doubt yer troth again." He gestures toward the edge. "Come now."

Eyeing him doubtfully, I make the mistake of looking down as Steffan swings himself over the edge. While I'm not particularly afraid of heights, the dizzying drop down the side of the chimney is enough to make my stomach clench. My face gives away my fear.

"Shall I carry ye on my back?"

I raise an eyebrow at him, fully aware he's mocking me.

"Don't you dare," I warn.

With a look that says, *Well then, come on,* Steffan disappears from sight. Securing my dress in my belt, I scoot over the edge, knowing it isn't only the climb that has my heart hammering in my throat.

Dafydd rakes the charcoal across the stone, obliterating his floundering attempt at shape and shadow. "'Tis nay bloody use!"

I sit back on my heels and wait for the tantrum to stop; arguing, cajoling, reassuring, scolding, and encouraging are pointless. I've already tried them.

Difficult describes my student about as well as nuisance describes me. In the hour since our daily lesson began, I've witnessed the boy hit, kick, cough, spit, fart, cry, stomp, and try to tie up a cat to keep it still. He's also astoundingly gifted and struggles to recreate the world around him with all the passion of his temperament.

So I wait. After slapping the slate shingle, Dafydd sniffs,

wipes the palm of his hand across his face, and is once more the picture of calm—except for the ash smeared from chin to forehead.

"If you hold the charcoal like this," I say, demonstrating the posture, "it will give you more freedom. See?"

Screwing up his face, Dafydd mimics my hand position.

"Now practice making bigger arches using your wrist, not your fingers."

To Dafydd's credit, he does as instructed, and the earthen jug perched in front of us comes to life under his small hands until it doesn't and the fury at his own limitations threatens to ignite again. We've been through this often enough that I know what not to do. Giving him any attention during a meltdown only makes it worse, so I stand up.

"I'm going to use the privy. I'll be back shortly," I say, hoping Dafydd won't sniff out my lie. Much to Efa's chagrin, I have so far avoided using the manor's public necessary room and had no intention of starting now. Or ever. "I'll look in on your progress in a few minutes."

I leave Dafydd on the floor of the dank little storage chamber where we conduct our lessons. Little more than a cellar on the ground floor of the manor, the room smells of mold and rust but nonetheless provides privacy and was procured by the amiable, if lecherous, falconer Rhodri Moel. Exactly why he chose to help us, I still don't know. Nor do I want to. But the light from the slit window is surprisingly adequate, and no one seems interested in our use of the room. Who am I to complain?

Silence follows me out the door and down the hall before I hear the steady scrape of charcoal on slate. I smile and hide around a corner for several minutes before returning.

"That's good," I say peering over his shoulder.

More than basic, the sketch captures the true shape of the

vessel and shows skill well beyond the boy's years. Dafydd regards the image with a scowl. Shifting shadows wash over his face, creating the exaggerated sorrow of a mime.

"It is okay," he admits. The boy's a remarkable mimic and has taken to copying my speech.

I can't tell if his modesty is false or not but decide it doesn't matter. "The thing is," I say, kneeling next to him, "your passion is important. It could make your work great." I hesitate, knowing the wrong words will be cast aside. "But only if you learn to control it."

"Great?" He repeats as he so often does.

"Could be. Someday." I emphasize. "If you learn control."

His mouth pinches in at the correction. "I need not do as ye say."

"No," I say. "You don't. But you should, and we both know it. Milord."

Dafydd sucks in a breath to argue, but the wheezing takes him first. I sit back to wait again. Any effort made to help just infuriates him more and prolongs the attack. I don't always like the skinny, red-faced creature hacking away in front of me, but I admire his tenacity. I don't know the source of Dafydd's illness, though I suspect severe asthma at least, but one thing is clear: the kid has guts.

Soon Dafydd's breathing slows, and his color returns to normal. "Ye should not stare."

I make a show of staring at the ceiling. "Fine."

"Fine," he mimics and pushes at his floppy hair. Now slick with sweat, the dark sheen around his temples deepens his pallor.

Fed up with the stale air and the darkness, I stand up. "Come on. Let's get out of here. Get some fresh air. Once upon a time, making art was enjoyable."

He stares up at me, his brandy brown eyes narrow and suspicious. "Where shall we get in?"

I shrug. "Anywhere with a breeze that doesn't smell like something died nearby. Where do you want to go?"

Asking is a gamble since, the last time Dafydd chose, I was screeched at by a bird of prey and groped by our would-be benefactor. There's no telling what this outing holds. Dafydd chews his bottom lip in consideration, nods, and leaves the room without a backward glance.

Something nearby is definitely dead. Fortunately, the sight before us makes up for the stench.

"It's amazing," I say and step closer to Dafydd's chosen subject.

"Nay. 'Tis *cyll*."

Tucked into the far corner of the bailey between the stables and the barracks—which would explain the smell—the tree hardly resembles a tree at all. Lacking a central trunk entirely, the cluster of narrow limbs thrusts up from the earth like the petrified tentacles of a kraken. Clumps of tiny red-orange flowers sprouting along each branch only add to the cephalopodian resemblance. Eerie and beautiful, the young hazel aches to be drawn. That does not mean I relish the task of shepherding Dafydd through such a difficult subject.

"The bailiff had it planted ... for a kindling coppice ... but 'tis too *bach* yet." Winded from our long descent into the bailey, Dafydd shuffles around the tree breathing heavily. "Milord father said ... it be mine till then." The boy's tempestuous face warms as he examines the tree, and I wonder just exactly how little attention the motherless, sickly, bastard son of Owain Glyndwr receives under the Arglwyddes' roof. I'd learned that illegitimate children had the same legal rights in Wales as those born in wedlock, but that didn't necessarily mean they enjoyed the same familial affection and Lady Glyndwr didn't strike me as someone willing to forgive so easily. As we watch the branches sway, a splinter-sharp memory stabs my chest without warning.

"It's almost as beautiful as you are, Meggie."

I blushed with pleasure even as I whined, "Mom."

Ignoring my false embarrassment, she stepped back to admire our work. But I saw only her. No more than a few inches taller than my prepubescent self, I noticed how the black soil settled into the delicate creases around her eyes and along her knuckles. The dogwood tree was a surprise birthday present for Dad, but I already thought of it as my own since I had cradled it in the earth.

Her hand fell on my shoulder, warm and steady. "Will you help me with it?"

I nodded, the cloud of pink blossoms swaying at the edge of my vision. Yes. Anything.

"Athrawes? Athrawes!"

Dazed, I look at Dafydd who gestures at the tree.

"Right." I give a forceful exhale to purge the memory. "Wait. What did you just call me? We talked about the insults, Dafydd."

"Be nay insult," he says, looking shocked that I dare assume such a thing.

I arch an eyebrow at him. "What does it mean then?"

Dafydd flails his arms with impatience. "Gog's bones, I know not the *twp Saesneg* word."

I cross my arms and glare. "Try."

He glares back. "One who ... tells another how to do a task."

My brain whirs like the arrow on a compass until it lands on a single, unexpected word. "Teacher?"

"Teacher?" Dafydd shrugs at the word. "Mayhap. Ye be mine."

The idea of being considered Dafydd's anything is disconcerting, but as the title and its implications settle over me, I feel a surprising comfort at their weight.

"Well." I clear my throat. "You need to work fast to get an outline done." I squint at the watery afternoon light. "What angle should we take?"

Dafydd rolls his eyes as if this is obvious and points. I move to stand behind him and catch my breath. Backlit by the sun, the young hazel blazes like a torch, and the sting of the burning-not-burning yew rushes forward in my mind. Will I never escape these trees? These endless vessels of memory?

Mutely, I nod my agreement before we settle onto a pair of low stones and begin. Dafydd moves his charcoal across the slate with the deft, raw brilliance every artist covets. I swallow the tang of jealousy in my mouth and focus on the kind of work he could produce with the right tools. I'm wondering how to get some pigments for paint when a horse in the stables next door gives a sharp neigh.

Startled, Dafydd's hand slips, obliterating the beautiful sketch. With a snarl of anger, he throws the precious charcoal against the side of the stable with a bang. It shatters in a spray of black powder. Then Dafydd slumps to the ground, face in his hands. Bug-eyed with surprise, my attention swings between the shattered stick and the trembling boy.

The words make themselves. "I bet that felt good."

He glances at me through blackened fingers, both defiant and wary of reproof.

"No, really," I assure him. "I've wanted to do that so many times and never have. Well done."

His bony face folds into a smile.

I return it before sighing. "You might drive me crazy, milord, but I'm going to miss you anyway," I say. "But now you're without charcoal. Again. Let's go—"

"What be 'miss'?"

The question isn't a surprise. Dafydd routinely latches onto unfamiliar phrases and demands explanation after explanation, sucking in the information like a parched root.

"To miss someone means ..." I trail off, thinking, "to long for them when you don't see them anymore. Like *hiraeth* but for a person," I say, pleased with the use of my new vocabulary.

At that moment, the sun slips beneath the treetops, splashing Dafydd's face with shadow. He wrinkles his brow. "Can ye miss what be nigh?"

"I think sometimes you can miss what's still close by but not often. Most of the time you miss people and places far away. Not nigh."

Relief floods his face. "Then ye shall not miss me."

Now it's my turn to look at him quizzically. "What do you mean?"

"'Tis as ye say. Ye cannot miss what be not gone, aye?"

Unease prickles along my scalp as I weigh my next words. Every instinct in my body is trembling with the sense that the ground is about to disappear from under my feet. "Dafydd, I will leave someday. This isn't my home. Not right now, but I can't teach you forever."

The shadows of the approaching twilight deepen and sink into Dafydd's eyes. His lips pale. "Ye shall stay."

I give him a long look. Charcoal and tears streak his face. "Dafydd, meeting you has been amazing. Truly. But I need to get back to my family. I don't belong here."

His mouth falls open. "Ye have kin?"

Well, shit. It's in that moment I realize I'm nothing more than a mushroom to Dafydd, a charming apparition devoid of history. A rootless oddity. I simply sprang up for his own usefulness. A heaviness settles in my stomach.

"Of course I have people, Dafydd. And they're waiting for me."

He turns toward the inky snarl of branches. "When?"

The wind picks up then carrying a sharp breeze over us. I fold my arms to warm myself. "I don't know exactly. It depends on the Arglwyddes."

His shoulders sag.

"I'll miss you too," I say and lay a hand on his arm.

Dafydd explodes off the stone, hurling the slate shingle at the ground, where it splits in two. "Nay! Ye shall not miss me," he screams, his cheeks already wet with tears. "Ye hate me, and I hate ye back!"

He runs.

"Dafydd!" I call as he stumbles and coughs across the bailey but never stops moving. Used to his antics, no one spares the volatile princeling more than a glance.

I shout his name again, but the wind snatches my words, hurling them away from us like a ball. I don't think he heard me at all.

STICKS, STONES, AND BROKEN BONES

"Meg."

I sit up and nearly knock the rushlight from Efa's hands. She doesn't have to tell me something is wrong. Her use of my given name tells me immediately.

"What is it?"

"Mistress Niassa hath asked for ye."

I squint at her, still half asleep. "Is the baby coming?"

"Nay." Light from the tiny flame quivers against Efa's pale face. Her bowtie mouth is pinched. "'Tis her husband."

My mind flounders, grasping at possible explanations until it latches onto a scene from the night before. Still fretting about the argument with Dafydd, I spent most of the evening meal sulking over my rabbit pie. Niassa was too busy with the children to pay me much mind until several men sitting nearby stood and left the hall in a rush. Across the table, a furtive glance passed between Steffan and Arthur. They too stood as one. Arthur leaned over and murmured something to Niassa before brushing his beard playfully along her cheek. I looked up at Steffan, my eyes questioning, but he only looked at me— vivid and steady—before they were gone.

I turned to Niassa, confused.

"They be men," she said as if this explained everything. Perhaps it did.

By the thin glow of Efa's rushlight, I pull my gown over my shift and slide into my shoes without lacing either. Dread seizes my tongue as I fasten the belt that holds Steffan's dagger and my purse before following my friend into the dark hall. The walls are solid, but we creep along in cooperative silence. We descend the stairs and make our way across the great hall where the sleeping figures of men-at-arms litter the rushes, giving the impression of a battlefield. I shiver at the idea. Efa speaks quietly to the guards on duty, and we pass under the portcullis into the chill black of night. Stars glimmer overhead like shattered glass.

The question teetering on my lips tumbles out. "Is he dead?"

Efa pauses and looks up at the sky. "Nay, though he hath a grave injury."

"What happened?" I ask, wrapping my arms around myself. The night air is clean and biting as any mountain lake.

"'Twas an ambush on our scouts by Lord de Grey's men."

My stomach plummets to my feet. "Was anyone else ..."

She looks back at me then, her eyes shining coins in the torchlight. "The lads live."

I nod, though I understand nothing, and follow behind as Efa hurries down the long ramp toward the bailey.

The hand is gone. It's not the first time I've seen a grotesque injury, but can't stop staring even as the bile geysers into my throat. I run to the far corner and retch.

"*Sglyfath*," hisses Viviane. "If the Saxon milksop shall be greensick, then get her gone!" she says as Arthur screams through clenched teeth.

Steffan says something in a tense rumble, only to be cut off by his friend's anguished moans. I spit, take a deep breath through my mouth, and turn around. Steffan and another dark-haired man I recognize from the archery range hold Arthur down as Viviane works on the place where his right hand used to be. Efa assists Viviane while Niassa holds his head. No one speaks except Niassa, who hasn't stopped speaking, her voice a low hypnotic hum in her husband's ear.

My vision swims, and I claw my palms against it, focusing on the bite of my own pain to steady myself. When the dizziness passes, I go to Niassa and kneel. I wrap one arm around her shoulders and place my other hand over hers, cupping Arthur's blood-splattered cheek. She never looks away from his face, even as she leans heavily into me. I welcome the weight and hold us both steady.

Trying not to look at Viviane's gruesome work, I stare at Steffan across from me. Only yesterday, we perched on the roof together, drinking in the vast, wild beauty around us and sharing our thoughts. Now, firelight flashes across his face where rivulets of sweat cut tracks through the grime. His bottom lip is split wide, the left side of his shirt covered in blood. Panic flares through me, hot and acrid. Is it his blood or someone else's? Even as I help hold my new friend's maimed husband, selfish relief floods my system. Steffan is alive and whole. For now.

Viviane turns sharply, drawing my attention. With her back to us, she braces Arthur's upper arm against her body.

"Hold him," she commands to everyone one as she raises the violent red tip of a hot poker.

Collectively, we throw our weight forward. As Arthur's heels and shoulder blades dig into the massive table, a guttural howl rushes past his teeth and mingles with the hiss of burning flesh. Nausea threatens to overtake me again, and I press my face into Niassa's neck, breathing in the tang of her sweat.

Then Steffan starts to sing. Gravelly and tender at first, his voice rises like the wind as Arthur bows into the table again. Niassa takes up the song, then Efa, and the other archer. Only Viviane and I remain quiet—her intent on cauterizing the wound, me on not vomiting. I hum along though, rhythmless, until it's over.

After a time, Viviane gives Arthur something for the pain that lulls him into fitful sleep—an opiate of some sort I assume— before leaving with Steffan and the other man to tend those less seriously injured. Efa cleans the bloodied instruments and looks after the fire while I sit in the corner of the hut with Niassa's head in my lap. Apparently, the Lady Glyndwr had the children of the wounded collected into another's care, so once Arthur dropped into unconsciousness, Niassa followed. Wisps of ruby hair flutter around her face as she snores gently against my leg.

Unable to relax, I lean against the daub-and-wattle wall. Looking around the surgery, I notice things I didn't when I'd been the patient myself. Set down into the ground a good foot, the packed earth floor is bare and cool except for the corner full of rushes where Niassa and I huddle. Rows of shelves occupy one wall, each one more crammed with earthen jars than the last, and bundles of dried herbs hang from the rafters. Despite the large hearth, skeins of smoke drift into the room and curl around the massive table where Arthur lays. The space is dark and homey and, though it distinctly lacks food or cheerfulness, gives the overall impression of a Hobbit hole.

Shouts from outside drift in. It's expected. Even mundane news spreads faster than disease through the compound, and an ambush by Reginald de Grey, who I learned is Glyndwr's traitorous neighbor to the north, is more than noteworthy. Efa and I exchange looks of concern but don't speak. After what feels like hours, Viviane bursts through the tiny door. Niassa twitches.

"*Byddwch yn dawel,*" Efa hisses.

With uncharacteristic obedience, Viviane slows her gait. After retrieving strips of cloth, garlic cloves, and a bundle of herbs from a shelf, Viviane peers at Arthur and touches his head. Satisfied with whatever she sees there, she turns to Efa, and the striking black head bends to the delicate sandy one in quiet conference.

Niassa stirs again, and her eyes flutter open.

"Hi," I say looking down at her.

She blinks before straining her gaze toward Arthur.

"He's well. Just sleeping," I say and help her to sit up slowly.

The women turn at my voice. Viviane's eyes cut hard to mine before resting on Niassa. "The Saxon speaks true. Yer man be strong. Keep the wound clean and poulticed. If we can keep the ague from him, he shall heal."

Niassa swallows hard, but her expression is steady. "I would see to my babes now."

Efa wipes her hands on her apron. "I shall ask the Arglwyddes for ye."

Niassa shakes her head and rolls onto all fours. Her belly nearly touches the ground. "I would speak to her myself."

"But you need more sleep," I protest even as I help haul her up.

"I have rested my fill for now." She kisses my cheeks and waddles over to stare at her husband's unconscious face. "There be naught for me to do here," she says before kissing his slack, pale mouth. "I shall tell the children o' their sire."

"I shall go with ye," says Efa, lacing her arm through Niassa's.

Niassa allows this and turns to Viviane. "The house o' Vaughn be in yer debt, mistress."

She curtsies deeply.

Viviane tips her head in acknowledgment. "*Mynd ymlaen.* Settle yer mind that naught be amiss with yer babes and break yer fast. If there be need, I shall send for ye."

With that, Efa and Niassa go out into the gray light of dawn. The door slides shut, and Viviane returns to her work. I want to leave, to get away from the smells of battle and sickness, but pride binds my feet.

"I'm sorry I made a mess," I say. "I've never ... How can I help you clean up?"

Viviane doesn't look at me. "A girl shall come in time."

I stand my ground. "Is there something else I can help with? Anything?"

"Nay." As she speaks, Viviane fills a crude cup with broth from a small cauldron and stretches it toward me. "Drink."

My hesitation betrays me.

"Fie," she hisses, retracting her offering. "If it served me to poison ye, I would have seen it done by now."

Somehow, this both frightens and comforts me.

"I never meant to offend you. Over anything," I say and reach out for the cup.

Standing near the fire with potion in hand, her milk-white skin glistening and a tangle of black hair trailing to her waist, Viviane ferch Gruffudd looks every inch a witch. Her eyes flash, but she extends the broth. I don't hesitate to accept this time.

Crossing her arms, she watches me drink. "I do not spin or weave or knit."

Wondering where the conversation is going, I let the warm, salty stock fortify me for a moment before responding. "Neither do I."

"I cook naught but poultices and broth," Viviane continues. "I have refused to take holy orders, and though I can stitch a man's flesh, I shall not lie with one."

I drain the cup and hand it back to her. Part of me wishes she'd refill it with something stronger. She sets it aside before returning to the herbs and garlic. With a pestle and mortar, she grinds them into a paste before ladling boiling water over them.

"Ask me." She speaks without looking up.

Not knowing if I'm the hunter or the hunted in this game, I play along. "Why not?"

Viviane surprises me then by casting a scythe smile over her shoulder. "For the same reasons ye instruct the little lord bastard and tolerate his fits. We all have our arts, Saxon. 'Tis best we learn young who and what we be and hold fast to it."

She faces me again, and for a moment, I see past the exquisite outer beauty to what she is: a strong, fierce, intelligent woman surviving in a world that will never understand her.

I could learn a lot from Viviane.

Hollow with fatigue and hunger, I emerge from the surgery as if from a long sleep and squint at the frosted sky. Looks like yet another day of rain. My stomach squeezes and rumbles after the intense night, and I strike out into the bailey, intent on finding food. I don't make it five feet before Madoc rushes toward me, eyes blazing.

I give him a tired smile. For today, he is safe. It will have to be enough.

"Are you well, Madoc?" I ask.

He shakes the damp from his hair. He smells of smoke and

horses and blood. "Aye, and by the rood, ye be a fair sight." His celery green eyes glow hot as he grabs my filthy hands and kisses them. "Where have ye been hiding? I thought to see ye in the hall this morn."

My smile drops. "I was with Arthur and Niassa most of the night."

Madoc shakes his coppery head in dismay. "Oh, aye. Be a goddamned loss, it be," he says. "Methinks I should rather die than suffer the shame."

I jerk my hands from his as anger spikes through my blood. "How can you say that? There's no shame in being wounded in battle. It could have been any of you."

He blinks, startled at my tone. "For certes, I meant no offense, Meg. 'Tis only, to nay longer swing a sword or tend yer stock or"—a blush leaches up his dirty neck turning his eyes pink— "or touch a woman. I would not feel a man, ye see?"

The thing is, I do see and am sure Arthur will too once he wakes up. I really look at Madoc then. He's a burly, affectionate boy on the verge of manhood and prone to taking risks. I tried to use him for it too. I admire his fire and humor and strength, but there's no natural sympathy between us. No spark. And somehow, I knew what he didn't—we could spend a lifetime together and never understand each other's thoughts because our bodies didn't speak the same language of desire. Leading Madoc on hadn't gotten me back to the yew, and even if it had, enough was too much.

"Listen to me, Madoc—I've been meaning to tell you something, and it can't wait any longer." I look down to gather my nerve, and suddenly Madoc's arms are around me. I flinch, putting my hands to his chest to hold him away.

"There now, *cariad*," he croons as he pulls against me, misunderstanding my intent. "I shall not aggrieve ye."

"Stop, Madoc," I say, pushing at him again. "Let me talk first."

Gentle but undeterred, Madoc lowers his face to mine. "I understand, Meg. I care for ye as well and would that ye be mine for all to see and—"

"I don't want you."

That stops him. Pulling back, Madoc's bloodshot eyes find mine.

"I don't care for you in the same way," I hurry on. "I'm grateful to you for so many things, but I only think of you as a friend or a brother."

His face is so close I could map the freckles dusting his nose and cheeks. Madoc's hands fall away, and I step free from him.

"I've been an ass," I say. "I should never have led you to believe I felt more than I did, but I—I needed you," I confess. "You risked your life to help me, and I used you." Shaking, I pull the love spoon from its hiding place in the pouch at my belt and hold it out, hands trembling. "I'm a coward, Madoc. You deserve better."

The heavy mists escalate to a drizzle, and the sound fills the silence left behind by my words. Madoc stares at the ground, jaw clenched. I want to run and never face him again, but he has a right to his anger and we both know it. So I hold still and wait.

Finally, he looks up at me. Rain drips into his eyes. "Be it him?"

My pulse whooshes through me as I struggle for calm.

"Who?" I manage to ask.

Madoc's nostrils flare as disappointment morphs into anger, twisting his charming face.

"Play me the fool nay longer. I see that ye keep his gift but not mine," he spits, casting a baleful look at my waist.

I follow his gaze to Steffan's dagger. "It's not what you

think," I insist, but even I hear the defense in my voice. The note of pleading that does, and doesn't, belong.

"Nay?" he snaps. "So my affections are to be cuckold in word if not in flesh."

"Madoc—"

"Do not lie to me!"

The sky opens as if responding to his rage, even as my own temper rises to meet it. "I'm not lying to you! I'm trying to finally tell you the truth!" I shout over the downpour and thrust out my hand again. "Take it back and free us both."

With a roar, Madoc snatches back the precious gift.

"So be it," he hisses before stalking off like the wounded animal he is.

Drenched and shaking, I swallow the bitter tears pressing against my throat. I will not cry over his anger. I don't deserve to. Thunder ricochets across the sky as I wrap my arms around myself and run for cover.

CHAPTER 21
BLOOD WILL OUT

"Damned fool babes shall not leave," says Niassa, looking down at the bedraggled little bodies asleep in the hay beside her. Gwilym, with his thumb hanging half out of his mouth, is curled tight as a field mouse while Fiona sleeps flat on her back, arms spread as if in flight. "Forsooth, as stubborn as their sire, they be."

Pride lights her tired face even as she throws a worried glance at the table. Arthur, though placid and cool, has not stirred.

I smile at the children from my place by the fire. After fleeing Madoc, I sought shelter from the rain under the eaves of the bake house. Pitiful as I was then, the smell of baking bread proved a siren's call, and I knocked. A kitchen urchin answered the door and was so taken aback by my presence that she screeched, threw the loaf of bread in her arms at me, and slammed the door. Drenched and once again on the verge of tears, I clutched the hot loaf to my chest and skulked back to the surgery like a shamed dog. Viviane didn't ask questions. Soon, Niassa showed up with the children, and we all ate fistfuls of the yeasty treat before Viviane left to check on her other patients.

Rubbing my hands against the cold, I put aside the problem of Madoc and think about the danger and hardship that surround my friend's future. That surround my own. "Will it be difficult for him?" I wonder aloud and immediately regret it. "I'm sorry. I only meant—"

"Aye," Niassa interrupts. "Especially for a man such as he." There's no anger in her voice, but a naked heaviness lays over her like a shadow. "But I be fortunate yet. Methinks Arthur shall not leave the babe unseen."

As if on cue, the occupant of Niassa's abdomen undulates.

"Soon?" I ask.

She nods, pressing her hand against the feisty inhabitant.

I really look at her then, this woman who befriended me. I notice the swollen veins pressing up against her freckled skin, at the chapped hands and firm limbs that testify to her strength. And I understand. In the half-light of that earthen surgery, I realize for the first time, why nearly every culture in history worships a Mother entity. Even at rest in a pile of straw, everything about Niassa's waxing womb feels sacred and powerful as her fecund body strains against itself to create new life.

I haven't even seen a photo of Meredith's pregnancy. I refused every offer, claiming I wanted to be surprised in person. It was only an excuse. Remembering this, I burn with remorse.

"What's it like?" I ask, glancing at her roiling abdomen.

Niassa studies my face before answering. I wonder what she sees.

"The first time, ye be as raw and bewildered as the babe ye have born," she says with a rueful smile and watches the dwindling fire. "A grand and terrible thing it is, for certes. Ye shall ne'er know how brave or brutal ye can be till ye have born a babe."

I feel the gravity of her words in my belly, even if I don't fully understand. "And the second time?"

Still staring at the weary flames, Niassa's eyes are twin sparks in the darkness. "'Tis always the first time."

Not knowing what to say, I get up to stoke the fire. The orange-gray embers crackle like fast-rising yeast and quickly consume the new kindling. I add another small log and fan the flame with my damp skirt.

"I know ye long for yer true place."

Her words hit my back like an unexpected snowball, and I turn. "Do I seem so miserable to you?"

She smiles faintly at that. "Nay—ye look well," she says, her voice neutral. "Better than when first ye came, for certes. 'Tis plain to see though, for I oft feel the same."

My momentary irritation turns to surprise. "You do?"

"Aye. Some days I would that I be a raven and could fly back to my own land and kin. To my life as a wee lass." She chuckles softly, as if remembering something sweet. "But I be here now, aye? With Arthur and the babes."

Gwilym stirs slightly before nestling closer to his mother. "Listen now, for I trow little else but this," Niassa goes on as she looks at her son. "The Fates make nay promises, aye? Take what ye would from this day, girl, for it may be snatched from ye on the morrow."

Then she leans back into the hay, breathes out a long sigh, and closes her eyes. Alone in my wakefulness, I sit again and press my back against the stones of the hearth. Warmth seeps into me as the weight of all that's happened pulls my eyes closed against both the future and the past.

I lurch out of a deep sleep as a door scrapes open. Blinking incomprehensibly, I look around, unsure of where I am. A woman with raven-feather hair snores in a chair to my right; three figures lay in a pile of straw to my left. Straight ahead, yellow light falls through the open door where a small, silhouetted figure stands holding a torch.

The figure beckons to me. Efa.

Stiff and cold, I peel myself off the earthen floor and cross the room, careful to avoid the table, where a huge man lays on his back. I glance down, and his name returns to me. Arthur. Flecks of dried mud still cling to his beard, and I gently brush them off. His arm is still bleeding a little from the wound, making a dark ink blot of blood on his bandages. I look at his face once more and then follow Efa outside.

Night's falling, and although the rain has stopped, the chill air is thick with moisture, frosting my breath. Efa has the cloak Cai gave to me slung over her arm, and after handing it to me, she pulls up the hood of her own. The tip of her nose is pink with cold.

"Here," she says, drawing a ruler-length stick from her belt. "'Twas left on the stoop."

I take it and examine the odd offering. It's a sturdy switch made from the hazel tree. The tip has been whittled into a point and carefully blackened.

"Dafydd," I breathe and look at Efa. "Have you seen him anywhere?"

"Nay, though the boy be bound to surface afore long." Her brows knit together then, and my battered nerves cringe, anticipating another blow.

"What's happened?"

"Be not what hath happened, but what shall happen." She leans closer then as if not to be overheard. "Lord Glyndwr hath commanded a company o' men north to Ruthin."

I squeeze my eyes shut against the futility of it all.

"What's in Ruthin?" I ask, not sure I want to know.

"Lord de Grey," Efa whispers. "The *bradwr* who started this whole mess."

"When?"

"Afore dawn. There be a feast to honor the men now."

"Holy fucking shit," I hiss.

"Aye."

We stand for a long moment in the twilight. Just stand there, not knowing exactly what to do next. The normally bustling bailey is subdued and almost empty, a sense of foreboding electrifying the stillness as sure as a coming storm. Even the livestock have gone quiet.

"Should we go up?" I ask.

"Aye," she says again. "Most already have."

Still a little dizzy with fatigue, I lace my arm through hers as we start across the grounds. The soft earth squelches under our feet and I think about Madoc. "I'm a terrible person."

Efa looks up at me. "Why do ye say such a thing?"

"Because I'm sending a boy off to war with a broken heart over someone who didn't deserve his attention in the first place."

"Ye spoke the truth then?" Efa says sidestepping an errant chicken. "Even *y Goch* shall see the kindness o' that someday."

I shake my head, unconvinced. "He might not have a someday. I shouldn't even be here."

Efa stops and holds the small torch up to see my face clearly. "How do ye know?"

I frown into her penetrating, toast-brown eyes. "I just do."

She cocks an eyebrow at me but says nothing as we move up the ramp to the great hall, but her question and its implications ring through me like the toll of a chime.

The room is packed. Young, old, noble, serf, and soldier crowd together so tightly that everything except the high table had to be removed, making it impossible to eat properly.

Kitchen urchins laden with platters of food roam the assembly, doing their best to avoid vagrant elbows and ankles. But the most obvious change is the noise. Or, more accurately, the lack of it. For the first time since I arrived, there's no harp or story, no argument or bawdy laughter. Only the low hum of anxious voices and the shuffling of feet clip the air.

Efa replaces the torch in a low sconce and grabs two cups of mead off a tray. She offers me one before draining her own in a single pull. I bury my face in the honeyed fumes and long for an oblivion I can't afford. After a few sips and a deep breath, I survey the room. Steffan is standing with Madoc on the far side of the hall, his wide mouth drawn tight.

I'm tempted to go to them when Efa touches my arm.

"'Tis time," she says.

Even as she speaks, commotion ripples across the room, and Lord Glyndwr enters from his personal chambers and mounts the dais. Like an eagle surveying his domain, the lord of the manor takes his place at the high table while his entourage files in beside him. When the Arglwyddes, artfully dressed in a copper brocade gown, and the eldest son whose name I can't remember, take their places, Owain Glyndwr begins.

"*Y Ddraig Goch ddyry gychwyn!*"

The hall erupts.

"What did he say?" The last time something like this happened, a man was murdered in front of me. I have no desire to repeat the experience.

Efa's eyes, though wary, shine with an unexpected rapture. "He says the red dragon awakes."

"What—"

The man in front of us shushes me in a great cloud of spittle. I get the message and scan the crowd for clues. Steffan and Madoc have been swallowed by the crowd, but all around us, expressions are lit with everything from ardor to terror. A few look smug. Others, resolute. But every one of them is enthralled by the man who carries himself like a king. Moments later, a riotous cheer goes up. Weapons and fists beat the air as the chant "Glyndwr! Glyndwr!" rises across the hall like sea mist above the waves.

"What. Is. Happening?"

Efa looks at me then, her eyes glistening. "He means to take de Grey for ransom. At all cost."

Blood rushes to my feet like water to a drain, and I know it's the beginning of the end. I close my eyes, picturing the now familiar faces of those being sent off to destroy or be destroyed, and a tremor ripples through my limbs as the grim days to come stretch closer, nearly touching me, like shadows growing bold in the dying light. When I open my eyes, Efa's facing me, but I stare past her.

In the mouth of a dark passageway, Steffan stands tall and solitary as an oak. His eyes look cave-black, and when they catch mine, the world shifts. Acknowledgment passes between us like an electrical current, and I know everything I need to in that moment.

"Thank you for taking care of me," I say, lacing Efa's small rough fingers through mine. "You're a good friend and deserve to be happy however possible." I squeeze her hand once before I let go and cross the crowded hall to Steffan.

Someone begins playing a pipe. The joyful notes trip across the air, and the great hearth fire takes up the tune, crackling and spitting in time with the music. As if in a dream, I move through the smoky room toward Steffan and then, with the quickest flick of my eyes, continue past him into the dark passageway. I don't look back, but my hands tremble when I hear it—the steady drum of boots. My pulse surges as we leave the great hall and wind our way through the tangled warren of corridors. Only when the music thins and the blazing light dwindles to a faint glow do I slide around a final corner and stop.

In front of me, shadows hang across the hallway like jungle vines and hide Steffan's expression when he comes into view. With the cold wall pressed against my back and my heart pounding, I extend a hand, beckoning him. Silently, deliberately, Steffan laces his long fingers through mine and steps into the dark with me. It's not the first time his big body has been pressed to me, but as I bury my face in his shoulder, I know each rise and fall of his chest poses a question my body is aching to answer. Freeing his hand from mine, Steffan drags gentle fingers through my hair, around the shell of my ears, down my cheekbones, across my lips, down the column of my throat until they rest gently at the base of my skull. Every inch of skin he's touched is already blazing.

Cradling my head in his palms, fingers splayed in my hair, Steffan tilts my face up.

"Megan?" His voice is a growl of desire, but I don't miss the question in it. At least in this I am completely free.

"Kiss me."

I feel the chuff of Steffan's laugh against my lips as he finally lowers his mouth. He means to be tender, I think, as his lips brush mine, but I'm having none of it.

Because my wanting is not a gentle thing. It does not bloom, fragile and orchidlike, but stabs deep and hard until my knees loosen and I'm standing in a pool of my own lust as I fist my hands in his shirt and open my mouth to him. He tastes of wine and yeast and need, responding to my demands by sweeping his tongue into my mouth, deftly, tasting, angling me to go deeper.

A moan rumbles out of me, and Steffan goes rigid against me, breaking the kiss just long enough to grab my wrists and trap them over my head with one hand. His other hand grabs my waist, pinning me to the wall as his mouth moves down the line of my jaw to my neck. When he drags his teeth across my throat, I start to shake, arching into him. Steffan hisses with pleasure.

"Ellyll," he breathes. "Yer taste. Yer smell. By Christ, I could live a hundred years and ne'er be satisfied," he says, voice a deep rumble in the dark.

Desperate to touch him, I free my hands and plunge them into his hair. It's soft and long enough for me to fist as he takes my mouth hard this time. Pleasure shoots through my core, and now it's my turn to run my hands down his neck, chest, waist. All I can think about is getting my hands on the tight muscles of his abdomen as I grab at his shirt and pull it from his breeches.

With a sharp inhale, Steffan steps back, freeing himself from my touch. Seconds pass as we face each other in the dark, unmoving, our breaths heaving in the quiet corridor.

"Did ... did I hurt you?" I ask, embarrassment staining my cheeks.

Steffan gives a rough chuckle and runs a hand down his face.

"What's wrong?" I ask. Every nerve in my body sings as I reach for him.

But he gently traps my wrists again, bringing them to my sides. His hands are rough and warm, scraping the tender skin of my wrists. I shiver.

Leaning forward he kisses my forehead and whispers into my hair, "I shall take ye back to the hall."

Now it was my turn to look at him in question. Had I misunderstood his intent?

"Why?" I don't bother to keep the edge out of my voice.

I watch Steffan's strong throat bob in the shadows as he slides his hands up to my shoulders, kneading the tender muscles there. I can't help tipping my face up to him, naked pleading in my eyes.

"'Tis not right," he murmurs.

This brings me up short. Not right? Does he regret being here with me? With chafed feelings and lips, I pull back. "Then why did you follow me?"

Steffan's face is no more than an outline in the dingy light, but the gleam of his eyes disappears in a long blink before he speaks. "I would that I had not."

My entire body flushes with embarrassment. "I see. My mistake."

Not trusting my voice anymore, I push past Steffan, but he catches my elbow before I can run.

"Be still, Ellyll. I mean ye nay disrespect. By God's bones, if ye knew all the ways I want to claim ye in this black corner. The way I would—" He cuts himself off.

Desire snaps through the air, electric and simmering. I can practically feel it rolling off him and settling in my core. I lift my chin in challenge. "Why don't you then?"

Steffan drops my arm as if stung. "I shall not cause ye to lower yerself."

"Lower myself?" I parrot and don't know whether to be furious or touched. Either way, I understand his meaning and soften slightly. "Steffan, I'm not a … a maiden." I wonder if this will shock him, but I press on. "And I don't believe that sharing yourself with someone you care about is anything to be ashamed of."

"Nor do I," he agrees without hesitation, surprising me, "but I would have all o' ye, Meg."

Warmth effuses my body as I take his beautiful hand and bring it to my lips. I kiss each battered knuckle before turning it and pressing my lips to his palm.

"You can have me," I say, almost surprised at my willingness to be with him. I'm far from innocent, but neither have I ever been one for casual partners. Not that anything about my encounters with Steffan was casual.

He cups my cheek. "Then stay with me."

The words buffet my heart with a gale force. I pull away. "What? That's—impossible. I have to go home."

Steffan doesn't move except to drop his hand, but I hear the rasp of his breathing in the dark.

"You don't understand," I say louder than necessary. "I made a promise, and my sister ... she's ... I'm ..." *She's me, only better, and I need her.* I shake the thought away in frustration. "I can't promise you that, Steffan. But I'm here now. Doesn't that matter to you?"

"Aye," he says. "It matters. And ye offer me the fairest o' gifts, Meg Quinn, but know this: 'tis not the fair vessel alone I desire but the creature within. Ye have not yet offered me her."

His meaning worms into my marrow, and I go very, very still. "You don't understand what you're asking of me."

"Then tell me," he pleads. "Let there be nay more half-truths betwixt us."

So I do. Everything. Like a cloud heavy with rain, the story pours out unchecked until every last drop has been released. When the words finally run dry, I look up from my feet to find Steffan staring off into the colorless distance, his eyes shards of wetness in the half-light.

"I—I ..." he stutters and then goes as still as new fallen snow.

And something breaks loose in my chest, stabbing me. I think it's disappointment. Steffan is the most deliberate person I've ever met. He does not fumble. He does not balk. In that moment, I know he doesn't believe me. So I run down the corridor as my bruised heart curls back into its shell. Steffan lets me go.

Sleep skulks around my chamber for a long time, never drawing close enough to swallow me down into oblivion. When I finally do fall asleep, there's no rest to be found amid the nightmares: gnarled, fairytale trees reach for me as I flee some unidentifiable evil through a dark wood, only to plummet into a river dark as blood, my scream silent. Thrashing, sinking, I feel myself drowning, only to break the surface of sleep with a feral noise roaring in my throat.

Chest heaving but awake, my hands are clenched in the rough blanket now tangled around me. Slick with sweat, I don't have time to think before pain radiates through my back and abdomen. I curl in on myself with a moan as the cramp peaks and then fades into a twinge centered in my womb. What the fuck is happening? Gently, I unspool myself until a familiar, sticky wetness between my thighs stops me. Reaching under the blanket, I touch my shift, and sure enough, my fingers come away damp.

"Balls," I curse before swinging out of bed to look for the rushlight. Shamed and heart-sore from my earlier encounter with Steffan, starting my period is not a welcome addition to the night. Once lit, the tiny flame reveals a macabre stain across the white material. Annoyed, I strip off the garment in the faint light and clean both myself and the worst of the stain in the wash basin, the water turning murky with blood. But as I spread the soiled garment out on the wood floor to dry, another ferocious ache starts to build.

With fear gripping my throat, I press both hands to the wall and ride out the pain as it swells and peaks, radiating into my legs, before quieting once again. Sweating and breathing heavily, I shuffle to the narrow window, blood trickling down my thighs. Stretching up, I force open the latch on the tiny window and brace myself as a welcome gust of night air blows into the room, cooling my forehead and diluting the smell of blood. A fat, white moon hangs in my window like a paper lantern, and I know with the certainty of death that Meredith is in labor with her sons.

And I'm missing it.

I've failed. Worse than failed, as I added to her grief.

My throat closes with emotion as I choke back a sob, but there's no more time to waste. No time for tears or playing politics. Lighting a second rushlight, I get to work. The twin tongues of flame lap at the darkness as I fashion my shift into a shoddy menstrual belt and get dressed in the overdresses. Both the bleeding and the pains have eased for now, but I don't expect that to last long. With a handful of stolen coins tucked away and Steffan's dagger at my side, I pace my way through another tandem contraction, hissing at the pain, before grabbing a wine skin from under my cot. The last thing I do is wrap Cai's precious cloak around myself and snuff out the flames with my fingers, savoring the bite of pain as punishment.

The hard edge of early spring has been blunted, but it's far from warm as I stride past the men-at-arms and into the night, my breath leading the way. I'm surprised at first when no one questions me, but it makes sense. Compared to the impending raid and its ramifications on the revolt, my movements are of little concern, even to the Arglwyddes. After Efa cleared my name of spying, the Lady of Glyndwr seems to have forgotten I exist. Which suits me just fine.

But when I reach the dark expanse of the bailey, a jittery, exposed feeling takes hold, and I remember another night I tried to sneak away through the dark. Unbidden, an image of the soldier in Bala wells up, a beast from a nightmare bog, and grabs hold of me. I push back at the memory, wanting it gone, but the images start to flash. Before I know what I'm doing, I break into a run until the sharp whicker of a horse cuts through my panic. Instinctively, I veer toward the sound. A horse. If I can only get a horse.

Another neigh comes, closer now, and soon the indigo swell of the stables appears out of the moon-bleached night. Coming to a stop, I struggle to slow my frantic breathing and listen at the door. Save for the shuffling of hooves and the creak of cold wood, all is quiet. I ease my way inside.

The familiar, musty smells of horse and hay envelope me, and I'm instantly soothed by the big-bodied beasts. Making my way deeper into the stables, I hear various steeds toss their heads at me in greeting. There are no torches, but long swaths of moonlight lay across the packed ground and guide me as my eyes adjust. I stop near a particularly large smear in the dark. The mount's eyes gleam white, and after feeling the warm, wet breath of the animal on my hand, I scratch the underside of its velvety chin.

"You're the one, aren't you?" I whisper to the horse. "You'll take me home."

"For certes, child," says a soft, whistling voice nearby.

I jump, craning my head toward the sound. "Who's there?"

A dusky, squat form steps forward. His white robes glow in the moonlight. "A friend."

The hair all over my body bristles at the unexpected sight of Brother Gwyn. "What are you doing here?"

He smiles. "*Maleficos non patieris vivere.*"

I edge back along the stall door, ready to run. The memory of his predatory stare, the *wrongness* of his presence, comes back tenfold. It's as if I was looking through a veil then at the danger that is now on full display.

"Come now, cunning woman. None o' that. A witch ye may not be—I care little—but since I am to be paid handsomely for fetching ye, I cannot be havin' ye disappear nonetheless."

I whirl at the same moment pain explodes across the side of my head. I'm falling, falling, falling as the mad world goes black.

CHAPTER 22

INTO THE WOODS

I open my eyes to a flat, cindery haze. Pain blitzes my skull, and my vision blurs, nausea roiling in my gut. *Steffan. Meredith. Niassa. Efa. Madoc.* The names filter down through a knot of confusion, and I notice my heart thumping. Once, twice. I swallow hard and breathe, trying to feel all my limbs, even as pain jabs my head. I'm alive. In pain but whole. Breathing deeply, I feel myself sitting unsteadily astride something but can't remember leaving the stables.

The stables. I reach up to touch my aching head, only to have both hands move.

I freeze. My wrists are bound. Jerking back in a panic, I have the sudden, dislocated feeling of tipping over in a chair just before a biting pressure on my forearm and thigh shove me back upright. Now fully lucid, I know I'm blindfolded and on a horse. My scream comes out as a garbled sob against the gag trapped between my teeth.

That fucking monk.

"Good morrow, poppet. Yer senses be restored, I see."

The sound of Brother Gwyn's voice sends my stomach

plummeting with dread as my lungs squeeze out wispy gasps, making it difficult to think.

"'Tis sooner than I had hoped, for certes, but be nay matter. Methinks ye shall not be missed afore sext."

Sext. I swipe at the word, trying to remember what it means. Noon? Franticly, I try to recall what happened. I went to the stables sometime after midnight. Brother Gwyn had appeared then—a nightmare framed in moonlight. I couldn't find a memory after that, but if we'd been traveling since then ...

Struggling to calm down, I take stock of my condition: my head pounds, matted hair sticks to the back of my neck indicating blood, my hands and feet numb with cold but don't feel injured. Wiggling my toes on impulse, I discover a new insult. The son of a bitch took my shoes and stockings. I thrust my tongue forward, trying to push the reeking cloth from my mouth.

"What be that?" he asks, mocking my inability to speak. "Oh aye, when last I saw, the red boy be deep in his cups and beating his dashed hopes out against his manhood." Brother Gwyn laughs.

At the mention of Madoc, I go very, very still. Dear God, this lunatic's been watching me. *No, no, no, no,* my heart beats in time with my dread.

"The breeding, speckled bitch be tending her crippled husband—stroke o' fortune, that—and the unnatural wench-es." He makes a derisive sound. "They be most occupied as the dark beauty shall follow the men's camp to tend the wounded."

At his description of my friends, my mind flies back over the past few weeks in the compound, pinpointing every prickle of skin, every moment of unease, and I wonder how I could have been so stupid not to know someone was following me? But even after the creeping sounds outside my cell, the niggling sense of eyes on me, I never would have suspected this.

"As for the wolf," comes Brother Gwyn's whistling voice. "He shall come a hunting in time. One hopes."

Steffan. My hands start to shake. I pull them close to steady myself, but the trembling only spreads to my torso.

"Lo, abide. Ye have yet to hear the grandest part!" The monk's voice sounds closer now, right at my knee. "For ye see, mistress, that glutton o' baubles Godfrey Holloway shall be payin' me twice when yer archer arrives. Jealous fools, both o' them."

I suck in a sharp breath at the sheriff's name. The filthy rag in my mouth coats my tongue, and I swallow, willing myself not to vomit. I don't need to see the monk's satisfied smile to feel its sinister press.

"Aye, 'tis true. Yon sheriff lived. 'Twas the towering tree up his lofty arse, I say. Too full o' himself to die." Brother Gwyn continues, monologuing like the stupid villain he is. "After leaving that mountain hovel for Bala, I be in the middle o' a shave with the village barber when this demon nay bigger than a dog burst in. Men-at-arms followed, carrying a tall whoreson with a dagger buried in his neck. The *twp* barber left me half-tonsured to stitch up his bloody flesh."

Too stunned to do anything but listen, I suddenly pitch forward as the beast carrying me stumbles.

"*Bydd yn ofalus!*" Brother Gwyn barks, grabbing me again and forcing my bound hands to the front of the primitive saddle. "Hold on, *twp* girl. Ye be worth naught to me dead," he says and slaps my thigh hard enough to sting through both cloak and skirts.

I hate myself for cowering but can do little else while the monk clucks over the creature that can only be his beloved mule, Horace.

When we start moving again, the monk picks up his story. "After the barber stitched up the sheriff, he came back to me and I asked after the identity of the long-shanked patient, obviously being a man of means. The barber gave me the most peculiar tale he'd heard from the sheriff's dwarf. A story about a strange Saxon wench and two brothers who broke free from the stocks," he pauses, chuckling as if amused. "Sheriff Holloway hardly stopped bleeding afore I availed my services to him—for a price."

Then Brother Gwyn's voice drops as if sharing a secret. "For a Cymry Cistercian can go where a Saxon lawman cannot, aye? For ye see, I shall deliver ye to Bala for the sheriff's entertainment, and when yer captain comes for ye—and he will—the wolf shall be turned o'er to the crown. Bolingbroke shall reward such loyalty once this sousepot o' a revolt be crushed and that fool Glyndwr be hanged."

The mule trips again. I hold on this time, but Brother Gwyn isn't satisfied.

"Shh, *bach,* I see her bones be a burden to ye," he croons as we stop. "Walk," he says to me before pulling my head forward by the hair to rip off the blindfold.

My eyes stream, and I blink to clear them. Flecks of gray sky are visible through the trees as the dank smells of rotten wood, leaf mold, and spring mud confirm what I was afraid of. We're deep in the woods. I listen for any sounds of the compound. But there's no rush of the river. No bleating of sheep. No way of knowing where I am. Swallowing hard, I look down at my captor. Standing just next to my leg, Brother Gwyn smiles his soft, toothless smile. Hate, thick and slippery, wells up in my chest. I can taste it behind my teeth as I struggle to speak.

"Scream," he invites, untying the gag. "Not a soul be nigh."

Free from the binding, I cough and spit the vile taste from my mouth before turning back to him.

"You've wasted your time. Steffan won't come for me. He's

halfway to Ruthin by now." I don't know if this is true or not, but I'll be damned before I let this pig turn me into bait.

"Oh, methinks he shall," the monk chuckles. "Rutting dogs always find their bitch."

Blind with fury, I pull back my knee and kick out as hard as I can. My heel catches him in the mouth, splitting his lip with a satisfying pop. The monk stumbles back with a grunt as blood drips onto his robes. He examines the crimson stain. Touches the dark trickle from his mouth, and slowly looks up at me.

"Be that the way o' it?" he asks in a menacing whisper and wraps his bloody fingers around my ankle.

I rear back, nearly falling, but it's too late. He yanks me off the mule with surprising ease. I hit the ground hard and jam my shoulder, skirts flying into my face. Crying out, I flip onto my back, pushing at my skirts in time to see his Brother Gwyn's crystal blue eyes go wide at my nakedness and then tighten into points of steel. He swallows hard.

I scramble up in terror, turning to run, but he's faster. Grabbing a fistful of my hair, Brother Gwyn spins me to face him and slaps me. Fresh pain unfurls across my face as I fall again.

Then he's on me. He isn't particularly strong but denser, heavier and has me by the hair.

When his stubby hand trails up my thigh, I freeze. Brother Gwyn's fetid breath is hot on my face, and bile rises in my throat.

Wrenching my head to the side, I vomit neatly on the ground.

"Filthy whore!" he cries, rearing away. Some distant, removed part of my brain where my soul is hiding notices that his hand is red with blood. My blood.

Rolling over, I crawl through my own sick toward the mule. Brother Gwyn grabs at my ankles, but this time, my kick connects with a crisp snap. He howls in pain. The sound fuels me as I surge to my feet. I lunge for the mule, gasping, just as a flickering ball of twilight light materializes in front of me. The wisp.

My eyes go wide in shock as the wisp rests on the rough saddle before disappearing again. My mind whirls. The monk's close behind, cursing, stumbling, too close, and Horace couldn't—wouldn't—run if I got on him.

I understand. Darting my still-bound hands into the saddle bag, I clasp the familiar shape of a dagger. I yank the knife out just before the spooked animal shimmies sideways and bolts. Clutching the blade to my chest, I savor the press of the handle against my mother's ring, still tight on my finger, and give one long exhale as the world slows on its axis.

Brother Gwyn's hand closes over my shoulder and jerks me around. Propelled by his movement, I swing my arms and slash Steffan's dagger across the soft flesh of Brother Gwyn's throat. His eyes bulge grotesquely as he lets out a rush of sour breath and spittle. Vivid lifeblood pours down his dirty robes, and the monk hits his knees. Pitching forward into the gore-soaked earth, Brother Gwyn prostrates himself at my feet. He twitches as a gurgling sound rises from him and then goes silent and still as death.

I run. Straight into the opaque wall of trees, paying no attention to the whipping of branches against my skin. The metallic tang of death fills my nostrils, and I gag but keep running, wilding guessing at which direction we came from. Limb and leaf and shadow blur together as I tear through the thicket, stumbling over mossy rocks and logs, heedlessly moving in no particular direction except away. *Please God, please God, please* runs on an endless loop in my mind.

Too soon, a wave of dizziness crashes down and sends me sprawling. I have nothing but adrenaline pulsing through my system, and I know I can't stop now.

Get up, I command myself and stagger to my feet.

The lightheadedness passes, and I start moving again, slower now, knowing that Brother Gwyn accomplished at least one of his goals: I'm lost.

My face flames at the mere thought of his name. I'd been hurt before. Emotionally. Physically. But never had I felt so violated as I did now. Not even by the soldier in Bala. I don't make it much farther before sharp cramps pierce my side, and I stop to double over. Looking down, I discover I'm still holding the gory knife and the stench of death is coming from me. From the blood covering my hands and sprayed across my chest. Unable to go on, I lean against a tree and drop the dagger.

Images of the dying monk crumpled in the decomposing undergrowth flash like a strobe in my vision.

I killed him.

From somewhere deep in my chest, rage and disgust and relief boil up together, and I start to shake. Choking on the foul taste of revenge, I slide to the ground and cry.

Time is malleable as the mountain mists. I cannot hold it in my mind. Hours or minutes might have passed before I open my eyes. There's no way to tell. The primal rush of panic has died, leaving behind a cold, terrified, exhausted shell. I look around. Benign tree limbs unfurl their talons and innocent knotholes morph into yawning, black mouths as carrion birds cry overhead.

But this is no enchanted forest, and no knight errant is rushing to my aid. There is only me. The thought sends a cold wind through my chest, but I refuse to let all hope gutter. I have survived worse, and I will survive this too. Somehow.

As if in bleak agreement, the sky rumbles. I glance up. Through the thick canopy, a torrent of rain is released. Tentatively, I sit up and lift my hands. The rain falls hard, stinging every scratch, but as the evidence of my vengeance washes from my hands into the soil, I feel it fall away from my heart as well.

I lift my hands higher and open my mouth to receive.

When the skin of my hands and feet is once again visible, I pick up the discarded dagger. Positioning the knife with care, I saw at the cord around my wrists. It's awkward work, but I only nick myself once and, within a few minutes, am free. I'm soaked and shivering but feel steadier as I get to my feet.

I have to keep moving. More than once, a twig snaps nearby and sends me whirling in the endless greenery. But each alarm proves false, cutting my reality more clearly.

I am alone.

Soon, a chilly mist is all that remains of the storm. The vapor hangs low between the black trees and obscures my view, so I don't notice the spider web until its cloying strands wrap around my face. I leap backward with a shriek, only to land in a patch of sweetbriar. Something sharp sinks into my heel like a knife in cold butter.

"Fuck!" I cry in pain and fall to my knees.

Still swatting at the invisible strands of silk, I bring my foot around to examine it. A broken thorn casts a deep shadow in my pale flesh. I try squeezing out the sliver. But my fingers are clumsy, and bits of Brother Gwyn's blood still cling to the dagger's hilt, rendering it useless. The only choice is to hobble on.

Unfamiliar terrain spreads in every direction. This knowledge sits heavy as a stone on my chest. I do not turn it over to see what creeping consequences lurk beneath.

Several things, however, are alarmingly clear: I need food, water, and warmth. Soon. Not to mention that I could just as easy be moving away from Glyndyfrdwy as toward it. I stop abruptly at the thought. Brother Gwyn—may God damn his soul—had, in fact, delivered me to my escape.

Over and again, I've failed to get home. Over and again, I've caused more damage both to the present and the past, even as the line between the two blurs. Furious tears prick my raw throat as I consider it all. The grief and anxiety I heaped on Meredith at such a tender time, the devastation I brought to Steffan and his family, the responsibility I feel to set things right for both, and the apparent impossibility of doing so.

"How can I fix anything when I don't even belong here?" I rage in response to my own thoughts.

How do ye know?

I stop as if struck. Efa's words boomerang back to me as a possibility opens, crisp as an unread book. In truth, I don't know. What if traveling through the yew wasn't a mistake? What if I was meant to be here? To be now? Opalescent as a bubble, the notion materializes in midair before me until I'm staring at what Mrs. Jones called an *ellylldan*.

A wisp. The glowing periwinkle orb hovers at eye level several yards to my right.

I wait, barely breathing, as the filmy brightness drifts backward, fading into the mist. Either the apparition is intentionally leading me astray, or something else entirely is happening.

Staring hard at the spot where the light vanished, I notice the trees look sparser. The mists thinner. I know if I want any chance of navigating, I need to get out of the woods. Barefoot, bloody, and undecided, I offer myself to fate and seek the light.

The wisp puts me on a path leading straight to the tree line. Stepping through the russet trunks, I find myself in a clearing that slopes into a shallow valley before rising back up to meet another thatch of trees on the opposite bank. With the sun still hidden behind thick clouds, I cast the die and choose a direction to travel in, hoping to better orient myself soon.

I walk for a long time. My head throbs, but the soft grass feels good on my tender feet, so I quicken my pace to chase the numbness from my extremities. I manage to sate the worst of my thirst by licking rainwater from every non-poisonous leaf I can identify, which isn't many, and am hunting for more when an unusually large tree root juts into my path. Stepping over it, I stop short. Mushrooms. My stomach twists in hunger as I crouch to get a better view. Half a dozen soggy white caps huddle in the shadows. A few tilt sideways, displaying their pink gills like can-can ruffles.

I've been without food for nearly twenty-four hours and every fiber of my being wants to shove them in my mouth with both hands. Anything to ease the jabbing pains in my stomach. But I hold back. On that not-so-long-ago day, Steffan gave the final say on each mushroom we collected. I learned a lot, but I'm not positive I can identify the safe from the deadly. Plucking one from among its friends, I brush off flecks of bark and take a long, sobering look.

"Which side of the mushroom indeed," I say and pop the entire thing in my mouth. I'm going to survive or die trying; either way, time is wasting. Without knowing the consequence of my choice, I gather up all the fungi I can carry and turn to go.

As I stand, something shifts in the corner of my vision. Tensing, I look over to find a man standing just outside the forest wall on the opposite bank.

I drop the mushrooms and run. Down the slick slope of the emerald hill, dashing here and there like a fleeing rabbit. He vaults off the embankment in one smooth movement and tackles me, knocking us to the ground. Grass-stained and muddy, we slide to a stop in the center of the dell, and for several long moments, neither of us can do anything but clutch at each other and stare.

"Meg. My Meg. Be ye aggrieved?" Steffan asks, his voice rasping with exhaustion and terror as his hands and eyes skim me, taking in my blood-covered dress.

Hearing him speak my name unhinges the hammered tin box containing my heart. The lid creaks open, and I am undone.

"No. Yes." I sob and wrap my arms around his neck, trembling with relief.

Steffan eases back and pulls me into his lap as if he's done it a thousand times before. Without reservation, I press myself as close as possible and breathe in his familiar smell of salt and leather, now mixed with the bite of sweat and fear. The fragile, terrified part of me wants to crawl inside his skin and be safe forever. With a gentleness that only comes with tremendous strength, Steffan touches my hair, arms, and back rubbing soothing circles over my skin while whispering Welsh nothings to me as I settle my fractured nerves.

Finally, when our breaths rise and fall as one, I look up at him. The hollows of his cheeks seem deeper, the flesh around his eyes shadowed and sunken.

"You came after me," I say in disbelief and hiccup loudly.

Steffan's elegant hands cup my face, his eyes ferocious. "Ye doubted?"

I can't meet his gaze. "After the things I told you. And the raid ..."

"Megan Quinn, do you know naught o' me?" He sounds genuinely wounded.

Unsure what to think, I touch the warm white skin of his neck and feel soothed by the contact. His pulse beats strong under my fingers. "But how did you find me? How did you even know that I'd been ..."

At my hesitation, Steffan presses his lips to the inside of my wrist and gently untangles himself from me. We stand up together.

"To my shame, ye found me, Ellyll," he says, retrieving his bow from the ground before starting to string it. As he works, his face changes, tightens, and I realize his relief in finding me has shifted to the business of hunting.

I lay a hand on his arm. "He's dead."

The words slide out in a sour wheeze.

Stepping back to really look at me, Steffan examines my mud and vomit-smeared dress, my chafed wrists and bloody neck. "For certes?"

I exhale hard and nod. "Pretty damn."

He takes my hands then, gently.

"Where?" he asks. He means to make sure.

"Please don't go," I say. "It was a trap. The monk is—was—working for Sheriff Holloway."

Steffan's head snaps around, his expression a jagged blade. "Holloway be alive?"

I nod. "He hired Brother Gwyn to kidnap me to lure you out of the compound. And it worked. We have to go before they come looking for us. This isn't just about the soldier. He means to give you to the king."

Steffan's only reply is a gruff nod before slinging the bow across his back and gesturing for my dagger. I glance down at the blade tucked into my belt but don't move to relinquish it. Something cold slithers down my spine even now. Even with Steffan.

Understanding me better than I do myself, Steffan lowers his arm. "I mean only to finish cleaning the blade. Ye shall have it back. 'Tis yer right, and I shall not take it from ye."

My grip tightens around the hilt, even as I offer up the weapon in faith. Steffan wets the blade in the grass before scrubbing it on his boots and then his leather jerkin. When the last of the gore is removed, he presses it into my hands. "Well done, Ellyll. Ye did as ye must."

With my jaw clenched, I slide the naked weapon back into my belt and wonder if I'll ever be comfortable without it again. "You didn't answer my second question. How did you know I was gone?"

After a long, pointed look around, Steffan sits on a nearby stone and unfastens his boots. "From a featherless bird."

I gape at him, incredulous. "Rhodri Moel helped the monk? Why?"

I knew someone had to have. Brother Gwyn couldn't very well have knocked me out while spitting witch-hunting texts in Latin. But the idea that the falconer had helped harm me hurt.

Steffan shakes his head, his face darkening. "Nay. Rhodri saw Dafydd with the white demon at the feast. When ye did not return to yer room, we loosened the lad's tongue. Dafydd claimed the monk promised to keep ye locked away for his lessons after speaking with you on an important matter."

Gingerly, I touch the back of my neck. It's still flecked with crusted blood, and a surge of sadness rushed forward at the knowledge of sick, sad, brilliant, mean Dafydd striking me such a blow. Wanting to cage me like a bird of prey. Tears of anger and hurt burn my throat, but I swallow them down. I will not cry for my student. Not after this.

I let my hand drop. "What did you do to him?"

Steffan removes his second boot and starts rolling down his own thick stockings. He pointedly does not look at me. "I gave him to Madoc."

I sway, nearly staggering. Regardless of what passed between me and Madoc, there's no doubt in my mind Dafydd's tongue isn't the only thing loosened after it's said and done. My gut twists, but I steady myself.

"What are you doing?" I ask suddenly as Steffan now stands barefoot in the grass.

He hands me his stockings and boots. "I left the horse in a thicket some ways back to track on foot," he says and looks down at my frozen, battered toes. "Ye shall be needing these."

"I can walk."

"Aye, ye can. But ye shall wear those or be carried."

I suck in my cheeks but decide my feet hurt more than my pride for once.

"Thank you," I say and accept the stockings.

Once Steffan has fastened the huge shoes around my feet and calves, he stands up. "Meg?"

Memories from the night before rise to the surface like good cream: his taste, the pressure of his fingertips, his stubborn refusal to make love to me, my own jumbled confession. I raise my eyes to his, questioning in turn.

Hesitantly, and with great tenderness, Steffan leans down and kisses my scratched cheeks. Like molten dross before a blazing forge, the barrier around my heart melts away. Unaware of his effect, Steffan straightens up and holds out his hand. With tears gleaming in my eyes, I take it as we move up the embankment together.

CHAPTER 23

FOREVERMORE

Thankfully, I chose the mushrooms well. After a scolding from Steffan for my "foolhardiness," we retrieve them and eat several handfuls each before moving on in relative silence. When we escaped from Sheriff Holloway in Bala, there was no time to recount our separate stories. It's the same now. Perhaps someday Steffan and I would share those tales, but there was no need at the moment. I had been taken, abused, and killed a man. Steffan had abandoned his lord and comrades to find me after turning a child over to interrogation. Neither of us were ready to discuss the consequences.

Soon, we reach the clearing where Steffan left the horse and drink our fill from a nearby stream. The mists are burning off, and welcome sunlight trickles down our backs as we mount the horse and turn north—the direction of Glyndyfrdwy. The inevitability of this sits heavy on my conscience. But I don't protest.

We travel slowly. As night falls, we camp in a grove of young oak. Once our stomachs are reasonably full of salted meat and stale bread Steffan finds in the saddle bag, we settle down without a fire. There's a solid chance the sheriff is looking for us by now, and we're in no hurry to attract attention. Stars blaze in cold disinterest as Steffan and I nestle into our den of grass and tender branches. Imagining myself a small, burrowing animal, I watch the rise and fall of Steffan's broad ribcage as he faces away from me. In, out. In, out. Overhead, new leaves rustle in the wind. But my head and foot still ache, and sleep won't come.

"Tell me a story," I whisper, not sure if he's awake.

In, out. In, out.

"What kind of story?" Steffan asks in voice thick with weariness.

I don't need to think long. "Tell me about your mother."

In, out. Steffan rolls onto his back, and I watch the movement of his belly as he begins.

"I remember more o' how I felt around her than the woman herself. How ye remember a song, though ye cannot recall the tune, aye?" His voice tells me he's smiling. "She smelled o' beeswax and was quick to laugh. And her hair, 'twas like mine, always about her face and loose under her coif. She slapped me once."

"Why?" I ask, surprised by the sudden shift.

"The year afore I fostered with Cai's kin, a badger had been after the hens. I left the pen open one night, and by morn, the coop, 'twas covered with blood and feathers. She made me wash each stone. I thought myself a man then and above women's work."

I cringe. "And you told her this?"

"Aye and with many a curse against the Blessed Virgin. I had not been thrashed in some time, and it shocked us both," he says with a chuckle.

My skin prickles with cold, and I inch closer to his heat. After a moment's hesitation, Steffan raises his arm, and I scoot under it, his warm hand pressing against my shoulder. Conscious of his hard body under my head, I try to lie still instead of squirming closer the way I want to.

"She died abed with Gwenhwyfar. I fear I be cursed and the women I love as well."

He says this without evident pain, but I know the kind of scars such things leave.

I splay my hand over his heart. "You're not cursed, Steffan. She must have loved you so much. They both did. I'm sure of it."

Steffan covers my hand with his and after a long silence, we sink into sleep.

In one palm, a soft skull tufted with chestnut hair. In the other, a crest of dandelion fuzz. With a baby cradled in each arm, Meredith guides her sons' greedy mouths toward her dripping nipples until the three are pressed together, the line between breast and cheek blurred into one flesh. Behind them, a tall shadow lays a hand on her white shoulder. Meredith tips her head back as a smile, raw and sad and radiant, molds itself to her mouth. The figure dips to meet my mirror image with a kiss.

I open my eyes, and the dream blows away like a puff of smoke. All that remains is a gentle ache at the tip of each breast and the assurance of Meredith's heartbroken happiness. Smiling my own sad smile as tears slide down my temples, I stare up at the slice of moonlight slanting into our den, the same moonlight that somehow cocoons my sister and her new family.

Against my side, Steffan sleeps warm and solid as a sun-drenched rock, despite the cool night air. Turning to him, I watch his pulse ripple under the translucent skin of his neck and marvel at him. Sculpted from a life of labor and war, his long muscles remain taut even in sleep, but his wide mouth relaxes into a pout that reveals the dough-faced child he must have been.

Slowly, I push myself up and brush my lips against his.

Immediately, Steffan opens his eyes. His arms slide around my waist and draw me on top of him as my hair falls around us, mimicking the shelter of the trees. Intensely aware of his shape pressed against me, I nudge his chin upward and kiss his neck where the blood beats between us.

Steffan's big hands cup my face, guiding me to his mouth.

Warm and sweet, every kiss grows more urgent. A desperate clash of tongues and teeth until a moan hums through me and Steffan breaks away. Again.

"Be still, my Meg," he pants, clearly trying to master his lust.

"I don't want to," I say and slide my hands under his shirt to his powerful chest. Heat coils tight in my core.

Steffan sits up, causing me to straddle his lap where the evidence of his desire presses against me, and I can't help but rock into him. With a hiss, he holds my body away. Once again, the bite of his reluctance takes hold, and I drop my hands. He would never force me, so I stop moving and try to understand.

"Don't lie and tell me this is about sin," I say. "You've killed for me. Twice. If you don't want me, then just say so, but please don't claim rejecting me is about morality."

Steffan takes a deep, shuddering breath. "'Tis not a lie." He catches my chin and forces me to look at him, his features divided by the moonlight like a theater mask. "If defending ye from harm be a sin, then on my soul alone let it rest. Have nay doubt that I want ye Meg Quinn. I long for ye, body and soul.

God save me, I burn with the wanting. But by my troth, I shall not lay with ye and dishonor us both."

His eyes shine like gray stones, ardent. I couldn't look away if my life depended on it.

A night breeze scuttles through the branches and tips my heart into its final, fatal plunge. "I don't have that kind of power over anyone, Steffan. Least of all you."

"Ye be wrong," he whispers, letting his hands fall away. "For if we become one, I shall lose myself to ye forevermore. And ye have not promised me that."

Knowing I could never dishonor such a man, I let him cradle me and lay us back down to sleep. Love, after all, is never a dishonor.

I wake again early in the morning to feel my old life slip behind the horizon with the setting moon. Cold air stings my nostrils, but with each exhale, I feel brittle shards of grief and insecurity, displacement and misdirection, slough off. Blinking against the gray light, I imagine myself sliding across the forest floor, slick and glistening. A new creation. Tears prick my eyes, but for once, they aren't tears of frustration or pain or sadness.

There's only one thing left to do.

I sit up and nudge Steffan. He opens his eyes without moving, a dagger already in hand. Then he sees me and gives two slow, sleepy cat blinks.

"I need to say something," I tell him.

An odd expression of interest and dread settles over Steffan's tired face as he pushes himself up. I face him, open my mouth to speak and promptly close it, my neck flushing. How am I supposed to ask something impossible?

Sensing my struggle as he so often does, Steffan laces his chilled fingers through mine.

"Be not affrighted, Ellyll, whatever it be," he says and gives me a small, brave smile.

I nod and let the words fall free. "I know you think I'm mad after what I told you about where I come from. But I'm not. It's the truth."

Silence unfolds between us, eating up the moments. Finally, Steffan meets my gaze. "I do not understand." He pauses. Breathes. I hold my breath. "But do not believe ye to be mad, Ellyll. So, tell me yer truth, and I shall believe it."

My throat tightens with something like hope even as my hands shake. "I think the yew in the churchyard marks some kind of doorway between our times. I don't know how or why it works, only that I was in my time and then the tree brought me here."

Steffan frowns thoughtfully. "The day at St. Melangell's. 'Twas then that ye ... traveled?"

I nod. "It was just a few minutes before I came into the church and found you."

He takes back his hands and crosses himself. "*Alban Eilir.*"

"What does that mean?"

"'Tis the old name for spring's first day. Stories abound o' folks being carried off by *y Tylwyth Teg* at such times." He pauses. "And o' such creatures moving among us."

"Like Cai's story about the Lady of the Lake?"

"Aye."

"So you believe me?" I wait, suspended in time, my heart vibrating in my throat.

Steffan's pewter eyes trace my features, searching. He nods, and I know he's telling me the truth. I exhale, my relief a near violent thing, and reach out to hug him. He flinches away, and my momentary joy bursts like a dropped plum.

"Steffan. It's just me. Please." Again, I reach out.

He doesn't pull away this time but watches my fingers as if they might sink into his chest and emerge with his still-beating heart. Fighting back a sob, I let my hand fall away just as Steffan catches it in his own, crushing our fingers together.

"Forgive me. I know well what ye be. I always have, in a way. 'Tis more than I can understand, but I shall not make light o' the old stories or o' yer word." Easing his grasp, Steffan rubs my knuckles with his thumb. "Shall I take ye there then?" he asks, no longer looking at me but at our joined hands. "Back to yer place?"

There it is. The thing I've been yearning to hear for nearly a month. Someone I trust deeply is offering me passage back to the yew tree and, with it, the chance to return to my own time. To safety and prosperity. To Meredith and her new family. I close my eyes and imagine it: barging in on Reverend Fitzwilliam and Mrs. Jones; trying to give the police a plausible explanation for my disappearance; forgiving Meredith for leaving me to care for Mom as she died; holding my nephews; going back to school and moving on with life as if the people I've met, the things I've seen and felt here, don't exist. Because they wouldn't. Not for hundreds of years.

I open my eyes. Over Steffan's shoulder, through a gap in the trees, molten sunlight crests the horizon carrying the possibility of a new day—and a new life—on its back. I stare, picturing it, until a dark form streaks across the sky. For one confused moment, I assume it's an airplane until the darting object comes into focus. Just a hawk. Nothing more than talons and sinew, feathers and blood. And with the realization comes a bolt of relief and my answer.

"Meg?" Steffan's voice is rigid with fear.

I turn and see my new life unfurling before me.

"No." I speak quietly, tasting the word and its consequences.

Steffan's eyes sharpen even as his mouth opens in disbelief. "Nay?"

Breathless with fear and joy, I smile and don't bother wiping away the tears that spill down my cheeks. "No. I don't want you to take me back. I will stay."

Like a man struck down, Steffan presses his face into my lap. "Truly?" he asks, kissing my palm. "Be ye certain?"

I run my fingers through his hair and feel the crisp snap of my heart: part blooming, part withering as love and loss flow in equal parts. There is no clear joy, no easy choice. Only the one I can live best with.

"No," I say. "But I'm going to stay anyway."

Grim, obstinate, stoic Steffan lifts his face and flashes the brightest smile imaginable, his eyes glassy. "Will ye have me? Will ye let me love all o' ye?"

My pulse jumps as heat floods my body. I nod. "Yes."

Reeking, hungry, sore, and grinning like fools, Steffan and I kneel among the trees and kiss until an irrevocable yearning rolls over my heart and I know I'll love him for the rest of my life.

"Would ye have us wait for a priest?" he asks between kisses. Even as he sucks on my bottom lip, I know Steffan would remain abstinent indefinitely if I asked.

I am not so longsuffering. "Don't you dare."

Steffan laughs as he tucks a tangled strand of hair behind my ear before lacing his fingers through mine. He's trembling. "Shall we be handfast then? Will ye hear my vow?"

Vows. My mind trips back to Meredith's rose-and-lavender-laden wedding the summer before, and a sliver of my pride objects. I'd never imagined an elaborate wedding but would have liked something memorable. Something beautiful. Then my gaze drifts up, and I notice the pink light spilling over us. Hear the tinkling of new leaves and the chorus of bird songs. Smell the fresh, dew-damp grass under me and know there is no more perfect fairy bower than this.

Steffan senses my hesitation.

"A moment," he says and darts from our hiding place, returning seconds later with a handful of yellow-and-white wildflowers, their star-shaped petals splayed.

I smile at his understanding and reach for them. "They're beautiful."

But Steffan keeps hold of the flowers before tucking a single stem behind my ear.

"Ye be most fair, Ellyll, always. But today ye shall be a fae queen," he says and proceeds to spangle my hair with blossoms.

My head spins with the tenderness of it, and I can't help watching as he works. The concentrated set of his mouth, the flecks of gold in his slate eyes. The care he takes to place every blossom just so and brush the tangles from my face.

"Will you help me with the words?" I ask when he's finished.

"Always," says my fierce, ragged bowman, and he presses my hands to his chest before crossing himself. "Be ye ready, Ellyll?"

I swallow and lick my lips, my mouth suddenly dry. "Yes."

Steffan nods and steadies himself with a breath. "I, Steffan ap Hugh Goch, take ye, Megan Alice Quinn, to be my wedded wife, to worship with my body and endow with my riches, according to God's holy law, and thereunto I plight ye my troth."

For a moment I can't breathe, let alone speak, but when I find my voice, it's steady as I seal my fate. "I, Megan Alice Quinn, take you, Steffan ap Hugh Goch, to be my wedded husband, to worship with my body and endow with my riches, according to God's holy law, and thereunto I plight you my troth."

Steffan crosses himself again, and I lean in for a kiss. But he's already undoing the laces at the front of his jerkin.

I furrow my brow in amusement. "Well I'm in a hurry too, but you could at least kiss me."

With a lopsided grin, Steffan pulls one of the laces free. "'Tis not quite as the lady supposes," he says with a wicked smile before wrapping the strand of material around our joined hands. "Now ye be blood o' my blood and bone o' my bone. I give ye my body that we might be one."

With my palm pressed to Steffan's, I repeat the words and feel an unexpected prick of shyness as we exchange a gentle, church-worthy kiss. My bleeding seems to have stopped with the phantom pains from Meredith's labor, so there's no point in waiting. I scoot onto my hip and push off Steffan's boots. The oversized stockings slip down my calves unaided, but the laces on my bodice tangle as I tug at them. A blush spreads up my neck, despite the pooling desire in my belly. I've wanted him for so long now but suddenly feel shy.

Steffan sits still, watching. So still that I jump when he stops my attempt at undressing. I let my hands drop, expecting him to take over the task. He doesn't. Instead, he crawls outside the bower and, standing in the middle of the dawn-drenched meadow, unfastens his belt. Then his jerkin and heavy outer shirt drop to the ground. Then his linen undershirt. Standing bare chested, the smug asshole smirks— actually smirks—as he takes off his dark breeches. Piece by piece, Steffan shows himself to me so I don't have to be the first.

Moved and emboldened by his tender offering, I let my eyes wander, drinking in his beauty. Chestnut curls fall around his ears and down his neck while auburn whiskers stand out on the clean lines of his jaw and chin. Steffan's milky, battle-scarred skin—marred by whirling cowlicks of black hair across his chest, forearms, thighs, and groin—hold powerful muscles tight against long bones. I watch as his flesh goose-pimples in the open air and his hard cock twitches under the heat of my open gaze.

Still staring at the proof of his desire, I rise to my feet just outside the bower. Looking down at my tangled laces, I choose one with care and unsheathe my blade. Then I find Steffan's vivid gaze and hold it, unflinching.

"I love you, too," I say and cut the lace. My hands tremble with longing as I unfasten the belt and push down my outer gown, filthy and ruined as it is. The breeze molds the thin underdress to my skin before I drop that too and step into the morning, unencumbered.

Steffan's gray eyes devour me like a starving man presented with a feast. He steps forward.

"Let me warm ye," he says, voice jagged with lust.

I do. Pressing myself against him, I inhale the musky tang of Steffan's scent as his hands roam the plains of my torso, bringing heat to the surface. My nipples tighten against the hair of his chest, and a growl escapes him before his mouth crashes down on mine again. I open for him even as his elegant fingers slide down my spine and into the warm crease of my buttocks before grabbing my ass in both hands. I gasp at the intimate touch and move my fingers from Steffan's shoulders to his hair, pulling. Closer. I need him closer, my blood sings. Wolflike, Steffan kisses me with teeth and tongue until my need fists inside me, building to a throbbing ache.

I break the kiss for a second.

"Hold still," I command and jump, wrapping my legs around his waist.

We both feel my slick heat against his belly, and Steffan makes another rumble in his throat that has me panting. Big hands splay against the back of my thighs as he carries me back to the cover of the trees and lays us down on our bed of cloaks, careful of my injuries.

Sitting back on his heels, Steffan looks down at me greedily from between my legs. "Let me look upon ye, wife."

His voice no longer holds any question. Gone is the humble farmer. The gentle brother. No, the man in front of me is pure warrior, pure captain of archers, and I am his treasure to both plunder and protect.

Heart racing, I lift my arms over my head to display my breasts and let my legs fall open to his gaze. With one hand, Steffan lazily strokes himself as he reaches out and runs his other hand across my breasts, pinching each bud in turn, down my ribs as if mapping them, across my belly, and finally through the curls at my sex. Pleasure rockets through my body at the touch, and it's all I can do not to thrust up to meet his hand. More. I need more.

"Steffan," I pant as he drags a finger through my wetness, gently exploring, up and down, only to circle my clit once before moving away again. "Please. I need you."

His soft eyes sharpen with hunger, his jaw flexing as he learns my body, applying devilish pressure right where I need it most when I buck at the brush of his calloused fingertip. I want to watch his face, but he starts circling my tender core, faster and harder until my head lolls to the side, the orgasm building.

Then he's leaning over me, braced on one hand as his other works me. "Look at me," he commands, and I do. "And I need ye, *cariad*. More than I have e'er needed anything afore. But I shall love ye for the first time only once, and I mean to take my time."

At his words and the sudden, hard pressure of his finger, release explodes through me, rolling down my limbs until I'm quaking. Steffan catches my cry in his mouth with a kiss that goes from wild and claiming to soft, dragging kisses that quiet as my body goes still. Chest heaving, I stare up at him in awe, my heart so full of love it brims in my eyes.

"I love you," I say, cradling his beautiful face in my hands.

The face of my husband.

The face of a good man I would give over heaven and earth to stay with.

Steffan's eyes fill with tears. "God may have my soul, Ellyll, but my body, my heart, and my life belong to ye."

Then he thrusts into me in one long, swift movement that has my head tipping back, body bowing against the thick pressure of him inside me. My words evaporate. He's large, and the stretch burns just this side of pain before he slowly eases himself out only to thrust back in.

I hiss in pleasure as Steffan pins my hips to the ground with his big hands and finds his rhythm.

I grasp his forearms for purchase as Steffan angles his hips slightly and drives deeper still, the slap of our bodies unrelenting as he picks up speed, chasing his own pleasure. I try to meet his thrusts, but he's too strong, too fast. All I can do is hang on and let him fuck me soundly until my moans tangle with his roar of release as we tumble into ecstasy together.

Hyperalert to every nuance of temperature, light, and texture, I decide that making love out of doors is highly underrated. Lying next to me, Steffan smells like winter sunshine; lemon leaves, warm pine needles, and melting snow seem to seep out of his pours and into mine, binding us together. We spend the morning hunting and making love under the climbing sun until once again crawling into the bower to rest and hide from the world.

Enjoying his nakedness, I finger the wiry hairs around his navel. "You're all black and white like a zebra."

Steffan scrunches up his face at me. "Zebra? 'Tis one o' yer faerie beasts, aye?"

"No," I say in mock annoyance. "They're living on the African savanna as we speak. It's a small wild horse with black-

and-white stripes all over. I'll draw you one when we get back." So far, we've avoided talking about our imminent return to the compound, but I can feel it hanging over us, real as the sun.

"Africa? Be that part o' the holy land or the orient?"

"Closer to the holy land, but it's an entire continent that stretches farther south." As I say this, an unexpected wave of sadness laps at my back. In all likelihood, I'll never see animals or cultures outside of this one again. In light of giving up Meredith and modern amenities, a hypothetical zebra is nothing. But the slight sting is real, and it seems the full ramifications of my choice will take some time to set in. And I can't help but wonder if me staying will change anything in my own time, even though there's no way to know for certain.

Steffan toys with the knobs of my spine, causing my toes to curl with pleasure. "What troubles ye?"

I smile to shake off the feeling. "Just getting used to being here. I used to imagine going to Africa someday."

He frowns. "Then ye shall still go."

I smile a little sadly. Flying to Africa for a photographic safari in the twenty-first century is one thing. Traveling such a distance in the fifteenth century is quite another. My hand slides down to rest in the groove of his hip. Smooth and faintly blue, the skin feels like the inside of a seashell as I run my fingertips over it. "No, I won't. It's thousands of miles away."

Steffan's hand falls away from my back, and I can feel his spirit drift from me, troubled.

"Hey." I turn his face toward mine. "This is my choice. It may take a little while to get used to it, but I'm not leaving so you can stop looking at me like that."

His expression doesn't soften as he rolls on top of me. "Looking at ye like ..."

"Like you think I'll regret staying."

He frowns. "I would have ye want for naught."

I smile. "Then choose me as I have chosen you."

"As ye wish, wife," he says with great solemnity before dipping his head to take my nipple between his lips.

Arching to the warm, tugging heat of his mouth there is only this: teeth and tongue, fingers pressed deep into flesh, his hard length sliding home for the third time today with an anchoring thrust that scatters any thought of elsewhere to the wind.

We break camp in the early afternoon and ride for hours. Chalklike clouds scrawl across the bluest sky I've seen since leaving Tucson, all variegated bands of aquamarine and cobalt as though a tropical sea was cast into the heavens. The wind still blows cool, but the unfiltered sunlight warms my head as I soften into the sway of the horse beneath me like taffy against a puller.

"Tell me again o' yer desert." Steffan has proven curious about the future in general and places I've been in particular, peppering me with questions about everything from farming to weaponry to clothes. He scoffed at the idea of airplanes and telephones but was fascinated by supermarkets, libraries, and hospitals. I do my best to answer him without condescending, but Steffan isn't bothered by my knowledge. He knows the world as he knows it and takes my word on the rest.

"What do you want to know?" I ask.

He counters my question with a sly smile. "What would it please ye to tell me?"

Considering the request, I close my eyes and picture Tucson. I feel a tug of sadness, yes, but not the stab of longing I expect. More than anything, the memories of my former home are soothing as good lotion to long neglected skin.

"Well," I begin and gesture upward, "the sky is like this most of the year. Except for sometimes in the summer when the heat makes it hard to even move and the rain clouds turn wicked shades of violet and even green."

"The sky be green, but the land be brown and full o' plants covered in thorns?" he asks, incredulous.

I nod. "Sometimes."

Steffan shakes his head as if this is truly bizarre. I suppose it is for him. "Other than missin' yer kin, what grieves ye the most?"

Sensing where he's going with this, I say the first flippant things that come to mind. "Sunshine, indoor plumbing, and drawing paper."

Steffan looks at me, confused. "Do we have nay sun?"

I laugh at his indignation. "Of course, but it isn't the same. Where I'm from, hardly a day goes by without sunshine, even in winter. As for the others, well, you can't imagine the convenience of both."

Steffan nods thoughtfully.

"But there's nothing like this," I add as we approach a field of golden gorse blossoms. A scent like warm butter wafts up from the hillside as if it's covered in sponge cake. "This is truly incredible. I don't think I'll even get tired of this beauty."

Steffan turns to survey the land stretching away from us. "Aye," he agrees and looks back over his shoulders at me. "Do ye not feel such affection for yer place? Yer time?"

Denying it is pointless. "Yes and no," I answer. "I'm not attached to the land the way you are. We live ... well, removed from it. Place is more about your work or what you enjoy doing. So, yes, I have affection for the desert, but I have more affection for—" I pause, searching for the right words. "For the person I've become here. And for you."

He clears his throat. Doesn't respond.

"Why, Steffan Blaidd, have I embarrassed you?" I tease as

the horse, who I've taken to calling Winifred, tosses her head merrily.

Steffan shoots me an amuses glare over his shoulder again before pointing toward the next heavy patch of trees. "Yestin and Indeg's farm be through yon woods. We shall be needing food and drink afore long." He looks down at my bare feet swinging behind his and frowns. He's still upset at my refusal to continue wearing his boots. "And shoes. Methinks Lord Glyndwr shall not strike again so soon after facing Lord de Grey. A sliver o' time be ours yet."

The revolt, which has been simmering in the background of my bliss, boils over in a scalding, attention-grabbing hiss at Steffan's words. Ignoring what comes next is no longer an option.

"Steffan." His back goes rigid at my tone alone. "There's something I need to tell you. About the revolt."

He's quiet for a moment, stilling his breathing as if bracing for the blow. "Tell it then, Ellyll."

"The rebellion is going to fail." I bite my lip as if to punish the bearers of such terrible news.

Steffan sigh, but reveals no other response. A breeze rushes across the gorse and into our faces like a slap.

"When?" he asks, voice low and careful. Too careful.

Dread coils in my belly, and I don't want to say. I press my forehead into the groove between his shoulder blades as if burying my own head in the sand. "I don't know the exact year. It will go well for a while. A few years, I think. Glyndwr will win several battles and most of Wales will join the fight, but in the end ..."

Steffan doesn't move. His breath doesn't so much as hitch as the news sinks in. But when he glances back to meet my eyes, his face is laid open with anguish. "Shall we ne'er be free?"

I swallow, weighing the potential damage of each word on

my tongue. "In my time, many hundreds of years in the future, Wales is its own nation in many ways but still part of something called Great Britain along with England, Scotland, and the north of Ireland. But there are Welsh universities and a Welsh government. Welsh is still spoken. It ... does get better in many ways."

Steffan adjusts the bow slung across his lap. After a moment, he says, "A man be free, or he be not. There is no better."

And I understand that, for Steffan, nothing but complete independence will do. I don't know what else to say.

"'Tis right o' ye to tell me these tidings, Ellyll." He turns his head and offers a sad smile. "Ye should not bear such burdens alone," he says before kicking the horse into a trot. But as we enter the shadowy woods, a dense silence descends. I don't dare break it.

CHAPTER 24

AN UNKINDNESS OF RAVENS

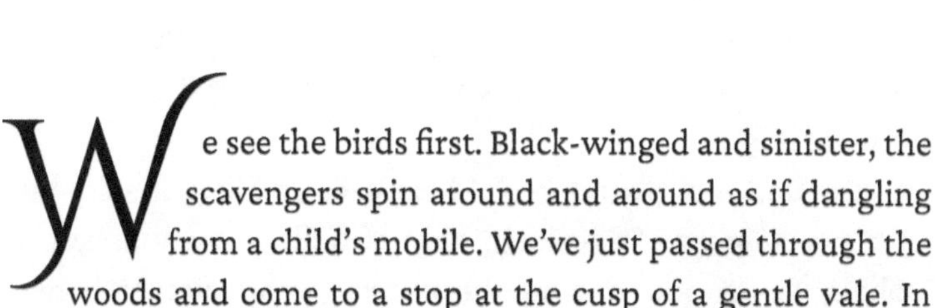

We see the birds first. Black-winged and sinister, the scavengers spin around and around as if dangling from a child's mobile. We've just passed through the woods and come to a stop at the cusp of a gentle vale. In the lowlands, where Yestin and Indeg's homestead should have been, only patches of blackened earth remain.

"Holy Mother o' God," Steffan prays and curses together.

The only reply is a cruel *caw*.

Without another word, we launch ourselves toward the carnage. The stench of ash and carrion stands up in greeting as we close in on the scene. Steffan pulls the mount up hard from its thunderous pace. I slide off Winifred and grab the reins as Steffan leaps off, heading for the central house at a run. All around us, the scorched ruins of a life lie in stinking heaps: the livestock hastily butchered and left to wolves and birds of prey, the kitchen garden and storehouses looted, the house ransacked and torched.

"Who did this?" I ask, but Steffan is already wading through the skeleton of the house, unreachable. I have my ideas but don't know if Sheriff Holloway's retribution or English raiders are to blame.

The horse, unnerved by the smell, skitters and neighs as I tie it off away from the destruction. Winifred's powerful muscles quiver, and I press my cheek against her neck, breathing in the warm, musky scent of her life. Then Steffan begins to keen, and every other thought disappears.

"Steffan!" I scream. Terror fists inside my chest as I run toward the sound, heart leaping wildly into my throat.

Feral as the shrieking birds, Steffan's seldom raised voice overtakes the silence as I skid to a stop just short of where he scours the wreckage like a man possessed. Something hangs from his closed fist. I step closer through the acrid stench and see what it is.

"Oh God, no. No, no, no," I hear a voice like mine cry but have no memory of speaking, only of falling to my knees, of looking down and finding the charred remnants of bones. Human bones, small enough to be a forearm. My body splits, drifting above myself for a moment as I watch my hands reach out to touch the remains, only to pull back.

When I come back to myself, I look up to see Steffan going about the gruesome work of collecting what's left of his family.

"Steffan," I call, trying not to sound as frightened as I feel. He doesn't respond. I'm not sure he can. "Steffan. Look at me. Look over here at me, my love."

Soot-smeared and terrible as a ghoul rising from its grave, he straightens and peers at me through a face contorted by remorse.

"Let me help."

He makes a strangled, vicious sound I've never heard and shakes his head. "There be nay help to give now, Ellyll. They be with God. And ye cannot take this from me." He turns away, pausing. "If ye must work, pray for me. Then gather stones."

Steffan resumes his eerie lamentation of song.

I do both. Hours later, when every last bit of bone that can be found is buried under a large cairn, an eternal sentry at the edge of the woods, we stand in front of it for a long time, too stunned to weep.

We bathe fully clothed in the first stream we come to. With each baptismal dunk, more and more ash and filth swirl off us, hanging on the surface of the water like an oil slick before drifting away. Then we strip bare and bathe again like kelpies, our clothes discarded skins on the shore. Shivering hard from shock and cold, I crouch in the shallows and scrub my fingernails. I can't get them clean. Most have been ripped ragged in the past weeks, but a few are just long enough for a thin layer of grime to stick under the nail. I need it gone.

"Meg."

I look up to see Steffan emerge from the depths like a river god, dripping and fierce, his dark hair matted against his pale skin in hypnotic whirls as he strides out of the water. Retrieving his knife from the bank, Steffan takes my hands and pulls me to my feet. Gently, he scrapes away the filth. Feeling the knife press so carefully to my skin, I think of the day he shaved me and am stunned to realize little more than two weeks have passed since then. It might as well have been two years. Not sure if I want to scream or laugh, I do neither as Steffan finishes and drops the weapon.

Then he dips his head to kiss each of my fingertips in turn before taking the last into his warm, pliant mouth. My eyes snap to his face, but Steffan is already watching me. Holding his desperate gaze, I make a small sound of pleasure as the scrape of his teeth begins to thaw the numbness at my center.

In the span of one breath, our arms are wound around each other, hungry. One of Steffan's big hands cups the back of my neck as he kisses me with teeth and tongue and heat, while the other hand drifts lower to grab my hip, long fingers pressing into my flesh. Lost in my own urgency, I rake my hands through his hair, pulling him closer before freeing one hand to snake between us and wrap around him. Steffan's smooth and hot and shudders under my touch.

"Christ, *cariad*, the things ye stir to life inside o' me. It would shame me to tell ye o' them," he breathes as his mouth works across my jaw, down my neck until he lets go of me to palm both breasts, his face kissing the tender skin between them.

"Look at me," I say, the one in command now. He obeys. "I'm still here, Steffan. *You* are still here. There is only now."

His face breaks. I watch as he chokes back the sob before his hands are around me again, spinning me so my back is pressed against his front, his hands gently kneading my breasts.

"Will ye let me love ye, Ellyll?" His voice is ragged with grief and desire. He can barely get the words out.

"Yes," I say, and immediately he picks me up and places me on the grass on my hands and knees. I'm surprised at the position change but feel his heat behind me, and I lean into it.

"Then I shall have all o' ye whilst ye be mine," he growls between clenched teeth as he slides inside me. "Do ye hear, my love? Just as ye have all o' me."

I can only nod before the pleasure of our frantic, rough joining takes over, and I dig my hands into the ground for purchase. Holding me in a bruising grip, Steffan thrusts hard and fast until I'm sobbing his name into the earth and he finds his own completion as if his life depends on it. I think perhaps it does.

It's sometime later before we extract ourselves from one another. Then without speaking, we splash in the creek for a third time and struggle into our wet clothes.

"Do you think we'll make it back to Glyndyfrdwy before dark?" I finally ask, climbing into the saddle behind him. The breeze chills me through my still-damp clothes, and I press tightly to his back.

Steffan glances at the sky and turns the horse slightly east. "If God hath any mercy."

It's the last thing he says until the church comes into view. My mouth goes dry with shock. Steffan had avoided the open moors, so I didn't know where we were until the trees thinned and I saw it squatting in the valley like a gray-stoned night-mare, the yews encircling it.

Waves of blossoming broom stretch down the hillside, and the hum of the bees echoes the rumble in my ears. I just stare at first, wondering if the mirage will fade. When it doesn't, I close my eyes and picture Meredith and her family, myself with a fulfilling art career and comfortable modern existence. But Steffan's face—hell—the faces of every person I've met here invades my mind. Even the wild, vivid landscape presses to the front of my thoughts, and I don't need long to consider.

I'm the first to speak. "You've wasted our time. I won't leave."

"Ye must go." His voice is hard and flat. Unfathomable.

I shake my head against his rigid back. "No, I don't."

Body locked, Steffan spurs the horse down into the vale.

"You can't make me," I seethe as we thunder toward St. Melangell's, the trees the only barrier now.

The church looks deserted as Steffan slides me off the horse before following, letting the reins hang free. In the corner of what will one day become the churchyard stands the yew, varicosed demi-god to which even time does not apply. Staring at it, I realize generations will live and die and the damn thing will still be there, ancient and ageless. My throat burns as I look at it, unwilling to cross into its shade for fear the phantom limbs could pull me into their red core like an octopus devouring its prey.

Steffan follows my gaze, his eyes hard. "'Tis the one?"

I don't answer.

"Megan—"

"Why?" I round on Steffan and shove him as hard as I can. "Look at me, goddamn you." I can't keep my voice from breaking at the expression on his face.

Steffan is no longer here. In front of me, is the merciless wolf.

Blank and cold and determined.

"Ye do not belong here. 'Tis death to stay. Ye spoke it yerself." Steffan's deep voice holds steady, but something behind his eyes belies the calm. And it's my turn to have the truth.

"So that's it? You just convinced me to marry you so you could fuck me without guilt and then send me away?" I goad him.

His head snaps back as if I've slapped him. "Do not speak such lies!"

"I'll say whatever the hell I want, especially if it's the truth!"

Steffan grabs my wrists, yanking me close.

"'Tis blasphemy, and ye know it well," he snarls into my face.

Good. Angry is better than the unfeeling blankness of before.

"I know no such thing if you send me away," I challenge and meet his unbending stare. "I may owe you my life many times over, but you owe me yours right back." I smack his chest with my palm, ready to beat sense into him if I must.

Dropping my wrists, Steffan stalks back and forth across the ground, eating it up with his long legs. Wolf indeed. "Aye, there be blood betwixt us and ye be hale and full o' wit, but we Cymry be naught but shite under the boot o' war. Ye told me yerself."

I fling my arms wide in frustration. "Life's going to be hard, so you think you can just send me away like a dog and I'll obey?"

A sardonic laugh burst from Steffan's mouth. "Obey? Nay, woman. I have ne'er known ye to do as ye be told, but I did not take ye for a fool."

"Now you listen to me, *husband*. You are the fool if you think there's a chance in hell I'm going back now." I blink hard against the tears building inside. "Because I have grieved for that life every single fucking day since I was ripped from it. I have lost my family three times over, just like you," I hiss, and jab my finger at him, unable to keep the tears at bay any longer.

Steffan stops pacing, his face a serrated knife, but I hold up a hand.

"I'm going to want them back for the rest of my life, but I have found things here—now—that are greater than my grief. I found my own strength. I found friends," I say, not realizing the truth until I've spoken it. "I found you. And I won't give any of it up just for your peace of mind."

Steffan clenches his fists. The horse shakes its bridle, startling a group of tiny, dust-colored birds from a low hedge. The flock darts up, splashing Steffan's face with shadow. As if enjoying the warmth, he tips his head back and closes his eyes. Breathes deeply. Then he opens them and covers the space between us in two strides. Through flecks of smoky quartz, he stares into me, and I know I'm no longer looking at my beloved Steffan, but Blaidd the warrior wolf.

"Fair words may slide from yer sweet tongue, but there be naught but ruin in yer touch, woman. Ye bewitch me nay longer, and I want naught to do with ye. My people be at war and what ye want matters not. Be gone back from whence ye came." He turns and, without looking back, mounts the horse. Kicking the amber beast into a gallop, Steffan leaves me screaming his name in the shadow of my fate.

I face his departure, eyes streaming, voice raw, until my legs buckle beneath me. I lay in the damp grass for a long time. The sun remains warm, the air cool, but nothing penetrates the numbness seeping from my chest into my limbs like poison.

Finally, mercifully, twilight's gloom stretches across the land, quieting the wind and birds. I sit up. My throat burns and my stomach pinches, but I ignore them. It doesn't matter. A thin mist rises from the cooling earth, cloaking me. Without thought, I push myself up to standing and walk on wobbly legs to the largest tree. I watch as if outside myself as my hands grasp the red-gray bark. As I pull myself up the side of the forked trunk.

Then, perched like a flightless bird, I stare up into the canopy of black lace until the silver sky fades to night. With despair and rage and heartbreak coiled in my belly, I step down into the inky heart of the yew.

"Be she dead?"

"I dinna ken, man," answers a rumbling voice. "Ye be the physician."

"You know I be nay such thing, thank the saints," says the first speaker indignantly.

Their words seep into my consciousness like water through sand. I consider moving but don't. He left me. I retract from the thought as if it can scald me, hot as a coal. There's no time for that pain now. Not after I've gone and sealed my fate.

I almost did it. Almost went back to the too-full arms of my perfect twin and a home that never felt like mine. The fractious sister returning to the fold. I could have made it work. Nearly did. But the decision, when it came, was instantaneous. As the bark warmed unnaturally under my hands, dual images of the lives I might lead spun through my mind, relentlessly gaining speed until, without thinking, I leaped free from the tree trunk as the hard glow of possibility dimmed.

It was done.

Turning away from the pain of my new reality, I drift back toward sleep until something pokes me in the ribs.

"Ah! Ye see? The lass be braw enough. Although," the rumbling voice adds, "sleeping in the shadow o' yon tree canna be a blessin', aye?"

The first speaker makes a dismissive noise and calls gently, "Mistress?"

Resentfully, I peel my eyes open and stare at the two hazy faces looking down on me.

"Leave me be," I croak.

The men exchange wary looks. Whether their confusion is over my accent or my words doesn't matter.

"Ye need not be affrighted," assures the figure belonging to the first voice. "Can ye stand?" Shorter than his companion by a head, the man pushes back his cowl to reveal a shock of silver hair completely incongruent with his youthful, handsome face. Wide, dark brown eyes set over a fine-toothed nose regarded me with concern.

Next to him, the man with the rumbling voice hides his massive frame under a ratty black friar's robe. Framed by the dark hood, a pair of cobalt eyes twinkle down at me over a bulbus nose and impressive ginger-red beard.

"I don't know," I answer, beyond making sense.

"Hmph." The big man in the friar's robe leans down and gently hoists me to my feet.

Standing brings physical relief from my numb, aching limbs but causes my head to spin slightly from hunger and dehydration. Overhead, a raven caws, and I glance up, wondering if the wind will whistle through my empty spaces as it does the tree's. I need a drink but can't make myself form the words my head is in such a jumble.

"Be ye lost, mistress?" the young man with the silver hair asks.

I blink, coming back into myself and stare directly into the stranger's compassionate face. I have no strength for anything but the truth.

"Yes," I choke out as a surge of panic sweeps over me. What have I done? Anchorless on the tides of time, I slump against the red giant and weep.

EPILOGUE

The Reverend Clara Fitzwilliam sighed as she filed the last of the paperwork into the bottom drawer of her mammoth oak desk. Leaning back, she rubbed the bridge of her nose where her glasses sat and fought the urge to light a cigarette. The flesh is so weak, she reminded herself and sent a prayer heavenward for strength against more than the nicotine.

She surveyed her surroundings with satisfaction. Freshly dusted bookcases and alphabetized metal file cabinets zigzagged along the walls of the small room, making the diamond-paned windows at the end seem like jack-o'-lantern eyes. She'd even wiped down the computer, leaving the normally cluttered room spotless except for a stack of newspaper clippings teetering on the edge of her work space. Clara sent a weary look toward the mess before picking up the paperweight anchoring it. Rolling the clear crystal orb between her hands, she admired its solidity before setting it aside and retrieving the article on top. A smiling photo of Meg Quinn, taken the year before at her sister's wedding, stared out at her.

She'd told the police everything about that day. Every detail of their conversation and what she'd done after Meg left the church. Looking at the article, Clara reminded herself that she'd done all she could to help the authorities. Putting the clipping aside, she reached for another one, intent on filing these away too, when the metallic whine of the lychgate drifted through the open window. Really should get that fixed, she thought, but it was so helpful in notifying her of visitors. She hated surprises.

"God be with you, *bach*," she said to Meg's picture before putting her back on the pile and replacing the paperweight.

Clara smoothed her gray suit and cobalt scarf before exiting her office through a low stone arch. She walked past the shrine into the body of the church where a young woman stood looking up at the Giant's Rib. Clara coughed.

"Welcome to St. Melangell's," she said brightly to the stranger, who turned at Clara's greeting. The visitor was young and very pretty, with caramel-colored hair cut stylishly at her chin, wide, hazel eyes, faint a smattering of freckles, and a prominent cleft chin. Clara gasped.

"I get that a lot," said the woman.

"I'm sorry." Clara clasped her hands together. "The resemblance is striking. You have to explain often?"

"Yes," Meredith answered quietly. "It's a good thing though. If people are startled by me, then they're still thinking of her, right?" She lowered her sad eyes to the floor.

Looking closely, Clara noticed the differences now. The woman in front of her seemed shorter and curvy with heavy breasts pressing against her lavender sweater. The voice was slightly different too. But my how they were alike.

Getting a hold of herself, Clara extended a hand.

"You probably know this, but I'm Rev. Clara Fitzwilliam. Would you like a cuppa tea?" she offered.

Meg's twin shook Clara's hand.

"Meredith Quinn-Davies. But you already knew that, I

suppose. Um, yes that would be lovely," she said, her smile tight. She shifted her weight rhythmically as if rocking a baby.

Clara turned toward her office. "Why don't you come this way? I keep a hot plate to support my tea habit."

"Thank you," Meredith said, tucking her hair behind one ear, which sported a diamond stud earring.

Clara led the way, glad that she'd cleaned. Gliding into the tiny room, she swept the pile of clippings up and stashed them in a drawer before turning to the tea kettle. She'd been drinking copious amounts of black tea since giving up smoking.

"Please have a seat. Won't be but a moment," she gestured to the chair opposite her desk.

Meredith sat quietly and stared out the window into the churchyard where the twisted arms of the largest yew hung over the wall. The wind picked up and carried the tinny squeak of the old hinges into the office. Meredith's face remained smooth, but Clara could imagine the tenor of her thoughts and felt compelled to speak.

"Are you staying in the village?" she asked.

"No, I just drove down for the day. My sons are too small to leave for long," Meredith explained.

Clara glanced over, noting the deep shadows under the young mother's eyes. "It's quite difficult in the beginning, isn't it?"

Meredith nodded. "You have children then?"

"Aye, a son," Clara said, pouring the tea. "He's grown now, but you never forget the early months. Here. These aren't very proper, but they do the job," she said, handing Meredith a sturdy white mug. The rim was chipped, leaving a saw-tooth edge on one side.

"Thank you," Meredith said and sipped from the steaming cup. "Everyone thinks I'm hormonal and crazy with grief," she said suddenly.

Clara regarded the woman across from her. "Aren't you?"

Meredith set her mug on the desk and wiped her hands over her face. "Of course I am," she said, exasperated. "My mother died, my identical twin disappeared, and I gave birth within a six-month timeframe. Wouldn't you be?" Her cheeks reddened with emotion.

"Without a doubt," Clara answered, wondering what exactly this traumatized woman had come to hear or say.

Meredith picked up the cup and stared at it. "They've called off the search."

Now it was Clara's turn to set down her mug. "I heard that. I'm so sorry."

"Thank you. I understand the police have to move on. It's just—" She broke off and took a deep drink of the hot liquid as if it were whiskey instead of tea.

Clara waited. "Is there something specific I can do for you, Mrs. Quinn-Davies?"

Pressing her mouth into a tight line, Meredith reached into her purse and pulled out a folded sheet of paper. "I read that, before becoming a minister, you taught history at the Aberystwyth University," she said, unfolding a thick sheet of drawing paper. "I was wondering if you knew where this was."

She pushed the sheet across the desk toward Clara.

Adjusting her glasses, Clara examined the paper.

"Did you draw this?" Clara asked.

"Yes. I was never as good as Meggie, though."

Clara studied the sketch. Everything about the structure suggested thirteenth or fourteenth century, but she wasn't familiar with it specifically. "Well, there's enough detail here to narrow it down a bit," she said and looked at Meredith. "Was this taken from a photograph?"

Meredith shifted. "No, it's from a—memory," she said and sipped her tea.

Clara arched an eyebrow. "That's quite a memory you've got. Something from your childhood?"

Meredith chewed the corner of her lip.

"I only ask," Clara went on, "because the more information you can give me, the more likely I am to identify the structure." She gave the younger woman what she hoped was a reassuring smile.

Meredith drooped. "I don't have any other information."

"Well," Clara said, wondering what was really going on, "I'll see what I can find out anyway. May I keep this for now?"

Meredith nodded.

Clara tucked the sketch into the drawer with the clippings. "Would you like to look around?"

Meredith nodded but didn't move to get up. Again, Clara waited.

"Do you believe in visions, Reverend?"

Aha, Clara thought. Now we come to it. "I believe that sometimes God chooses to reveal his truth in mysterious ways," she answered carefully. "Have you had a vision?"

Meredith looked straight at Clara. "I've seen her."

Tread lightly, Clara thought and longed for a cigarette. "Sometimes, in grief, the mind creates what the heart wants to believe."

Meredith gave a harsh chuckle, and her eyes cooled like glassy stones. "I know what you're thinking," she said rather sharply. "And believe me, I've been telling myself the same thing for months. I'm already in grief counseling and have considered adding everything from hypnotherapy to getting a CAT scan to explain it."

Clara sat back and folded her hands. "I did not mean to imply that you were impaired. Only under great stress."

"I know. I'm sorry," Meredith went on. "But for the sake of my *entire* family, I decided to ask for your help first."

Clara regarded the woman across the desk. Meredith Quinn-Davies appeared tired and sad—not delusional. "Forgive me for making assumptions. But when you say that you've seen your sister, what exactly do you mean?"

Meredith looked out the window. "The first time, it was the day we reported her missing. I sat down to fold laundry while waiting by the phone—dear Lord, the laundry never stops— and I just saw her. It was like watching a movie reel inside my head," she said and looked over at Clara for signs of disbelief. Clara didn't move. "Before you suggest it, I was not asleep or hallucinating," she insisted, wiping her eyes. "Everything simply went black and then—then I watched Meg struggle with a strangely dressed man," she broke off. "He hit her, and I thought she was dead."

Clara felt as if her blood was draining out the soles of her feet. "You said the first time. Have there been others?"

Meredith nodded. "Three."

"Would you describe them to me?" Clara asked, shifting forward in her chair.

"The second was about a month later. It was dark, and Meg was tearing through the woods like the devil himself was after her." Meredith's voice cracked.

"And the sketch?" Clara asked.

"It's from the most recent. About a week ago," she wrung her hands in her lap.

"What was she doing?"

Meredith furrowed her elegant eyebrows. "It wasn't frightening like the others, just strange. She was wearing a long dress, like a costume, and standing next to a tall man. They were talking and it felt like there were people around, but I couldn't really see them. I just saw Meg and this man staring at each other, and they looked ..." she cut off and shook her head.

"What did they look like?" Clara pressed.

Meredith stared out the window again. "They looked very much in love."

Clara's breath iced over in her lungs. "And you believe these visions to be real?"

Meredith met her gaze, her eyes flashing. "Yes," she admitted and grew bolder with the confession. "I know how that sounds, but yes. And it isn't the first time my sister and I have experienced something like this," she said looking away. "It's happened since we were children but never like this."

Clara closed her eyes and for a moment was lost to the past.

"Reverend Fitzwilliam?" came Meredith's voice. "Are you okay?"

"Aye," replied Clara coming back into her skin. "Sorry. I was just ... remembering," she whispered when she was able to speak. Opening her eyes, Clara focused on the woman across from her and watched as one manicured eyebrow arched up and the corners of Meredith's mouth tightened.

"Oh my God," said Meredith. "You know something."

"I know nothing that will help the authorities find your sister."

"But you know what happened, don't you? Where she is?" Meredith's golden voice had gone cold as ice.

Before she knew she'd made the decision, Clara leaned forward, her black eyes never leaving Meredith's.

"I'm afraid the question isn't *where* your sister is but *when*." Her husky voice reverberated off the stone walls and rippled through the air, reaching into forever.

THE END

ACKNOWLEDGMENTS

I could write a novella naming each beloved who helped bring this book into being, but I'll be as brief as possible. First, I don't know how to thank God without sounding trite, but I can't leave it undone either. So, I'll quote the beneficent Julian of Norwich by giving thanks to the "...Force of Love moving through the universe that holds us fast and will never let us go."

Enormous thanks to Jeni Chappelle (and Sandy!), for her years of encouragement, kindness, and editorial genius. You're the literal best. Special thanks to Stefanie Saw of Seventhstar Art Services for the gorgeous cover art. The stars aligned for me to find your beautiful work. Thank you to my virtual hype women Cassie Miller, Erin Hahn, Trish Knox, Fiona Keane, Tamara Mahmood Hayes, and Brittney Arena—your kindness cannot go unnoted. Thank you to the authors who graciously answered questions and guided me through this journey—especially Amanda Adam and JoAnna Illingworth—and thanks to Starla DeKruyf for her amazing work formatting this book. I couldn't have done this without you all! Extra love and gushing to Erin A. Craig, Hester Fox, Paulette Kennedy, and Sarah T. Dubb for graciously reading the manuscript and writing blurbs. You all humble me with your generosity; I want to be you when I grow up.

Thank you to the staff of The Shrine Church of Saint Melangell and Centre for answering so many of my questions and for your good work in the world. All remaining mistakes and hyperbole regarding your beautiful site are entirely my own.

Writing is necessarily a solitary gig, but a writing life cannot be done alone. With that in mind, my eternal thanks to Caroline Elle Murphy for her endless enthusiasm and kindness—I am so grateful we picked each other up! And to C.B. Bernard, who is both an exceptional writer and friend, thank you for always metaphorically dusting me off and reminding me to be the wind, not the weathervane. To all my Very Early Readers, your gentleness meant the world when my little writer heart was so tender—thank you. You know who you are. To my Book Club gals, thank you for your friendship and themed snacks! I look forward to many years of community. And to my Hot Mom Squad—you've kept me sane through the years with laughter and shenanigans. Your friendship is a balm to my anxious little soul.

A special thank you to my parents, Bill and Merry Nebeker; my siblings, Travis Nebeker and Heather Davis and their spouses; my extended family, and many friends who encouraged my writing and loved me through life's ups and downs. I wouldn't be here without your love. Finally, thank you to my incredible daughters, Sophia and Violet, who have taught me more than I could ever teach them. I love you to the moon and back, my precious bits of stardust. I hope Mama made you proud. And to my ever-patient husband, Jeremy, who gave me the most precious gift a writer could ask for—time—a thousand thank yous would never be enough. I love you.

About the Author

Jeanne Renee can't remember a time when she wasn't in love with stories. After earning a BA in English Literature and Creative Writing from the University of Arizona, Jeanne worked as a bookseller, assistant magazine editor, and elementary school reading tutor. An eclectic reader, mediocre yogi, and admirer of sunsets and dairy-free lattes, Jeanne lives outside Tucson with her husband, daughters, and the best bad dog ever, Patrick the Fierce.